Lost in Bliss

Lost in Bliss

Nights in Bliss, Colorado Book 4

Lexi Blake
writing as
Sophie Oak

Lost in Bliss
Nights in Bliss, Colorado Book 4

Published by DLZ Entertainment LLC

Copyright 2018 DLZ Entertainment LLC
Edited by Chloe Vale
ISBN: 978-1-937608-98-9

Sign up for Lexi Blake's newsletter
and be entered to win a $25 gift certificate
to the bookseller of your choice.

Join us for news, fun, and exclusive content
including free short stories.

There's a new contest every month!

Go to http://www.lexiblake.net/newsletter/ to subscribe.

Dedication

No book of mine gets written without an enormous amount of support. I want to thank my husband, my mom, the best PA a girl could have, Chloe Vale, Jen Kubenka (who often entertains my kiddos), the Righteous Perverts chat group for their unflagging support, and my writer friends—Shayla Black, Kris Cook, Chloe Lang, and Jen August. I love you all!

Dedication 2018

Over the course of years, things change and people come and go. It doesn't make them not important. We learn something from everyone we meet. As I've heard before, some people come for a reason, some for a season, and some for a lifetime. Many things have changed in my life since I first wrote this book, but one remains the same. Always. Kim Guidroz. You are my rock and my guiding hand. You lift me up and never once in twenty years of friendship have you let me down. Except in pop culture trivia. You suck at that. But you are simply the best friend anyone could ever have. You're a gift from the universe and I'm so glad to have been the recipient of that present.

Prologue

Washington, DC
Five years before

Laura Rosen came awake to the sounds of familiar voices arguing.

"You're the one who needed to talk, Rafe." Cameron Briggs's voice held a level of anger she hadn't heard from him before. "We should have been there with her that morning."

"Do you think I don't know that?" Rafe Kincaid's question came out in a harsh grind.

Why were they here? Where the hell was here? The world seemed groggy and hazy. She couldn't quite feel her limbs. She tried to move them and…

Pain filled her.

It was wrong. She was supposed to wake up happy and warm, not every muscle aching. She was supposed to wake up to Rafe and Cam kissing her, not fighting.

"How do we tell her what's happened?" Cam asked. "Should we leave that to the doctors?"

A long sigh filled the air. "I don't know how to tell her, but it must come from us. We can't leave something like this to a stranger. How do we tell her she's never going to have children? God, we made love to her a few nights ago. How do we tell her?"

Nights ago? How much time had passed? The words didn't seem to penetrate her brain. Who were they talking about? Certainly not her. She remembered that they'd made love to her and then…

"I'll tell her," Cam offered. "I'll take care of her from now on. You should go."

"I'm not fucking going anywhere," Rafe snarled back. "And if you suggest it one more time, we're going to take this to a physical level."

"I'd love to see you try."

They were fighting. Over her. She'd known it wouldn't work. She'd known it was crazy to think they could share her.

She fought her way through a haze of pure agony. She forced her eyes open. This was everything she'd feared. They'd had one beautiful night together and now it was threatening to fall apart.

Except it already had. It had fallen apart the minute they'd chosen their careers over her.

No, I don't agree with Special Agent Rosen's profile. She's very smart, but I think she's wrong this time. Cam had spoken with his head up, eyes anywhere but on her.

I think Special Agent Rosen has an interesting theory, but it's too far out for any of us to pursue. We should stick with Edward's. He's got far more experience. Rafe had looked at her with sickening sympathy in his eyes.

They'd proceeded to tear apart her profile, not giving even a hint that a line of it could be true. They hadn't given her a heads up that they'd read her profile. They hadn't discussed it with her. No. They'd simply…

The truth flooded her system, the past few days playing out in her mind like a horror movie.

Except it had been real. The monster she'd been hunting had come for her. She'd been standing outside her apartment after the worst day. She'd been fired and then…

"*Bella?*" Rafe's voice cut through the terrifying memories. "She's awake."

Cam was suddenly at her side. "Baby? Baby, don't move. You need to stay still. We'll get a doctor. Rafe's going right now."

Guilt. It was right there in his eyes. Terrible guilt.

What had they been talking about? They'd been fighting and then they'd said something about what they couldn't tell her.

"What happened?" Her mouth was dry. The last thing she'd remembered was managing to get the ropes undone. The Marquis de Sade, the serial killer she'd profiled, had kept her for days in some warehouse. He'd tortured her. He'd taken…god how much had he taken from her?

Cam got to his knees by her bed, his big hand covering hers. "How much do you remember?"

She didn't want to remember anything at all. "No one believed my profile and I got fired and then he took me. I was standing in front of my apartment door and everything went dark. Then I woke up and he was there."

It had been the utter opposite of the night before when she'd fallen asleep cuddled in between Rafe and Cam. That night had been everything she could have hoped for, dreamed of. They'd held her and loved her, and in the morning they'd been gone. The next time she'd seen them, her lovers were telling her boss that her profile was shit. Oh, they hadn't used those words…

She was in a hospital. Everything hurt. She was in a hospital because the Marquis de Sade had tortured her and stabbed her and left her pinned to a table like a butterfly he'd been studying.

He'd stabbed her low, right above her pelvis.

"It's all going to be okay," Cam promised her. "You don't have to worry about anything except getting better."

Of course she didn't. She no longer had a job.

Then the doctor was there, checking her vitals and saying a whole bunch of stuff that made no sense to her. She was surrounded by men and she didn't want a one of them there. They were staring down at her with sympathy, like she was something to pity.

And maybe she was.

"Doctor, I would like to speak with you alone, please."

Rafe got down on one knee at her bedside. "There's no need to hide anything from us."

Cam was on her other side. "We're here to help you. You can't imagine how scared we've been. Baby, you have to know that we're going to be here for you."

At one point in time, those words would have been so sweet. Now they rang as hollow as the look in Cam's eyes. She turned away from him. She couldn't be around them now. There was too much pain in her body to handle the blows they would deal to her soul if she let them stay. She turned back to the doctor. "These men are not married to me and not related. I would like them removed from my room, and you don't have permission to share my information with them."

She heard Cam's gasp and then Rafe was standing over her. His eyes bore into her. "You can't get rid of us, *bella*."

"Laura, please. Don't do this. I'm sorry for what happened. Don't kick me out," Cam pleaded.

"I'm going to have to ask you to leave," the doctor said gravely.

"It won't work, *bella*," Rafe said even as he got to his feet. "We'll be back with the team to take your statement in a few hours. And we will discuss everything. This isn't over. Come on, Cameron. We'll give her space."

Cam looked back as Rafe led him out of the room.

"Don't let them back in." She couldn't deal with them now. She'd made a terrible mistake thinking this could work between the three of them. Even being with one of them would have been a mistake. She knew that now.

The doctor looked down at her. "Ms. Rosen, are you sure you want to keep those men out? They seemed extremely concerned about your well being."

Seemed being the operative word. "Could you please explain what happened? I assume I had surgery. I don't remember much right now, but I know I was in bad shape."

"Let me get you some pain medication. You have to be hurting," he said as though trying to stave off that moment when he had to tell her the whole truth.

She shook her head. It was time to rip the bandage off. It was time to discover exactly what had been taken from her. "Tell me, doctor."

He sat down, his eyes grim, and began to speak.

Four days later she stepped up into the cab of the truck, only wincing a bit. The massive eighteen-wheeler smelled of air freshener and stale French fries.

How the mighty had fallen.

"Be sure to buckle up, hon." The woman in the driver's seat had curly steel-colored hair. "I can take you as far as Oklahoma City."

"Thanks." She pulled the seat belt over her body but only because she'd been asked to. She was completely numb. It was funny because she knew what was happening from an intellectual standpoint. Trauma. She had loads of it. Trauma of the body. Trauma of the mind. So much trauma she could no longer feel anything. She was making decisions based on pure instinct, and that instinct told her to run.

All that mattered was getting the hell out of DC.

If she stayed, he would find her again. The Marquis de Sade wouldn't stop. She'd tried to warn them all and what she'd gotten for her trouble had been pain and loss.

He didn't get to take her life. He'd already taken her future.

And he wasn't the only one she was running from.

If she stayed, they would find her again. Rafe and Cam had tried to talk to her, to explain what had truly happened the day they'd thrown her under the bus, but she wasn't listening. She couldn't allow herself to. She had to hold herself together and find a place to lick her wounds.

Alone.

"How far are you going, hon?" the driver asked as they pulled out onto the highway.

"As far as I can," she replied.

As far away from those men who'd ruined her as she could get.

Chapter One

Cameron Briggs felt like he was storming the castle. His heart was beating, adrenaline coursing through his body as he charged through the double doors that separated the FBI offices from the lobby. It had been years since he'd walked through those doors. Hell, he probably didn't have clearance to be in this part of the building anymore, but he wasn't allowing anyone to keep him out today.

Luckily, the guard on duty was a small, gray-haired woman who smiled brightly at him as he strode through the double doors.

"Agent Briggs!" Helen Angelo exclaimed, getting to her feet. "It's been a long time."

Cam shook his head. "I'm not an agent anymore, Helen. Is Rafe in?"

If Rafael Kincaid wasn't in his office, then Cam would hunt his ass down. The bastard hadn't answered his phone, and Cam had left three messages. The printout in his hand nearly burned his skin.

Five years. He'd looked for her for five years.

Helen frowned, and Cam felt the weight of her disapproval. "Yes, I heard you had left the Bureau. I don't think it was a good career move for you."

He hadn't given dick about his career when he'd left the Bureau. There had been nothing for him here after what had happened to Laura. A vision of Laura Rosen leapt into his mind. Blonde, gorgeous, with a soft body and a softer heart. The vision didn't have to leap all that far. Every time he closed his eyes he saw her, smiling and looking down at him, her blonde hair around her shoulders as she rode his cock.

And every time he went to sleep he saw her another way—battered, beaten, and stabbed, being shoved into an ambulance.

"Where's Rafe?" Cam didn't have time to argue. This was the best lead he'd had in five fucking years. He wanted to follow it now.

He would already be on a plane if he hadn't made that damn promise to Rafe.

"Special Agent Kincaid is in a meeting. An important meeting with the director and the SAC and a task force. He and his partner are giving a briefing."

Yeah, yeah. They were all important. Everything was important to the goddamn FBI except the agents who didn't perfectly follow procedure. They could go to hell.

Or they could go to Bliss. What a fucking name. How on earth had his cosmopolitan Laura ended up in some podunk Colorado town?

He gave Helen a wave. "Thanks. I'll take it from here."

Cam took off. He heard Helen yelling behind him, but he wasn't about to sit in the waiting room for the briefing to be over. He wasn't Rafe's lapdog, as many had claimed. Sure, he'd taken money from Rafe over the years, but only because they had a single goal in mind. A goal Cam had accomplished.

He opened the door to the briefing room but was startled to find absolutely no one there. It was empty and silent, though Cam remembered a time when he'd stood in the room and listened for quiet words.

You don't believe me. How could you stand there and tell them all I'm wrong? How could you advise the chief to take

16

me off the biggest case of my career?

He shut the door quickly. There were only ghosts in that room. There were ghosts everywhere in this building.

He shook off the feeling. He still needed to find Rafe. If the meeting wasn't being held in the briefing room, then they were using the auditorium.

Maybe Helen was right. Maybe this meeting was important.

He slipped into the auditorium, where large-scale briefings were held. The lights were dimmed, and the only illumination came from the projector. No fun movies for the FBI. Only horror shows, and this was no different. He was assaulted by the picture projected on the wall, a woman, young, but no longer vital. Her glassy eyes stared out of the picture, utterly unseeing. Her flesh was a pale white, the only bit of color a shiny mauve-colored lipstick painted on her lips.

She was naked, her hands tied over her head. The victim's wrists had been bound so tightly that her hands were blue. She would have lost feeling in them long before she died. Her pale flesh was a map of cuts, some shallow, some terrifyingly deep. He knew this killer. This killer liked to start with small stabbing wounds to the lower abdomen, painful, but not fatal. Long strips of flesh had been lashed from the victim's breasts and thighs. This woman's death hadn't been quick. It had been a long, slow opera of torture ending in her throat being slit like a lamb led to slaughter. He'd seen it before. Cam let his eyes drift down as his stomach did a flip.

The Marquis de Sade.

Yeah, this was an important meeting.

"The victim was discovered outside the warehouse district on Tuesday morning. Her name is Christine Parker. She was a prostitute working the area."

He shrank back, all thoughts of breaking up this meeting gone in a tidal wave of fear and self-loathing. De Sade had been gone for five years. He'd been utterly silent, like a shark who feasted in the shallows of the beach before sinking back into the deep. The shark

17

was surfacing again. Cam had always known he would. De Sade loved his work too much to stop. Rafe had been watching for him, too. They'd theorized that he was in prison, or he'd moved to another city after his close call with the law. Five years had sped by with not a hint of the serial killer.

How was this happening again? How the hell was this happening just when he'd found Laura, the only victim of the infamous serial killer to have ever gotten away?

A tall, broad figure stood by the projector, his solid body almost ghostly in the shadowy light. Cam's former partner had been a bit like a ghost these last few years. He'd seen Rafe rarely and only to update him on the progress he'd made in finding Laura. Rafe had become a bank account Cam tapped into when he needed money to follow a lead. There was a man standing beside Rafe. Cam couldn't see his face, but he knew the name. Brad Conrad. Ex-college football star and all-around asshole. It was kind of hard to believe, but in another year's time, Brad would be Rafe's partner for longer than Cam had been.

Rafe Kincaid's deep voice continued. It was far steadier than Cam's heart rate, and, for a moment, jealousy and rage curled in his belly. Rafe had never loved Laura the way he did. How could he if he could stand there and talk about the man who had almost killed her the same way a college professor talked about a Shakespearean sonnet?

"As with all previous victims, this one was found with lipstick on her. Forensics has already verified that it's the same brand and shade as the others. Purple Passion. Also, according to forensics, the victim had been killed at least twelve hours before. Blood spatter indicates she was killed where her body was found."

That was the pattern. The lipstick. The victim was a prostitute. She'd been tortured before she was killed. Everything fit the pattern. He simply didn't want to believe it. "He's been quiet for years. Why has he started working again?"

At least twenty-five heads turned.

Rafe put a hand over his eyes as though trying to see across the distance. "Cam?"

Even in the low light of the auditorium, Cam could see Brad puffing up. "Briggs, this is a closed session. We don't need low-level PIs here. If you need information on something, please go and ask the secretary."

Rafe turned briefly and exchanged words with Brad Cam couldn't hear. Before Rafe could turn back, the lights came on. An almost relieved sigh swept through the room. The picture on screen seemed to recede a little, no longer the main focus of the world.

"Cameron Briggs, you son of a bitch!"

Cam turned and couldn't help but smile. Joseph Stone, his former Bureau chief, took the stairs two at a time, his familiar face lit with a smile. He'd aged very little since the last time Cam had seen him. Joseph was a big, athletic guy. As long as Cam had known him, he'd been bald, but even that made him seem a bit powerful. Joseph was the type of man other men followed.

"Special Agent Stone." Cam took his hand and shook it. Joe had always been a good boss. He was Harvard educated and highly connected, but he'd always known how to make a guy feel welcome.

Joe pumped his hand twice and slapped him gently on the back. "No need for formalities any more. Did Rafe call you? I have all the paperwork set up to bring you in as a contractor. We need everyone on this. It's going to take everything we have to catch this one. I don't have anyone on the team with your computer skills."

Cam looked to his former partner, who had his head down, one foot tapping against the floor. *Guilty as sin.*

"No, he didn't call me." Betrayal burned through him. Apparently, despite their oaths to one another, his former partner didn't think it was important enough to call and tell him that the man they'd hunted for years had resurfaced. "I was here on another matter, but I can see plainly that Special Agent Kincaid is busy. I won't interrupt him. Call me sometime, Joe. We can have a beer."

Joe's brows came together in a *V*. "What are you saying? You

19

do understand what we're talking about here? This is the Marquis de Sade's work. There's no denying it."

Oh, he understood. He understood perfectly fine. He also understood that he had played his part, and he was naïve for thinking Rafe would play his. Rafe's head came up, and those dark eyes of his narrowed for a moment. Ruthlessly intelligent, it wouldn't take long for Rafael Kincaid to figure out why he was here interrupting this briefing. It wasn't like Cam would come for lunch.

"I understand. De Sade is back." It was time to make a strategic retreat. His fist closed around the paper in his hand. He was gentle with it. He didn't want to crush it. It was the first glimpse he'd gotten of Laura in years. It was strangely precious to him. "Rafe's your man. He and Special Agent Conrad can handle this. You don't need me."

He turned and walked out of the door. If Rafe wanted to renege on their deal, he sure as hell wasn't about to give the man the keys to the kingdom. He would go after Laura himself.

It was better this way. Rafe could search for the killer and further his career. Cam could get what he wanted. He wanted Laura. Without Rafe around, maybe she would fall for him again. Yeah. He had a better shot without pretty, rich, smooth-as-silk Rafe around. It had been a flat-out miracle Laura had even noticed him.

"I need you, Cam." Laura had turned to him, her plump lips red and swollen from Rafe's kisses. Cam had kissed her and tasted the Scotch on her lips. Rafe's drink. He'd plunged his tongue inside, not giving a damn that Rafe was behind her, his hands playing with her breasts. Somehow, in that moment, it had felt right to be there with Rafe. It had been perfect.

"Cameron!"

He stopped, pulled roughly from his memory. His feet had known which way to go. He was standing in front of the doors that led to the lobby. Rafe put a hand on his shoulder and spun him around.

"I've been yelling for two minutes. Why didn't you stop?"

Cam shrugged, unwilling to betray his emotional state. He let his face go blank. He'd perfected it long ago so his father wouldn't gain any satisfaction from knowing how deeply his insults cut. He never thought he would have to go there with Rafe. "I didn't have anything to say."

Rafe scrubbed a hand through his perfectly cut pitch-black hair. "That's bullshit. You wouldn't be here if you didn't have something to say." He glanced down at his watch. "I know you're pissed at me. I would be pissed at me, too, but I have my reasons."

"Were you going to tell me?" Cam asked the question as if the answer didn't have the ability to rip his insides out. He also asked it as though he would actually believe any answer that came out of Rafe's mouth.

"No."

Well, at least the asshole was honest. "Then we're done here. I'll see you in the next lifetime, brother."

"Stop. Come on, Cam. You know we need to talk. Let me explain, and then if you don't want to talk to me, we can be done. I need five minutes, but I have to finish that briefing. I can meet you at Oscar's at four, okay?" Rafe was already backing up, his five-hundred-dollar shoes squeaking against the marbled floor.

Oscar's Pub. They had spent a lot of nights unwinding at Oscar's. For a while it had been their favorite hangout. They'd spent every night there after work. They joked that there was a booth with their names on it. He and Rafe had taken turns sitting beside Laura while they discussed the workday. "Sure. Four o'clock."

Rafe smiled. "Four o'clock. I'll be there."

But Cam wouldn't. He waved at Rafe and then walked out the door, hopped on his bike, and motored right past the bar where he was supposed to give his ex-partner five minutes of his time. He wasn't going to waste another second.

When he pulled into his rathole of an apartment complex, he carefully unfolded the newspaper clipping he'd printed from the

Internet.

Billionaire Artist's Bride-to-Be.

It was an article featuring someone named Jennifer Waters and her spectacular wedding plans. The picture was of the bride-to-be and her bridesmaids. There were five other women in the picture, but he only saw one one. She stood toward the back as though she didn't want to be in the photo, but a smiling red-haired woman held her hand, dragging her in. Her lips quirked up in a secretive smile. She looked different with her hair down and very little makeup on her face. She looked vibrant and happy and so sweet he could eat her alive.

Laura Rosen.

The only woman he'd ever loved.

"I'm coming for you, baby." He hopped off his bike and jogged to his apartment, eager to get the hell out of Dodge.

* * * *

Rafael Kincaid pulled his Benz into the parking lot of the Hampton Manor Homes and felt a bit of his rage morph into guilt. He'd been furious when he realized Cam had stood him up. He'd rushed through the meeting, anxious to talk to Cam, to clear the air between them, and that asshole had gone home. Cam had stood him up and gone home to a dilapidated fourplex that he wouldn't have let a dog live in.

Cam lived here?

Damn it, he should have known. Cam had sent him an e-mail with his new address, but he'd been far too busy to do what he should have done. He should have helped Cam move. He should have checked this place out. He slid out of his car, which might be worth more than the entire building in front of him. There were four units, and at least three of them had to be housing meth labs. What the hell was Cam doing here?

Spending every dime he has looking for your woman.

It was obvious that Cam had spent all of his money on the computer equipment he needed to perfect his facial recognition software. Cam had given up comfort and safety.

Rafe scrubbed a hand across his face and felt years older than thirty-four. He could swear he'd aged twenty years since the night Laura Rosen had been captured by the Marquis de Sade. The minute he'd realized she was gone, his soul had become something older, heavier, than it had been before. Guilt weighed on him. Now he felt its press as he walked up the steps that led to Cam's "home."

Damn it. Why hadn't Cam told him he needed money? He would have happily written a check.

He rapped his knuckles across the peeling paint on the door. "Cam? Cam, let me in. I'm not going away, and I can see that your bike is parked outside. I know you're in there."

"And I should care about that, why?" Cam shouted it through the door.

"Because I'll tell you what you want to know. I brought the files and everything." He felt infinitely weary. He'd wanted to avoid talking to Cam about this because he didn't need anything else tugging at his conscience.

"I don't want to know anything. I'm good. You could get in some serious trouble for sharing that file with me. I hope you catch the bastard."

He was about to protest, to start to coax Cam out of his shell, but he'd known Cam for years. When Cam felt slighted, he could hold on to it like a baby clutching a prized toy. He was also tenacious as a pit bull. Cam should be drooling over new information about the man they had been hunting for years.

Four years before, they had made a deal. It had been almost a year after Laura had walked out of her hospital room leaving behind nothing but a note that told them a simple good-bye. They had killed themselves, splitting their time between trying to catch the Marquis de Sade and trying to track their missing lover. Neither one of them had had a decent night's sleep. It had been time to make a change.

He had stayed on at the FBI to keep on top of the case, and Cam had devoted himself to finding Laura. Cam had started a private investigations business, but it was almost entirely funded by Rafe. Cam had also started writing a software program that scanned the Internet not only searching for any mention of her name, but more importantly, looking for her face.

Cameron Briggs was not a man who gave up. Unless he'd found a much bigger prize.

"You motherfucker, you found her." He pounded on the door, his prior guilt morphing into red-hot jealousy. He wasn't about to let Cam waltz away with information on Laura. Laura was his, damn it. His.

"I don't know what you're talking about."

Rafe heard the unspoken "sucker" in Cam's shouted words. He lifted his leg and gave the piece-of-shit door separating him from his ex-partner a well-placed kick. The door itself held, but it cracked up the middle. Cam stared at him through his now ruined door.

"You're an asshole, and you're replacing that door." Cam reached out, and after two loud clicks, the door swung open.

He wasn't about to feel bad about the fucking door. "Where is she?"

Cam's mouth became a flat, stubborn line. A long huff of breath came out of his chest, and he pointed to a table in the tiny kitchen. "Colorado."

There was a printout of a newspaper article on the table. It was a copy of an article from the Lifestyle section of a Denver newspaper. He couldn't miss her even though she was surrounded by other women. Laura Rosen. He could still remember the day she'd walked into the Bureau. He'd known the moment he'd laid eyes on her that she was the one.

Unfortunately, Cam had felt the same way.

Unfortunately? Was it really so bad? At the time, it had felt that way. At the time, all he could think about was how enjoying a three-way with his partner and his soul mate would affect his career.

There wasn't a single sitting Bureau chief openly involved in a polyamorous relationship. At the time, he'd been willing to fight his best friend over her. He'd been willing to throw her under a bus to get ahead. Oh, he'd told himself he was helping her, but he was only thinking of himself.

Yep. The guilt was back.

"She's calling herself Laura Niles. Why does Niles sound familiar?" Rafe asked, his finger tracing over the picture. He wanted to touch her, to assure himself that she was real and alive and whole.

"Her grandfather's name was Niles. Niles Rosen. She loved that old man." Cam stood at his side, his arms crossed over his chest.

Rafe looked at the man he'd once been closer to than his own brother. Cam looked tired. There was a set to his shoulders that he recognized as defensiveness. Cam stood there in the piece-of-crap kitchen, a big, unmoving block of wood.

He could now understand what had truly happened this afternoon. Cam had come to the office to tell him he'd found Laura. He'd run through the building with this printout in his hand, and when he'd found Rafe, he'd walked in on what Cam had to assume was a betrayal of the worst kind. No wonder Cam hadn't met him at the pub.

He had to play this carefully if he didn't want to get his ass kicked.

"Stefan Talbot." Rafe whistled as he glanced over the article.

"Who the fuck is Stefan Talbot?"

He felt a grin come and go. That was Cam. Despite the fact that he was built like a linebacker, Cam was a nerd. He was far more into his computers and watching bad sci-fi movies than art. And Cam couldn't care less about society and powerful people. "He's an artist. My mother has one of his works. He's very reclusive. Supposedly he lives in a weird town in Colorado. And, according to this, Laura is in his wedding party."

"What the hell is she doing in some backwater small town?" Cam's shoulders relaxed slightly as he stared at the photo.

"Hiding. From the Marquis de Sade. From the Bureau. From us." Laura had a lot to run from. "But if he's back, then he could have seen this, too."

"Yeah, nice to fill me in on that." Cam's eyes had sunken back into his face as though retreating. "I must have missed the message you left. You know how it is when your social life is as active as mine is. Oh, wait. That's you. So, you too busy kissing the brass's ass to give an old friend a call?"

Cam was firmly pushing a whole bunch of his buttons, but he was determined to be patient. "Please hear me out."

"I don't know what the fuck you think you can say that would make me care."

How did he put this? He'd been thinking about this every minute since last Tuesday when he'd gotten word of the new victim. "I'm going to be honest with you. We found the body a couple of days ago. We've kept it quiet. I was worried about you. I remember what happened the last time you were on this case. I remember the drinking and the fights. I remember you nearly died on that damn bike. When we found that girl, do you know what I saw when I looked down at her? I saw you. I saw you falling into bad habits and getting your ass killed."

"And that would matter to you?"

What the hell was he supposed to say to that? The asshole wouldn't give him an inch. "I give a shit if you die, Cam. You couldn't handle it the first time. I wasn't about to send you down that path again."

"I couldn't handle it?" The words came out clipped, each bitten off through clenched teeth.

Rafe had tried to give him an easy way out. Cam was too damn stupid to take it. "You know you couldn't. You punched another special agent in the middle of a briefing. You wrecked your bike twice. You got arrested for public intoxication. I'm not bailing your ass out again."

"I wasn't asking you to."

"Oh, is that what this is about?" He gestured around the room that seemed to serve as Cam's kitchen, office, and bedroom. The whole place was covered in computer equipment. Wires and cords ran along the floor like thick vines. There was no rhyme or reason or organization to the place. He wouldn't be surprised if Cam opened a window to pee. "You don't want to have to ask me for money?"

"No, I don't. I'm sick of living off you." Cam's booted feet widened to a predatory stance.

Rafe was sick of Cam's insecurities. He'd put up with them for years. He'd never been able to convince Cam that he didn't give a shit that he'd grown up in a trailer park. It was Cam's problem. Not his. "You weren't living off me, you stupid, overly proud prick. It wasn't charity. You were working to find her. We agreed to this deal."

Cam's lips curled up in a smirking approximation of a smile. "Yeah, we agreed that you would share information with me, but you don't have to uphold your end of the bargain, do you? You don't have to share with a guy you consider your goddamn employee. That's why I didn't want your money. I didn't want to be your butt monkey anymore. Tell me something, Rafe, you been fucking any admins with Brad there? Brad working out as your wingman? I'll be sure to tell Laura when I see her that you're fine, because you finally found a partner you could truly love."

Without another thought, Rafe pulled back his fist and plowed into Cam with everything he had. Cam's head snapped back with a crack, but his body stayed in place. Too late, he remembered why Cam had gotten into that fight with another agent.

Cam liked it.

A feral smile crossed Cam's face right before he reared back and let his fist fly.

A lance of shock speared through Rafe's gut. His breath shot out of his body, and he staggered back, hitting the wall with a thud. Cam pressed his advantage. He landed another blow, this one an uppercut to Rafe's jaw. The pain exploded in his skull, and he fought back.

He shoved against Cam's bulk. Did the country boy expect the city boy to play fair? Rafe was done playing fair. It bought him nothing with Cam. He shoved out with both hands, and Cam fell back, stumbling over his sadly worn duffel bag.

"What were you thinking, Cam? Did you already have your bags packed when you came to see me? Do you honestly believe you can waltz back into her life? What do you have to offer her? You going to bring her back here?"

Cam's leg came out, sweeping across Rafe's ankles and knocking him down. Cam kicked himself up, years and years of martial arts practice turning the move into a graceful dance. Cam moved well for a man of any size, much less for a man who weighed in at two hundred and fifty pounds of pure muscle.

"And what are you going to give her? Are you going to bring her back to your condo and turn her into some trophy for your goddamn wall? She never meant anything to you. She was nothing more than a prize. You only wanted her to fuck with me." Cam stopped, his face going dumb for a minute. "Damn it, Rafe. What the fuck are we doing? I'm..."

Whatever Cam was going to say was utterly lost on him. All he knew was they had had this fight before. He was so fucking sick of having his money shoved back at him like it was something to be ashamed of. Cam wielded his impoverished childhood like a sword, and Rafe was done with it. City boy was done taking country boy's shit. With ruthless precision, he brought his foot up and kicked out. His heel met with Cam's cock, and Cam went down with a long, animal-like moan of pure agony.

Rafe rolled over and shoved himself to a standing position. He wiped the blood off his face. It was time to have a long talk with his ex-partner. They used to be best friends, and damn, but he missed the dumbass country boy.

"You got any beer in this hellhole?"

Cam's face was mottled up in a mask of pain. He cupped his

crotch, but he nodded toward the fridge. "It tastes like piss, but it's cold."

Rafe grabbed two beers and helped Cam to the couch.

"You're a fucking bastard." Cam groaned as he gingerly lowered himself to the cushions.

"Yeah, because you're so damn upstanding." His jaw was still throbbing as he propped his feet on Cam's wobbly coffee table. He took a long drink of the beer. Cam was right. It tasted like piss.

"I don't try to come off as Captain America."

Rafe rolled his eyes. "Well, at least I don't try to be the tough guy every minute of the day. Look, I really was concerned about you. I don't want you going off the deep end again."

Cam was too obsessive. Now that he was looking around the tiny apartment, he was even more concerned. There were printouts stacked to precarious heights. The only books in the place seemed to be about coding, and stuck all over the walls were handwritten lines of code on sticky notes. Cam had always been the guy who sank into a case. He needed someone to pull him out, and Rafe hadn't been there.

"That was the best year of my life," Cam said quietly.

Rafe knew exactly what he meant. That year before Laura had left had meant the world to him, too. It started as a joke. They had dared the gorgeous blonde profiler to date both of them. She had told them she didn't have the time. They would have to date her together.

They had gone to a movie and then a bar. The three of them had sat and talked until they were kicked out at closing time. It had only gotten awkward when they dropped her off. No one had gotten a kiss that night. And then they had settled into a friendship.

Months had passed, and she somehow became the center of their worlds. He'd been unwilling to push her to choose because she seemed to care about Cam so much. Cam had come alive. His thick, protective shell had cracked. Rafe had felt like a better person for knowing her.

And they had fucked up everything in a twenty-four-hour period.

"I have to see her again." Rafe had to stand in front of her, if only to beg her forgiveness.

"Do you still want her?" Cam asked.

"More than I want my next breath."

A long sigh came from Cam. "I want her, too. I've tried dating. I've been so mad at Laura that I've tried to fuck her out of my heart. I just feel…god, this is stupid. I feel dirty after I sleep with someone else."

"It's not stupid, man. I feel the same way." His dick had languished in limbo for the last eight months. That had been the last time he'd gone to bed with a woman and it had been a spectacular failure. He belonged to Laura. It was wrong to sleep with someone else.

Cam ran a hand through his hair, an obvious sign of frustration. "What the hell are we going to do? She walked away from us. Even if, by some miracle, we can make her want us again, she didn't want to choose."

The answer was staring them right in the face. "Okay, so we don't make her choose."

Cam sat up. "Are you saying what I think you're saying?"

"If we want to have a chance with her, if we want to get her to forgive us, we're going to have to give her everything she wants."

"Everything?" Cam asked. "I thought what we did that night was perverted. That's what you said to me the next morning."

"Well, we fucked the same girl at the same time. I think that's a little perverted by anyone's standards." He let that sit for a minute. "But it was also hot. I liked watching. I think we can make it work. We can share her. People do it. Somewhere." Rafe let his head fall back. Damn, he'd missed Cam. "I think I have a plan on how to get her to accept us, well, force her to accept us. Though it will probably make her mad. We'll have to hang out in that little town of hers for a while. And it totally takes us off the case."

"I'm okay with that. Laura's the important thing here."

Cam was right. They had put the case above her feelings before. It was time the case took a backseat.

"So we're going to Bliss. What a name." Rafe tipped back his beer. "You know, we're going to have to be aggressive. We're going to have to go after her hard and fast and together."

Cam settled back. "That might not go over so well in a small town."

"So what? You aren't a guy who minds a little scandal."

"Nope," Cam agreed. "But I didn't mind being the bad boy of the Bureau, either. It might bother you."

"She's worth it." He wasn't going to let some societal taboo keep him from Laura. Never again. Five years without her had taught him what he wanted. He'd spent years feeling incomplete. He couldn't go the rest of his life without knowing where she was, and he was pretty sure that once he found her, he would do whatever it took to stay in her life. If he had to share her with his best friend, then that was what he would do.

An hour later everything was in place, including their airline tickets and a rental car. Within twenty-four hours, they would be in Bliss.

Rafe hoped Bliss was ready for a little scandal.

* * * *

Deep in the night, he watched. It was easy to blend into this particular part of the city. All he had to do was look hungry.

That wasn't hard. He was always hungry.

That little meal he'd had the week before hadn't even begun to take the edge off what he needed. The whore had gone down far too easily. A few taps and she'd knelt at his feet. The fight she'd put up had been halfhearted, as though she hadn't truly minded dying.

Oh, she'd minded the pain. She'd howled, but even that had been sad compared to his rabbit.

When he closed his eyes, he saw her blonde beauty stretched out on his rack. He saw her eyes filled with rage. She wouldn't have gone down easy. He could have played his game with her for days and never gotten bored.

Oh, the plans he'd had for her until the clever bitch had managed to escape.

She'd won that round. She wouldn't win again.

He'd known all he had to do was follow the horny men. They would do the work for him. The rabbit had run, but she couldn't hide forever.

Now all his plans were coming together. It was fate. He hadn't actually meant for the feds to find his latest kill, but he wasn't upset about it either. It would throw them off.

He adjusted the device in his ear as he took another long drink of the green tea he'd placed in a forty-ounce beer container. There he was another bum looking to get drunk on a Thursday night. He pulled the hood over his head despite the heat.

He'd listened in on Cameron Briggs's completely worthless life for years. Now he finally had something to show for it.

Bliss, Colorado.

He got up, and by the time he reached his car three blocks away, he'd shed his bum persona. No one would know him now.

He'd found his pretty rabbit. It was time to go hunting again.

Chapter Two

Laura Niles studied herself in the mirror. She had to admit the peach color Brooke Harper had selected for the bridesmaids' dresses warmed up her skin tone.

"I don't think there's enough fabric in the world," a sad voice said beside her.

Laura looked over at Callie Hollister-Wright. She was almost eight months pregnant, and she was lovely to Laura's eyes, but she was also very, very round. "You look beautiful. Brooke needs to let it out a bit, that's all."

Callie sniffled as she stared at herself in the mirror. She hadn't been able to zip up the back of her dress. "Maybe I should let someone else take my place. Brooke can't keep letting the dress out."

"Yes, I can," Brooke said with a vibrant smile. "For what Stef's paying me, I will happily let that sucker out twice during the ceremony if I have to."

Brooke patted Laura on the shoulder. She leaned in. "I need to take up your hem, but I'd like to get Callie done first so she can go rest. Do you mind?"

Callie needed to be off her feet. Laura took a step back. "Not at all. I don't have to be at work today. I'll sit down with Nell and Holly. You let me know if I can help."

Laura couldn't miss the way Callie gave her a once-over as she stepped away. She could guess what Callie was thinking. Callie was wishing she had her body. How could she tell Callie that she would change bodies with her in an instant? She would do it without ever missing her own body because despite her perfect size-six figure, she would never be round and full like Callie was now. She would never complain about swallowing a beach ball or how she waddled or how often the baby growing inside her kicked. She could never be pregnant, and Callie couldn't know how that made her ache inside.

"I think it is so nice of you to write that man," Nell was saying as Laura made her way from the makeshift dressing room through the souvenir aisle. Laura walked into the teeny-tiny tearoom at the Trading Post that overlooked Main Street.

"Well, I figured he must be lonely. He's in a foreign country after all," Holly said, taking a sip of tea as she looked over a letter.

Laura banished her sad thoughts and felt a smile crinkle her lips. Holly was such a bullshitter. "Are you seriously trying to pass off your prison love letters as some community service project? Nell, she and Alexei have been trading flirty letters. She's not trying to save his soul."

Nell looked up and smiled that ridiculously brilliant smile of hers. Whenever Laura got in a bad mood, all she had to do was get Nell to smile to force one of her own. Nell genuinely believed all the crap she pushed. She believed in the good of man. She believed in saving the Earth. Nell believed, and Laura thought it was a lovely thing. "Well, it wasn't like Alexei did something terrible. I mean the 'killing people' thing was awful and all, but have you heard about what the Russian mob does? It's horrible. And they don't recycle."

"And it's not prison love," Holly said with a prim sigh. "It's witness protection friendship. He's in witness protection while the trial is going on. I have no idea if this thing we have is going to go

34

anywhere once the trial is over. It's a friendship. With some flirting. Although honestly, I don't know if he's flirting. I still don't understand half the things he says to me. He doesn't write English any better than he speaks it. Like this—'Holly, you are very cold woman. I wish to see you once more to spend the times with you, not to do hooking thing, but to talk, to know the real womens inside you.' I think he might think I'm a cold-blooded prostitute with multiple personality disorder."

Laura let her head fall back, the giggle coming from a place deep inside her. It was easy to let go of the pains of the past when she was surrounded by her friends. "Oh, I don't think so, sweetie. Let me translate for you. He thinks you're a cool chick. He wants to spend time with you, but not to hook up. He wants to know who you are inside. He's crazy about you."

Holly flushed, her skin turning almost as red as her hair. "I doubt that. He's so young. I'm almost forty. I have a teenager."

Nell reached across the table, her hand rubbing over Holly's. "You're a wonderful woman, Holly. Any man would be lucky to be with you."

"Speaking of men," Laura said, reaching for the sugar, "has the doc finally gotten past the stuttering stage?"

Doctor Caleb Burke had been circling around Holly like a socially awkward shark.

Holly folded the letter and put it in her purse. She let her head sink down to her hand. "Well, he manages to start sentences, but then he always asks for coffee and then goes quiet again. I don't know what to do with him. Everyone says he likes me, but he never talks to me. My love life is sad. I have one man who can't get two words out around me and another who barely speaks my language. I'm going to die alone."

"Nope," Laura said to her best friend. "I'll be right there with you."

Nell and Holly both sat forward.

"Did the stud turn out to be a dud?" Holly asked, her eyes wide.

Nell shook her head Holly's way. "Wolf has a mind, Holly. It's not a good thing to sexually objectify the man."

The man in question chose that moment to walk across the street. Wolf Meyer was a stud. Nell was flat wrong. There was no way to not sexually objectify that hot hunk of man. The former Navy SEAL stood long and lean in his jeans and a T-shirt that hugged his strong, muscular chest. His hair was dark, but there was very little of it. He looked like the military man he was.

And he was coming her way. Laura gave him a wave through the window. They'd gone out on exactly two dates. She'd kissed him once before she had realized it wouldn't work. There was no spark between them beyond friendship, but Wolf Meyer was a good man to know.

"God, that man is hot as hell." Nell's mouth hung open. She slapped her hands across it as if she could push the words back in. "Please don't tell Henry I said that."

"Your secret's safe with us." Holly winked Laura's way.

It was always nice when Nell slipped a bit and proved she was wholly human. "He's a yummy man, but it didn't work out."

It hadn't worked out between Wolf and her for several reasons. Though they had a lot in common, they still felt more like friends than lovers, but she feared the reasons went far deeper for her. It hadn't worked out because Wolf wasn't Cameron Briggs or Rafael Kincaid. How could those two men still affect her all these years later? She'd told herself time and time again that she was over them, so why had she been unable to get them out of her head? Why had she seen their faces when Wolf Meyer had leaned over her and bent his head for a kiss?

"Ladies," Wolf said, the word rolling off his tongue with lazy charm.

"Hi," Holly managed to squeak.

Nell simply waved and took a long drink of her tea.

"What's up with you, Wolf?" Laura asked.

He gave her a sexy smile that had her wishing things were

different between them. "Well, I was actually looking for you."

"OMG! The dress is gorgeous. Brooke is a genius!" Jen Waters's voice rang out as she opened the door to the Trading Post and glided in with Rachel Harper in tow. There was a sling around Rachel's body, and a fat baby face peeked out. Paige Harper was the sweetest thing Laura had seen in forever.

But her momma did not look amused. "Nell, we need to have a talk."

Nell smiled up, seeming to not notice Rachel's narrowed eyes or the flat set of her mouth. "I would love to talk to you, Rachel."

Rachel was not amused. "What the hell are you doing? Midwifery? Seriously?"

Nell opened her arms as though ready to embrace anything that came her way. "Yes. I have decided to study the ancient art of midwifery since it seems we're having a baby boom in Bliss. I've tried to talk to everyone about population control, but I've given this a lot of thought. It makes sense that you and Max and Rye would have little Paige. And Callie is having her baby with two men. If you all weren't in polyamorous relationships, you might have had more children. When you think about it, it's a thoughtful way to raise a family. So, I think I should help bring this new generation of human beings into the world as naturally as possible."

Rachel kept one hand on her daughter as she stalked Nell. "Look, Callie is one of my closest friends in the world. She's one of the sweetest human beings I have ever met."

Nell nodded, her dark hair shaking. "I agree. Callie has a beautiful soul. Her aura is so pure. The shaman I've been learning from says a pure aura is important."

Wolf snorted and then sat down, his huge body perched precariously on the delicate chair. "You're learning to deliver babies from a shaman?"

"Oh, yes," Nell replied. "She's brilliant. She's in touch with all the ley lines that run through the valley. It's where she pulls her energy from. She's from Del Norte, like you, Wolf."

Wolf's eyebrows rose on his face. "Are you talking about crazy Irene? She works at the Dairy Queen."

Nell waved off that tidbit of information. "The universe leads us where it will. She's recommended a home water birth for Callie's son. Oh, and Rachel, she's already had a vision of your daughter and Callie's son. Don't tell Max, but they get married. And some guy named Charlie. I don't know who he is."

"I fucking love this place," Wolf said under his breath.

Laura stood, ready to throw herself in front of Nell if Rachel started playing Mama Bear, and it was almost a sure thing at this point. She liked Rachel, but more than that, she understood Rachel. Rachel was the alpha female of her group. Rachel led a tribe that included Callie and Jen. And Laura had found herself with Holly and Nell under her wing. Laura crossed her arms over her chest and sent Rachel a look, alpha female to alpha female.

"What do you think I'm going to do, Laura? I'm not going to murder her," Rachel said with a huff. "Not when I'm holding my baby."

"She's sworn not to kill anyone around her baby," Jen added with a serious nod.

Nell looked from one face to another as though trying to figure out where she'd gone wrong. "Don't worry. I'm prepared. The tub at Callie's cabin is too small, so I've found a biodegradable kiddie pool that I think will work."

Holly groaned as her head hit the table.

Rachel growled as she leaned in. "Look, Nell, feel free to prophesize all you like, but Callie is not having a water birth. She's my friend, and I have to look out for her. I have been lying to her for months, and I will continue to lie to her because I don't want her to be scared, but here's the truth. Giving birth hurts. I mean it really fucking hurts. Oh, I know that according to Callie, Zane and Nate have seriously stretched out that whole part of her body, but I refuse to believe that Zane Hollister's cock is as big as a baby's head." Rachel pointed to her daughter's perfectly round noggin. "Look at that. Oh, it's a little bigger than it was then, but not much. That came out of my vagina. And no one thought to lube her head up. You would think the way these men are in this town that someone would have a tube of K-Y on their persons, but no. No lube, Rachel. No whiskey, Rachel. No, you're giving birth. You can't have a hamburger in between contractions. Callie is going to the hospital. Callie is going to have drugs."

Nell stood up but didn't move past the safety of Laura's back. Despite her sometimes out-of-touch-with-the-real-world nature, she had a healthy sense of self-preservation. "But women have been giving birth naturally for thousands of years."

Rachel had an answer for that, too. "Well, people have been crapping in the forests for thousands of years, too, Nell, but I don't see you and Henry giving up your indoor plumbing. It's called progress. When Callie goes into the hospital, I'm going to tell those doctors to put all the drugs they have into her epidural. All of them. And don't you even talk about a silent birth. There's nothing silent about birth. It's loud. First there's the screaming because of the contractions, and then there's some man whining about me breaking his hand. That wasn't what I wanted to break that day, let me tell you."

"Hey, guys." Callie had a bright smile on her face as she made her way toward the table. She'd changed back into her street clothes, which included shorts and one of the new T-shirts from her husband's bar. It had the Trio logo and sported a new "tourist friendly" slogan that the town council had informed all of the business owners in Bliss they must use to rehabilitate Bliss's image.

Don't worry about the murder rate in Bliss
The wings are hot at Trio

"I bet the mayor adores that shirt," Laura said with a genuine smile. Zane Hollister was an asshole, but damn if he wasn't a lovable one.

Callie smoothed her T-shirt over her pregnant belly. "Well, Zane and Nate don't agree that we need to change Bliss's image as a place where tourists get murdered."

Holly leaned back, crossing one leg over the other. "Most of the murders that have occurred here weren't our fault. Rachel had to kill her stalker. That shouldn't count."

"They count him as a tourist because he bought some fudge from Teeny," Rachel explained. "And the guy Callie killed stayed at the motel. So did that Ivan fellow, who is the only one who killed an actual tourist."

Callie tapped a foot against the floor. "And those other Russian mob guys weren't in town long enough to buy anything before we killed them. They shouldn't count. I think the mayor is making way too much of that tiny article."

It hadn't been tiny. It had been a feature in *Time* magazine. The reporter, a woman named Mia Danvers, had wondered if Bliss, Colorado, wasn't the most dangerous place in the United States to visit. Strangely, Laura had noticed it hadn't really kept the tourists away. If nothing else, there had been an odd surge of thrill seekers, but the mayor and the town council were busily trying to refute the statistics.

"Zane wants to make sure no one else moves here," Callie continued. "He likes Bliss exactly the way it is. He and Nate are like those immigrants who come to a place and then want to build a wall to keep everyone else out."

Rachel sighed. "I think Max and Rye are right there with them. Are you ready for some lunch? Jen and I thought we could have some girl time."

Callie leaned over and kissed Paige's nearly bald head. "I wouldn't miss it for the world." She turned back to Nell. "I'll see you on Friday. I can't wait to start my breathing exercises. And tell Irene to bring me a double chocolate Blizzard."

As they left, Rachel turned back to Nell, her eyes silently promising retribution if Callie didn't get her drugs.

"Hey, Holly and Nell, I'm ready for you guys," Brooke Harper called out from the back of the store.

Holly got up. "Time to get poked and prodded."

"Darlin', it's always the right time to get prodded if it's with the right instrument," Wolf said with a grin on his ridiculously handsome face.

Holly shook her head and wandered off to her fitting. Nell gave Laura a hug.

"Maybe Rachel is right. Maybe I should think about my plumbing practices."

It was time to go a little alpha on Nell. "Nell, you are not getting an outhouse. No one will come to your place and make blankets for the homeless if they have to use an outhouse."

Nell bit at her lower lip. "I suppose you're right. Well, I like my bathroom anyway, and if it helps the homeless, then I'll keep it the way it is."

"You're good with her," Wolf said as Laura sat back down after her friends were gone. "And you were quite good with Rachel. You're a very intuitive woman."

Laura took a sip of her tea and wished with all her heart she could feel a deep connection to the man in front of her. Wolf Meyer was everything she could hope for. He was well educated, gorgeous, and kind. He was easier to get along with than any man she'd met in a long time. So why did she long for the fight? For the push and pull she'd had with Rafe and Cam?

Rafe and Cam had turned out to be assholes.

She stopped herself. She couldn't think that way. They weren't assholes. They were men looking out for their careers. That was the way it was in the real world. It hadn't been their fault that she'd been taken hostage and nearly murdered by a serial killer. They had followed their leads, and she'd followed hers. Her heart ached, but that was the way it was.

A callused hand slid over hers. "You're so far away."

"Sorry. I was thinking about something else."

41

"Or someone else," Wolf murmured. "I was going to ask you if you wanted to go out with me tonight. I think your answer is going to be no, isn't it?"

"Oh, Wolf, I am sorry."

He shook his head. "It's all right. I like you. I like you a lot, but I don't intend to be here for too long. I'm getting back in."

She doubted that. Wolf had been discharged from the Navy against his own wishes. He'd taken heavy fire in Afghanistan, and given his injuries, the Navy decided to decline his offer to re-up. He'd flown in to Washington weeks before to try to talk his way back in, but she doubted it would happen.

"I hope you do," she said.

Wolf seemed a bit lost. He'd come home to recuperate at his mother's house. He'd been working odd jobs in the months since he'd returned.

"It'll happen," he said with confidence. "Now, I was also looking for you for another reason. Do you have any idea why the feds would be looking for you?"

She sat straight up, every nerve in her body sparking with suspicion. "What feds?"

"I went by your place, and there were a couple of feds knocking on your door. They asked if I knew where you were, but I said no. I said I hadn't seen you in a couple of days, but they should go up to Mountain and Valley because you spend a lot of time up there."

And they would believe Wolf because he was an excellent liar. She sensed that about him. He wouldn't do it if he didn't have to, but when the occasion called for it, Wolf Meyer could lie and never bat an eye. He would have made an excellent CIA operative if he hadn't been a SEAL. She couldn't help it. Even five years after she'd been fired from her job, she still profiled everyone around her. "That should throw them off for a while."

Mountain and Valley was the local naturist community, a nudist colony on the mountain. Bill Hartman ran the place, and he didn't like feds, either. Bliss was a suspicious community. Bill would likely send them on a merry chase.

Wolf leaned forward in his chair, his dark eyes softening, drawing her in. He was also damn good at that. "I wanted to give you some time if you needed to get out of here. I don't have anything to do, Laura. If you want to, say, take a trip, I can go with you, make sure you're safe. I can take care of you."

Oh, yeah, she was a dumb shit for not falling for this guy, but it wouldn't be fair to him. "I'm not on the run, Wolf. Well, not in the way you think. I'm not wanted for anything."

"But you would prefer not to talk to the feds?"

Oh, she would prefer to never see a federal agent for the rest of her life. When she'd walked out of DC, she'd done it for good. She'd known she would never go back. That was why she'd changed her name and hadn't spoken to anyone she knew from there in five years. Her parents were gone. She had a sister who lived in France. Laura talked to her once a year, but Michelle had promised not to tell anyone where Laura was. They had agreed that it was best for Laura to hide. Given the fact that she was certain the Marquis de Sade was involved in some sort of law enforcement, she didn't particularly want them to know where she was hiding.

"No, I would rather not talk to them, but now I'm curious." And a little scared. Had he caught up to her? "Are you sure they were FBI?"

"If they weren't, then they were doing a damn fine impersonation. And that's the other thing I want to talk to you about. We need to get rid of those guys, whoever they are. Mel is out at my mom's, but he's going to come into town at some point in time today, and what's he going to see? Two dudes in suits and sunglasses riding around in a dark SUV."

She sighed. Mel wouldn't see feds. Mel was a lovely man, but he was also insanely paranoid about aliens and all the things that went with them. "Men in black."

Wolf pointed. "On the nose, love. My mom's boyfriend is going to flip out, and then he'll come and get my mom and they'll end up in the bomb shelter plotting how to survive the invasion, and I'll have to call my brother to talk her down. I don't want to call my brother. Every time I call my brother I get a lecture about moving on. I get some Zen-craptastic speech on how getting booted from the teams is the best thing in the world for me—or it would be if I would get a job. Like he has a job. Do you know what he does? My sainted brother works in a BDSM club spanking subs. Maybe if some dude was willing to pay me a ton of money to spank pretty subs, I would be fine with my military career being over. So we need to figure out how to get the feds into something less conspicuous than those suits so my mom's boyfriend doesn't freak. You see the precarious house of cards I live in?"

Wolf was talking, but his voice had faded to the background. Only one thing held Laura's attention as a big, black SUV pulled up, and she realized her time was up.

It was happening. Someone had found her.

Why had the FBI tracked her down? Had something changed with the de Sade case? Her heart fluttered at the thought of having to get involved in that again. She felt herself get a little faint. Best-case scenario—this was unrelated and someone needed to talk to her about the Russian mob coming through town a few months before. She'd stayed off the record, but someone might have mentioned her name. Worst-case scenario? She'd been right. The Marquis de Sade had tracked her down because he wouldn't want to leave loose ends.

"Laura? Are you okay?" Wolf stood and then knelt at her side, his hand grasping hers. "Maybe I should take you upstairs so you can lie down."

The door to the SUV opened.

"I'm sorry, sweetheart. I should have dealt with them myself," Wolf said in a deep, soothing tone. This was another reason Laura had known she and Wolf couldn't work out. He was so much more interested in her when she needed help. Wolf was looking for a damsel in distress.

Where the hell had he been five years ago?

44

"I'm fine. I'm seeing ghosts, that's all. I can handle them." And if de Sade had come for her, then maybe she had some unfinished business with him, too. But it was more than likely about the mob trials. Alexei Markov had set off a firestorm when he'd decided to turn on his mob boss. Nate Wright, Bliss's sheriff and Callie's second husband, had already had his fill of feds. He'd complained to Laura about it earlier in the day.

Except the minute the dark-haired man in the perfectly tailored suit slid gracefully from the SUV, she realized this had nothing to do with Alexei's case.

She'd left out a scenario.

Armageddon. In that scenario, Rafael Kincaid showed up and her past finally, truly caught up with her. Laura closed her eyes and prayed it was an illusion. That glorious man in the suit wasn't Rafe. She opened her eyes.

Shit. It was Rafe, and he wasn't alone. An enormous man walked behind him. His suit wasn't perfectly tailored. He looked uncomfortable in it, like any moment his body was going to burst from its confines.

Cameron Briggs.

Rafe was an elegant bird of prey, while Cam was a huge tiger stalking his next meal.

What the hell were they doing here? When she'd left, she'd made damn sure that the two men who had broken her heart into tiny pieces and then stomped on it in a public forum couldn't find her. Oh, sure, they'd been all tears and apologies after she'd been nearly murdered, but that had been nothing more than guilt.

"Do you know those men?" Wolf asked.

She knew every inch of those men. She knew how Rafe liked his cock sucked and that Cam could eat pussy all night long. She knew them intimately and far beyond the physical ways they liked to fuck. She'd spent a year getting to know them. She'd spent a year working and drinking and talking with them. She knew Cam was ashamed of how he'd grown up and Rafe hated that people knew he came from wealth.

She knew they valued their placement in the FBI far more than they could ever love a woman.

Laura nodded.

"From the look on your face, it wasn't a good thing. Do I need to kick some ass?"

"No," she said quickly. Wolf would do it, and he would get in trouble.

Rafe and Cam were looking up and down the street, their mouths moving in short, clipped words. Finally, almost in slow motion, Cam turned and stopped. He stood looking at her in the window, as still as a statue. Rafe watched him for a moment, and then turned as well.

"Laura." There was no mistaking the word Rafe's mouth made.

She stood, utterly panicked at the thought of them walking in and realizing that after five years she still wasn't over them. How pathetic was that?

Rafe moved first, followed by Cam. They stormed into the Trading Post, stalking through the tourist merchandise and the candy aisle until they made it to the tea room.

"Laura." Cam was the one who said her name now. "We found you."

"No thanks to him," Rafe said, eyeing Wolf, who stood beside her. "He sent us on a wild-goose chase. You look good, *bella*."

Bella. Beautiful. It was what he'd called her when they had made love. How dare he ever call her that again.

What if they had come after her? What if they had figured out what a mistake they had made? Rafe was eating her up with his eyes. Cam was pulling his alpha male act, staring Wolf down. What if they had searched for her, longed for her the way she'd longed for them?

"You know what you did was illegal," Cam was saying, his icy blue eyes laser-focused on Wolf. She stared at him for a long moment. His golden hair was cut short. She'd always wanted to see what it would look like longer, but Cam liked the simplicity. It highlighted his masculine face. Cam was all sharp angles with the exception of his sensual lips. God, she remembered what it felt like to have his mouth on her. "You impeded an investigation. You lied to duly appointed federal agents."

She felt her hope die. They were here on a case. Of course. How silly to think they still gave a damn about her.

"Who the hell do you think you are?" Cam asked Wolf.

"He's my fiancé." Laura said the words without really thinking. It was instinct that caused her to protect herself. She slid her hand into Wolf's and lied through her teeth. "We're engaged to be married."

Rafe's face fell. Cam took a step back.

Wolf hauled her close. "You know how it goes, gentlemen. I'm not one to let something like an investigation get in the way of true love."

Yep. Wolf Meyer was cool as a cucumber under pressure.

And she was definitely under pressure.

Chapter Three

Cam Briggs felt like his gut had been kicked straight out of his body.

Engaged? How the hell could she be engaged? He tried to wrap his brain around those words. He'd spent the last five years of his life thinking of nothing but Laura, and she had been getting engaged to some dickwad military guy.

He had to be military. Ex-military, Cam would bet. And that dude wasn't afraid of a little PDA.

"Sorry, I had no idea why you were looking for her," said the asshole who seemed to be trying to inhale Laura's hand. He'd brought it to his lips, and his other arm had snaked around her waist, drawing her close to his body. "When you have something this gorgeous, you have to take care of it."

"She's not an 'it,'" Cam snarled.

Rafe put a hand out, a silent request that he stay calm. It was a familiar gesture, one he'd seen a lot over the years. Rafe took over, all smooth professionalism.

"We understand," Rafe said, gesturing to the table behind Laura. "If I had a fiancée as beautiful as yours, I would protect her at all costs, too. Please, if you would sit with us, we do need to talk to

48

Laura."

Cam tried to get to that calm place that seemed to come so easily to Rafe.

As Laura and her affianced asshole sat down, Rafe leaned in and whispered in his ear. "Watch them. There's something wrong with this scenario. Look at her body language."

Cam settled down. Rafe had always been good at getting him to think. It had been that way ever since the first day they'd been partnered up. Somehow Rafe had known how to deal with him. Rafe had made him comfortable.

He hadn't been comfortable for five years. Maybe he'd missed more than Laura.

"Laura, it's good to see you." Rafe's voice had taken on that soft, soothing tone he used on reluctant witnesses.

Cam looked at her. Really looked at her. When he'd seen her before, all he'd been able to see was the woman he loved, her golden-blonde hair, her sky-blue eyes. She was curvier than she had been before. It looked damn good on her. She was wearing a form-fitting pinkish dress that hugged her new curves. And her breasts. Damn, they were bigger, too. Plump and round, they looked like they were about to pop out of her dress. They would fill his hands now.

She'd looked like a model before. She looked like a woman now, a delicious, luscious woman.

And she belonged to someone else.

She smiled, but it was her fake smile, the one she used on people who annoyed her but she had to put up with. It didn't reach her eyes. "You, too, Special Agent Kincaid. Apparently you've already met my fiancé, Wolf Meyer."

Wolf's lips curled up in a smirk. "He's had the pleasure. Though neither of you seemed interested in giving me your names."

Laura's manners seemed to take over. "This is Special Agent Rafael Kincaid and Special Agent Cameron Briggs. I knew them when I was in the FBI. We worked a couple of very important cases together. I take it that's why you're here."

Cam felt a foot nudge against his. It was a long-used cue for the bad cop to come out. In this case, the bad cop was the honest one. Damn, he'd missed working with Rafe. "I'm not an agent anymore."

Laura's eyes flared, and her mouth opened slightly.

"You're sure dressed like one, buddy." There was no way to mistake the mocking tone of Wolf's voice.

Laura didn't seem amused. She shifted slightly, as though uncomfortable. She didn't look like a woman who was used to the man beside her. Rafe was right. Something was wrong. Though he knew it made him a bastard, a fierce joy lit inside him. If something was wrong between Laura and her fiancé, then there was still a chance.

"What do you mean you aren't with the Bureau anymore?" Laura asked.

"I left," he replied. "I resigned about a year after you disappeared. I had a job to do, and I couldn't do it at the Bureau."

Rafe settled back in his chair. "We decided that one of us should look for you full time. Cam became a private investigator, and I stayed on at the FBI to watch the case."

Laura shook her head as though she was having a hard time understanding. "You've been looking for me?"

A small, older lady walked up, a pleated white apron wrapped around her slender form. "Hello, welcome to the Tea Room. Can I get you anything?"

Cam softened. The older woman reminded him of his mom. She looked a bit tired, but there was a smile on her face anyway. He hated tea, but he couldn't refuse her. "I'll take whatever she's having."

"And I would love a cup of chai, if you have it," Rafe added.

Laura introduced them, her Southern manners taking over. The woman in the apron was named Teeny Green. Cam shook her hand and assured her he was pleased to meet her.

"Anything for you, Wolf?" Teeny asked.

"I'm fine. Laura and I were discussing our wedding plans." Wolf's hand went to the back of Laura's neck, sliding over it as though he enjoyed the intimate touch.

Teeny stopped and stared for a moment. She looked from Wolf to Cam and Rafe. Her eyes narrowed. "Did you boys know Laura from her days in the FBI?"

"Yes, ma'am," Rafe said. "We knew her well."

"Oh, that's interesting. Well, we're so happy to have her in Bliss," Teeny said. "And we're thrilled to have so many weddings this year."

"Well, we were thinking of eloping," Laura said, fidgeting.

Teeny shook her head. "No, no, dear. I think it should be huge. We'll have to look over flowers and get those ordered."

"Absolutely," Wolf said. "Nothing but the best for my bride. We're going to fill the church with flowers. And we'll want to release doves at the end of the ceremony, won't we? To symbolize our love."

And he was crazy. Who released doves? Birds crapped everywhere. It didn't seem like a smart thing to unleash on a wedding party. If he was marrying Laura, he would do exactly what she'd suggested. He would take her to Vegas, sign whatever papers he had to, and then get to the good part. He and Rafe would keep her in bed for days.

It was getting easier and easier to think that way. She was theirs. Not just his. Laura belonged to them.

Teeny reached around and pulled two white T-shirts off a rack. "And Laura, you need to get those boys out of the suits. Mel is going to freak when he sees them, and the doc will have to tranq him again. They can have these. Why the mayor thought it was a good idea to let Zane head the Rehab Bliss committee, I have no idea. I knew that boy was up to something when he volunteered to do it. Now I have a hundred T-shirts. What am I going to do with them?"

Teeny held out the shirt.

The Trading Post
We make murder clean up easy

Cam couldn't help but laugh.

"You should see the shirts he made for Stella's," Laura murmured. "I'll make sure they're properly dressed before Mel sees them. And if you wouldn't mind letting Holly and Nell know I'm down here with my fiancé?"

"I intend to tell everyone, dear," Teeny said as she walked away.

"So why did you come all the way out here?" Laura asked, her voice crisp and tight. She seemed to be done with small talk.

Time for the bad cop again. "De Sade is back."

There was no way to soften it, and he wouldn't try. Rafe's approach worked on witnesses, but Laura was tough. She wouldn't want to be handled with kid gloves. She was smart and capable, and he wouldn't treat her any other way.

Her face lost every ounce of color, and it was all he could do not to take her in his arms. She might be capable, but that didn't mean he didn't want to shelter her, or at least let her know she wasn't in this alone. Fiancé or no fiancé, he wouldn't walk away from her. Not until the Marquis de Sade was dead or behind bars.

"We found a body last week in the warehouse district of DC. Same MO. The victim was a prostitute," Rafe explained in a calm, matter-of-fact manner.

Wolf sat up, his shoulders set in something other than decadent playfulness. "Who are we talking about? Does this have to do with a case Laura worked when she was in the FBI?"

Rafe turned, his brows up slightly. It was his what-the-fuck look.

Cam was sure the same expression was on his face. Laura hadn't told her fiancé about the biggest case of her career? She hadn't told the man she loved about the case that had almost gotten her killed? That was hard to believe. "Have you heard of the

Marquis de Sade?"

Wolf snorted. "Well, if you knew who my brother was, you would know the answer to that. Sometimes I think my brother works for the bastard."

Rafe shook his head. "Not the French aristocrat."

Laura held a hand up. "You'll have to forgive Wolf. He's been overseas for years. He recently got out of the Navy. He's not up on all the latest serial killers."

"Serial killers?" a feminine voice asked. "Why are we talking about serial killers?"

Cam looked up as two women entered the small dining area. They wore matching dresses, the same as the one Laura wore. One was a voluptuous redhead with a suspicious grin on her face. The other was a sweet-looking brunette.

"No reason at all, Holly," Laura said, standing up suddenly. "These gentlemen are with the FBI. Well, Special Agent Kincaid is. He's with a unit called the BAU. The Behavioral Analysis Unit."

"You used to work there," Holly said.

Cam studied the redhead. She had spoken of Laura's work with friendly curiosity. There was no horror or fear in the redhead's words. Laura hadn't told Holly what had happened to her, either. Had she told a single soul in this town what she'd been through? Had she held it in all these years?

"Yes, where I used to work. Special Agent Kincaid, Cameron Briggs, and I were friends," Laura said. "They thought I should know about what's been going on in the Bureau since I left."

Friends? Friends? He had a sudden urge to get up out of the chair, haul her into his arms, and remind her of how friendly they'd been. He could still feel her pussy clench around his cock, and he hadn't slept with her in five years.

"Our relationship was closer than that," Rafe said.

"This isn't some reunion, Laura. This is serious." He hadn't expected their first meeting in five years to go this way. Cam didn't know what he'd expected, but it certainly wasn't sitting in a tea room meeting all of Laura's new small-town friends. It sure as fuck hadn't included meeting her fiancé. Now she was treating them like they'd breezed into town for a chat and they would breeze right out. She was going to be terribly disappointed.

"How serious?" Holly asked.

The dark-haired woman next to her was gesturing wildly. Both Holly and Laura watched her.

"No, Nell, a serial killer isn't coming to Bliss," Laura said with a long sigh.

Holly shrugged. "Sorry, she's taken a vow of silence, and I think you know why, future Mrs. Wolf Meyer."

"You two are totally invited to our wedding," Wolf offered.

"What's this about a serial killer coming to town?" Teeny asked as she set down the tea. "Did they hear about the T-shirts? I don't care how big that Zane Hollister is, if we attract serial killers because of his smart mouth, I can put him over my knee. Has anyone told the sheriff yet?"

"No one needs to tell the sheriff," Laura said.

Rafe held a hand up. "Actually, we probably do need to liaise with the sheriff. Does anyone know where he is? There's a sign on the door that claims he's out fishing."

The brunette brought her foot down. Despite the elegant dress she wore, there was a pair of hippie-dippy sandals on her feet. She gestured around the room, her arms flying about and a wild look in her eyes.

"Sorry, she wants you to understand that she believes that the Rio Grande is overfished in this part of the world," Holly explained.

The brunette's arms went wide.

"In every part of the world," Holly corrected. She shrugged as though in apology. "Well, every part that the Rio Grande is in. Nell doesn't appreciate the sheriff's frequent fishing trips. Even though most of the time he catches and releases."

That didn't seem to satisfy Nell. She put her forefinger in her mouth like a hook and flapped her body around.

"No, Nell," Laura said. "I wouldn't like it either. It would definitely cause some psychological damage. You should talk to Nate about it, when you're back to talking."

"Okay." He knew it was a bad idea to ask the question, but he was so damn curious. Everything about this small town was starting to intrigue him. It was nothing like the tiny town he'd been born in. "Why won't Nell talk? Have we offended her in some way?"

It wouldn't be the first time he'd offended someone, though usually the offended party yelled at him rather than refusing to speak.

Nell chose to start dancing.

Laura's eyes lit up. It was so different from the tight expression that had owned her face since the moment he'd laid eyes on her again. Laura smiled, a light creasing of her lips that softened her whole face. Her shoulders relaxed, and she watched Nell with great affection. She turned her head slightly as she spoke with a wry tongue. "She's taken a vow of silence, but she can communicate through interpretive dance."

"Seriously?" Cam asked.

"Oh, Nell is always serious about interpretive dance," Holly explained.

"She says she can't talk in a world filled with lies," Laura said as Nell twirled around the room. "So many lies when only the truth should be spoken. She says that lies never work and only get people in trouble. She's very judgmental."

Nell stopped and stared.

Laura shrugged. "It's called interpretive dance for a reason. I'm interpreting judgment."

"She's got you there, Nell." Holly nodded along with her friend.

Nell stuck her tongue out, turned, and danced away.

"And that's my cue to change," Holly said with a wave.

"I'll come with you," Laura said, moving forward.

"Hey, *bella*, we aren't done here." Rafe had his hands on his hips, a sure sign that he didn't like the way things were going.

"Don't call me that." The words came out quickly, and Laura's mouth closed as if she wished she could call them back. She smoothed the peach-colored dress over her curves. "I need to change. Then we can all go back to my place where we can discuss this in a private setting. But you two need to put on those T-shirts or a very nice man is going to get tranquilized by the town doctor."

She turned on her heels, those superhot fuck-me shoes she'd always worn, and left as though her words made a lick of sense.

"So, gentlemen, what should we talk about while we wait for my bride-to-be?" Wolf grinned as he sat back in his chair.

"You better behave," Teeny said, shaking her head as she walked off.

Cam was left with a T-shirt and a bunch of questions. What was happening with Laura? Why was this town filled with crazy people? But there was one question that burned through his gut—why wasn't she wearing an engagement ring?

* * * *

Laura could barely breathe. She stumbled her way into the dressing room after telling Brooke she had an emergency and needed to leave.

"Calm down, sweetie." Holly's hands were on her back, tugging the zipper of the tight dress down.

Twenty minutes before, Laura had loved the dress, but now it felt like a cage hemming her in. She pushed the spaghetti straps off her shoulders and started shoving the dress down her body until she was only in her bra and panties. She let her back find the wall behind her and slouched to the floor.

They were here. Rafe and Cam were here in Bliss.

Nell got on her knees while Holly closed the curtains. God, she'd gotten naked in the middle of the Trading Post. Not that anyone would care. Well, Nate might write her a ticket for public nudity. Public nudity tickets had paid for the new park, but

56

otherwise no one would give a crap.

Nell's big brown eyes stared down at her. "Are they the reason you came to Bliss?"

Holly sat down beside her, leaning her head on Laura's shoulder while Nell stroked her hair. They were so affectionate. It had taken her a while to get used to how Holly and Nell hugged her and held her hand. Now she couldn't imagine life without it.

"I thought you weren't talking to me." She hadn't been surprised by Nell's sudden vow of silence. She'd known the instant Teeny had left the room that she would go straight to Holly and Nell to tell them the news of her sudden "engagement." And she'd known Nell would disapprove. Nell was a woman who would rather say nothing than allow a lie to pass her lips. But she would dance to show her feelings.

"I thought it best to be silent around the people you're lying to," Nell admitted. "I'm not good at lying."

"I'm with Nell on this one. Unless you actually fell madly in love with Wolf in the twenty minutes we were gone, and then I say congratulations," Holly added.

Laura sniffled. It was hard to be strong around Holly and Nell. She didn't have to. They didn't care if she cried. They didn't give a crap if she wasn't professional and tough. They loved her. "Nope. But he did come in handy."

"So these agents are assholes." Holly squeezed her hand. "What are we going to do to them? There's only one reason Laura would announce her engagement to a man she knows she's not in love with. One of those men broke her heart, and she couldn't stand the thought of him knowing she hasn't moved on."

"It has to be the gorgeous man of South American heritage," Nell said. "He's very international."

"He's half-Cuban, Nell, and he was born in Miami."

Holly leaned forward. "And I, personally, think that hot hunk of all-American beef is better looking. He's huge."

"You don't know the half of it," she said without thinking.

Holly grinned at Nell. "Told you it was the linebacker."

She could be honest with her girlfriends. "The only man who matched him was Rafe."

Nell's whole face lit up. "And that was before you came to Bliss. The universe led you here."

No, a bus had taken her to Alamosa and then a handsy trucker had left her in Bliss when she wouldn't crawl into his cab to pay for her ride. But if Nell wanted to believe some hand of fate had led her here, she would let it go. "But it was just a fling."

"Not for you it wasn't," Holly said. "You were in love with them."

She shrugged. There wasn't anything else to do. Holly knew her way too well for Laura to lie. "It doesn't matter. They're here to update me on a case. That's all."

If de Sade was back, then they probably wanted to grill her on what had happened during her time with him. God, she wasn't ready for that. She'd spent five years trying to forget. She'd given them everything she could remember from the hospital bed she'd recovered in. She'd spent hours with Joseph Stone going over the incident, from the time she'd been knocked out to the moment she'd managed to break free and run.

"Did they know you were in Bliss?" Nell asked.

Laura was surprised they'd found her. She'd been using her granddad's name. She'd tried to stay hidden. Maybe she'd been fooling herself and they'd known where she was all along. "No, but they're members of the BAU. They're smart guys."

"They track serial killers," Holly said, obviously impressed. "I guess I always thought you were like a secretary or something."

She'd always known that was what Holly thought, and she'd encouraged the mistaken impression. She didn't want Holly to think she'd had a high-powered career. Holly had several insecurities, mostly revolving around her lack of an education. Holly was incredibly well-read, but she felt her lack of a higher degree. Unfortunately, she couldn't hide it anymore. Rafe and Cam had seen to that.

"I was a profiler. I had moved up into the BAU, when I met Rafe and Cam. They were partners before they joined the unit. They flirted with me. A lot. We got to be friends, and then we had a slight disagreement over a case and we weren't friends anymore. That's all."

Holly's eyebrows had crept up her forehead. "Is that how the serial killer found you? Because you were hunting him?"

She'd only mentioned her career a couple of times before. Nate and Zane knew about it. Rye Harper knew. She'd always offered her experience to law enforcement, but she'd only mentioned it to the general population once during a town hall meeting. Still, it had made the rounds. It was a testament to Holly's and Nell's patience that they hadn't asked her about it until now. "I wrote a profile of a serial killer the newspapers named the Marquis de Sade."

"He doesn't sound nice," Nell said.

This wasn't a world Nell could even conceive. Laura groped for gentle words. "He wasn't. He killed a lot of women. I was new to the unit, and I had a radical theory. I thought the killer was a member of law enforcement or maybe in the military. There were things about the killer's MO that led me to believe he was intensely disciplined and knew forensic procedure quite well. Anyway, everyone in the unit, including Rafe and Cam, thought I was wrong. There was another profiler, a more senior profiler, who bought into the stereotypical 'highly intelligent, socially awkward, abused child' profile. No one wanted to believe one of our own could do it."

They had refused to believe her to such an extent that she'd been ridiculed. She'd felt so horrible about all of it that she'd made the biggest mistake of her life. She'd talked to a reporter friend who had written a story, and the next day she'd been fired for talking to the media. She'd topped off that wonderful day by nearly being murdered. She'd been taken, right outside her own apartment.

He'd worn a mask. When she closed her eyes, she still saw that dark, beaked mask, like doctors wore during the black plague. It had covered his whole face, and he'd placed dark mirrored circles over the eyes so she saw herself when he looked down at her. The nose of the mask had been elongated, making him look foreign and far from human. Of course, he wasn't really human at all. No human being could have done what he'd done to her. The mask, he'd explained to her, was because she was dirty and diseased. He had to protect himself. He'd talked a lot about how smart he was. He'd talked as he'd tortured her.

"Holly, could you please?" Nell asked.

Holly nodded. "They are sons of bitches. Assholes, motherfuckers, and I hate them."

Nell nodded solemnly. "What she said."

Laura had to laugh. Nell didn't curse, but she didn't mind when Holly did. "They'll be gone in a day or two. Don't worry about it. They want to see if I remember anything else. Please, don't worry about me. I'm fine. It's over. Talking about it won't hurt me."

She wasn't sure of that. And she wasn't sure this would be over in a day or two. Why was Cam here if he wasn't in the FBI anymore? She had a million questions, but she couldn't ask them without looking like an idiot.

"All right then, we'll play along with the whole 'you're marrying Wolf' thing," Holly said, getting to her feet.

Nell followed. "I'll stay perfectly silent around them. Henry will want a vow of silence in lieu of lying as well."

Laura gave Nell a thumbs-up.

Her friends got dressed and promised to help in any way they could, but both seemed to understand she needed a minute. The curtain closed behind Holly as they left, and Laura was alone.

The only two men she'd ever loved had turned up in the only place she'd ever really felt at home.

It was a recipe for disaster. Laura couldn't help it. She closed her eyes and thought about that night. The best night of her life, that led to the worst day.

The world receded, and she was loved again.

Chapter Four

Washington, DC
Five years before

Laura Rosen pulled the cork out of the second bottle of wine of the night and poured two glasses. Cam wasn't a wine guy, but Rafe liked it. After dinner, he would invariably switch to Scotch, but before they ate, Rafe always drank wine with her.

What a fucking day.

Her shoulders were bunched and knotted from twelve hours of pure stress. Looking at pictures of dead girls was no way to make a living. Why had she thought she could handle this?

If she thought today was rough, what was coming for her tomorrow? When Edward Lock read her profile, he was going to flip. She knew she was in for a fight, but she owed it to those girls. Edward might have years of experience over her, but he was flat wrong this time. She could feel it. At least she could count on Rafe and Cam to back her up. She hadn't showed them her profile yet.

She didn't want to ruin the night, but after a year of depending on those guys, she was sure they would stand by her.

"Hey, *bella*." Rafe's hands slid along the muscles of her neck. She could feel the heat of his body behind her. "You're so tense. It got to you today."

"Victim number five was barely nineteen," she replied. And Rafe was wrong. It hadn't merely gotten to her today. It got to her every day. Despite herself, she shivered as Rafe's skin pressed against hers.

It's a friendly touch. Slow down, girl. This is not a place you should even think about going to.

The trouble was, she'd thought about it far too much. She'd started to think of Rafe Kincaid as way more than a friend and a colleague. She hadn't missed the way he looked at her. He ate her up with his eyes, and it was killing her. She would have jumped into bed with him in a heartbeat if it hadn't been for one thing— Cameron Briggs.

How could she have been stupid enough to fall for two men? Two men she worked with.

"We'll catch him, *bella*." Rafe's hands rubbed down her back, soothing the muscles there. Every inch of skin he touched came alive.

"I'm not sure about that," she murmured.

God, his hands felt good. How long had it been since she'd been physically close to another human being? She hadn't dated for a year and a half. She'd been far too involved in her career, and then she'd been far too involved with Rafe and Cam to think about other men.

She'd kept it friendly. She was the only woman on her team. She was playing with fire by spending time outside of work with them, but she couldn't help it. They were funny and kind. Rafe was her gentleman, constantly smoothing the way for her. He opened doors and gave her his umbrella when it rained. They could talk about gourmet food and wine and books.

And Cameron. Cam was her protector. Cam was a huge hunk of granite that got between her and anything that came her way. Cam was the one who called her at night to make sure she'd locked the doors. He was the one who insisted on installing a security system in her apartment. Cam was the one who got pissed at her when she walked to her car alone at night because she didn't want to bother him.

She couldn't help but remember a case they'd worked in Detroit a month after she'd joined the team. It was a serial rape case, and they'd been put up in a motel that was seedy to say the least. She'd locked her doors, but when she'd emerged the next day, Cam had been sitting outside, his back against the moldy wall, a cup of coffee in his hand. His eyes had been so tired. He'd sat there all night because she had fit the profile, and he wasn't going to let that happen to her. The next night, both he and Rafe had slept on the floor of her motel room.

How could she ever choose between them? It was easier to put her hormones on hold and enjoy their company.

Rafe stopped what he was doing, and she mourned the loss of his hands on her, but it was better this way. She could already feel the wine lowering her inhibitions. Rafe had drunk even more than she had, and Cam had tackled several beers. He'd had to walk to get the pizza. It was best if Rafe didn't keep massaging her. It could go badly.

"You have to know that he'll slip up sometime. Killers always do." Rafe leaned back against her countertop. He'd shed his suit coat, and his dress shirt was partially unbuttoned, showing off a bit of his perfect olive skin. He was a paragon of modern masculine beauty. From his wavy, pitch-black hair, to his laser-focused eyes, to those lips that Laura stared at, he was utter perfection.

"I don't know that," she replied, trying to get her brain off those lips. What would they feel like on her mouth? God, what would they feel like on her nipples? The mere thought of his mouth suckling at her breasts made her nipples lengthen and rub against her bra.

He shook his head as he grabbed the glass she'd poured for him. "They all screw up in the end because they all want to get caught. They want the fame or they want to be stopped, but one way or another, they want to get caught."

"I think this unsub is different than anything we've come up against. He comes off like a mission-oriented killer, but I think he's a thrill seeker."

There were several small markers that led her to believe that the Marquis de Sade was playing a game. It went past the killing and the torture. He was playing a game with the FBI. If Laura was right, he was playing a game with his own family.

"Don't, *bella*. No more tonight. I can't take anymore." Rafe had been the one to take the call. Laura had only been forced to look at the pictures, but she knew Rafe had to walk into the room where they found the victim. He and Cam had to call the young woman's mother and tell her that her daughter was never going to get it together and come home. "Can't we wait until tomorrow to get back into this?"

Yes. Tomorrow was soon enough to cause trouble. Her profile was going to be controversial. "Sure."

She took a sip of the deliciously rich cabernet. Rafe got very quiet. Just like that, the room felt thick with tension. She was alone with Rafe. He was right there. So close she could feel the heat of his body. She'd been alone for so damn long.

"How long is this going to go on, *bella*?"

She felt tears prick at her eyeballs, and she took a longer gulp of the wine. She wasn't sure she was ready for this. Choices. She would have to make hard choices. Whether to leave her job wasn't as hard as she would have thought. If she got involved with one of them, she would have to ask for a transfer, but she'd been thinking about that anyway. She'd been thinking of using her degree in psychology in the victim's services department. All the death was getting to her.

It was choosing between them that would kill her. Either way she went, she lost one of them.

"I don't think it's a good idea, Rafe."

"Because of Cam?"

She nodded, unwilling to say that she was equally in love with two men. What kind of woman did that make her?

"What if I told you that Cam and I have talked about this? What if I told you that Cam and I are willing to give you some time to make your decision? We're not stupid, *bella*, and neither are you. We've both become very attached to you. Neither one of us wants to let you go, but we also have no interest in simply being your friend for the rest of our lives. I want you. I want you so badly I can taste it. Cam wants you, too." Rafe's hands came out and found the curve of her hip. He drew her forward until she was in the cradle of his body. He turned his head down, staring into her eyes. "Tell me you don't want me, and I'll stop."

She set the wine down before she lost the glass. She could feel the long, hard line of his erection poking at her through the wool of his slacks. Her head was swimming with arousal. Her whole body felt like it was being primed for pleasure. She needed to move away from him, but her chin tilted up and then there was no escape.

His lips brushed hers, a soft touch like silk kissing against her skin. Their noses scraped together. It was an innocent intimacy, but her heart was suddenly swollen with the sweetness of it. She lifted her head up and went onto her toes, silently requesting more.

He went slowly, his lips pressing down on hers, seducing her mouth. He didn't push her. He simply made love to her mouth with agonizing persuasion. He kissed her over and over, light touches to her lips. He pressed soft kisses starting on one side of her mouth, touching every inch, and then making the trip again once he'd gotten to the other side. His hands threaded through her hair, holding her still as he explored her face. He kissed her nose and her cheeks. She closed her eyes so his lips could touch her there, too. He kissed her forehead and then made his way back down. It was so much more than lust. Lust she might have been able to refuse, but Rafe's tender care sucked her in like nothing before.

"I want you so badly, *bella*." The words were lyrical coming out of his mouth. When he was aroused, his Cuban accent flared, giving a round seduction to every word that flowed. "You're so beautiful. I've never known a woman as beautiful as you."

She shuddered as Rafe's tongue played along the seam of her lips, lighting a fire in her pussy. She was softening, preparing for him, and it felt too fucking good to deny. Her whole body had gone languid, waiting impatiently for his hands to roam across her skin.

"Open for me, *bella*. Let me taste you."

She opened her mouth, and his tongue swept in. It glided across hers, begging her to play. It was wrong. She knew it was wrong, but it felt right. She cared about him. Hell, she loved him. Why was it wrong to have him? She needed him. The events of the day—of the whole last year—weighed on her so heavily that it was like a weight lifting to simply let go and feel. She gave in and let her hands cup his broad shoulders.

"Yes, oh yes, *bella*." He whispered the words against her mouth before he plunged inside. His tongue was rapacious now, as though he'd been let off a leash. His hands pulled her in as his mouth took hers. He pushed her against the countertop, taking up all the space. His cock ground against her pelvis. She heard herself whimper because his cock was hitting her clit, rubbing against it through his slacks and her skirt.

Too tight. She couldn't get her legs open. The pencil skirt she'd worn had seemed pretty and professional, but now it hemmed her in. She wanted to wrap her legs around Rafe's hips and feel that massive cock against her pussy. It felt huge and rock hard. It would feel so good inside her.

She let her hands run down his torso, deeply hating the fabric that covered him.

"Feel me." Rafe ripped open his dress shirt, the buttons pinging to the floor.

Laura looked down to see his perfectly cut chest. She ran her fingers over the muscles of his stomach and up along his ribs. Every part of him was smooth, the skin soft, but the flesh underneath was like steel. Rafe's hands went to his belt. He unbuckled it and undid the top of his pants, revealing a thin line of dark hair that led down.

She leaned over and did what came naturally. She kissed him from the hollow of his neck down, tasting his clean and masculine flesh. She licked at his flat nipples, loving the way they tightened for her. She gently worked her way around the nipple and then moved to the next one.

"Bite me, *bella*. I like it rough. I want to feel your teeth on me."

The idea made her clench. Moisture was making her slick and wet for him. She bit down on his nipple and was rewarded with a sharp hiss.

"Yes. That's what I want. I want you wild."

If he wanted her wild, he was going to get his wish. Her heart was pounding, and her skin felt like it might pulse off her body. His gorgeous form was all there for her delectation, and she wasn't about to hold back.

She pushed at his pants and shoved his boxers down his lean hips. His cock sprang free. Touch hadn't lied to her. He was huge and thick, with a spongy purple head. Laura shoved him back. In the small kitchen, there wasn't a lot of room to maneuver. Rafe seemed to know what she wanted, and he leaned back, spreading his legs as she got to her knees. Her skirt forced her to keep her legs together, but she could move a bit. She breathed in the scent of his arousal before leaning over and licking the head of his cock.

It jumped, and Rafe's groan reverberated through the small kitchen. His heavy balls pulled up as she looked at him.

"Please, *bella*. I need you. I've needed you for so long."

Laura let her mouth close over the head of his twitching dick. His arousal, thick and salty, spread across her tongue. She grasped the thick stalk of his cock with one hand as she worked her tongue over the *V* on the underside of his head.

Rafe's hands found the back of her neck and pulled her forward.

"More. Take more."

He was a ruthless son of a bitch. It made her even hotter. He forced her head forward. She opened wide because his dick was invading, penetrating inch by luscious inch. *Air*. She needed air. She forced herself to breathe through her nose. Rafe filled her mouth with his hard dick. She struggled but managed to whirl her tongue around the cock in her mouth. Rafe fucked into her mouth in hard, short strokes.

She gave up fighting him, allowing Rafe to take over. She softened her jaw and felt his cock sink further. Rafe's movements took on jerky strides. She felt him pulse, and then he cursed and pulled out.

Laura looked up. Her mouth felt empty without his cock in it. His face was bunched and tight. "You didn't like it?"

His hands came out, pulling her up. "I was too close, *bella*. I don't want to come in your mouth. Not this time. I want to get inside you. I want to feel your pussy around my cock."

He picked her up and settled her on the countertop, pushing her skirt to her waist.

"Lift up. You don't need this." He ran his fingers along the edges of her underwear.

She lifted her ass, and Rafe slid the offending silk panties off her hips. Cool air stroked over her heated flesh. Rafe forced her legs open. His cock thrust from the perfectly manicured nest of hair at the juncture of his thighs. She couldn't take her eyes off his cock. It was slick from her mouth. Suddenly Rafe palmed himself. He stroked his cock twice, the head weeping pearly fluid. He let go. There was the sound of a wrapper tearing, and then his hands were shaking as he rolled the condom over his cock.

God, was she doing this? Rafe Kincaid was covering his cock in a rubber so he could fuck her. What was she thinking? Her brain worked overtime.

"Don't." Rafe nearly groaned the command. "Don't think."

But she couldn't stop. There would be no going back. "Rafe, we should—"

"We should stop thinking and let it happen." He pushed her knees wide and lined his cock up. "I need this. I fucking need you, Laura. I'll stop if you want me to, but I think we both need this."

"I want you," she admitted, her hips moving, trying to welcome him inside.

He held himself there, right on the edge of her pussy. His big cock teased at her. Laura felt her pussy pulse as though demanding the same thing Rafe was. She wanted it so badly. Her body was begging for it.

"Look at it." Rafe was looking down. "Look at how beautiful it is and tell me it's wrong."

Laura let her eyes follow Rafe's line of sight down to the place where his cockhead sat poised at the entrance to her pussy. The head slipped inside the labial walls, threatening the channel with sweet invasion. As Rafe's hips moved, she could see that his cockhead was already coated with her juice.

"We're beautiful together. This isn't some one-night thing for me, *bella*. I'm crazy about you." He kissed her forehead. "But if you need more time."

Only one thing kept her from wrapping her legs around him. "Cam—"

"Thinks he wants to watch."

She felt her heart almost stop at the words that came from the hallway. Cam stood there, pizza in one hand and a six-pack dangling from the other. His whole body was still. It was almost as though he was stopped in his tracks, and he couldn't move. His handsome face was set in stone.

"Cameron." Laura tried to push her legs together, but Rafe was still there. "We can't. I can't hurt Cam like this."

Rafe's head turned, his dark eyes slightly desperate. "Cam, please tell her it's okay."

Cam set the pizza and the six-pack on the kitchen table. In two long strides, he crossed the space between them. They crowded into her tiny kitchen, their big bodies taking up all the space. Cam's eyes softened, and he towered over her. He was a good two inches taller than Rafe, his body thick and corded with muscles. His eyes were blue, and they ranged from an icy, arctic color when he was angry to the bright, inviting blue of a perfectly kept swimming pool. His big hand cupped half her face.

"I wanted to be first, but I had to go and get pizza. My momma always told me my gut would get me in trouble," Cam said with a chuckle. "Laura, baby, this has been inevitable from the moment we met. I know it's odd, but I think we're ready to try."

Were they ready to try to make it work between the three of them? "I want to try, too. I want you both. Yes, I want this."

Cam kissed the side of her face and then turned back to Rafe. "Give me a show, buddy."

The minute the words left Cam's mouth, Rafe thrust in.

She groaned at the invasion. He filled her, stretched her taut. He worked his dick in, thrusting back and forth with determination, trying to get in.

"You're so tight, *bella*. How long?"

Laura didn't pretend to misunderstand. He was filling her, making her ache with longing. "Years."

She'd paid attention to her career. The FBI was a rough environment. It was still, in many ways, a good old boys' club. She was a younger woman. She'd known if she'd wanted anyone to take her seriously, she couldn't date another agent. The job was so demanding that she didn't have time to meet anyone, and after meeting Rafe and Cam, she hadn't wanted to.

"I'm glad, *bella*." Rafe leaned over and kissed her while he pulled on her hips and thrust in to his balls. She could feel them resting against her skin.

"I told you she's been living like a nun." Cam spoke quietly.

She turned slightly, and Cam was looking down. He was watching the place where Rafe's cock disappeared into her pussy. His eyes were sleepy, and Laura could see his cock was pressing against his jeans. Something about Cam watching made her feel ridiculously sexy. He ran his tongue over his plump lips.

"He likes it, *bella*." Rafe's voice had gone hoarse. His hands trembled as he pushed her back so her body was laid out on the counter like a feast about to be devoured. "I think you like it, too."

She wrapped her legs around his hips and thrust her pelvis up. There was way too much discussion going on. Her pussy was begging, and Rafe held himself there. Now that she knew Cam wasn't going to hate her, she wanted to move on. "I like it. I would like it a whole lot more if you would fuck me."

A rough look crossed Rafe's face. His hands tightened on her hips and he pushed in even further, impaling her as far as his cock would go. "Demanding thing. Lucky for you, I'm in a mood to be giving."

He pulled out almost to the brink and thrust back in with a powerful swivel of his hips. Laura gasped. It felt so good, so right to have him deep inside her. He rammed his cock into her, his beautiful head thrown back as he fucked her. Over and over, he thrust, his cock hitting someplace deep in her pussy that she'd never known existed. It made her shake. Rafe adjusted his stance and thrust in one last time with a groan as he fingered her clit and sent her over the edge.

She let the orgasm pulse across her flesh. Rafe was still thrusting, holding their hips together as he pumped out his own orgasm. His whole body went rigid, and then he let himself fall forward so they were chest to chest.

"Thank you, *bella*. I've waited a long time for that." He kissed her and then pushed himself up.

She started to struggle to adjust herself, but suddenly strong arms lifted her off the counter, and she was cradled against a big, muscular chest.

"He was rough on you, baby." There was a hint of rebuke in Cam's voice as he cuddled her close. Laura threw her arms around his neck. Cam hadn't given her a chance to fix her skirt. Her bare ass was hanging out, but he started toward the hallway. "He didn't even get your clothes off. What was he thinking?"

She was dazed as he kicked open the door to her bedroom and gently laid her on the queen-size bed. Only the light from the hallway penetrated the bedroom. Cam's body was a huge shadow towering over her, but his hands were gentle as he reached out for the buttons of her blouse.

"I wasn't thinking," Rafe said, stepping into the doorway and blocking the light. "I wanted to get inside her."

Rafe flipped the light on, and Laura got a good look at him. He'd shed his shirt and his slacks. He walked into the room wearing nothing but his dark cotton boxers. Cam's hands released the buttons on her blouse and smoothed it back, his touch light against her skin. After the storm of making love with Rafe, Cam was so soft and tender that Laura relaxed into the bed.

It seemed unreal, like a fever dream, but she didn't want to wake up. Her body had hummed with satisfaction only a moment before, but another wave of arousal swept over her. As Cam looked down, she got restless with desire. Cam was here. Rafe was here. They weren't rejecting what she needed.

"And I want to make it last." Cam sat on the bed beside her. "I want to see her. I've waited forever to see her without all these clothes."

Cam was different than she'd expected. He was so big and badass that his sudden tenderness disarmed her. When she'd thought about making love with Cameron Briggs, she'd imagined it would be wild and tempestuous, but emotion flowed from Laura as Cam flicked open the front clasp of her bra and uncovered her breasts. His eyes flared, and his hand trembled slightly as he brought it to her breast. He grazed the peaks with his fingertips. She groaned as her nipples tightened under his touch.

"Do you want me to go away?" Rafe stood at the edge of the bed. His eyes shifted from her to Cam. There was an awkward hesitance in his stance that she'd never seen before. Rafe was always confident.

Cam turned slightly, and she got the feeling that Rafe hadn't been talking to her. He was talking to Cam. "Do you want to stay?"

"I do. I wasn't sure I would, but I do. I want to watch you with her."

Cam nodded. "Then stay. But we'll have a lot to talk about come morning."

Laura would have asked about that, but Cam leaned over and put his mouth on her breast. She couldn't think past that tongue licking on her flesh. He was stretched out beside her, still dressed. The rough denim rasped against her side. She wanted him on top of her, but he held back. She wiggled, the sensation causing her to move. Cam's hand came down on her arms.

"Don't move, sweetheart. I want to enjoy you. Let me make you feel good." He spoke the words against her skin, lighting it up with prickles of fire.

She relaxed and let her hands find his hair. Cam kept his golden hair short, but it was soft. The lips at her nipple suddenly pulled and tugged. She felt the soft scrape of his teeth on her flesh. He sucked the nipple into his mouth and lavished it with affection. He whirled his tongue around and around before kissing his way to the opposite breast and starting the process again.

She was helpless to do anything. Where Rafe had been aggressive and quick, Cam was slow and seductive. Time seemed to still as he played with her. He licked and nipped at her breasts while his hands ran all over her torso. He finally kissed his way up to her neck and nuzzled her there.

"You're killing me," she managed to whisper. He was making her tremble. Her every nerve was past ready for him to move to her center, but he kissed the curve of her neck and ran his tongue along the shell of her ear.

"No, I'm *enjoying* you." The words were spoken softly into her ear. The heat of his breath was another decadent sensation to be had. "You see, I know that Rafe is the gourmet. I know I sit in a fancy restaurant like an idiot and order a hamburger when I could have something froufrou. I'm not that classy. I don't care what wine tastes like as long as it gets me drunk, but this—this I want to savor. I'm a connoisseur of you, sweetheart."

He planted his lips on top of hers and took her mouth. His tongue slid in, gliding along hers, not allowing an inch of her to go untasted. Laura heard Rafe leave the room. The door to her bathroom squeaked open. Cam kissed her, slanting his mouth over and over as he got at every angle possible. His hands played in her hair.

There was a sudden warm, wet sensation at her pussy.

"It's a washcloth, *bella*." Rafe was at the end of the bed. "If what Cam says is true, I think he's going to spend some time here. Let me get you ready for him."

Cam turned, and they both looked down her body at Rafe. He was gently washing her pussy. The sensation left her feeling raw and exposed, but it wasn't a bad thing. It was a sweet ache.

Cam turned back, a smile on his normally hard face. "I'm definitely spending some time down there. I bet you taste sweet."

He stood and began to quickly shrug out of his clothes. He pulled his T-shirt over his head and shucked his jeans and boxers in one smooth move. Cam was the only one of them who had changed after work. He always changed out of his suit and tie as quickly as he could, sometimes ducking into a bathroom before they even left the office. He preferred street clothes, but now she knew what he looked best in.

Nothing at all.

Cam stood over her. He was enormous in every sense of the word. His shoulders were wide, the muscles bunching as he tossed his shirt off the bed. His cut chest tapered down to lean hips and strongly muscled legs. And his cock. *Damn.* She'd thought Rafe had the largest cock she would ever see. Cam topped him. His cock was thrusting up, bobbing, the head close to his navel. His thick, heavy balls had pulled up against his body.

"Give me the clothes, sweetheart," he said softly, his voice belying the rough, masculine look of his body. "I want to be skin to skin."

With shaky hands, Laura pushed herself up and let the blouse fall off her arms. She shrugged out of the bra. She felt a little self-conscious. Rafe and Cam were ridiculously perfect. She tried, but she knew she wasn't really in their league. She was attractive, but they were practically Greek gods.

"You're beautiful." Cam pulled the skirt off her hips and reached for the rest of her clothes. "You're so fucking beautiful to me."

"I call you beautiful all the time, *bella*," Rafe added.

It didn't make sense to her, but she wasn't about to argue. Then she couldn't think at all because Cam was climbing on top of her. He'd said he wanted to be skin to skin, and suddenly it seemed like he was kissing every part of her. Their chests met, and their bellies snuggled. Their knees knocked together, and his feet played against hers. His lips covered her mouth in a soul-sinking kiss.

The world melted away as he kissed his way down her body. It narrowed and got smaller and more intimate. The case and all the stress fell away until all that was left was her and Cam and Rafe.

Cam settled between her legs and shoved his nose into her pussy, breathing in her scent.

"This vintage has an excellent nose," Cam said, grinning. He had said it with a hint of Rafe's inflection, poking fun at Laura and Rafe's recent wine experiments. "And I love the flavor."

His tongue came out, and he licked a long, slow path through her pussy.

She felt her back bow. Cam set in, eating her pussy. She let her head roll from one side to the other, the pressure building with every swipe of his talented tongue. She was wetter than she could ever remember being. She opened her eyes, and Rafe was sitting on the chair by her bed. It was the same chair where she sat every night trying to read before she went to bed. Now she wouldn't be able to think about that chair without seeing Rafe in it. His boxers were shoved down, and he had that magnificent cock in his hand, pumping it slowly as he watched Cam devouring her pussy. His eyes were half lidded, but there was no doubt that he was focused. That hand moved up and down, from base to tip, over and over.

"He's thinking about fucking you," Cam said, his eyes on hers. "He's remembering how tight this pussy is."

Laura groaned as he worked two fingers deep inside her.

"She was so tight, Cam. That pussy of hers clamped down on me so hard," Rafe said on a guttural groan.

"I bet she's tight everywhere." There was suddenly a dark, delicious pressure on her asshole. "How about here, sweetheart? You ever been fucked here before?"

"No." The word came out in a breathless squeak. She squirmed. It was so wrong, that finger teasing her there. Still, she couldn't help but wonder what it would be like to have Rafe in her pussy and Cam in her ass.

"A virgin asshole. That gets me hard, sweetheart. But it'll have to wait. I won't hurt you." Cam surged up and was spreading her legs before she could take another breath.

"Cameron, suit up before you get inside her." Rafe's rough voice reminded her that he was here, watching as she was about to fuck his best friend.

Cam grabbed a condom from his discarded pants and rolled it on. "I can be satisfied with this pussy for the night, but you should know, I will have that ass, Laura. It's going to belong to me."

He thrust in, his cock splitting her in one long stroke.

His pelvis ground down in perfect harmony with that hard cock hitting her G-spot. She called out his name as she came.

Cam seemed to let himself go. He thrust in over and over again. His head dropped as he groaned and every muscle stiffened. He fell forward, his weight pressing her into the mattress.

"My turn." Rafe stood over them, his dick standing at rigid attention.

Cam's head came up. "You won't get any sleep tonight, sweetheart."

He'd barely rolled off her before Rafe was on top, his mouth coming down on hers.

Laura sighed and gave herself over to her men.

Chapter Five

Bliss —Present day

Rafe felt totally out of his element in expensive slacks and a T-shirt that proclaimed The Trading Post was Bliss's one-stop murder clean-up shop. He made his way out of the bathroom, the suit coat and dress shirt he'd previously worn tucked over his arm.

"See, that looks much better," Wolf Meyer said with a sarcastic grin on his face. "Much more comfortable than that suit."

Rafe stared at Wolf. What kind of name was Wolf? And what the hell had happened? How was Laura engaged? His heart constricted at the thought, but he didn't buy it. She didn't have a ring on her finger. "I prefer the suit, but if this is what Laura wants me to wear, I'll suffer through it. She knows the town and how to fit in. I see she likes to be comfortable, too. She used to dress even better than I do. And, of course, she loved jewelry. I'm surprised she isn't showing off an engagement ring."

Rafe had quickly figured out that Wolf Meyer was a possessive son of a bitch. He'd spent the last ten years of his life on a BAU team. He knew how to read people. Wolf Meyer was former military, possibly Special Forces. The man was all alpha male with a strong streak of snark. No way did the man in front of him not buy the woman he was going to marry a ring. He would want some physical mark of his ownership. Rafe would, too. If he managed to convince Laura to marry him, he would have a ring on her finger in a heartbeat.

Of course, Cam would probably take it a step further. He would want a tattoo on her ass, something that couldn't slip off her body.

Wolf didn't even blink. "You know how we country folk are, Special Agent. We tend to downplay things like that. Our love is far more important than a ring. At least that's what she told me. We're saving up for the downpayment on a bigger cabin."

Bullshit. Rafe didn't believe that for a second. If Wolf Meyer wanted a ring on her finger, it would be there. Rafe had a lot in common with Wolf.

Something was off with Laura's engagement.

And something was definitely off with this town.

"Here's some fresh baked cookies, Special Agent." Teeny Green placed a plate on the bistro table. "I, personally, am glad you're here. Oh, I know that everyone else will go into lockdown mode, including my wife, but something has to be done. We can't keep having all these murders. First it was that dreadful man after Rachel and then those bikers. They needed to bathe more often, I tell you. If you're going to murder someone, at least have the common courtesy of smelling nice, I say."

Rafe listened to the woman go on about the grooming habits of the Russian mob and realized that he hadn't met a single person in this town who he wouldn't flag as potentially insane. From Wolf Meyer, who lied like a pro, to that dude who greeted them with his dick hanging out at that Mountain and Valley place.

Rafe looked around. Where had Laura gone? Two women whispered outside a curtained-off section on the second floor of the store that seemed to sell everything from souvenirs to groceries to fishing equipment. Rafe could see them from the ground floor. They were Laura's friends, the redhead and the one who previously couldn't speak. She didn't seem to have that trouble now. Charm hadn't worked on them. Maybe it was time to take a play from Cam's book and be a bit of a bully.

He couldn't let Laura go. If she slipped out the back, he might not be able to find her again. He needed to know she was safe. The sick feeling he'd had in his stomach every day since she'd walked out was back. He'd gotten so used to it, it had felt normal, only going away when he'd set eyes on her.

"Do you think I should make more cookies, Special Agent?" Teeny asked. "Your partner looks like a man who likes to eat."

Cam was still in the bathroom putting on his undercover wear. Cam would probably be thrilled to do the whole assignment in jeans and a snarky shirt. "Cam can put away more food than an elephant, but he's not the only one."

Wolf Meyer looked up, his face a mask of innocence. All six of the cookies were gone. "They were awfully good."

Rafe turned away as Teeny began to nag the big guy about sharing.

He clenched his fists at the base of the stairs and made his decision. Laura wasn't getting away. All this time he'd blamed himself for her running, but wasn't she to blame, too? He'd fucked up. He knew that. He'd fucked up, and she'd paid the price, but she was the one who left without a word. She was the one who had punished him and Cam for five long years. She was the one who hadn't wanted to listen to explanations or apologies.

He wasn't letting her go.

Rafe took the steps two at a time, never letting his eyes leave those women. They turned as though sensing something was stalking them. Two pairs of eyes widened. They were shocked and not a little frightened. He could sense that easily. Neither one moved, however. They stood their ground. The redhead even firmed her stance, as though guarding something precious.

"Special Agent Kincaid," the redhead said in a too-loud voice.

Holly. Her name was Holly, and she'd given Laura away. Laura was obviously behind the curtain, and her friend wanted to warn her of encroaching danger. *Nice.* He didn't mind that at all.

"I was looking for Laura." It was a leading question. He wondered if Holly would attempt to lie to him.

Guileless green eyes looked up at him. No lies in those eyes. "She's changing. I think she would appreciate it if you gave her a moment. She wasn't expecting people from her past to show up here today."

She'd placed careful emphasis on the word "past."

"Yes, I doubt she ever expected to see me again," Rafe murmured. He wondered if she was changing clothes. He wanted to see her again. She'd changed. She was softer, more round. She was older, but it looked good on her. She was even more beautiful than he remembered. Damn, he needed to get his head back in the game. He couldn't think about sex. He needed to stay in control or he would lose her.

Nell, whose voice had disappeared again, patted her friend on the back, and they seemed to have a whole conversation with a series of looks and gestures.

Finally, Holly turned back. "Nell and I would like to know why you're here."

That was a question he needed to answer carefully. Especially since he knew Laura was behind that curtain, probably listening. What should he say? Well, he'd told Cam they needed to be aggressive. "I'm here because I love her. I've loved her since the day I met her, and I've missed her every day she's been gone. I'm here today because yesterday Cam discovered her location. We've been looking for years."

Let her stew on that for a while. Or, perhaps, she would come barging out of her hidey hole, and they could have the fight they'd needed to have for five fucking years. Yeah, he was looking forward to that. He had the distinct feeling that they wouldn't get anywhere until they had that fight.

The curtain opened, and Laura stepped out, dressed now in tight jeans that accentuated her new curves and a plaid shirt that opened low enough to show off the slope of her breasts. Her hair had been pulled back in a ponytail. Her beauty had always been soul deep, but there was a strength in her eyes that hadn't been there before. It was apparent that she'd been crying.

Fuck, that hurt.

"It's good to see you, too, Special Agent Kincaid." She stepped into her heels. They were the only thing left from the outfit she'd been wearing.

The words were said with a flat cadence that told him she was simply being polite. She was fooling herself. It was obvious to Rafe that she still had some sort of feelings for them, whether good or bad. She'd been crying. There was still something between them. He wanted to take her in his arms, but it wasn't the time or the place.

"We need to find someplace where we can talk. Cam and I need to go over a few things with you," he said.

She glanced down at her watch. "Sorry, I have a lot to do today. All week, actually. I have a friend who's getting married on Saturday, and I'm in the wedding party. Tonight is the Big Game Dinner. That's serious in these parts. If you want to talk, you're going to have to do it at my place while I get ready."

With that, she dismissed him. She gave her friends hugs and then walked right past him.

He felt his blood pressure tick up as she walked away. He caught her in two long strides, gently clasping her elbow and turning her to face him.

"I came all this way, searched for years to find you, and you can't give me an hour to explain things to you?"

"I think you made everything clear to me back in DC. I understand that something has come up with the case, but I have a life here now. I have a job."

He knew about her job. Once he'd figured out what name she was using, he'd found out everything he could about her. It had been very surprising to discover that one of the most driven, ambitious women he'd ever known worked at a place called the Stop 'n' Shop. "Yes, you're working at a gas station. I'm sure that degree in psychology comes in handy when you're using a cash register."

She flushed but stood her ground. "I make no apologies for my life. I do a damn good job. I like the people here. If you have a problem with it, the highway can take you anywhere you want to go. I suggest you use it."

"That would be easy for you, wouldn't it, *bella*?"

"Nothing about this is easy for me, Rafe."

At least she'd stopped calling him special agent. "I'm not going anywhere until we talk, and I don't mean about the case. I don't care that you're involved with that man downstairs. I want an explanation. I want to know why you walked out on me."

"On us." Cam stood at the bottom of the stairs, looking up. He appeared to have utterly dumped his coat, and Rafe prayed he hadn't actually tossed it out. The T-shirt Cam had been given was the tiniest bit too small. "You walked out on us."

Rafe saw Laura soften for a moment, and then her stubbornness set back in. "I was fired. As I didn't have a real relationship with anyone outside of work, I didn't think I had to leave a forwarding address. And you should get your hand off me. You're hurting me."

"Hey!" Holly said.

"Put the fishing pole down, Holly." Laura sighed as she looked over Rafe's shoulder.

He turned to see the redhead with a fishing pole in her hand, apparently ready to defend her friend. He released Laura's arm.

"I don't think that would have done a lot of damage." Laura smiled at the two women who had been coming to her rescue.

Holly shrugged as she reset the fishing pole. "Next time you get assaulted, make sure it happens deeper in sporting goods. Then I could have picked up a hockey stick or a baseball bat."

"There won't be a next time," Laura promised. "I'll see you two tonight. Holly, you're going, right?"

"Oh, yes. Stella's Café is responsible for dessert. And Hal has come up with something called venison tapas. I have no idea what it means, but Zane made the sheriff promise to give it a try." Holly pointed a thumb back toward Nell. "Nell and Henry are protesting."

"Excellent. See you there." Laura started down the stairs.

"Laura, we're not done here." He wasn't about to come all this way only to be dismissed.

"I told you, I'm going home to change. I'll be at the Big Game Dinner this evening. It's going to be on the fairgrounds. We can talk there."

"If you run, I'll come after you."

She stopped halfway down the stairs and turned those blue eyes on him. "Why would I run? This is my home."

"You left your last home."

"DC was never my home. It was just a stop on the way to Bliss. This is my home and nothing and no one is going to make me leave it." She stepped down the stairs and nodded at Cam before she walked out.

Cam turned as if to go after her. Rafe raced to stop him.

"We can't let her go," Cam complained.

"She isn't going anywhere." He understood Cam's urgency. Now that he was close to her again, the idea of letting her out of his sight rankled. "I have it on the highest authority that this is her home."

Cam smiled, his face opening in a way Rafe hadn't seen in a long time. It made him look years younger. "Well, you've got to admit, it is kind of cool."

"I don't have to admit anything."

Cam slapped him on the back. He didn't seem at all upset with his too-tight T-shirt or the woman who spoke through interpretive dance. "Come on, it's gorgeous. It makes me miss Arkansas. Hell, I never thought I'd miss Arkansas, but the mountains here are beautiful. And the air is amazing."

Rafe frowned. "The air is air, Cam."

"Nah, it's different in the mountains. It's cleaner." Cam turned and stared after Laura. She almost walked out the door and then seemed to remember that she had left something behind. Her fiancé. She awkwardly returned to Wolf Meyer's side. "What is she doing with that asshole? I don't buy the whole 'we're getting married' thing. She hasn't got a ring on. She doesn't look comfortable when he touches her. And did it seem to you like everyone was surprised when they talked to her and she mentioned her wedding?"

Rafe hadn't missed the storeowner's slight double take. He was glad that Cam hadn't missed it either. He might have been out of the BAU for a couple of years, but Cam still knew how to read body language. "I don't know what's going on, but I want to take a close look at that guy. He was the only one who didn't flinch. That makes me interested in him."

Cam held up his phone. "Already on it. I'll run a search on the fucker the minute I get decent access. We should have a nice-size file on him by the time night falls. I sincerely hope he's got a record."

"Well, we can hope." Rafe started to walk toward the front of the store. He would check out this place Laura wanted to go to tonight, but he wasn't going to let her shut him out for long. She was in danger. If they had found her, it was a good bet that the Marquis de Sade could find her, too. He wouldn't underestimate the fucker again. The serial killer had gotten his hands on her once. He wasn't getting a second shot.

Wolf casually looped an arm around Laura's waist. He didn't seem uncomfortable with her at all. If it hadn't been for that small space she kept between them, he might have bought that they were a happy couple. He was willing to bet that they weren't sleeping together.

Wolf leaned over to whisper in Laura's ear, but something caught his eye. He moved fast. One moment he was cuddling up to Laura, and the next he was rushing out the door.

Laura turned to them, a stern look on her face. "Well, now

you've done it."

"What?" Rafe felt like he hadn't done a damn thing right since the minute he'd stepped off the plane. It was unnerving. He wasn't the guy who fucked up. He was cool and smooth. He took care of things. Cam was the guy who unraveled from time to time. It was the way their partnership had worked for years. Cam screwed up, and Rafe smoothed it over.

But Cam had been taking the lead since they crossed over the Bliss County line.

Now he wondered exactly what he'd screwed up this time. Laura stomped out of the store.

"Come on." There was a bounce to Cam's step as he jogged after Laura.

Rafe followed, but with trepidation. He hoped no one was naked. There was no way he would be able to unsee that. He'd thought a nudist colony would be filled with hot women. Nope. Middle-aged men. With their dorks hanging out.

Rafe pushed through the door and saw what had Wolf and Laura up in arms. A tall, thin man was walking around Rafe's rented black SUV, an odd instrument in his hand. It was shaped like a small satellite connected by a wire to a box that beeped like mad.

"Now, you see here, Wolf, it only beeps like that in the presence of extraterrestrial materials."

"Mel, it beeps like that all the time." Wolf spoke in a long-suffering tone.

The older man was dressed in a mechanic's jumpsuit. He had a trucker's hat on, but there was a glint of thin silver peeking out from the cap. Was that tinfoil?

"Well, of course it does, son. You're full of all kinds of alien stuff. Half your DNA is alien," the man named Mel said with a fond smile. "It goes off around you and your brother, but you're a good boy."

Rafe heard Cam snort beside him. It was pretty funny. Wolf Meyer was an enormous, badass-looking man being called a "good boy" by a man half his size.

Laura's foot tapped against the sidewalk, her pretty face masked in an irritated frown. "Mel, they aren't aliens. They're worse than aliens."

"Ain't nothing worse than aliens, Laura," Mel argued, running his instrument over the hood of the SUV.

"They're feds." The word dropped like a lodestone.

Mel backed up, his eyes widening in obvious horror. "Well, hell. That *is* worse."

Cam covered his mouth but walked forward. "We're sorry to disturb you, sir. We recently got in from DC to talk to a former special agent about an important case."

Mel's eyes narrowed. "I've given the FBI at least fifty important cases, and they ain't never called me back. You ain't with *The X-Files*, are you?"

"*The X-Files* is a TV show." Rafe was at a loss.

Mel nodded. "Yes, sir. That's what they want you to think."

"My momma loves that show." Cam's Southern accent was suddenly thick. "Now, I'm not an agent any more, but I still have contacts. I can call and ask about where your cases have gone."

Mel's eyes narrowed. "You would say that if you were an alien."

He held out his beeper. It went off, but weakly.

"I spent all morning in that car," Cam explained. "We rented it out in Alamosa."

"You got the rental agreement?" This Mel person wasn't about to give up.

Cam nodded steadily. "It's in the glove box. I assure you, I am one hundred percent Southern boy. And self-employed. I left the FBI years ago. You can't trust big government."

Now Mel was all smiles. "Well, hell, I came from the south myself. I was from Georgia until the mothership picked me up and dropped me outside of Denver. Now they don't usually do that. They're usually real good about dropping you back off right where

87

they took you. But they were sneaky with me. You see, I managed to stay awake through my probing. Now, that wasn't all unpleasant. I mean, first you're scared and all, but there are times when it feels nice. I wish they wouldn't play all that Britney Spears. Those aliens really like that Britney Spears. Come on, son. Let's go get some lunch at Stella's, and I'll tell you all about it."

Cam turned his head and gave Rafe a helpless smile as he allowed himself to be walked off. Mel started in on what alien lubrication was like, and Rafe stood there feeling like the biggest idiot in the world.

Laura had a grin on her face that would have made the Cheshire Cat proud. "Guess your brand of charm doesn't work here in Bliss."

She placed her arm through Wolf's and walked off after Cam and Mel.

The cell in Rafe's pocket buzzed. He was grateful for the distraction. He looked down at the number. His chief. Joe's voice cracked over the line.

"You ma…okay?"

Yeah, well it was far too much to ask for good cell reception. "Joe, I can't hear you."

"Wha…can't…where?"

"You're cutting out." He raised his voice, somehow hoping that louder would be better.

"On his…Bliss. New information."

"What information?" He was screaming now, frustration taking over. Was it on the case? Was it about Laura? His hand tightened on the worse-than-useless phone.

There was a click and a buzzing sound as the call disconnected.

Someone slapped him on the back. Rafe turned and saw a man with a cowboy hat on his head. He was dressed in khakis, and there was a gold badge on his chest.

"You know yelling at it doesn't fix things. If you want to yell at someone, yell at the Farley twins. They had the brilliant idea to turn our nearest cell tower into a SETI receiver. I have no idea how those boys managed to screw it up so badly, but it doesn't work anymore. The phone company says they're working on it, but because we're small, I don't think we're a priority. We're all scrambling," the man said. The badge on his chest proclaimed him to be the sheriff of the town. "We've had to make do. Now, if you want good reception, there's this hill right outside the Harper Stables. You tend to have to stand on one leg, and it's best if you take a friend with you because the really good spot is about four feet off the ledge, but as long as someone holds on, you should be all right."

The sheriff tipped his hat and started to walk off. He didn't look back as he said his final words of wisdom. "And watch out for bears! And Max Harper. He can be worse than a bear. If you see him coming, I would shoot first and ask questions never."

Yeah, Rafe fucking hated this place.

* * * *

"Are you planning to tell me why we're lying to federal agents, or have you had an abrupt change of heart? Because if the latter is true, then we have to talk about the way you proposed. A guy needs some romance with his marriage proposal. And you didn't get down on one knee."

Normally, Laura would have laughed at Wolf's teasing. Instead, she found herself frowning his way. She shouldn't be pissed at him, but he was the only one around. "If you could please play along, it will only be a couple of hours. I assure you, once they tell me what they need to say, they'll be right back on a plane to DC. Those two are very career oriented. They don't belong in Bliss."

Wolf helped her step up the curb as they walked toward the parking lot beside Stella's. Holly had driven Laura into town, but she'd decided to let Wolf drive her home, all the better to keep up her little deception. She couldn't feel too bad about it. After all, Rafe and Cam had deceived her. At least she hadn't slept with them before she lied to them.

89

Wolf walked her toward his dually. The massive black truck was a lot like Wolf, enormous, powerful, and surprisingly comfortable on the inside. He opened the door and handed her up.

"I'm surprised you didn't listen to them." Wolf stood outside her door. The height of the seat allowed her to look straight into his calculating, dark eyes. "If what you say is true, then one conversation could clear everything up and send those boys on their way. Makes me wonder why you put them off."

Bastard. He shut the door and walked around the truck. She didn't want to think about that. She wanted to stew. She wanted to rail. Why had she decided to let Wolf drive her? If she was with Holly, she could simply sit and fume. Holly would fume with her. Wolf was far too busy psychoanalyzing her.

Wolf hopped into the driver's seat and started the truck to purring. "No answer for that?"

"Is one required?" She hadn't meant to sound that icy, had she?

He turned to her, one eyebrow climbing up his handsome face. "No, but some courtesy would be nice."

And she finally figured Wolf Meyer out. He'd always reminded her of someone, but she hadn't been able to put her finger on it. That arched brow and the demand for courtesy did it. Stefan Talbot. Oh, yeah, Wolf Meyer was a Dom. He'd mentioned that his brother was in the lifestyle, but he'd conveniently left out his own interest in BDSM. She sighed. "I'm sorry. I didn't mean to be rude. I'm afraid they threw me for a loop." She allowed her lips to quirk up a bit. "Will you forgive me if I call you Sir?"

His cheekbones stained a slight red. "Gave myself away, did I? Well, I always knew you would be hesitant about that part of my life. It was never going to work, was it?"

He pulled out onto the road.

"Sorry, I'm afraid that's not my cup of tea."

"But I'm guessing ménage isn't out of the question."

Now she was the one blushing. "And you go there, why? Most normal people would ask which one I'd been involved with."

"I'm not normal, and both of those men want you. They both wanted to murder me. You don't get that possessive about a woman unless you've had her—or you're completely insane. Given where we are, it could be either option."

"It was a fling." She heard the hollowness in her voice. *Damn it*. She'd been good at hiding her emotions once. Now they were hanging out all over the place.

"Do you honestly believe that?" Wolf asked as he turned toward the valley where a small cluster of cabins lay. "I don't know if we were listening to the same conversation. I heard that they'd been looking for you. The big guy quit his precious job in order to spend all of his time trying to hunt you down. The other guy practically ate you up with his eyes. They didn't seem to be disengaged agents doing a job."

She wasn't falling for their crap again. She wasn't sure why they were here, but it didn't matter. If anything, it was guilt that caused them to search for her. They'd felt guilty when she'd been kidnapped. She could still remember waking up after surgery to the sounds of the two of them fighting about who was at fault. Cam had blamed Rafe for selling her out. Rafe had pointed out that Cam hadn't believed her profile either. It had been a nasty way to wake up.

And then the doctor had told her the bad news.

"When a member of one of the teams gets injured or dies, do you feel bad about it?"

Wolf's face shut down, his jaw forming a hard line. He kept his eyes on the road in front of him. "Of course. Your team is your family."

"Well, consider the BAU my team."

"If that's the way you want to play it, who am I to stop you?"

Wolf was quiet the rest of the drive. He turned down the dirt road that led to her cabin. Holly's cabin was beside Laura's. Callie and her husbands lived close, but Laura always felt like she was the only person in the world when she shut the door to her cabin. It was her sanctuary.

As she got out of the truck, a wave of guilt rolled over her. Wolf was a nice man, and she was using him. "I'm sorry. I don't know what came over me. I didn't want them to think I'd been pining for them."

She hadn't. She didn't think about them every day anymore. She'd gotten used to her life here in Bliss. She didn't need them coming in here and disrupting everything. She was over them.

Liar.

Wolf smiled at her. "It's all right. I knew it wouldn't work out deep down. I find you incredibly attractive, and women around these parts can be a little...interesting. I would move on and ask Holly out, but I hear she's taken, even if the interested parties are unavailable or so whacked out they can't talk around the girl."

It was an apt description of Holly's plight. Wolf pulled the truck into her driveway and stopped.

Laura slid out of her seat. "Well, I thank you anyway. I'll tell them the truth tonight."

"Don't. I enjoy subterfuge as much as the next guy. Let 'em sweat." Wolf winked at her. "I'll be back to pick you up for the dinner. It'll be fun to see what your friend is like after a couple of hours of Mel."

Wolf pulled back out, and she was left alone.

She tried not to think about what he'd said. After a long time staring at the river, she walked into her cabin to get dressed.

Chapter Six

Cam pulled the SUV into the parking lot, gravel crunching under the wheels. Lights sparkled in the distance like fireflies, and the hum of music could be heard even through the heavy doors. Cam squinted, trying to make out the individual forms swaying in the distance. The fairgrounds were lit with a mixture of twinkle lights and the full moon shining down. He craned his neck to look through the windshield.

Damn. The stars didn't look like that in the city. They were like jewels in the sky here in Bliss.

"Are you ready to go?" Rafe's voice seemed caught in his throat. He'd been quiet for hours, sitting in the booth of the diner while Cam talked to the insane dude.

He'd actually learned a lot while talking to Mel. He'd learned that everyone in town loved Laura. Mel had talked about her with great affection. The woman who ran the diner had talked about her, too. Laura had formed real connections in this community, connections she'd never formed in DC. Laura hadn't known her neighbors in DC. Cam understood. He didn't particularly want to know the people he shared his rattrap complex with, either. He'd already had more conversation with Mel, the conspiracy kook, than he'd had with anyone in the last year or so. It made him realize how isolated he'd become.

Cam watched as Rafe checked the clip on his Glock. "I feel weird not carrying."

Rafe shook his head. "They would never have let you on a plane with a firearm."

Rafe looked around the place, his dark eyes hawk-like.

"What are you looking for?" Cam hadn't seen anything in this place that worried him. Sure, some of the people seemed weird, but they were harmless. He had to wonder if he'd been out of the game too long. Was he missing something?

"If you found her, de Sade could find her," Rafe pointed out.

"I doubt that," Cam assured him. "She's pretty isolated here. If she hadn't taken that photo, I wouldn't have found her. I can't imagine that de Sade has written a software program that scans the net and identifies missing people through facial recognition."

Rafe shook his head, a slight nod that let Cam know he disagreed. "That software exists, Cam. I heard recently there's a group in Dallas working on something similar. You remember Alex McKay? He's in private security now and one of the men on his team is writing a program like yours."

"I know all about Adam Miles. We've exchanged some emails. But I assure you my program is better than his. I tried several of the ones on the market before I gave up and built my own. What do you think I spent my money on?" It had taken him about a year and a half to design that software. His training in communications had been the reason the Bureau was interested in him in the first place. He'd left his actual programming jobs behind when he joined the BAU. He'd concentrated on keeping the hardware up and the use of communications in the field, but he'd realized that he needed something more than what the market had when he couldn't find Laura. He'd sold almost everything he had to make the software work, but it had paid off in the end. He'd found her.

94

And now she was with a former Navy SEAL.

She swayed in Wolf Meyer's arms in the middle of the small dance floor. *Fuck*. He hated that man. Cam had spent the afternoon in their tiny motel room using freaking dial-up to come up with everything he could on Wolf Meyer. Of course, it wasn't much. The Navy kept a lot of things classified, and Wolf Meyer seemed to be one of them. Unless he wanted to hack into the Navy's classified files and risk bringing the wrath of God down on himself, he had to let the particulars go. He didn't care that Wolf was a badass who had honorably served his country for years. The asshole was horning in on his woman, and he wasn't going to sit back and let it happen.

"If you'll let me borrow your sidearm, I can take care of one of our problems," he said between clenched teeth.

"You can't shoot him," Rafe replied with a disappointed sigh. "I wish we could, but we need to concentrate on what's important."

"Protecting Laura." It was all that mattered.

"Gentlemen, can I help you?"

Cam turned and saw a man in a khaki uniform.

Rafe nodded. "Sheriff Wright."

Cam held out a hand. Rafe had made contact with local law enforcement. Nathan Wright, according to Rafe, was deeply concerned about the problem.

"Have you done a perimeter sweep?" Rafe asked.

A long, slow smile crossed the sheriff's face. "I've walked around the fairgrounds and said hello to everyone, if that's what you're asking. Look, my deputy and I are both on the job tonight. You can relax. This isn't a tourist event. If someone new shows up, every single person here is going to have questions."

Small towns could be like that. His hometown hadn't been easy on newcomers, but they tended to take care of their own. "Have you let the gossips in on what's going on?"

"Small-town boy?" The sheriff glanced Cam's way.

"Green Line, Arkansas, population three hundred fifty-two."

Rafe looked between the two of them. "What does gossip have

to do with anything?"

The sheriff shook his head. "Big city?"

"Miami." Cam shared a look with the sheriff. "I'm afraid my partner here is pure city. He was born in Miami and moved to DC. Rafe, in a small town, if you want everyone to know something, you usually only need to call one person. If you let the worst gossip in town know something, an hour later everyone knows."

"Hell, Callie is way better than that. She had everyone in the know in half that time. Trust me, Zane and I keep certain things very, very quiet around our wife. Don't worry. Everyone knows to watch out for Laura. Logan and I will keep a close watch on things." The sheriff tipped his hat and began to walk away. "And you boys mind your manners around Wolf Meyer. I don't want to have to break up any fights. You don't need to fight him, you know. There's two of you and only one of him. That should be enough to take her down."

Rafe turned on Cam as the sheriff walked toward the gathering. "See, this is why this place irritates me. What the hell did he mean by any of that? It's like they speak a different language. I don't get it. Why would he refer to his wife as 'our' wife? Do these people get along so amazingly well that they keep in touch after a divorce and become best friends with the ex-husband?"

Cam wasn't sure about that, either, but there was a much more important problem. "Why does this place bug you so much? We've been in way worse places. We've been in even smaller towns, and it never upset you."

Rafe stared at the scene in front of him. Vivacious music floated across the fairgrounds, and Cam could hear the sound of people laughing and talking. The sweet smell of barbecue made his stomach rumble. It was a perfect little world to his mind, but Rafe was frowning the way he did when they walked into crack houses or slums.

"She's not going to leave with us," Rafe said after a long pause.

Cam sighed. It came from deep within his body. He'd known

that the moment they walked into town. "No, she isn't. But the point might be moot. She hasn't shown a lot of interest in us."

Oh, there had been that moment when he'd locked eyes on her. He would have sworn he'd seen something on her face, some spark that nearly leapt through the window that had separated them. She'd quickly locked it down, and all he'd seen from her since was a mixture of deep sadness and anger.

"I love her," Rafe said quietly. "I thought that when we walked in, she would fall into my arms. I guess there was a part of me that thought she was waiting for us."

Cam leaned against the SUV. He'd had that dream, too. Somewhere in the back of his head, he'd imagined she was waiting for them to find her. "We should have known better. She went through a lot. My god, she was lying in her hospital bed, and we were fighting over her like dogs fight over a bone."

"I know. I know we fucked up, but she ran. She walked out and didn't even let us know she was alive. How could she do it?" Rafe asked, his voice tortured.

"Come on, man. I know you. You ran from Miami as fast as you could. The same way I ran from Arkansas." Rafe's parents had been a bit controlling. After they had divorced, he'd been trapped in the war zone. He'd talked about it extensively over the years. And Cam had taken the first scholarship out of his one-stoplight town and never looked back.

"But I call my mom and my dad. I might not like either of them, but I let them know I'm okay. What does that say about the way she feels about us? I thought a good argument would solve this, but now I have to wonder."

"I'm staying." Cam was sure of that. He didn't have anything to go back to anyway. He had a crappy apartment and no friends beyond Rafe. He had a PI license but not a lot of clientele. "Until de Sade is caught, I'm going to stay right here."

He would find a job, and he would watch over her.

"Are you going to go to her wedding if we're wrong and she's truly involved with Meyer?" Rafe asked.

The whole idea made his chest constrict. God, he couldn't watch Laura walk toward someone else while she wore a white dress, her face shining with love. It would tear him apart. "Yes. I'll do it. I owe it to her."

He owed her everything. Guilt weighed on him, stronger now that he could see her again. He couldn't help but remember that day after they had made love for the first time. He and Rafe had gone out for breakfast to discuss what had happened, and they hadn't seen her again until the briefing. Laura had looked so fragile as she turned in her first major profile. She'd looked worse than fragile when everyone had turned on her.

"Do you think she's right?" He'd made himself sick over this question. "Could we have been wrong while she was right?"

"About de Sade? God, Cam, I've thought about that every single day. If I could change one thing in my life, it would be the way we handled that fucking profile, but Edward was sure."

Rafe's whole face had aged in a minute. Lines formed on his forehead and around his mouth. This was why they hadn't seen each other much in the last several years. Neither of them wanted to talk about what had happened. It had been easier to concentrate on finding Laura. They'd drifted apart because staying close had been painful.

But why had it been that way? Why hadn't they been able to talk about it? They'd managed to spend a lot of time drinking and fighting, but not once had they had an honest conversation about what had happened.

"Even Joe went with Edward's profile. There wasn't enough evidence to push the notion that de Sade was law enforcement." Cam hadn't wanted to believe it, either. It was too horrifying to think about the possibility that one of their own could do that. He'd grasped on to Edward Lock's alternative profile. He hadn't meant to hurt Laura, but he'd truly believed what Edward had said.

"Besides, after what happened with that reporter, can you still believe Laura was right?" Rafe asked.

Cam couldn't help the way his fists clenched when he thought of the Washington reporter who'd written a story on Laura's profile. She had been a friend of Laura's, a long-term friend, and she'd betrayed her for a headline. The story had hit the next day. Laura had been fired for leaking information, and twelve hours later, she'd been a guest of the Marquis de Sade.

What if Cam had supported her? What if he'd put his career on the line to back her despite his own beliefs? She probably wouldn't have felt the need to call her friend and commiserate. She wouldn't have gotten drunk and confided in that vicious bitch. She wouldn't have had her face plastered across the papers like a road map leading the killer straight to her.

"I've read that letter a thousand times." Cam straightened up. The Marquis de Sade, or someone claiming to be him, had sent a letter to the FBI and the reporter responsible for breaking the story, claiming he was insulted to be called law enforcement. He'd written a long diatribe on how he was smarter than any of them and the woman who insulted him would pay for her crime.

"We've all gone over it a thousand times. The fact that de Sade took her because he was insulted she'd said he was in law enforcement fits Edward's profile," Rafe argued.

But Cam had finally pulled out Laura's profile a couple of months before. He'd been obsessing over it. And he'd been questioning the entire case. "Or he fits Laura's profile and he's trying to throw us off."

Rafe's fist came down. "I've thought of that, too. This is getting us nowhere. We have to convince her to come home with us. She isn't safe here. If she's right, then she needs to be protected."

"I disagree. Not that she doesn't need protection, but I think taking her back to DC is a mistake. He got to her in DC."

Rafe obviously wasn't buying it. "And you think he can't get to her here? Have you looked around this place? The door to her cabin was unlocked. There's no way she should stay here."

"I'll stay with her," Cam offered. "I can protect her, and the sheriff was right. A stranger will stick out like a sore thumb here."

"This isn't about protecting her, is it? This is how you plan to win."

He went toe-to-toe with his old friend. "I'm not trying to win anything. I'm trying to keep her alive. I think what you're trying to do is have your cake and eat it, too. You want to haul her back to DC and turn her into a sweet little wife. She was never going to be your trophy, Rafe."

Rafe's face went red. "She's not a trophy. I never wanted her to get fired."

"But you thought it was a dangerous job for her."

"I was right. It *was* dangerous."

"She should have been at home baking cookies?" Cam asked, feeling his blood pressure rise.

Rafe got right in his face. "Fuck you, Cam. How are you any better? You're the one who wanted to get her pregnant. I had to remind you to wear a condom that night. Do you think I don't know why you wanted to do that? You thought if you tied her to you, she would pick you."

He felt his whole body flush. He hadn't meant to do that, had he? Sure, he'd thought about getting her pregnant, but he had just forgotten in the heat of the moment. Of course, after what had happened with de Sade, that wasn't a problem anymore. He hated to think about everything that bastard had taken from her. "Well, it didn't take long for that whole sharing thing to get tossed out, did it, Rafe? If you get her back to DC, we would always have to hide. No one would understand. I'm going to assume since you're the one with the fancy job that you would be the one to legally marry her."

Rafe shrugged as though it was a forgone conclusion. "It makes sense. I make more than both of you combined. I seriously doubt the FBI will promote me if I'm flaunting the nation's polygamy laws."

"And no one cares what I do?"

"What do you want me to do? I can't force society to accept

what we want. I'm willing to sit down and work it out. There's not a place in the world where we could live openly. It probably doesn't matter anyway since she's made it plain she doesn't want to have anything to do with either one of us."

"Damn, brother. This is some entertaining shit."

Cam turned and saw two cowboys walking toward them with a red-haired woman in between them. One cowboy wore a black T-shirt and the other had on a denim Western-style shirt, but other than that they were perfectly identical.

"Nate said they were going to be trouble, Max."

The one in the Western shirt shrugged. "I find trouble highly entertaining. Hey, you think I could get one of those boys to fight?"

"Maxwell Harper, you promised me you wouldn't try to start another fight until after Stef and Jen's wedding." The redhead with a baby in her arms gave the one named Max a dirty look. "I am serious, Max. I do not want Jen's wedding pictures marred by you having a black eye. If that happens, I'll substitute Rye in with Photoshop. And we will have a conversation, you and I."

The redhead started to stomp off.

"But I like our conversations, baby!"

She turned and stared at Cam for a moment as though assessing him. "If you hit him, you go for his gut. If you touch his face, I will find you. Do you understand me?"

"Yes, ma'am," Cam said immediately. Everything the redhead said had an air of Southern authority. Cam responded. He backed off of the cowboy who he had zero intention of fighting. It had the added effect of making him back off Rafe, whom he had kind of been planning to fight.

The cowboy in the black T-shirt smiled. "You're going to sleep on the couch tonight, brother."

"Damn, Rye, I wasn't really going to fight. I promised Rach. You're trying to get our wife all to yourself. When this edict of Rachel's is no longer in effect, I'm going to kick your ass."

"Not if I kick yours first, Max."

"Stop, both of you," Cam commanded. That was the second time some dude in this town had mentioned sharing a wife. "What do you mean by 'our wife?'"

Identical faces turned to him. Cam felt Rafe move beside him. All thoughts of beating the shit out of Rafe fled in a rush of curiosity.

"Rachel, that hot redhead with the gorgeous baby, is our wife." The man in the black T-shirt whom Max had called Rye crossed his arms over his chest. "And before you start calling in Johnny Law, you should know we do things differently in Bliss."

Max snorted. "What's the sheriff going to do? Arrest us? How is he going to lock the cell door from the inside?"

"Stop. Are you two talking about polygamy?" Rafe had a hand on his hip. It was his cop stance.

Rye Harper didn't seem scared. "The technical term for what we do is polyandry. And we're perfectly legal. Max married Rach legally, and we're not defrauding the government. We're not illegal, just on the fringe of what society finds acceptable."

"No one cares in Bliss," Max said with a questioning look aimed at his twin.

"Yeah, well, Bliss isn't exactly society," Rye returned. "If we left Bliss, people would think we're freaky."

"There's no reason to leave Bliss anymore. Not since we got cable."

Rye turned to his brother. "I have a reason. Reliable cell service. I spent two hours on the landline trying to lodge a complaint with the company. Seriously, how long does it take to fix one tower?"

"I don't care about that," Max said. "I don't want to talk to anyone outside of Bliss. Hell, half the time I don't want to talk to people inside Bliss. It's all gossip. Rach spent thirty minutes on the phone with Callie talking about some weird plan Laura's cooked up where she marries Wolf so two dudes don't know she's been alone for years."

A sly smile crossed Rye's lips. "Yeah, now, I did hear about that. I heard those men had been looking for her for a real long time. It occurs to me that two men who spent all that time looking for a lady must have some pretty strong feelings for her, and a woman who hasn't dated in a long time usually is hung up on a man—or two."

Cam went still. "Laura hasn't dated anyone?"

"Well, she did go out with Wolf," Max replied. "But as far as I can remember, no one else. We were all surprised she said yes to him."

Rye shook his head. "Rachel wasn't. Rachel told Jen that any woman in her right mind would be after him."

Max whistled. "Is that why you spanked her?"

"Damn straight. But she knew I was listening. She even winked at me when she said it and slapped her own ass." Rye adjusted his Stetson.

Everyone in this town wore a hat. Cam's own head was starting to feel bare. Damn, he hadn't worn a cowboy hat in years, not since he left Arkansas.

"She is getting saucier with age," Max said with a grin. "Oh, well. There's no way around it, Rye. She's the boss of our family. What she says goes. We need to be careful. She told us not to give up Laura's secret."

"I won't tell. Now let's get going, brother. That damn bear won't eat himself."

Max elbowed his twin. "He damn near ate you. You were lucky the rangers came along when they did or Rach would be down a husband and little Paige would only have me for a dad."

The twin cowboys sauntered off talking about all the weird shit they planned on eating this evening.

Rafe turned his head, a grin crinkling the corner of his mouth. "She's not engaged."

A light happiness threatened to take over Cam's body. She wasn't engaged. She wasn't even sleeping with him. According to those two cowboys, she hadn't really dated for a long time, maybe since she'd left DC.

"There's only one real reason for a woman to lie like that," Rafe continued.

"She still has feelings for us," he said, a smile spreading across his face. She'd lied to protect herself. "She still gives a damn, and we just landed in a place where no one is going to blink an eye if we share her. Hell, now I have to wonder how many of these people are in weird-ass relationships. I saw a girl wearing a collar in town."

Rafe shook his head. "Yeah. I'm still not sold on this place, but at least we can go after her without any shame. We can do it completely in the open."

Cam suddenly wanted to get started on that project. It was time to show Laura that he wasn't going to wait another five years to get inside her again. He turned to his partner, all previous anger gone. They might have to revisit that fight, but not tonight. "What's the plan?"

Rafe leaned in and started to speak.

* * * *

Everyone was looking at her.

Wolf twirled her around the dance floor, his big hand leading her this way and that in time to the music, but her focus was on the multitudinous eyes that tracked her.

"Congratulations, you two!" Hank Farley said as he danced by with his wife. "You should know our barn is available for the reception."

"We'll think about it," Wolf said with an easy smile.

He steered her toward the middle of the dance floor. Right where she didn't want to be. Wolf seemed to be enjoying the attention far too much.

"Laura, Wolf." Stef Talbot held his fiancée in his arms as they swayed to the music. "Jennifer and I have talked about this, and we want to offer to include your own nuptials in our wedding. It can be a double ceremony. I'll cover all the costs."

Jen Waters had a smirk on her face. "And Brooke said she can put together a dress in no time flat. We want to make this as easy on you as possible."

No, they didn't. They were being righteous bastards. It was the whole damn town's way of letting her know they disapproved of her lying. She wasn't stupid. No one in Bliss would blink twice if she was lying to save a friend or protect herself from real harm, but the minute her heart got involved, everyone became a shrink.

"They're going to give you hell, you know," Wolf said as he led her off the dance floor.

"I'm beginning to see that. I've already received lectures from Marie and Stella on how I need to face my past if I ever want to move on." Getting married had turned Stella into the world's biggest authority on relationships. She was madly in love with Sebastian Talbot and wanted everyone in town to be as happy as she was.

It was annoying.

Even Mel had thrown his two cents in. Apparently lying left her open to alien death rays or something. And Cassidy had called to let Laura know that she didn't appreciate her son being used as a beard and offered her other son's counseling services. Laura wasn't sure, but she might actually have an appointment with a man named Leo Meyer in Dallas to discuss her relationship issues.

It wasn't what she'd had planned. It was supposed to be a simple deception. Nothing was simple in Bliss.

"You could come clean," Wolf offered.

Laura frowned. "They seem to be pushing me that way."

Wolf leaned against an empty picnic table. "That's the trouble with family, isn't it? They always think they know what's best for you."

"And they think it's best that the men who broke my heart know that I haven't been with anyone since I left them? They think it's best that I look utterly pathetic?"

"I think they want you to not think of yourself as pathetic. I think these people love you, and they want you to love yourself. Whatever happened to you hurt you deeply. That's not pathetic. They want you to see yourself the way they do. Do you know what they say about you?"

Damn, tears were pricking at her eyes. "No."

"They say that you're brave and you don't hesitate to speak your mind. They admire you for that."

"I didn't speak my mind before I came here. The one time I stood up for myself got me into serious trouble. It isn't like the movies, you know. The FBI is like any other business. In the end, they want good soldiers who follow orders. It's hard to do one thing all day and then come home and be a different person. After a while, the act seems like reality. Trying to fit in changes a person." The only time she'd truly been herself was with her friends. With Rafe and Cam, she hadn't needed that armor she put on during the day. She didn't even think of Jana Evans. Jana had never been her friend. She'd been a reporter waiting for a story.

"Well, I don't think you're the same person you are now that you were back then."

It was true. Bliss had changed her. The first couple of years had been rough. She hadn't wanted to let anyone in, but they had wormed their way into her heart. Slowly, she'd become more open and willing to talk about her past, to mesh the woman she'd been with the woman she was becoming. She'd stopped hiding in her cabin and talked to people.

The truth of the matter was she was a bit surprised that Cam hadn't found her. She'd kept off the radar as much as possible, using a fake social security number to work, but she'd talked openly about her life. She guessed Bliss was more isolated than she'd believed.

"I don't suppose anyone would be the same after what I went through." Maybe it was time to be honest about it. She wasn't sure she was ready to tell everyone what had happened, but she didn't have much of a choice.

"No, sweetheart, being betrayed by a friend and then captured by a serial killer would change the best of us." He sighed at her gasp. "I can use a computer. I knew you lived in DC five years ago and you worked for the FBI. A quick Google search of Laura plus blonde plus FBI brought up a shocking number of prostitutes and your story."

She tried to recover from the shock. "Well, I'm glad the rest of my friends aren't as tech savvy as you are."

"Oh, I wouldn't count on it. I'm pretty sure the sheriff has figured it out, and if the sheriff knows, then Zane knows. I would bet that every man in this town knows to watch out for you. It's the way they work."

The fact that the sheriff knew brought with it an odd mix of anxiety and security. She didn't like the fact that her secret was out there, but the way the sheriff seemed to have handled it made her feel respected and protected. It was the way Bliss worked.

"Hello, happy couple!"

Holly walked up, a broad grin on her face. Nell and Henry followed. They wore their typical Big Game Dinner protest-wear of black pants and T-shirts with the words "Animals Have Voices, Too." Their mouths had been duct-taped closed to show that these poor animals had been silenced forever. Despite their dark and brooding wardrobe choices, Nell's eyes were lit with mirth, and Henry carried a bright yellow legal pad that he flashed quickly.

Congrats on your fake engagement. I will give you a fake present! Here is a toaster.

Henry mimed giving them a gift.

"They intend to have a whole fake ceremony for you two," Holly explained.

Wolf laughed. "Well, hell, Henry, you couldn't do better than a fake toaster?"

Holly and Nell both shook their heads. "Oh, no," Holly said.

"Henry is very frugal, even when it's fake."

Laura watched as Holly's whole body seemed to go on full alert.

"Doc." Wolf nodded a greeting as Caleb Burke walked up.

The town doctor was wearing his usual uniform of dark-washed jeans and a Western shirt. When he was working, he sometimes put a white coat on, but mostly it was jeans and Western shirts and worn boots, even when delivering a baby.

"Wolf, Laura, Holly." His throat seemed to close over the last name, though he managed to get it out. Laura couldn't help but smile as he scrubbed a hand through his hair. Caleb Burke was a glorious hunk of man, but he had issues. He also had a small bowl in his hand, and he passed it to Nell. "It's peanut stir-fry with quinoa and tofu. Perfectly vegan."

Nell quickly pulled the duct tape off her mouth. "That is so sweet, Caleb."

The doctor suddenly found his feet endlessly fascinating. "Well, I figured you wouldn't have a lot to eat here, so I made something for you."

Nell thanked him. Henry gave the group a thumbs-up and they walked off to find some silverware.

"That was thoughtful," Holly said.

Caleb flushed, his face redder than his gold and red hair. "Well, you can have some if you want it."

Holly bit her lip. "Um, I'm not really into tofu, but I would love to try it."

"Oh, I'm sure it tastes like shit," Caleb said. "I mean, why eat that when you could try bear?"

A bright smile lit Holly's face. "Come on, then. It's actually really good, and the bison burgers are amazing."

She was about to say something when she caught sight of Rafe and Cam walking onto the fairgrounds. Holly and Caleb left in search of exotic meats, but it wasn't the smell of barbecue that had Laura's mouth watering.

Why did those two men have to be so damn delicious? They were almost perfect opposites. Rafe was smooth where Cam was rough on the outside, but then they changed roles when they got to the bedroom. Rafe had taken her with the ruthlessness of an invader, and Cam had made her feel utterly worshipped.

"You should see the look on your face, Laura." There was a wistful quality to Wolf's words. "Damn, I hope a woman looks at me like that someday."

"I don't love them." She forced herself to say the words. Maybe if she said it enough, she would believe it.

"Life is way too short to lie to yourself, sweetheart. And it's too short to sit on your ass because you're scared. Could they hurt you again? Oh, yeah. What's going to hurt worse? Your heart breaking or waking up one day and realizing you didn't try?"

"Were you this mouthy in the SEALs?"

He shrugged. "Can't help it. I'm brilliant when it comes to dealing with other people's problems. It's my alien DNA. It helps me see to the heart of the matter and makes me very intuitive. Damn, there's my mom. And she has beets. I fucking hate beets." He pushed away from the picnic table and smoothed out his shirt. "I don't think you need me to handle this one, but if you choose to go with the fake fiancé thing, know that I am going to require an enormous amount of filthy, disgusting fake sex."

She couldn't help but smile. He really was adorable. "Got it."

He backed away with a wave of his hand. "And I'm the best fake sex you've ever had."

"Damn straight," Laura returned.

And then all she could see was them. They had lasered in on her and walked side by side with purpose, ignoring everything else around them.

They were the best real sex she'd ever had, and they were headed her way.

Chapter Seven

Rafe didn't miss the way Laura's body went still, her muscles stiffening where a moment before she'd been laughing with her friends. She changed the second she became aware of them. It wasn't the greeting he would prefer. Back when they were friends, when she would see him coming, her whole body would go soft and a welcoming smile would transform her face from something professional to an intimate visage, one only meant for someone close to her. He'd taken great pride in the fact that he'd only ever seen that look on her face for one other person.

"Hello, *bella*."

She frowned at him. Even with her lips turned down, she was stunning. She looked only slightly out of place in her yellow heels. The rest of her outfit was charmingly Western. She had on a full cotton skirt, a yellow tank top, and a light denim jacket. It wasn't far off from what many of the other women were wearing, yet Laura made it seem elegant. Everything she did had an air of grace to it, even when she was bitching at him.

"I thought I asked you to stop calling me that."

He wasn't going to let her push him. He gave her what he hoped was an easy smile. "And I asked you to stop calling me asshole. I doubt you've done that. Dance with me."

Her eyes widened, a look of horror crossing her face. "No."

"Come on, baby. Don't say no." Cam crowded her, but she held her ground. Those heels were planted firmly in the grass beneath her. "I can't dance with you until you dance with him. I lost the coin flip."

"Oh, that's romantic." Her hands found her hips, and those gorgeously full lips pursed. "Every woman in the world wants to be won by the flip of a coin."

"We didn't have time to play cards," Rafe admitted. He was well aware that people were listening in. Oh, they were pretending to be doing other things, but they leaned over and then talked behind their hands. The citizens of Bliss seemed to be enjoying the drama. Damn, he couldn't get used to it. In DC, no one paid a bit of attention to what was going on around them. He tried to ignore it. "We weren't sure how else to handle it, *bella*. You have to teach us."

Her lips rose in a sarcastic grin. "See, that's easy. Let me teach you how to handle a situation like this. You both turn around and walk out the way you came in. You get in your car and drive to Alamosa and get on a plane back to DC."

Cam sighed. "That's not going to happen."

Cam ran a hand up her arm, and Rafe was satisfied with the way she shivered. She still responded to Cam. Would she respond to him? He reached out and took her hand, studying it. Her hand was small in his, her skin fair against his olive tone. Her nails weren't as long as she used to keep them, but they were still manicured and painted a pretty pink. "Come on and dance with me. We came all this way. We've looked for so long. Can't you spare a moment of your time? Your fiancé is otherwise occupied, and I promise to behave."

He wouldn't behave. He had every intention of reminding her of the chemistry they'd had, but he wasn't going to announce it.

Her eyes strayed to where Wolf Meyer seemed to be having an argument with a small woman with steel-gray hair. She was giving the big man hell, and Rafe was glad to see it.

"Fine." She pushed off of the picnic table she'd been leaning against. "One dance and that's all."

"With both of us," Cam added quickly, pushing the advantage. "It's only fair. Otherwise, we'll both dance with you here and now."

There it was. Rafe's heart soared. Her eyes had flared momentarily, and it wasn't with disgust. When they had checked into the odd motel at the edge of town, they had decided it would be best to come at her together. She'd been turned on by sex with both of them. They needed to remind her of what they had to offer. "I'll spare the world that sight. One dance, with both of you, and then you'll go?"

She was going to be difficult to the end. Rafe decided to press his second advantage. It wasn't truly an advantage, but he knew she wouldn't be able to say no to them. "You know we can't do that. We need to talk. It's important, *bella*. De Sade is working again. He's been quiet for years, but he's back. I would do anything to spare you…"

She held up a hand, her face taking on a blank, professional stare. "How many?"

"One that we've found so far." He was certain the victim they'd found wasn't the only one. De Sade was back in DC and on the hunt.

Her expression remained blank, but he could see the way her pulse jumped in the vein in her neck. Her heart was pounding. He had to stop himself from hauling her into his arms and promising her that it would be all right.

"I didn't see his face," she said, her tone as bland as her expression. "I went over all of this in the hospital with Joseph. De Sade wore a mask the whole time. I would have given you a description if I'd seen his face."

Cam's hands fisted at his side. Rafe was pretty sure he was

resisting the urge to touch her, too. "We don't want to go over what happened to you again, baby. We want to go over your profile."

She shivered slightly. "I don't have it anymore. I left everything behind."

Rafe knew that well. He'd spent days going through everything in her apartment, trying to figure out if she'd left anything behind that would point to where she'd gone. He and Cam had sifted through her belongings, and finally, after a year of making sure her rent was paid and her place kept the same, they had been the ones to box her things up. Rafe was still paying for the storage shed where he kept her belongings and her furniture. He kept her very personal items in his own house, her pictures and keepsakes. He hadn't been able to put them in the shed.

She shook her head. "We can talk about this later. In the morning, perhaps. This party isn't the place to discuss it."

Cam relaxed, his face opening up a bit. He hopped onto the picnic table. "What is this party anyway? Do ya'll do this kind of thing often?"

Laura looked over the crowded fairgrounds with a fond smile. "It's a rite of summer around here. It's called the Big Game Dinner. When the rangers have to put down an animal, we process it and freeze the meat. Some of the locals hunt, too. It's considered wrong around here if you merely hunt for sport. We eat what we kill, whether it's a bear or an elk or a deer or a squirrel. We encourage hunters to donate their kills if they were looking for a trophy. That's why the meat processor is next to the taxidermist. Of course they're both next to the vegan café. That was some interesting planning on their part."

"Squirrel?" Rafe was pretty sure he didn't want to try squirrel.

"Now, don't you go talking bad about squirrel. My momma used to cook up some squirrel and rabbit, too." Cam's Southern accent was suddenly thick.

Laura slid Cam a look as a laugh escaped her lips. "I bet you paired beer with squirrel."

Cam winked her way. "Only Milwaukee's finest goes with squirrel, baby."

He felt a deep gratitude to his partner. Cam had gotten her laughing. "Come on, let's dance while Cam walks around trying strange meat."

He took her hand and started to lead her toward the dance floor.

"It's all right, *bella*," he said in what he hoped was his most soothing voice.

She was skittish about this. She walked beside him, but he could feel her reluctance. It wasn't surprising after everything she'd gone through. He pulled her into his arms just as someone changed the song. Before it had been a two-stepping country song, but now the music slid to something slow and sexy.

"Busybodies," she said under her breath as she allowed him to put his arms around her. Her hands wound almost reluctantly around his neck.

He let it go. There was a lot he didn't understand about this town and Laura's place in it. "Cam and I have been talking. We mishandled everything on the day you turned in your profile. We're sorry."

Her face was stony even as she swayed to the music. "I don't know how to take that. Should I forgive and forget when it cost me my career?"

It had cost her much more. That truth lay between them like a brick wall keeping them apart.

"No one wanted to believe that it could be one of us," he said, wishing he had never opened the subject.

"I didn't want to believe it, either."

He pulled her closer, loving the feel of her body against his. "I don't want to fight. Can we have one night where I'm simply happy to see you?"

She moved stiffly in his arms. "Tell me why you're happy to see me and maybe we can talk."

Rafe felt his eyebrows creep up his face. "What do you mean?"

114

She stared at someplace past his shoulder. "I mean I want to know why you've been looking for me."

Was she high? Had the altitude affected her brain? "Because that's what people in love do, *bella*. They look for their loved ones when they disappear. Cam gave up his job to look full time. We've done nothing but think about you and search for you."

"You weren't even in bed with me the morning after we had sex."

Relief flooded his system. That he could address. "We woke up early. We weren't exactly sure how to handle it. It's odd waking up in bed with a naked man."

"It didn't seem odd to me."

At least there was a hint of a smile on her face. "Well, the way I was raised, it is definitely odd. My culture isn't big on sharing."

"I don't think any culture is."

"This town doesn't seem to mind. I talked to two cowboys earlier who share a wife."

"Ah, met Max and Rye, huh?" Her movements became more graceful as the music seemed to take over.

"And the sheriff, if I'm not mistaken. Tell me something, I can almost understand the twins. I've heard twins have deep connections. But what about the sheriff? He seemed so normal to me."

"That's because you don't know him. No one's normal, Rafe. Haven't you figured that out yet? Here in Bliss, we don't even try to be. We fit together because no one tries to fit in."

He doubted that seriously. Even in odd communities, there was a certain amount of fitting in. He couldn't believe that Bliss was different. But discussing Bliss with her seemed like a bad idea. He concentrated on his previous line of questioning. "So the sheriff is bisexual?"

She stopped in the middle of the dance floor and laughed.

Embarrassment flashed through him. "No, then? Well, how am I supposed to know?"

She put her arms back around him. "I guess you aren't. No, Nathan Wright isn't bi. He's totally hetero, just a little kinky. He and his partner, Zane, have been best friends since they were kids. When they fell in love with the same woman, they decided to share her. The sheriff says it's the best of both worlds. He gets to hang with his closest friend all the time, and he gets his girl. It works nicely for them, and here, no one blinks an eye."

It sounded nice, but he wasn't sure if it would work for them.

"So that morning after we had sex…"

"Made love." He wasn't about to allow her to cheapen it.

Her blonde hair shook. "Whatever. That morning, the two of you couldn't figure out how to share, so you left?"

It had been more complex than that. "We went to breakfast to talk. It seemed like something we should do."

He and Cam had ordered breakfast, but neither had eaten it. They had stared at each other over the tabletop.

"And it never occurred to you that I should be in on that conversation?"

It hadn't. It still didn't. "It was between me and Cam."

He and Cam had sat in a diner a block from her place and talked. It had been an odd and stilted conversation that ended in a fight. Neither one had been willing to give her up, and neither one had been willing to share long term. The entire idea had been foreign. It was fine for one hot night, but they both wanted a lifetime with her. They'd argued over how to proceed. Neither could stand the idea of the other winning. All of that had changed when she was taken. When she'd been taken by the Marquis de Sade, Rafe and Cam had been inseparable. They'd practically clung to each other.

Over time, they'd begun to see less and less of each other, as though their guilt had become a wall neither wanted to climb. He wondered what would become of the sheriff and his partner if something happened to their wife. Or to the brothers. He doubted they would fall apart the way he and Cam had.

He'd missed Cam. He'd missed Cam as much as he'd missed

Laura. The idea kicked him squarely in the balls. He didn't have sexual feelings for Cam, but he did have feelings. Serious feelings. What did that make him?

"It's only guilt, you know," Laura said softly. "Some bad stuff happened to me, and you feel guilty about it. I'm okay now. You can stop worrying about me. I'm safe here."

It seemed to Rafe that she was gently giving him permission to go. She had no idea what he was feeling. He pulled her into his body, thrusting his pelvis toward hers. "Does this feel like guilt, *bella*?"

He let his hands drift to her hips, pressing them together. His cock responded immediately. It grew long and hard. Rafe could feel it jump in his pants like it was a heat-seeking missile that had finally found a target.

Her gasp filled him with hope. It was the same breathy sound she made when he touched her clit or sucked on her nipples. His cock hardened painfully. It had been on full alert since the moment they had found her, and being close, being able to touch her and breathe in her scent, wasn't helping.

"I still want you. I never stopped wanting you."

"I've changed," she said, but she didn't pull away.

"You couldn't possibly change enough for me to stop wanting you."

She bit into her bottom lip as her eyes turned down. "I'm a different person now. And I gained twenty pounds."

He chuckled. She was worried about that? "I can see that. It looks good on you. You're beautiful. Every inch of you calls to me. I didn't come here out of guilt. I came out of desperation. I've missed you."

She turned her head up, and his lips were so close to hers. He could feel the breath coming from her body. Everything inside him stopped, as though frozen and waiting. He leaned over to press his mouth to hers.

"Hey, Laura, heard about the wedding." A smiling couple

danced around them. They were middle-aged and looked like the oddest couple. The man was expensively dressed, but the woman looked like she'd been cast as Annie Oakley. She wore all-white Western wear, with the exception of her shiny red boots and cowboy hat. The woman was the one who had spoken. Rafe kind of wanted to punch them both.

"I've reserved the diner for your reception. I don't think you should hold it in a barn, dear. And Pastor Dennis said he would perform the ceremony, but you have to give him a couple of days' notice because he gets feed deliveries every Thursday."

"I am not getting married in the Feed Store Church, Stella," Laura said flatly.

The woman named Stella simply gave her a bright smile. "I don't see why not. Stef and Jen are. It's lovely once you get rid of the smell. Jen selected a nice potpourri to mask that horsey smell. Why does feed smell like horses?"

"She could use the estate," the older man interjected. "Stefan wouldn't mind. He didn't use the estate because it wasn't Bliss-oriented enough. Oh, it would be lovely. Especially in the spring."

The minute that couple danced away, another took their place. A man in a cowboy hat swayed with a tall, lovely brunette. She was dressed more chicly than the rest of the group.

"I've already got plans for your wedding dress! And I already have your measurements, so I can start working as soon as possible. I'm seeing something fitted and very elegant. How do you feel about a satin sheath?" the brunette asked.

"I don't feel any way about it, Brooke," Laura said on an obviously frustrated sigh.

"Now Brooke, I had plans for you after this wedding business is over," the cowboy replied, seemingly just as frustrated.

The brunette rolled her eyes. "That's not happening, James. I told you once before, I am not going to be your next one-night stand, and I have no intention of staying in Bliss. And you should be happy about it because both of my brothers would kick your ass if I played

118

around with you."

"They could try." The man named James nodded Laura's way. "Congrats, Laura. You're getting an amazing man in Wolf. I heard the town is going to throw you an engagement party next week."

Laura stopped in the middle of the dance floor. She fairly vibrated with frustration. "I am so done with this."

Rafe wanted to protest the loss of her closeness, but she was already leaving.

She turned and stomped toward the raised stage where there was a microphone and a DJ. The DJ, who appeared to be a teenage boy, and his twin brother stopped the music right in the middle of the song as though they had been planning for this particular eventuality. All heads turned Laura's way.

"What the hell did you do?" Cam asked as he forced his way through the crowd.

"I don't know. She said she was done with this." He was at a loss. "I was actually getting through to her."

Cam's eyes narrowed. "Yeah, I saw how you were getting through to her. You practically humped her leg."

"I did not."

"You were rubbing your penis all over her," Cam complained.

"I was dancing with her." And if dancing had happened to bring his penis in close contact with her body, then so be it.

"Well, you didn't do it right. Now I don't have a chance to rub *my* penis on her. How is that fair?"

He was about to reply when Laura began to speak.

"Good evening, all you lovable busybodies," Laura announced, looking perfectly comfortable taking the stage. She adjusted the microphone like a pro.

"Hey!" one of the cowboys, Rafe couldn't remember if it was Max or Rye, called out. "Shouldn't Wolf be up there with you if you have a big, formal announcement to make?"

"No, asshole," Laura said and flushed suddenly. She looked back at the boys standing by the stereo. "I am so sorry to have cursed like that."

One of the boys waved his hand. "We've heard them all."

The other nodded. "Yeah, we actually thought asshole was Max Harper's name for a couple of years."

"Bobby!" a woman's shocked voice rang out.

"Sorry, mom."

The crowd hooted, even Max.

"Well, I'm sorry, anyway. I do have an announcement to make. I would like to tell you all that you suck. I'm not engaged. I was trying to keep my pathetic single status under wraps, but I know you all believe that the truth will set us free." Another loud cheer went up, and Rafe heard Cam breathe out. "There. Now Nell can start talking again. My little lie was the only thing that kept Nell and Henry from vocally protesting, so please enjoy."

"Animals are people, too!" Nell yelled.

A collective groan went through the crowd. Laura gave them a jaunty salute, a wide smile on her face.

"She's happy here," Cam said, his lips spread in a wide grin.

Yes. She was happy. And he had to figure out how to get her to come home with him. Rafe realized he had his work cut out for him.

* * * *

Laura winked at the Farley brothers and started down the steps. A hand came out to help her down the last step, and she looked into the eyes of Stefan Talbot.

"Congratulations on coming clean," he said in that deep voice of his.

"Well, I didn't have much of a choice," she replied. "If I hadn't, this town would have planned the whole wedding and sent me a bill."

His lips quirked up in an affectionate smile. "You might be right about that. I'm afraid this whole town takes an active interest in you. Nate's already called all of his old contacts at the DEA. He managed to get the details on those two feds sniffing around you."

She felt her stomach turn. This was exactly what she hadn't wanted to happen. She didn't want her two worlds to meet. She wanted her old world to go away and her new world to not ask any questions.

Stef put a steadying hand on her elbow. "Stop. I can see by the look in your eyes that you're worried about Nate finding out about what happened in DC. Well, you should know that almost all of the men know."

"They do?" Wolf had told her, but she hadn't wanted to believe it.

Stef shook his head. "No one comes into my town to stay without a background check."

There was a reason his fiancée called him the King of Bliss. Stef took his town seriously. "Well, I'm glad to know I passed the test."

His face lost its previous bright smile, but he continued to look at her with a softness in his eyes. "What happened to you wasn't your fault. Not even the part where you got fired from the FBI. You didn't realize that reporter was taping you, did you?"

Shame filled her. She didn't like to think about Jana. "No. Jana had been my friend for a long time. I was a bit surprised she sold me out the way she did. But it was my fault. I shouldn't have talked about it."

Stef patted her shoulder. "Well, I understand how hard it is to forgive yourself. I really do. Anyway, it was obvious to me that you needed a place to stay and maybe a second chance. Why do you think the cabin you're in was so cheap?"

Laura stared at him for a moment, surprised he would even make the statement. "It was part of the deal I made with Bart Vickers. He needed someone to work the day shift at the gas station, and he happened to own...damn, I'm stupid. You own it all, don't you?"

His head tilted slightly in acknowledgement. "I have my fingers in every pie in this town. I'm Bart's silent partner in the gas station, and I owned most of the cabins in the valley at the time. I've sold them off as needed. I like to take care of my family."

She knew she should be upset about the deception, but there was genuine love and compassion behind most of the things Stef Talbot did. "Well, I thank you. And I would like to buy my cabin. Now that everything's out in the open, there are a couple of old bank accounts I can get into. I should be able to come pretty close to market value."

He nodded. "I'll have my lawyer draw up the paperwork immediately. I am glad to know you won't be leaving us."

She was startled at the thought. "Why would I leave?"

His shoulders moved up and down negligently. "It's obvious to anyone who sees you with those two men that you have a past."

"Yes, and that's what it is—the past."

It wasn't going any further. It didn't matter that her libido had come back online for the first time in years. For five long and lonely years, she'd had nothing but her vibrator. Even that hadn't gotten much use. At first, she'd tried because she wanted to make sure everything still worked. Her parts functioned, but her heart wasn't in it. The only times she'd worked herself up to a froth had been when she thought about them. When she'd pictured Rafe's handsome face working over her or the way Cam's shoulders bunched as he climaxed, that was the only time she could enjoy it.

"You know we found out a lot of things about those two," Stef said, his voice all smooth and silky. "They appear to have spent an enormous amount of time and money searching for you."

"They feel guilty." But the words were starting to ring hollow.

She let her eyes seek them out. They stood together talking. Rafe looked intent on what Cam was saying. They had always been an odd partnership. Rafe was the big-city hottie who understood fine wine and good clothes. Cam was a backwoods, gorgeous nerd who cared far more about his computer than when a wine was bottled. He liked beer and watched an enormous amount of science-fiction television. Yet they fit together. Somehow, someway, Rafe and Cam had become halves of a whole.

Once there had been three pieces to their puzzle. Had they honestly missed her? Were their emotions more than simple guilt?

Stef's voice broke through her thoughts. "They put their lives on hold. Can I ask you a question?"

She wanted to say no but had a feeling Stef would press anyway. "All right."

"Did you love one of them?"

Tears clouded her eyes as she shook her head.

Stef nodded. "That's what I thought. You loved both of them."

Her throat felt far too small. She couldn't even manage a yes. She looked at them. Really looked at them. They were older. Rafe had lines across his forehead that hadn't been there before. There was a slump to Cam's shoulders that she didn't remember. She'd missed them. God, she had missed them so much.

They started to walk toward her. She took a short step back, but the stage was behind her.

"You could run again." Stef didn't sound enthused about that choice.

"No." She was done running. She'd found her home.

"Then I want you to think about what you were looking for when you came to Bliss. You were looking for a second chance."

She had been looking for a place to hide. "They hurt me, Stef. They just about killed me."

She could have sworn his eyes misted for a moment before he spoke. "We do that sometimes. We do it to the people we love the most. We do it precisely because we love them. I know you're scared. In the end, this is all the time we have. I would take it if I were you. I would take it and milk it for every moment it's worth, and if it all falls apart, at least you have a home now and people whom you can always count on. Holly will stand by you, and Nell will protest at their front doors if they hurt you again."

She couldn't help but laugh at the thought. She'd never had

friends the way she had them here. And she'd never loved the way she had with Rafe and Cam. What if she could have it all? Even if only for a few days?

Stef leaned in. "It's better to hurt because you tried with every ounce of your soul than it is to regret not trying. My wife taught me that."

"She isn't your wife yet." The wedding was still a few days away.

"Oh, but she is. I see now that she was always my wife. She's the other half of my soul. The wedding is merely a party. The marriage is already well under way. It was rocky in the beginning, but I wouldn't change it." Stef took a step back as Rafe and Cam walked up to them.

Cam strode up like an angry bull, his eyes assessing Stef the way he would a perp in an interrogation room. "What did you say to her?"

Rafe was all about her. His hands found her shoulders. "*Bella*, you're crying. Are you all right?"

Rafe's hands on her felt wonderful, but she was worried that Cam was about to start a fight. She moved between them. "He was saying that I should dance with you. It's only fair. I danced with Rafe."

Cam turned, his attention shifting from Stef to her in the blink of an eye. "What?"

He stared down at her like he couldn't quite believe what she'd said. And his eyes weren't exactly on her face. A laugh escaped. That was Cam. He wasn't good at hiding what he felt or wanted. He'd never been able to play the games he needed to play to move up with the Bureau. Rafe had smoothed the way for him because they were friends. She loved the fact that Cam almost never had a mask on.

She reached out and took his hand. "I said I would like my dance now."

He nodded. "Okay."

She had to lead him to the dance floor. He shuffled behind her, an almost shy look on his face. She moved to the center and stepped close to him, putting her arms around his neck. His handsome face turned mulishly stubborn.

"If this is some trick, you should know that I'm not leaving. You can't say that you gave me my dance and now I have to go. If you think that you can send me back to DC after one measly dance, then you don't know me."

She laid her head against his chest. It felt good to hear the beat of his heart. "I know you, Cameron Briggs. I would have to get a tow truck to haul your ass out of town if you didn't want to go."

Slowly, his arms came up and surrounded her. He clutched her like he was afraid she would slip away. "I missed you, baby. I missed you so much."

"I missed you, too, *bella*." Suddenly Rafe was right behind her. He stepped in, and his arms circled her waist. He was careful to move in time with Cam, and soon they were swaying to the music. All three of them were dancing together, the men forming a protective circle around her.

"Well, that was fast. It didn't take those two long to move in once the truth was out," Holly said as she danced with Pastor Dennis, who ran the Feed Store Church.

She felt Rafe stiffen and start to move back.

Laura took a deep breath, thinking about Stef's words, and let her hand drift around to Rafe's waist to keep him close. He moved back in.

Pastor Dennis took them in with a smile on his face. "All good things flow from admitting the truth with an open heart."

"Not all of them," Holly grumbled.

"Crap, what happened with Caleb?" Laura tried to look around, but she couldn't see the doctor.

Holly shrugged. "Same old, same old. I asked him if he wanted to go back to my place and talk, and he suddenly remembered some very important surgery he had scheduled. For tonight. Without a nurse. Or a hospital. I give up on him. I'm going to satisfy myself with my prison love letters."

Holly gave her a sad smile as the pastor danced her away.

Poor Holly. Caleb was breaking her heart, and they had never even gone out. Would Holly be happier if she had at least gotten to be intimate with the man who hurt her? Would she regret it? Or would she do what Stef had said and forgive herself and be happy that at least she had tried?

"Did you come back for the case?" She didn't pull her head from Cam's chest. She simply asked the question and prayed they had the right answer.

Cam's head touched the top of her own. "I don't care about the case anymore. Don't get me wrong. I want to kill him for what he did to you, but I'm here because I'm crazy about you, Laura Rosen or Niles, or whatever you call yourself."

Rafe breathed against her neck, the warmth reassuring. "We're here for you, *bella*. Nothing else. We talked about the case because we thought it would force you to spend time with us. We've been looking for you for years because we don't want to live without you."

Well, that was a pretty fine answer. Tears in her eyes, she stopped dancing, disentangled herself, and started toward the parking lot. She'd gotten ten feet when she realized they weren't following. She turned, and they looked like lost puppies.

"I'm going home. I thought we could talk better at my place. Do you want to come home with me?" It was as plainly as she could put it. She wanted them. Life was too short to not try. If it all went bad, she would always have Bliss. She and Holly could be nuns together. Maybe Alexei had a friend in witness protection who needed some letter loving.

But before she tried that, she was going to have at least one more shot with the two who had gotten away.

They ran to catch up, each taking one of her hands as they walked into the night.

Chapter Eight

Cam slid into the back of the SUV beside Laura, his hips brushing against hers.

Rafe turned the engine on, though Cam could see plainly through the windshield mirror that he wasn't thrilled about being left with driving duties.

Cam didn't care. He wasn't about to let her sit by herself. She'd invited them back to her place. He wasn't exactly sure what that meant relationship-wise, but the look in her eyes had dared him to try. He wouldn't turn down that challenge.

Rafe turned the key in the ignition, and the SUV purred to life.

"You need to take a left on the highway to get back to the valley." She sat forward, her body bending over.

"I know how to get to your place." Rafe's voice was flat. His whole body betrayed his lack of enthusiasm for the current seating situation. Cam had been faster. He'd tossed Rafe the keys and climbed in the back with Laura. It was only fair. Rafe had gotten to dance with her first. "I can be there quickly."

Cam didn't need a long time. He had her to himself for the time it took to get from point A to point B. He wasn't going to waste a minute.

He scooted over, unwilling to give her space. He slid his arm over the backboard of the seat, his palm covering her shoulder. She stiffened slightly, and Cam was about to take his arm back when she finally snuggled against him. She turned her head up, her bright eyes finding his in the intimacy of the car. It was dark, but he could see her. He couldn't miss the way her eyes widened and softened as she looked up at him.

"Laura, I want to tell you—" he started.

He wanted to tell her everything that had happened since she'd left. He wanted to know everything that had happened to her. He wanted to know what it was like to live in this town. He wanted to know why she'd walked away. The five years they'd been apart felt like centuries, and he needed to fill in the history.

She held a hand up to his lips, the pads of her fingers sparking against his flesh. She might have kept the touch gentle, but Cam's reaction was like a fire lighting his skin. His cock was at full mast, straining against the material of his pants.

"Not tonight. I don't want to talk about it tonight." Her voice was breathy with longing.

His heart rate skittered. That sounded like an invitation. "If we're not going to talk, baby, then what exactly are we going to do?"

"You said you missed me." Her fingers skimmed across his face.

"So fucking much." She'd left a huge hole that had only started to shrink the minute he saw her.

"Show me how much you missed me."

Cam felt like he'd been let off the leash. He grabbed her and hauled her into his lap. "Straddle me, baby."

She threw one of her long legs over his hips so she straddled him like a horse she was about to ride. Her skirt bunched around her knees. There was absolutely nothing between them but her panties and his slacks and underwear. He could feel how hot her pussy was.

"Damn it," Rafe cursed, hitting the steering wheel with the palm of his hand. "I should have made you drive."

He didn't bother to reply. Rafe had made his bed, and Cam had no intention of lying in it with him. Laura had given him permission, and he was taking it. He thrust his hands into her hair. It was soft and silky, and he used it to pull her mouth toward his. He felt like a starving man who'd been put at the front of the line at an all-you-can-eat buffet. He wasn't sure where to start. He wanted to inhale her.

Everything about her called to him. Her scent, the touch of her skin, the sight of her breasts threatening to overflow her shirt. He was on sensory overload.

Laura took the choice out of his hands. She leaned over and pressed her lips to his. It was a soft touch and not nearly enough. She seemed hesitant, brushing their mouths together as though trying to remember how to kiss.

He hadn't forgotten. He dreamed about it every night. He let his hands tighten in her hair and ran his tongue over her plump bottom lip. She shivered and softened, giving him control of the kiss. Cam surged into her mouth, her taste filling him.

Cam took her mouth, slanting over her again and again. Their tongues met and mated, sliding against each other. Laura's arms wound around his neck. He loosened his hold on her hair and trailed down, seeking her breasts. He cupped them. They were bigger, rounder. The weight she'd put on had gone to all the right places. She was a sexy handful.

"Show me your breasts, baby." He pulled away from her mouth, needing to see them. He wanted her naked.

She leaned back, and he could see the worry in her eyes. He brushed his thumbs across her nipples. They tightened to hard nubs.

"Come on," he cajoled. "You're gorgeous, baby. I think you're so gorgeous. Five years has only made you more beautiful to me. Let me see them."

He knew why she was hiding them. He'd read all the reports.

She would have scars, but she needed to know that no amount of scars would make her less lovely.

"Please, *bella*. I want you naked by the time we get to your place. Enjoy her now, Cam. I'll be inside her as soon as I park the car." Rafe's voice had taken on a guttural tone. Cam could see his eyes through the rearview mirror. He wasn't sure what Rafe could see, but Rafe was obviously trying to be a voyeur.

Cam chuckled. "I think he wants a show, baby. Let's give him one."

She bit into her bottom lip, tugging it into her mouth. "It's been a long time for me. I haven't actually been with a man since…"

He forced himself to slow down. He wasn't terribly surprised she hadn't had sex. Laura had been picky. She hadn't dated anyone the whole time he'd worked with her, though many men had tried. But that hesitation in her voice could be more about de Sade than them. That worried the hell out of him.

He softened his hands on her body, touching her in long, slow strokes. He needed to be careful. He didn't want to bring back any bad memories. "Baby, we don't have to do anything you don't want to do. We can take it as slow as you want. Hell, if you're not ready, I can just hold you."

"Do you really mean that?" Her face was close to his. He could feel the warmth of her breath on his skin.

"Yes. I do. Rafe and I can take you to bed and cuddle you." It would be hard, but utterly worth it if it brought her a moment's peace. He'd spent years wondering if she was alone and scared. He'd wanted to hold her so much. He could put his own needs aside if she needed it.

Her hands went to the bottom of her shirt, and she began to tug it over her head, revealing creamy-white skin and a lovely white lace bra. Her breasts threatened to overflow the cups, and then they bounced free as she undid the front clasp. The scars from the night she'd been tortured had faded to white lines that did nothing to distract from her beauty. Those scars were a testament to her strength.

He looked past the scars to her breasts and nipples. They were gorgeous and round. Cam's cock ached at the sight. He wanted to lube up her chest, hold those tits together, and fuck his cock in and out of their pillowy softness. Then maybe she'd understand how much he loved her breasts.

"I don't want to cuddle now, though I might want to after," she said.

"Anything you want." He wasn't looking at her face. He couldn't take his eyes off her breasts.

"Describe them to me," Rafe ordered.

"Fucking amazing," he said, looking at the bounty offered up to him. He brought his hands up and cupped her breasts. "They're so soft."

"I have scars, Cam." Laura whimpered, a sexy sound that made his cock strain. She was grinding a little, her hips moving, forcing her pussy against his cock.

"I don't care, Laura." He pinched her nipples, loving the moan that came out of her mouth. "Her nipples are hard. You remember how much she loves having her nipples sucked?"

"Oh, yes. Her breasts are incredibly sensitive." Rafe's voice was tight as he turned onto the highway.

"Please." The word came out on a cry as he thrust his pelvis up, hitting her pussy with his cock. "Oh, please, Cam."

"You tell me what you want, baby. You know I want to give it to you." He pushed her hips down, grinding her pussy against his rigid erection. He wanted to impale her on it, but she had waited for him. He owed her way more than a quick roll.

"Kiss me." She balanced herself by putting her hands on his shoulders.

"Where?" He ran his fingers over her straining nipples. "You want me to kiss you here? You want me to suck your pretty nipples into my mouth?"

"Yes, Cam. Please. Lick them. Suck them."

He pulled her close. "Anything you want, baby."

He licked a nipple, a long, slow stroke of his tongue.

"Oh, god, that feels so good," she moaned. Her hands found his hair. She thrust her chest out, pressing her breasts to his mouth.

He licked around the areola before sucking the tight bead into his mouth. He sucked her deep, enjoying the sounds she made as her hands wove into his hair and tugged. He whirled his tongue around, biting down lightly. While he sucked and bit at first one nipple and then the other, his hand made its way under her skirt to the edge of her panties. He teased his way under the cotton to find her pussy drenched in moisture. He inhaled, the scent of her arousal filling his senses.

"Baby, your pussy is soaking wet." He breathed the words across her breasts. His hand slid between her legs, brushing her clit.

"Fuck," Rafe cursed as he made another turn. "You're a lucky bastard, you know that."

"I can smell and feel how hot you are," Cam said, fingering her folds. "This greedy little pussy is begging for a cock, isn't it?"

"Cam." She wiggled against his fingers.

"Yeah, baby, you need a big, hard cock to fuck." He shoved a single finger in, her heat nearly scorching him. She was so ready, but he wanted to play.

"Give it to me," Laura said, her eyes closed. She bounced a little, trying to fuck that single finger.

Cam pulled out and let his soaking wet finger trace back to the cheeks of her ass, cupping them. Fuck, that got him harder, and he hadn't thought that was possible. The thought of burying himself in her pretty ass made him ready to come then and there.

"Still a virgin here. I have to do something about that." He licked her nipple one last time as he gave her cheeks a squeeze. He was going to have to go slow, to prepare her. "I'm going to have this ass, Laura. I've waited years to fuck you here, and I won't stop until I know what it feels like to have my cock so deep up this ass that you forget a time I wasn't there." He pulled his hand away. "But not tonight."

He scooted back slightly, putting a tiny bit of necessary distance between them. He tore at his pants, freeing his dick. Laura leaned back, giving him access to his cock. It sprung free, bouncing in between them.

"You suit up before you shove that cock in her." Rafe opened the glove box and tossed a condom to him. They had bought a box at the airport, telling themselves to think positive. Up until this moment, Cam had thought they would go unused.

"Nice to know you guys came prepared," Laura said, taking the condom out of his hand. She held it up for his inspection. "Here, let me help with this."

She opened the condom, and Cam prayed he wouldn't come in her hands. His cock was weeping. With shaky fingers, she placed the condom on his dick. It took her a moment of pure torture to roll and tug it down to the base of his cock.

The minute he was sheathed, he pulled her forward and impaled her on his cock.

A low moan came out of her throat.

"Fuck, you feel good, baby." He gripped her hips, pushing his cock further into her wet heat. She was tight around him, so fucking tight he felt like he would explode. Her pussy sucked and gripped him until his vision started to go. The backseat was small. He couldn't move her around the way he wanted, couldn't shift her to her back without losing her, and he wasn't about to lose her.

"Ride me." He shifted his pelvis up and slid in all the way to his balls.

Her head fell forward as she started to fuck him. She ground down on him and then pulled back, every muscle in her pussy sliding in a silky, gloved grip.

He wasn't going to last. Being close to her was making him crazy. It was everything he'd needed for five years. She was here, and she was safe. He could touch her, feel her, love her, and he wanted to mark her. He wanted to make her scream so she would never again forget who she belonged to. He wanted to drive into her so she never walked away again.

He shoved his hand between them, his finger finding her clit and pressing against it. He rubbed a circle, never letting up on the pressure. Her hips lost their rhythm, and she cried out as he drove hard into her one last time. She shook as she came, and he felt his balls tighten, pleasure suffusing his every nerve. The orgasm shot through him like a bullet. He twisted almost helplessly, trying to get it all out, trying to give her every drop.

She slumped forward, her weight a sweet burden. He couldn't help himself. He toyed with her a bit more. Her body spasmed every time he hit her clit. He finally put his arms around her and held her close, their breaths and heartbeats mingling. He kissed the side of her face and inhaled her scent.

The car came to a stop, and Rafe slammed out.

Cam brought his head up. They were parked in front of Laura's small cabin, a lone light shining from what was probably her kitchen.

"Are we home?" Laura asked quietly.

He nodded, unable to speak. He was home. Finally home.

* * * *

Rafe's hands were shaking as he got out of the car. He raced around to the passenger side. He couldn't breathe, could barely think about anything beyond getting inside her. He knew he should want to pound Cam into the ground, but all he could think was to be grateful to the man. Cam had made sure Laura was prepared. He'd given her a killer orgasm from the sound of her moans, and Rafe wasn't sure he would be able to last long enough to give her one. He needed her.

Fuck. He needed her so damn bad.

He opened the door, and there they sat, like puzzle pieces nestled together. Laura's face was buried in Cam's shoulder, her legs on either side of his hips. Cam's arms clutched her in a tight embrace. He looked up at him. A solemn silence passed between the two men, and he felt something powerful flow between him and Cam.

"Baby, we're back at your place." Cam's voice was soft. Cam could be one intimidating dude, but he was always soft and gentle around Laura.

Rafe let himself touch her. He smoothed a hand along her golden hair. In the moonlight, it looked almost silvery. She turned and opened her eyes. She looked like a sleepy princess to Rafe.

"Hi." She said it, and Rafe took it for what he hoped it was. A second beginning.

His heart softened. "Hello, *bella*. Let me take you inside."

He reached out for her.

"I can walk." She sat up and started to look for her shirt. "I'm fine."

He wasn't about to let her walk. He wanted to hold her. He lifted her up and off Cam. He couldn't miss the fact that Cam's cock was covered in her arousal. It should have disgusted him, but damn, it made his own cock harden. He wasn't interested in Cam sexually but watching him fuck Laura through the rearview mirror had gotten him hot as hell.

"Rafe, don't," Laura protested. "I'm half-naked, and, well, I'm messy."

"Not an excuse, *bella*." He hoisted her up, loving the feel of her pressed close. "I like you half-naked, and I'm not going to bother cleaning you up. I'm going to make sure you get even messier."

She sighed. "I like the sound of that."

He couldn't help it. He leaned his head in and kissed her. "I'm glad because I think Cam and I can keep you busy for a few days. You might regret those words."

Her arms floated up and around his neck. "I don't think I will. I missed you. I missed you both. I tried not to think about you, but I couldn't."

"I thought about you every day," he admitted. "I even told my mother if I found you that I intended to marry you."

"Really? And what did you tell your momma about Cam?" There was a mischievous smile on her lips.

That took the wind out of his sails. What would he tell his mother? His father was a bit more open. He would probably find an enormous amount of humor in it, but his mother was devoutly Catholic. Rafe doubted she would ever accept that he was sharing a woman with his friend. He wasn't going to think about that now. He gave Laura a smile.

"I don't think my mother can handle that news right now. But she will be thrilled to know that I found you." Rafe moved toward the front door of her small but well-kept cabin. He had introduced Laura to his mother as a friend and colleague, but she hadn't been fooled. His mother had immediately known that he was crazy about her.

He still was. Years hadn't changed the fact that he loved this one woman. She had been the one for him when she was a big city, high-powered FBI agent, and she was the one for him as a sweet, small-town girl working in a gas station. It went far beyond her beautiful body or gorgeous face. He loved her soul. She was kind and smart. She challenged him on every level. They could talk for hours, and he would never get bored.

He even loved the fact that she loved Cameron.

"I'll tell her about all three of us, *bella*." He made the declaration with all the solemnity the moment required. He loved his mother, but he loved Laura as well. Laura would never be happy without Cam, and he was rapidly discovering that he felt the same way. They were connected, the three of them. It wasn't optimal, but it was true.

He was going to ask Laura to sacrifice, to come home with him. He had to be willing to sacrifice as well.

Cam suddenly hurried past them. He had managed to get his pants done up, and he turned when he got to the door. "Keys?"

"I didn't lock it." She said it as though it was an everyday, normal occurrence to leave the door unlocked.

Cam opened the door, but he managed to send her a stern look.

She shrugged, utterly unconcerned. "I don't lock it because Holly lives next door, and she's always out of something. How would she get in to borrow coffee if I locked it all the time?"

"You're going to lock it from now on," Rafe ordered, horrified at the thought that she was so unprotected. Anyone could walk in. "And we'll get a security system as soon as possible."

She wouldn't need it for long. His house in Virginia had an excellent monitoring system. If they moved in order to buy two homes close together, he would simply ensure that a state-of-the-art system was installed. But for now, he wanted to feel secure.

"Nothing ever happens in Bliss. This is a quiet town," she said.

Rafe exchanged a look with Cam. They would deal with the problem. Holly would need a key if she wanted to steal some coffee.

He walked through the front door. Laura's cabin was tiny, with one room serving as both living room and kitchen. He walked through it. It was neatly kept, but there wasn't a bed in sight, so it wouldn't do. There were two closed doors. He picked the one on the right.

Laura's bedroom was small but ultrafeminine. There was a queen-size bed that dominated the room. It filled up most of the space, and the rest seemed taken up by a dresser and small lounger. He tossed Laura on the bed with its richly decorated quilts and stared down at her.

She was stunning. Her skin was rosy from the sex she'd had with Cam. She looked beautiful and well loved.

"I want you, *bella*."

"I want you, too, Rafe."

"Show me. Spread your legs and touch yourself." He had watched her give to Cam. He needed to be in control now. He needed her to give to him.

Cam walked into the room. He clung to the wall, his expression almost apologetic. He started to turn and walk back out.

"Where are you going?" He didn't want Cam to leave. He wanted Cam to help him. He wanted a partner. "Get behind her. Spread her for me."

"Are you sure?" Cam asked.

"Do I often say things I don't mean?"

Cam gave him a silly grin and jumped on the bed behind Laura. He wrapped his arms across her chest, her back to his front. Laura relaxed against him. They were happy together. They were relaxed and happy and willing to play.

"Spread your legs, baby. Rafe wants to see your pussy." Cam's fingers found the hem of her skirt and pulled the cotton fabric up. Her small black undies were bunched up and soaking wet. It looked like Cam had merely shoved them to the side in his haste to get inside.

Rafe corrected the problem. He knelt on the bed and let his hands slide up her long legs, reveling in every silky curve. He took a long, slow tour before he drew the small piece of cotton off her body, leaving her perfectly plump pussy in full sight. It was a vision. She was shaved and glistening. The lips of her pussy were slightly swollen from Cam's use, and her juice made it look slick and inviting.

He couldn't miss the long, thin scar that ran an inch above her pelvic bone. There were other scars from where de Sade had stabbed her repeatedly. Emotion choked him. He leaned over and kissed that scar.

"I don't want to think about that tonight. Can't we just have fun?" Laura asked, her eyes pleading with him.

He nodded and forced himself to look away from the scars. He wanted her, and beyond that, he wanted to please her. He let his fingers slide across her clit. He wanted to dive into that dessert, but he needed something from her first.

His hands went to the front of his slacks. He carefully pulled the zipper down while he watched Cam turn Laura's head toward his.

His partner took their lover's mouth in a long, slow kiss. Rafe shoved his slacks off along with his boxers. He toed out of his loafers, and then his shirt hit the floor, too. He felt better naked. God, he always wanted to be naked with her.

"I think Rafe needs some attention, baby." Cam let go of her mouth. He palmed her breasts one last time. "You better give him some."

Rafe knew exactly what he wanted. He wanted to feel her mouth on his cock before he took her pussy. "Come on, *bella*. Get on your hands and knees."

Her eyes were languid, her movements lazy as she did what he asked. Cam pulled her skirt off her body so she was totally bare except for the sunny yellow heels she wore.

"Where do you keep the lube, baby?" Cam asked.

"In the nightstand." She flushed. "I only use it when I..."

Rafe petted her hair as he moved into position. "You use a vibrator?"

Cam pulled out her purple rabbit-head vibe and a small tube of lube. "It's a bit small. I don't suppose you have an anal plug?"

"No," she said on a breathy huff. "I play around with a vibe from time to time. I do not anally plug myself to have fun on a Saturday night."

"Well, *bella*, I think that sounds like a very fun Saturday night. We'll need to go shopping." He widened his stance and took his cock in hand. It was pointing her way like it knew the way home. "We might have to go to Denver. I doubt this place has a well-stocked sex shop."

"I think you would be surprised what you can find here." Her tongue peeked out from her cherry red lips. His cock jumped.

"Come on, *bella*. Lick me." He didn't want to argue Bliss's many attributes. He wanted a blow job.

That little pink tongue swiped over the head of his cock, and he counted himself lucky he didn't spew right then and there. He forced the need down. He wanted to make this last.

Laura whimpered.

"It's all right, baby. It's lube. I'm going to get your ass ready. I won't take it tonight, but soon. It's nothing more than my fingers tonight." Cam was on his knees behind her, his hand hidden behind the luscious curves of her heart-shaped ass.

"What's he doing to you?" He wanted to hear her voice as she talked about getting her ass ready to take a pounding. Fuck, he couldn't wait for it. He wanted to watch as Cam pounded into her and know that it would be his turn to shove his hard dick up her sweet ass.

"He's pushing his fingers in. I don't know if I like it or not." She wiggled as though trying to accommodate him.

"Let me play, and then I'll eat your pussy. You like that, don't you? You like when I eat your sopping wet pussy like it's a slice of pie I can't get enough of." Cam's eyes were looking down. Rafe could imagine. He was looking down, watching his fingers disappear into her tight, puckered hole. "Let me play, and I'll give you what you want. Now suck Rafe's cock."

She leaned forward and pulled his cockhead between her lips.

Rafe shoved his hands in her hair and gritted his teeth. Her tongue was lighting sparks all over his cock. She teased him with little licks that never stayed in the same place, but dashed and tantalized all over. She licked a path from the tiny slit of his cockhead down to his balls, where she traced the line that separated them with her tongue. It felt so good. Rafe's cock was pulsing in anticipation.

She sucked his balls, causing them to tighten with pleasure. She popped one and then the other into the heat of her mouth, lavishing them with affection.

She groaned suddenly, the sound reverberating across his taut flesh.

"Sorry," Cam said with a grin that told Rafe he wasn't at all sorry. "I added finger number two. She's really tight."

Rafe eyed his partner. "Stop playing and give her what you

promised. I'm not going to last forever."

Cam frowned, but he pulled his fingers out of her ass. "Fine, but we do have all night, you know. I don't intend to sleep."

"Says the man who already came inside her." He was on edge. He needed to come. He needed to fill her up, but he didn't want to do it if she didn't come along for the ride. Cam could take care of her while she took care of him.

Laura looked up at him, her blue eyes half-closed and a smile on her face. With a deliberate wink, she reached out with her tongue and delicately licked at the arousal pooling on the tip of his dick.

She was playing with him. He wasn't having that. The caveman that was always lurking under his very modern surface surged to the forefront.

"You take me deep," he growled.

He shoved his hands in her hair and guided his cock to her mouth. He wasn't going to play. He was going to invade and conquer.

She groaned as he thrust in. Cam had disappeared. All Rafe could see of him now were his knees sticking up. He'd done exactly what he'd promised and buried his face in her pussy. Cam was making a meal out of her.

"You take care of me," Rafe ordered. He would take his turn pleasuring her later. He would eat her pussy and suck her breasts. He would rock into her until he hit that special place that sent her soaring, but for now, he wanted to fuck her hard.

Laura's mouth opened obediently, and he thrust in. He was immediately assaulted by how tight and hot she was. His balls drew up. He pushed in another inch and then two, all the while praying he could last. He wanted to do this forever. Her tongue laved the underside of his cock. Even the brush of her teeth against him was sensual.

He pulled back and thrust in.

Her tongue managed to whirl around him and sucked him deep. Her mouth pulled on his cock. She moaned around him, and he found a soft place at the back of her throat. The orgasm shot from his balls outward. He could feel her throat working around him as she swallowed everything he gave her.

He shook as she licked him clean. She groaned, and her face was tight with pleasure. Rafe's cock popped out, and he could see that Cam was eating her pussy with great enthusiasm. Her whole body was flushed, and she ground her pelvis down. She was incredibly beautiful as she took her pleasure.

Rafe got on his knees and kissed her. He could taste himself in her mouth, and he felt his cock start to twitch to life again.

When she came, he drank down her cries of pleasure.

* * * *

The plane dipped slightly, turbulence making for a shaky flight, but he didn't mind. The agent seated next to him had long since turned a faint shade of green, but it didn't bother him a bit. He was meant for far greater things. He wouldn't go down in a government-owned airplane.

It was late in the night, but luckily the higher-ups had decided this particular errand couldn't wait. It was an hour longer to Colorado, and then they still had a drive ahead of them. He wouldn't be able to see her until the morning. He couldn't get off the plane and rush to her doorstep the way he wanted to.

He had to play it carefully.

"Here are the portfolios I had made." The unctuous little ass passed him one of the manila folders. "It has all the latest updates."

The Marquis de Sade smiled blandly as he took it. He had another name in this world, but secretly he preferred the one the press had given him. Oh, he preferred when they referred to him properly with his full name. That dumb bitch reporter had Americanized it by calling him "de Sade" as if it was simple slang. She obviously needed some remedial French to know she was calling him "of Sade."

He took a deep breath and forced himself to calm down. He couldn't do anything about it. The name had stuck, but one day he would make the reporter pay.

Still, mangled or not, it had a ring of authenticity. In the old days, society knew how to take care of its dregs. Men of power made the decisions, and they were carried out in the most brutal way imaginable. Justice was swift, and no one apologized for it.

They certainly didn't spend hours pulling together files and worrying and hoping that they had their shit together. The FBI was a joke.

But it did pay the bills.

He let his fingers drum across the small tabletop in front of him before opening the file. It was everything the team had been able to pull together on Laura Rosen's new friends.

Laura. He could still see her laid out on his table. He could still see the intoxicating mix of fear and outrage in her eyes. She had been a lovely woman, elegant and perfect. She'd cared for herself in a way few of his victims ever had. He'd culled from the lowest of society. Laura had been a bit of caviar among the hamburger meat.

She'd fought him like the others hadn't. There hadn't been crying and begging from her. She'd cursed him the entire time. Even when he'd forced a knife through her womb.

She'd taught him he could be something more, something grander than he was. She'd moved him in such an elemental way that he'd stopped his work for years, only taking it up again when he thought she was gone forever.

His little rabbit had taught him so much.

It was almost time to take a final lesson from her. It was almost time to break free.

One of the many suited agents stood up. "We'll be landing in Alamosa in a bit. Some of the agents from the Denver office will meet us there. They've been fully briefed on what's happened and are ready to back us up if we require it. They say this town she's in is known for being a trouble spot."

143

He'd read up on Bliss. It seemed they liked to think of themselves as true, pure Westerners. They tried to take care of their own.

They hadn't met anyone like him.

His rabbit thought she'd found someplace safe to hide away. She was about to find out how wrong she was.

He answered a question someone posed to him, carefully keeping on his outward mask. No one here had ever seen his real face. They never would because they would never catch him. He was smarter than all of them combined. These sad men around him couldn't conceive of his greatness.

Only one woman had ever come close. The one who got away.

Killing her was going to be bittersweet. There was a part of him that wanted to force her by his side. She was a woman worthy of him, but her adherence to morals kept them apart.

He would kill her. He wouldn't underestimate her this time. He would take her, let her see his real face, and he would put her down. She was really too lovely for the world, anyway.

And when she was gone, he could finally continue his work.

Maybe he would start in Bliss.

Chapter Nine

Laura thought seriously about climbing back into bed. Rafe and Cam looked scrumptious lying together. She stared at them for a moment, enjoying the way the early morning sunlight caressed their naked flesh. Cam was lying on his stomach, his arm outstretched. It had been wrapped around her waist, but now it looked as though he was reaching for Rafe. Rafe's dark hair fell over his angelic face. He looked years younger while he slept, as though all of the worries he normally carried fell away when he closed his eyes. She had the urge to kiss those gorgeous lips of his, but she knew where that would lead her—on her back, where she'd spent the majority of the night before.

Four rounds of nasty, athletic, sweaty sex had left her a little bit sore. A nice, hot shower had taken care of the sweat, but she was still moving slower than normal.

She glanced up at the clock. *Damn it*. She needed to hurry if she was going to make her shift. The fact that she'd broken her five years of celibacy didn't mean that the gas station was going to run itself. If she didn't make it in, Bart would either have to call in someone else or work himself. He was almost seventy-two. He didn't need to be on his feet like that, so this time, she got to be the one who walked out the morning after sex.

Cam shifted in his sleep, a huff coming out of his mouth as his hand found Rafe's stomach and wrapped around his waist. Rafe turned, but his hand slipped over Cam's. She could have sworn he called Cam *"bella"* in that deep voice of his, and then they stilled again.

She wished she had a camera.

She slipped out of the bedroom, leaving the men to their much-needed rest. *Coffee.* She needed coffee. Damn, she could even smell it. She shut the door, careful to not make a sound, and then nearly screamed when she turned and saw a man sitting at her table.

"Wolf," she hissed the words out. "You nearly gave me a damn heart attack."

Wolf took a long drink of coffee. "Sweetheart, you have no idea. First, I suppose this means our fake engagement is truly off. I'm deeply wounded. I expected you to take at least a few days to mourn our lost love before you hopped into bed with actual, real human beings."

His sarcasm was getting on her nerves this morning. She strode across the room, grabbed a mug, and poured herself a cup. She had to give it to Wolf. He knew how to make coffee. "I thought we worked this out last night."

Had she been thinking last night? She stared out her small kitchen window as she sipped her coffee. The Rio Grande was visible, the river shining like a jewel in the early morning light. The river was always in motion. Was that what she'd craved the night before? She'd been stagnant for a while. She loved the peace of her new life, but everyone else was moving forward. In the years she'd been in Bliss, she'd watched Max and Rye find their perfect woman, Callie had come out of her shell for Nate and Zane, and Stef had finally stopped hiding from his love. Even Holly seemed to be moving on. Only Laura felt like she was stuck.

"Was it bad, sweetheart? Did they hurt you?" Wolf was studying her with a single-minded intensity.

She shook her head. "It was wonderful. I'm just thinking about what it meant. Why do I do that? Why can't I simply enjoy it? Why do I need to put a label on it?"

His lips curled slightly. There was a beard coming in across the skin of his jaw. He looked the slightest bit scruffy and it suited him. "You're not a good-time girl. You're always going to want a home and a family. You're always going to seek out stability."

Was that what she was trying to find with them? Was she racing headlong into another disaster because she needed a family? She had a family. She had Holly and Nell, and even Henry. Henry stopped by Laura's cabin at least twice a week, a toolbox in his hands. He did it because Nell loved her and Henry loved Nell.

Damn it, she wanted that.

Wolf leaned forward, his elbows making contact with the table. "Your brain is racing, but I wonder if you're making the right connections. I want you to think about this, sweetheart. You didn't rush into a relationship with the first man you saw. You waited. You want them. Those two men in there aren't interchangeable for anyone who would put a ring on your finger, or you would have been dating all this time."

"Maybe they just showed up at the right time." She'd needed a while to get over what happened to her in DC. Hell, she wasn't sure she would ever get over it, but last night had proven that at least she was ready to get physical again.

"Don't fight this," Wolf said with a sigh as though he knew his words would go unheeded. "You're only going to cause more trouble for all three of you. Now, I came out for a reason."

"Other than to scare the crap out of me?"

He grinned. "That was a bonus." His face lost its jovial expression. "The feds took over the Movie Motel last night. Men in suits rented out every room Gene had."

A cold chill crossed her skin. "Did Gene get them talking?"

Gene liked to talk to everyone who came to his place. The Movie Motel was the largest inn in town. It was pretty much the

147

only inn in town.

"They followed Rafe and Cam out here. According to one of the lead men, your boys were well aware that the team, as they called it, was on their way. I take it they didn't bother to mention that they were bringing all their friends out here?"

She tightened her grip on the coffee mug. There was only one real reason to bring the whole crew out here. She was pretty damn sure de Sade wasn't working here in Colorado.

"Did they tell Gene if there had been a threat made against me personally?" It would explain a lot.

"No," Wolf replied. "But they did ask for directions out to your place. Gene had never heard of you. Strange."

She couldn't help a little snort. The feds were going to find Bliss a bit hard to manage until she'd gotten the word out that she was cooperating.

Was she cooperating?

Damn it. She couldn't think straight. All she could think about was the fact that Rafe and Cam had lied to her. Again.

The sweet feeling she'd had looking at them together dissipated, replaced with a hole in the pit of her stomach.

"The minute my momma heard the news that the feds had descended, she and Mel took to the shelter. She's sending out radio messages that anyone in town who wants protection from the coming invasion should come out to Mel's place. On the plus side, she made pecan pie. I love pecan pie."

Laura turned to Wolf. Her current dilemma was going to have consequences for everyone in town. Just as she had the thought, a Bronco with the logo for the Bliss County Sheriff's Department rolled into her driveway. Logan Green slid out of his vehicle looking a bit cranky, but then he was always cranky these days. She was pretty sure what he was here about. If she let them, the feds would have everyone in town on edge.

"I'm sorry. I don't know how long they're going to be here. Maybe if I go to DC with them, things can go back to normal," she said as she walked across the small room to throw open the door for Logan.

Whatever they wanted to do, they could do in DC. She didn't have to upend the whole town.

"Don't you even think about that." Wolf stood, his face set in hard lines. "You are not leaving this town. We can't protect you if you're off in DC."

Logan jogged up the steps, pulling the aviators off his face. "Wolf is right. I read that file this morning. You nearly got killed in DC. No place is safe anymore, but at least here you know everyone will watch out for you."

She opened the screen door and allowed Logan in. His big frame filled the doorway. In the last several months he'd gone from lanky boy to muscular man. He'd put away his precious comic books and now spent a lot of time in the gym. And at bars, if the rumors were true.

"Are you here to bring me in?" Laura asked the deputy.

Logan settled his hat on his head. "It's not like that. Nate's got a whole bunch of men in his office who want to talk to you. He wouldn't tell them where you live. He sent me out to see if you want to talk or if you would prefer to join Mel and Cassidy. No one is going to look for you there. You could hole up for a week or two, and this should blow over."

"It's not so bad," Wolf offered. "Mel's made that place quite comfortable."

"I'm not going to hole up in a shelter and hope they go away," she said with a long sigh.

She'd dreaded this moment. It was so much worse because, once again, Rafe and Cam were involved in her utter humiliation. "It was far too much to think I could hide forever. I'll go talk to them. Who's the agent in charge?"

"A man named Joseph Stone," Logan replied.

Wolf suddenly held up his right hand, making a fist.

"Is he going to punch someone?" she asked.

149

Wolf shushed her and started to move around the table. His voice was low. "Someone's outside. They're moving slow and quiet, but they're not used to rural terrain. He's making a bunch of noise, and he doesn't even realize it."

Logan's face had gone stony, and he had his gun in hand. "I thought I was being followed. Damn. Back of the cabin?"

Her heart rate sped up. The whole world suddenly seemed far too quiet. Every small noise felt like a threat.

"You protect her," Wolf said, his voice a mere whisper.

"You don't have a gun." Logan pushed her none too gently to the nearest corner and placed his big body in front of hers.

"Since when does a SEAL need a gun?" Wolf asked.

He opened the screen door and disappeared. As far as she could tell, he didn't make a sound.

She stood there feeling like a coward for hiding behind Logan, but she didn't have a gun, and she was out of shape. Bliss had made her feel secure. She'd stopped practicing judo and given up on lifting weights. It was so much nicer to sit with her friends at Stella's and have pie and think about summer. Laura blinked back tears. She'd gotten too used to Bliss. She'd forgotten how crappy the world could be, but now it was crashing in on her.

Suddenly, the door to her bedroom opened and Cam stepped out, a gun in his hand. He wore his boxer shorts and nothing else.

"Put it down," Cam growled at Logan. The Glock in his hands was perfectly aimed at the deputy's head.

"You put it down, motherfucker. I don't see a badge on your chest." Logan didn't move an inch to put down his gun, and she could feel the tension tighten in the room. "I'm giving you to the count of three before I blow your fucking head off. You understand me?"

"Logan, please, he's not here to hurt me." She needed to defuse the situation.

"I don't give a damn," Logan replied. "He's threatening an officer of the law. I don't have to take that."

She looked to Cam, hoping he would be the reasonable one. "Cam, please."

Cam's gun didn't waver. "Not on your life, baby. Someone is moving around outside. Rafe is taking care of it. I'm taking care of you."

"Everyone can stand down." Rafe showed up in the doorway. He had put on some pants, but he was barefoot and bare-chested. He pushed someone through the doorway. All Laura could see was a man's dark suit and his head covered in one of her pillowcases. Rafe had a gun to the back of the man's head, and Wolf followed after them.

"He didn't need a gun, either," Wolf said with a smirk on his face. "It was actually pretty cool. I was edging around the house to catch this guy when the fed here managed to get out that tiny window of yours, jump him, take the asshole's gun, and get a damn bag over his head."

Rafe tightened his grip on the pillowcase. Logan finally stood down, but she could feel the tension pouring off of him.

"Can you vouch for these guys, Wolf? This one pulled a gun on me." Logan practically snarled the words.

The man Rafe was holding had his hands up, and he seemed to be trying to shout something through the case on his head.

"They're law enforcement," Wolf explained. "The sheriff should have warned you they were in town."

Logan holstered his weapon. "He didn't warn me that they would come at me with guns and their dicks hanging out."

Cam looked down and readjusted his shorts. "I'm sorry about the hard-on. It's the adrenaline. I'll put on some pants as soon as we figure out if we need to bury this asshole."

Rafe gave his partner a stern glare. "We're not burying anyone. We'll take him into custody."

Wolf pointed to Cam. "I like that one, Laura. He's the one you should keep. Sorry. I'm really good at burying bodies. I was looking forward to it."

151

"No one's burying anyone. Cam, get the hood, and let's see what we caught." Rafe forced his prisoner into the kitchen chair and took a step back.

Cam pulled the hood off, and the man suddenly had two guns pointed at his head, and he had a pair of her socks stuffed halfway down his throat.

"Well, if it isn't Brad," Cam said, shaking his head. "I should have guessed you would show up like a jealous girlfriend."

Rafe lowered his gun. "Brad? What the fuck?" He pulled the gag out of the man's mouth.

Laura studied the newcomer. She hadn't met him before, but she knew a fed when she saw one. He wore the uniform, dark suit—not too expensive, not too cheap—comfortable loafers, white shirt, and bland tie. He was built, but there was something about his face that reminded her of a weasel.

"You nearly killed me, asshole." Brad spit the words out along with no small amount of phlegm.

"What the hell were you doing sneaking around like that?" Rafe asked. The guns had all been lowered. The tension notched down.

"I was trying to figure out where our target was," Brad replied. "No one around here seemed willing to help. The whole damn town seems intent on interfering with a federal investigation."

"He followed me from the station house. I remember you," Logan said. "You were the jerk who wanted us to haul in an innocent citizen. He argued with Nate that we should put out an APB and treat Laura like a criminal."

The man named Brad's face twisted. "She can't be too innocent. She's done a hell of a lot to cover her tracks. I've found innocent women don't walk away from their lives and go off the grid. Innocent women don't get the locals to cover for them. This whole damn town has made sure no one can find this bitch."

Rafe's fist came out and made sharp contact with Brad's nose. She stepped aside the minute she saw Rafe draw back. Rafe knew how to punch. Brad's head snapped back, and his nose crunched, a splatter of blood flying out.

"You broke my nose," Brad said, though it sounded more like "nobe" instead of nose.

"I'll break more than that if you refer to her that way again," Rafe said.

"I'll do worse than break your nose," Cam threatened.

"I'm your partner," Brad said, looking up at Rafe.

So the asshole was Rafe's new partner. That was interesting news. Cam was staring at him like he couldn't stand the man. She walked into her kitchen and grabbed a kitchen towel. She grabbed some ice and wrapped it up before she handed it to Brad.

He put it to his nose. "You need to think about why we're here, man. The whole team is holed up at that shithole sheriff's office waiting around with their dicks in their hands because you won't answer your damn phone."

The words kicked Laura squarely in the gut. So Rafe had known they were coming. Well, she'd pretty much figured that out. Hearing it hurt, though.

"The team was supposed to wait for us to call back," Rafe said. He was looking at Brad. His eyes seemed to be avoiding hers.

"We have some new information. I'm not talking about it here," Brad said, his mouth setting in mulish lines. "Now, maybe you can do your job, partner, and bring this...lovely woman in where we can talk to her."

"That's up to Laura," Logan said.

"What new information?" Cam asked.

"Rafe didn't share that news with you?" Brad asked, smirking. "Joe called and talked to him yesterday. I guess he decided to withhold that nugget. I would have done the same. Rafe is a Bureau man in the end. Now you need to step back, Mr. Private Investigator, and let the real men take over."

Cam's face flushed. She knew that look. Asshole McSmartypants was about to get a fistful of Cam. She'd had enough testosterone for the morning.

153

"I'll ride with you, Logan." Laura walked past Cam. "You should get dressed. Both of you. Wolf, can you give my boss a call and explain why I'm not going to be at work?"

He nodded. "Sure thing. I'll find someone to take your shift. Everyone is going to want to help out. You be sure to take care of her, Logan. Call me if you and Nate need some backup."

Brad stood up. He still held the icepack to his nose. "You are not going to interfere with an official investigation."

Cam moved into Laura's space. "You're not going anywhere without me."

"Everyone stop," Rafe ordered. Even dressed in nothing but his slacks, there was an indefinable air of authority about the man. "Laura can ride with us. We'll get dressed and get to the station house. We will sort this out."

She nodded. It wouldn't do any good to argue with him. It was far better to let him believe that she would be reasonable. Of course, she was being reasonable. Last night she'd been naïve, thinking that they could try again.

Rafe tried to lean over and kiss her, but she pulled away.

Rafe's eyes narrowed. "We'll talk about that, too, *bella*."

Cam stared at her for a moment before they both walked back into the bedroom to get dressed.

She grabbed her purse the minute the door closed behind them. "I'm ready, Logan."

"Hey," Brad muttered before Wolf put a hand on his shoulder.

"I would keep my mouth shut, G-Man," Wolf said. "I wouldn't want my fist to slip and take you out."

Brad sat his ass back down.

"I promise, I'm going to be a good girl and talk to the SAC." It shouldn't be hard. Apparently the special agent in charge was her old boss, Joseph Stone.

She stared at her cabin as Logan pulled away. She wondered how long it would be before she could sleep there without feeling their arms around her.

* * * *

Cam heard the car pull away and cursed as he zipped up his slacks from the night before. He shoved the feminine curtains aside and watched the deputy's Bronco pull out of the drive and fly down the road. He wasn't stupid. He knew the deputy wasn't alone in that car. Laura was gone, and it was Rafe's fault.

"You knew the unit was coming in?" Cam finished getting dressed in a hurry, his hands closing buttons in angry, impatient motions. Rafe had known all along and he hadn't bothered to tell him.

"No, damn it," Rafe replied. "I got a call from Joe yesterday, but you can't get decent cell service here. All I knew was that there was some new information. I didn't know that he was coming here."

Cam sat down on the bed he'd shared with Laura last night. Rafe had been there, too, but he didn't want to think about that right now. "You told me we were coming out here to talk to her, to make sure she was safe."

Rafe didn't look up from tying his loafers. "Yes, that's what we came out here to do."

"You're not telling me everything." He could hear the hesitation in Rafe's voice. There was something the bastard was keeping from him. Maybe he would have seen it before if he hadn't been thinking with his dick.

"I was supposed to bring her back to DC for questioning and, if the SAC deemed it necessary, protective custody."

Cam got up, clenching his fists at his sides. "And you didn't bother to tell me that we might have to drag her kicking and screaming back to the city where she was nearly killed? There's a reason she was hiding. You know I didn't want to tell the Bureau at all. I didn't see that we had any reason to. She didn't do anything wrong. If she feels safer in this tiny town, then what's wrong with that?"

Rafe stood, his shoulders set for a fight. "What's wrong with it? First, she is not safe here. That lock on her door wouldn't keep out a toddler. Second, as long as that asshole is out there killing and torturing women, there's the possibility that he finds her. Do you think he's happy that she got away? This killer is obsessive. He won't be happy that she's still alive. He'll feel the need to tie up that loose end."

Cam was sick of it. It was an excuse. An ugly suspicion was forming in the back of his mind. "Don't feed me that profile crap. This is about getting Laura back to DC where you think you have the advantage. If she goes into protective custody, where does that leave me? I'm not on the payroll anymore. I guess it gives you a lot of time alone with her."

Rafe's eyes narrowed. "What exactly are you accusing me of?"

"I think you know."

"Are they going to hit each other?" A feminine voice spoke from outside the bedroom door. Holly stood there in the kitchen with Wolf. There was a small loaf of bread in her hand and a worried look in her eyes.

He wasn't sure when the bedroom door had come open, but it was obvious those two had heard more than he wanted them to. "I don't have time to beat him up right now."

"Like you could," Rafe growled under his breath.

"Maybe you should put the fight on hold for a second. We have another problem," Wolf said. "Holly had a woman knock on her cabin door a few minutes ago."

Holly's hair was up in a messy ponytail, and she gestured toward her own cabin as she spoke. "She said she was with a news station in Washington. I thought she was talking about the state and maybe they had heard how great our coffee was here. It's really good. Everyone says so. There's something about the way Stella…"

"Holly, stay on task, darlin'," Wolf urged her.

"Oh, well, I started talking about how nice Bliss is, and how very few tourists have met grisly deaths. That part is totally exaggerated, but then she started asking about Laura. She said she'd heard I was her best friend and how did I feel about potentially being the target of a serial killer."

Fuck. There was only one person that could be. "Skinny? Long, flat blonde hair?"

Holly frowned. "I'm ashamed to say I barely got past her boobs. I'm not interested in females, but those boobs were...well, I couldn't take my eyes off of them."

Cam shuddered. "They're fake. Yours are better."

Holly's smile lit up the room. "Thank you."

Rafe's mouth was a flat slash as he brushed by Wolf and Holly and walked straight to his partner. Brad still had the ice pack on his nose. What had he been thinking, sneaking around the side of the cabin?

Rafe's hands came down on either side of the table, and he looked at Brad the same way Cam had seen him look at a suspect. "What the hell is Jana Evans doing here? Who gave her the tip-off?"

Eyes wide, Brad leaned back in his chair. "Now, Rafe, you know I can't stand that bitch. She's always on us, calling us incompetent fools. Why the hell would I give her a tip-off?"

Rafe pressed on. "Someone is tipping her off. This was supposed to be a secret."

Yeah, even for him. Cam didn't like any of it. He absolutely didn't like the fact that Jana Evans had shown up. That reporter was trouble. It had been her story that led to Laura's kidnapping. He could still remember getting that note. It had been sent to the SAC, but he and Rafe had been called in. The note had explained that de Sade was angry. He was far smarter than anyone in law enforcement, and Laura Rosen would pay for the insult.

That note had been the beginning of the worst years of Cam's life. Now the trouble with de Sade was all starting all over again.

Damn. He wanted to be in bed again. He wanted to be snuggled beside Laura in this quiet, safe place. He wished he'd never woken up.

He was wasting time. God, he was going to look like an idiot. His day-old clothing was wrinkled, and he hadn't managed a shower or a shave, but he wasn't going to let her face the unit alone. He was going to have to suck up his pride and ask for a favor. He looked at Wolf.

"Could I get a ride into town from you?" Cam sure as fuck wasn't riding with Rafe.

Rafe sighed. "Don't do this. I told you I didn't know they were coming. I didn't cut you out of this. I convinced them to let you come in with me."

He didn't even look back. "And I found her. Don't pretend like you were doing me a favor."

"I'm going, too. I have banana bread. Everyone likes banana bread," Holly said. "From what it looks like, Laura hasn't had any breakfast. So, I'm coming, too."

"Ma'am," Brad began in that whiny voice of his, "this is serious investigative work. Stay in your cabin, and I'm sure there's a secretary who can keep you informed."

Holly stared at him for a moment, then turned back to Wolf. "If he touches my banana bread, I'll kick him in the balls. Can we go now?"

Wolf nodded. "Come on, Cam. I'll give you a ride in."

Rafe pulled on his arm. "Don't do this. The last thing we need is to let this thing come between us. I never meant to leave you out. I would think last night proved that."

Cam wanted to believe him. He did. The night before had been the best of his life, and part of that had been sharing Laura with Rafe. Perhaps Rafe hadn't lied to him, but he hadn't been truthful, either. "I think you need to take a step back and decide what's more important to you, Laura or your career. I know where I stand on that. I'll see you at the station. I understand that I'm not on the 'team.' I'm strictly there to provide support for Laura. And to keep that fucking reporter off her back."

"I'll get rid of her," Rafe promised. "I know no one in this room is going to believe me, but my main concern is Laura. However, I believe the best way to keep her safe is to catch this killer. I'm going to do it. I'm going to do it because I know he's going to come after her, and I'm going to get to him before he does it."

"Would he come for her here?" Holly asked, a tremor in her voice.

Wolf's arm went around her. As far as Cam could tell, there was nothing in his stance but friendly concern. Wolf Meyer seemed to like to touch the women around him. As long as he kept those paws off his Laura from now on, Cam didn't have a problem with it. Holly didn't seem to have a man to watch out for her. That meant every man who knew her should watch out for her.

"Laura's going to be okay," Wolf promised. "We're having a town hall this evening to discuss the situation. Stef called it."

Rafe groaned. "There's no need to bring the town into this, Mr. Meyer. We're working with the sheriff. He'll keep you updated."

"That isn't the way things work here in Bliss." Wolf started to lead Holly to the door. "We'll grab some coffee from Stella's. That crap Nate drinks is like motor oil. You coming?"

Rafe stood there, his eyes on the table in front of him. His face was stony, but Cam could feel the anger practically vibrating off of him.

He wanted to believe Rafe, but it had been one deception after another with him. How much was he supposed to take? When would Rafe decide to fully cut him loose?

"Yeah, I'm coming." He followed Wolf out the door. He had enough problems to deal with without sorting through all the things that were wrong between him and Rafe at the moment.

He'd woken up cuddled around the dude. That was wrong.

"Shit, I take it that's the reporter?" Wolf asked.

And there was another problem Cam didn't need. Sometimes he thought his life had been a fuckload easier when it was just him and his computers. He'd had a promising career as a hacker. He could have had all the Hot Pockets he could eat and all the comics he could read, but no, when the FBI had recruited him, he'd had to go. Now he had to deal with waking up with his dick on his best friend's thigh and catching serial killers and dealing with ninety-two pounds of pure evil in designer clothes. Yep, he should have gone the geek route.

"Well, if it isn't the FBI's least wanted," Jana said with a wrinkle of her cosmetically perfect nose. She'd once told him she had Reese Witherspoon's nose, Angelina Jolie's lips, and Halle Berry's chin. She might have paid for all of that, but she hadn't had to pay for Hitler's soul. That, she'd been born with.

"You're going to get your ass thrown in jail for obstructing a federal investigation."

Jana smiled, but it was more like a snake baring its fangs. How had Laura ever considered this woman her friend? She waved her hand, and her cameraman appeared. He was a lanky guy with stringy hair poking out of his baseball cap. He didn't say anything, merely shoved the camera on his shoulder and looked through the viewfinder. "You should know I'm always rolling tape of one kind or another."

Yeah, he knew that all too well. "Even when your best friend is pouring her heart out to you? Tell me something, Jana, how do you sleep at night? How do you rest knowing that your story almost got Laura killed?"

She shook her head, but her hair didn't move. It was like the rest of Jana, utterly and perfectly under control and potentially very fake. "I didn't kidnap her. I was trying to help the public. That monster had been killing for years, and you guys couldn't get your thumbs out of each other's asses long enough to find him. The public had the right to know that there was important information the BAU was overlooking because the profiler was female."

"That had nothing to do with it, and you know it." At least Cam hoped it didn't. Laura had always been treated like a valued member of the team, yet Joe and Edward Lock, the senior analyst on the case, had utterly discounted everything in her profile.

Jana looked down at her nails as though the whole conversation was boring her on a fundamental level. "Seemed like a cover-up to me. It's my responsibility to keep the public informed. The FBI sat on Laura's information because she's a woman, or they hid it because they were trying to protect their own. Either way, it was wrong. I got her information out to the public. I did her a favor."

Cam had to clench his fists to stop from winding them around her neck. He wouldn't need both hands. He could crush her throat with one. "Yeah, I bet she felt like you helped her out when she was fired and humiliated and then nearly killed because your fucking news report gave out her address."

Wolf was in his truck, revving the engine. Holly had been perfectly still beside Cam, but now she took his hand.

"Come on, Cameron. I think you've said enough. Let Rafe handle her." Holly's hand was shaking as she started to pull him away.

"Yes, Cam, run away. I don't need you. I want to talk to a real FBI agent," Jana said. "You're useless now, but then you've always been useless unless someone needs their computer fixed or backup in a bar fight, you hick."

He followed Holly because she wouldn't let go of his hand. There was a rigid set to her jaw as she climbed into the backseat, leaving him sitting next to Wolf. Wolf stared holes through the reporter, and he hadn't even heard everything she'd said.

"I'm sorry you had to hear that, Holly," Cam said. Humiliation flowed over him. "Uhm, I should have walked away. You're right. Rafe is the agent. He should handle her."

She slapped at his shoulder. "I wasn't saying that. I think Rafe deserves to have to handle her. She's a horrible human being. I needed to get out of there or I was going to stuff my banana bread down her throat. And it's good bread. It shouldn't be wasted on revenge."

He felt a deep surge of gratitude for his woman's best friend. It looked like Laura had been much more fortunate in her choices of friends in this place. Even that kooky Nell seemed sweet and loyal, if a bit insane.

His stomach was in knots. How was he going to convince Laura he hadn't tricked her? He couldn't lose her again, but how could he keep her after this?

And Rafe. *That son of a bitch.* The betrayal burned in his gut. Had Rafe really used him? It would be easy to get rid of Cam once the feds swooped down. He wasn't on the team, and he wasn't local law enforcement. He had not one lick of clearance or standing when it came to the case, and after this morning, he doubted Laura would even consider him a friend. He could get frozen out entirely.

He looked out the side mirror back at the cabin where he'd almost found heaven. Rafe was getting into their rented SUV. He shouted something at Jana before slamming the door.

Cam forced his eyes forward.

He couldn't think about Rafe now. Laura. Laura was all that mattered.

And keeping her alive had just become Cam's full-time job.

Chapter Ten

Rafe got into the SUV and put it in reverse. "Is there a reason you can't take your own vehicle back? Won't you miss it? Where did you park, by the way?"

Brad frowned as he snapped his seatbelt closed. "Down the way a little. I didn't know what I was getting into, and you hadn't been in touch. I can get it later. Why the hell is News 9 out here?"

Rafe shot Jana Evans the finger as he drove by. The very sight of her made Rafe want to put his fist through something. This had to be one of Laura's worst nightmares, and he'd brought it down on her head. Now everyone was pissed at him. "That's a good question, one of many I have to ask Joe."

"Well, I have a couple of questions for you. You want to explain to me why you were in the same bedroom with Cam Briggs? Seriously? Give me another explanation, man. I knew you two were close, but…"

"I don't owe you any kind of explanation," Rafe stated flatly.

He didn't want to go into it. A couple of people knew he was involved with Laura, mostly coworkers who had been around when Laura was a member of the team, but he'd never talked about her with Brad. Brad was his partner, but Rafe had kept his distance. He'd kept his distance from everyone for the last several years.

Until last night.

Brad kept droning on about some shit, but Rafe's brain had gone back to the night before.

It had been perfect. He'd taken her, his cock sliding in and out until he couldn't tell where he began and she ended. He'd pumped into her, giving her everything he had while his tongue slid against hers. He'd tasted her at one point. Cam had held her, her back to his front. Cam's legs had held hers apart, her pussy on full display and available to his lips and tongue. Her pussy had been sweetly pink and swollen from use. Rafe had tenderly washed her with a warm cloth before he'd settled between her legs and licked every inch of her. When he'd looked up her body, Cam's hands had been there, holding her down when she tried to wiggle, keeping her still so Rafe could have his way.

Cam was his partner.

Brad was nothing more than a fellow employee.

"What's this new information?" he asked, cutting off whatever diatribe Brad had gone on.

Brad stopped and turned to him. His eyebrows rose over his angular face. "You like this girl, don't you? Were you involved with her before she left?"

He tightened his grip on the steering wheel as he turned out of the small cluster of cabins in the valley toward the center of town. He'd been here less than twenty-four hours, but he was learning his way around. "It doesn't matter."

Brad's eyes narrowed. "It matters. If you're involved with this woman, it affects this case. She's the only person we know of who's survived this guy. She's a victim. You don't fuck victims."

He stopped the SUV in the middle of the highway. "She's Laura Rosen. She has a fucking name, and you're going to treat her with some goddamn respect."

Brad's whole face fell. "Shit, you're in love with her."

Rafe cursed himself. Brad was a thoroughly "by the book" kind of agent. Joe knew about his relationship with Laura, but Joe understood. He'd agreed to keep it quiet and not take Rafe off the case. Brad could make a stink. He didn't want to find himself on the sidelines. This was one of the reasons he hadn't gotten close to his "partner." He would never have been able to keep something like that from Cam when they had worked together.

There was a long sigh. "I'm not going to say anything. I don't know why you think I'm such a dick."

Rafe slid a glance his way.

"Fine, I'm a dick," Brad replied. "I'm a thrice-divorced dickhead with very few friends. I'm not going to out you. You're my partner."

"Joe knows." He'd poured his heart out to the SAC after Laura had disappeared.

"Then you're fine. I'm not going over Joe's head, but you have to be careful. There's a reason we don't get emotionally involved with any case." Brad sat back. "Okay. As long as we're putting all our cards on the table, I received a package yesterday. It came to my apartment, but it was addressed to Laura Rosen."

His gut clenched. "Why would he send a package to you? He doesn't send packages. He's sent notes before."

De Sade had sent a couple of notes to both the Bureau and the newspapers, but he'd never sent a package before. And why would he send one addressed to Laura?

"I think I know why." Brad gingerly touched his nose, looking in the passenger side vanity mirror. "I don't have a family, and my building doesn't have security cameras. And I've filed the last three official updates on the killings. I think de Sade has been watching for any sign of her."

"How could he have known?"

Brad slumped back. "Because we have a leak somewhere. Jana Evans being here in this tiny piece of hell proves it. I'm sure she's already filed a report back home. It will be the top story on the evening news. If reporters already have the story, why couldn't de Sade? The package was sitting in front of my door when I went home yesterday afternoon."

That would have been right around the time Joe had called. They had moved damn fast. And de Sade had done his homework, as always. He was everything Laura's profile said he would be. Ruthless. Intelligent. He had to have known that Brad's building didn't have great security. Damn, he probably had a file on every agent on the case. It would be easy if he were law enforcement. "What was in that package?"

There was a hesitation that let Rafe know it was going to be bad. "A single pair of women's underwear. A small, pink thong."

Fuck. Laura had been found naked with only a thin sheet wrapped around her bleeding body. Among the clothes she listed as missing was a pink thong. He had to swallow back the bile that threatened to come up. "No note?"

"No, but the message was clear. He knows we've found her. We have the lab working on DNA, and the box has been sent to forensics, but you know we won't get anything off it. He's too careful."

"He does seem to have a working knowledge of forensics and how to avoid detection," Rafe murmured.

"Yeah, anyone who watches TV does these days. I don't buy that this guy is one of us. And you shouldn't, either. I don't want to argue about this. The Marquis de Sade is not an agent. He's some asshole who has connections. I can buy that. We need to check into Jana Evans."

He'd already thought of that. Jana wasn't capable of breaking a nail, but it was obvious that whoever de Sade was, he was carefully watching the reporter. "I agree. Run a check on everyone around her, including that cameraman of hers."

She'd worked with this particular cameraman for as long as Rafe had known her. Bob Lewis or something. It couldn't hurt to run a check. Including financials.

Brad pulled out his phone and started making notes. Rafe had to give that to Brad. He was an asshole, but he was organized. He was always on top of things. Cam forgot. Cam's brain was always flitting around. Rafe had been the one to write things down. Sometimes Brad's brutal efficiency bugged the shit out of Rafe.

He sped down the road. It wasn't like the locals were going to pull him over. The sheriff had his hands full of feds, and the disgruntled deputy had Laura. "So why did Joe decide to go mobile?"

"Joe was worried about that package. He thought it was best if we came out here and talked to the vic...to Laura again. She's our only connection. We need her." Brad was silent for a moment. "We need you, too. I need to know that you can keep your head on straight."

Up ahead, Rafe could see the truck Wolf had driven off in parked in front of the sheriff's office. Two Broncos sat in the parking lot, too, and several black SUVs. It looked like the gang was all here. *Woohoo*.

"My head is on straight," he assured his partner. "I promise you, my brain is thinking about this case twenty-four-seven."

"That's what I want to hear, man."

He pulled into a parking space. His brain might be on the case, but he had the sinking feeling that his brain wasn't in charge anymore.

He knew he wasn't in charge of anything when he walked through the double doors of the Bliss County Sheriff's Department. It was utterly transformed from the quiet station house he'd visited yesterday. He'd dropped by the station to officially introduce himself and inform the sheriff why he was in town after Cam had finished talking to the conspiracy kook.

There were folding tables and laptops everywhere. The sheriff stood in the middle of it all, a pained expression on his face. A small brunette in a long skirt and a button-down shirt stood next to him, a clipboard in her hand. She chewed on her lower lip as she carefully wrote on the paper. Rafe sought his memory. *Hannah? Hope.* The sheriff's secretary's name was Hope something. She'd been quiet as a mouse during yesterday's interview with Nate Wright.

"Special Agent Kincaid," Nate called out. He pushed through the crowd, his hand out. "Am I happy to see you."

That was a surprise since the sheriff hadn't been happy to see him yesterday. Rafe shook the man's hand. "Sheriff, I'm sorry about this. I had no idea they were coming. Despite what everyone thinks."

Nate had an easy smile on his face. "I believe you. I know how service is out here. Though you folks don't seem to have the same problems. Your boss brought satellite phones."

"Well, we have the best equipment. We're not going to rely on locals when we can bring our own things. You should sit back and watch how it's done, Sheriff." Brad patted the sheriff's shoulder condescendingly and walked off.

"Don't shoot him," Rafe said with a sigh. "He's arrogant."

Nate shrugged it off. "I've dealt with worse. Hell, I've been worse. We need to talk."

Rafe nodded. For some reason, he trusted Nate Wright. He'd learned a couple of things about the sheriff. He was once a DEA agent. He wasn't some lightweight. "And we will, once I get a lay of the land. And it's best if we don't do it here."

He wasn't sure what the FBI coming to Bliss meant yet, but it never hurt to have allies. He had a feeling the sheriff would prove to be a powerful ally.

"Sure, I suspect we can sneak off for lunch and no one will notice. Your boss has already ordered in. He's taken over my entire office. Seriously, I hope I didn't fucking act like this when I was a fed."

Rafe could only nod. He knew how it went. When the FBI decided it was taking over, local law enforcement was pretty much fucked. Up until now, it seemed like the right thing to do, but he kind of liked Nathan Wright. He seemed competent, but Rafe knew that Joe would cut Wright out. He would do it because no FBI SAC was going to truly trust the locals. And he was pretty sure, in this case, that was a mistake.

"Where's the special agent in charge?" He'd already looked around the small office and hadn't seen Laura. Joe would have her. Rafe had worked with Joe for years. He knew how Joe operated. Joe would have been all over her the minute Laura entered the room. "Do you have an interrogation room?"

"A small one." Nate pointed down a narrow hallway. "She's in there. Briggs went in with her. I thought she was going to punch him at first, but he managed to smooth talk her into letting him in there with her. The SAC said you could go in when you got here. Do you need anything? Hope is making a run to Stella's for coffee and breakfast."

His appetite had fled long before. There was nothing now but an angry lump in his gut, but he hoped it was different for Laura.

"Laura likes her coffee dark with a hint of sugar. Can you make sure Hope brings her a dark roast with one sugar packet? And a bagel. She likes bagels with cinnamon cream cheese."

A hint of a smile played on Nate Wright's mouth. "I believe that's what she asked Hope to bring her, though she didn't ask for the bagel. I think she's eating Holly's banana bread."

Rafe nodded and walked through the hall toward the small closed door. He stopped. It felt like the walls were closing in on him. He'd been here before, back in DC. It was all the same. Narrow hallways and neutral colors leading to a room where questions were answered in monotones. He'd been in a hundred of these rooms. The fact that Laura sat in one now made him edgy. She was on the wrong side of the table. She was on the vulnerable side.

He hated that.

There was a weird feeling in the pit of his stomach. There was one reason and one reason only for the BAU to come out here and talk to Laura Rosen. She'd given them all the information she had. Her case was five years old. There was a chance they had come out here to simply talk to her—but he discounted that possibility. Brad's snippet of information made that scenario implausible. They didn't want to talk to Laura. They wanted to use her.

For bait.

Fuck. Why had he told anyone? He should have taken a leave of absence and come here with Cam with no further agenda than seeing her again, holding her again. He'd fucked up, and Cam and Laura had every right to be pissed with him.

And yet, a certain amount of rage choked him. She'd walked out. She'd left without a goddamn word. Didn't he have the right to be angry?

She wouldn't be safe until he took down the Marquis de Sade. She'd be looking over her shoulder for the rest of her life.

He walked through the door.

"And you're sure you haven't had any communication with..." Joe stopped in the middle of his sentence, his face serious as he glanced up.

The small room was filled to capacity. There was a long wooden table. A recording device was sitting in the middle, the red light flashing, indicating that it was on. Laura's golden-blonde head was turned away from him, but there was no mistaking who sat beside her. Cam's broad shoulders filled up too much space. He'd obviously moved his chair so he could sit as close as possible. Cam's hips brushed against hers.

A burning jealousy filled his soul.

"Special Agent Kincaid, it's nice of you to join us," Joe said with a welcoming smile on his face.

On the other side of the table, Edward Lock sat beside Joe. Edward was an older man, but there was nothing soft about him. He kept in shape, both body and mind. He was studying Laura, his razor-sharp gray eyes assessing her the way he would an unsub. Rafe had the sudden urge to punch him in the face.

"Come and join us, Special Agent," Joe offered. There was one chair left to the right of Joe. "I was filling in Special Agent...I mean

Laura on the case. It's been a while. We've been catching up a bit while we waited on you."

Laura finally turned, her blue eyes shifting up. Her face was utterly blank, but he didn't miss the way her hand curled around Cam's.

Fucker.

Rafe had a choice, and it was so clear to him now. He had to choose between the career he'd spent years building and the woman he'd obsessed over. She seemed to have already made her choice. It should be simple. She'd chosen Cam. Rafe could move to the FBI side of the table with no remorse, just a never-ending ache in his heart. She'd made her choice without even bothering to listen to his side of the story. It was the same thing she'd done when she'd walked out of the hospital. She hadn't bothered to let him know if she was alive or dead. She hadn't given him a single thought.

He could choose his career with the same ruthless selfishness that she'd used when she'd walked away.

Rafe walked around the table, pulled out the chair—and moved that fucker, because he was done with picking his job over the needs of his heart.

She'd walked out on him and ripped his heart in two. She was currently choosing his best friend over him without giving him a chance to explain, and he would sit at her side until he keeled over because he loved her. He knew that now. He knew it in a way he couldn't have known before she'd left. The last five years had taught him something. He was ready for a marriage. He was ready to move on to a place where his job was something that took care of the people he loved. Hell, that was all this place had been for the last five years, anyway. It had become a place that paid for Cam to look for Laura. He and Cam had been functioning as a unit. Rafe wanted his place acknowledged.

Laura slid a glance his way.

Rafe kept his eyes on Joe. "Perhaps you would like to bring me up to speed, Special Agent. Special Agent Conrad told me some new evidence has come to light that makes the unit believe de Sade is working again and taking an interest in former Agent Rosen."

"He had her panties, Rafe," Cam said with a brutal frown.

Laura sighed. "Yes, I wish the bastard hadn't kept those."

At least Cam was looking at him. There was a file in front of Joe that Rafe reached for. There was a stack of photos. On top was an evidentiary photo of a small, pink piece of silk.

"Do you recognize this?" Rafe asked, not quite able to look at Laura.

There was a long, charged pause. "Yes."

Edward sat forward now, pushing his glasses up his elegant nose. "You were wearing these when the Marquis de Sade took you?"

"She said she recognized them," Cam said with a frown.

"I need a formal acknowledgement that these belong to you, Miss Rosen," Edward said with his usual condescension. "There's no point in denying it. We'll have DNA confirmation by tomorrow. There was a drop of blood on the waistband and other biological excretions on the lining of the drawers."

Laura flushed, and Rafe thought seriously about putting the Harvard-educated agent's nose through the back of his head.

"They were mine," Laura said with a huff. "I was wearing them when he took me. He gave me some form of sedative. When I woke up, he'd taken my clothes off. Hopefully the next package contains a Michael Kors dress. I miss that dress. It made my boobs look spectacular."

It was all he could do not to laugh. That was his Laura. She was rebellious to the end. She'd faced de Sade and lived. She could certainly handle the FBI. She didn't need him to be her protector. Was that what she'd tried to tell him by walking away? Had she really simply not wanted him after he'd failed her so miserably?

"Why Brad? Why would they send it to Brad and not me or Rafe?" Cam asked.

"Well, son," Joe said, leaning forward. "I think this boy likes to

172

screw with us. He genuinely enjoys playing the game, and you aren't FBI anymore. I have to ask you something, Cameron. Have you talked to that reporter at all? Have you mentioned Laura's whereabouts to anyone at all?"

"He barely managed to tell me," Rafe muttered.

Cam's face reddened, and Rafe didn't miss the way Laura's hand tightened over Cam's. She seemed to be reminding him he was on a leash.

Edward tapped his long fingers along the table. "Let's not get ahead of ourselves with accusations. The Marquis de Sade is nothing if not organized. It wouldn't shock me at all to discover he's been watching. This is all a game to him. He would keep tabs on the major players. Despite Briggs leaving the FBI, I think the killer would still watch him. After all, he's a potential link to the most important person in de Sade's life—Laura Rosen, the one who got away."

"It doesn't make a lick of sense," Cam said, his previous irritation seeming to dissolve into frustration. Laura had handled him perfectly. "He's been quiet for years. He gets one sniff of her and he's back?"

"It's possible that the incident with me threw him off his game," Laura said. "Serial killers have been known to stop killing for years and then start up again."

Edward adjusted his glasses in that scholarly fashion that set Rafe's teeth on edge. He was always so far above everyone else. "I believe he simply entered another portion of the game and changed his tactics a bit. He's smart."

"Yeah, you've said that before," Rafe replied. Edward had always seemed fascinated with this particular case. Edward had also been the one to declare that Laura's profile was amateur and unworthy of real assessment.

Joe sighed as he looked around. He finally focused in on Laura. He pushed the folder toward her. "I would like for you to look at the evidence we've gathered since you left. I would appreciate your take

173

on this. You, of all the people in the world, know this guy. Help us. Help us catch him."

"She needs to stay out of this," Cam said.

Laura let go of his hand. Her fingers crept across the table toward that folder.

Rafe's heart rate shot sky high. "She needs to come into protective custody. We need to get her out of here."

Laura's eyes never wavered from that manila folder. Her hands caught it, and she slid it toward her. "I've tried hiding. It didn't work. What I'm rapidly discovering is that no matter how hard you try to hide, your past always catches up to you."

Joe's face was in a brutal frown. "We need her, Rafe. You have to see that. She's the closest we've ever come to catching him. He wants her."

Laura casually opened the folder. "He'll come for me."

Cam looked at Rafe over her head. His blue eyes were practically begging him to do something, anything.

His fists clenched into tight balls of anxiety. He'd brought her to this. "You are not using her for bait. I won't allow it."

"You don't allow or disallow anything, Special Agent Kincaid." The fine edge of authority bit through the air. Joseph Stone had been a special agent in charge for a very long time. He hadn't gotten there by allowing his underlings to tell him what to do, but Rafe didn't have a choice.

"Nor does he have any control over me." Laura's voice had gone cold, professional. She opened the file, and Rafe knew he'd lost this particular war. "I'll need an hour or two to go over this. I know this isn't standard procedure."

"Letting a witness read confidential files?" Joe relaxed back into his chair. "No, but you're not any witness. You know I never agreed with the decision to fire you."

She waved it off. "It doesn't matter."

"Then I'll leave you to it." Joe and Edward got up.

"I'd like to be alone," Laura said, never looking up from the file.

"Laura," Cam started.

But Rafe knew she was done for now. He would have to find another way to get to her. If he pushed, she would retreat even further. It was time to regroup.

"Come on, brother," Rafe said. "Let's go see what's going on out there. She's safe enough in here."

The door closed between them. Rafe prayed it hadn't closed forever.

Chapter Eleven

An hour later, Laura finally closed the folder and tried to take a deep breath. It felt like the walls were closing in on her. Five years. She'd hidden for five years, and in an instant, it was all coming back to her. She'd been safe here, and now she had to wonder if he was going to find her again.

She stood and smoothed out her shirt. She made sure the file was in pristine order and turned on her heels to walk out of the quiet interrogation room. She was pretty sure it had never been used to actually interrogate anyone. Mostly Nate simply locked people up and let them go after he'd either calmed down or they had paid their legitimate fines. The citizens of Bliss had quickly gotten used to the sheriff's temper. They knew if they were wrongly jailed there would be a nice free meal and a beer waiting for them at Trio. Laura had a sudden desire to be there. She could sit at the bar and joke with Callie and Zane while she sipped the chardonnay Zane kept behind the bar for her.

Why had this followed her home?

Laura stepped out of the door, looking for Joe. She knew he wanted to ask her some questions. She wasn't looking forward to any of this.

A hard hand clamped down on her elbow, pulling her toward an open door.

Rafe sent her reeling into Nate Wright's office. He closed the door behind her, the discipline of his action telling her exactly how pissed he was. He shut that door with a quiet intensity.

She wasn't having it. He'd been the one to pull her back into this world. Cam had explained his part. He'd practically tackled her and begged her forgiveness. She believed him that he hadn't sicced the feds on her, but Rafe was another matter. Rafe was the one who had always been devoted to the job. He'd been the true believer. At the time, she'd seen his devotion to justice as something intensely noble. She still did, but damn, if she didn't wish he had been a little more devoted to her. She would have enjoyed the chance to decide for herself if she wanted to be a part of this again.

"What do you want, Rafe?" She was alone in a room with him. A tiny room. A room that suddenly seemed far too small for two people.

His face was set in tight lines, his jaw painfully stubborn. "I want a lot of things, *bella*. I doubt you'll be willing to give them to me."

There was no mistaking the hard edge of his tone—or the line of his erection. Rafe was angry, and it was doing something for him. The sad thing was it was doing something for her, too. "You can't seriously think I want to be alone with you."

Where was Cam when she needed him? Oh, yeah. She'd told him to leave her alone. Well, she'd gotten what she wanted. She'd claimed she needed time to think about the new facts and the case, but what she'd really needed was time away from both of them. Yet even as she had sat there staring down at proof that her worst nightmare was still at large and at work, she'd thought about them. When was she going to learn?

"I don't care what you want at this moment." His back was to the door, as though guarding it. She was suddenly extremely aware of how alone they were. "I'm going to talk to you, and you're going to listen."

"Well, it doesn't seem like I have a choice." She crossed her arms over her chest and hoped she was giving him her absolute most intimidating glare. He hadn't been huge on giving her choices. Resentment started to bubble up. "What's wrong, Rafe? Are you afraid if I'm given a choice and treated like an actual functioning adult that you'll lose out? You're probably right. If you weren't standing in front of that door, I would be out of here."

His lips curled up in a bitter imitation of a smile. "Yes, *bella*, you've made that plain to me. But I do take offense to the accusation that I've taken away your choices."

She allowed her eyes to widen in suspicion. "What exactly did you mean to do by storming into Bliss the way you did? We have phones, you know. A simple phone call would have saved all of us time."

"Would it? Because you would have answered and been so reasonable. If I am not treating you like an adult, *bella*, it's because I haven't known you to act like one."

Her fists clenched. It was ridiculous. She was one of the most responsible people she knew. She always made the responsible choice. The craziest thing she'd ever done was sleeping with Rafe and Cam, and it was clear where that had led her. "Fuck you, Rafe."

She started toward the door, rage riding her. She wasn't a child. She didn't have to stay here and listen to some lecture he seemed to need to get out of his system. He would move out of her way or she would see if she remembered anything from martial arts class.

Rafe had her pinned to the desk before she could take her next breath. Unlike her, it seemed Rafe had never stopped training.

He invaded her space, his big body holding her down. Though he'd slammed into her, his hands had come around and taken the brunt of hitting the desk. Even when he was being violent, he made sure she didn't get hurt. "Very mature, *bella*. I should have expected that. Let me explain a few truths of the world to you. Mature people do not walk out of their hospital beds leaving everything they own and love behind."

"I didn't give a shit about my belongings, and I sure as hell didn't love anyone." She was lying, but she wasn't about to admit it to him.

"I don't believe that for a second," Rafe replied, his voice low. He was between her legs, and his cock jutted up as though seeking her pussy. His hands gentled and smoothed back her hair. "You loved me. You loved Cam. But you were angry with both of us. You chose to punish us."

"I chose to walk away from a life that didn't work for me anymore." She averted her eyes. It was another lie, but Rafe wasn't completely correct, either. "What should I have done? I didn't have a job. I was completely free to do as I chose."

"What should you have done?" He repeated the question as though the answer should have been evident. "You should have stayed. You should have fought."

But she'd been fighting so hard and against so damn many things. "You have no idea what he did to me."

"I know what he did, *bella*. And I know you punished me by not allowing me to take care of you." He was unwavering. Rafe was the rough one. If this had been Cam, Laura had no doubt he would already be whispering to her, trying to soften her. Rafe seemed to want her angry. "Ask yourself how you would have felt if Cam or I had simply vanished without explanation. Be honest, *bella*. You might not be honest with me, but be honest with yourself. If you loved someone and they disappeared without a trace, how would you feel?"

Betrayed. Angry. Panicked. Sad. So fucking sad. She'd felt every single one of those things along with an aching emptiness that she was sure had never really gone away. She'd told herself at the time that it was better to leave. They obviously didn't really love her, so she was free to go. Was there any truth in what he was saying? Had she punished them?

179

"Keep silent." Rafe's fingers sank into her hair. "I can see it on your face, you understand. I also know that you're questioning everything. You're wondering if I ever loved you. But I'm not the one who walked away."

This she could deal with. "No, you're the one who threw me under a bus at the first given opportunity."

"I can admit my mistakes, but I was still there, ready to talk it out. Cam and I called you over and over again. You wouldn't answer the phone. We intended to explain everything to you that night, but it was too late."

She shrugged. "Sorry I missed our meeting. I was busy being tortured."

That was a direct hit. He actually eased up a bit. "And you think I don't feel that every day of my life? If I hadn't made the decision to go with Edward's profile, you would never have been taken. But I won't allow that to hold me back another second. You are going to listen to me. I'm putting aside this bullshit. You are going to go back to your cabin and very quietly pack a bag. Tell Joe that you're tired or you've forgotten something. I'll drive you."

She knew exactly where he was going with this. "And I suppose once we have this bag I'm supposed to pack, we'll keep right on driving."

"Yes. I won't allow you to be used in this fashion. I don't care that you don't believe me, but I never meant for you to get involved in this again. We'll drive and call Cam. He can run interference for us and meet us when we find a place to stay."

Tempting. So tempting. But she'd done that once, and the past had still caught up with her.

His hands caressed the line of her throat. His eyes had gone sleepy with desire. She wanted him. Bastard that he could be, she wanted him. The last hour had shaken her to her core. She wanted more than mere sex. She wanted to feel grounded and whole, and she wasn't sure she could ever feel that way without the two of them in her life. But if she ran with them, she would pull them into her trouble. Rafe couldn't leave the FBI. It had become his home. Cam wouldn't be happy on the run, and that's what they would be.

"You know I can't do that," she said as he pulled her legs up. She didn't fight him as he wound her legs around his waist, his cock shoved against her pussy.

"I know you will do it, *bella*," he replied, his voice deep in his throat. "I'll make you do it."

His hips slid against hers in an easy, smooth rhythm. She had no doubt of how he intended to impose his will on her. He would fuck her into submission if she let him. He was already pulling the light, flowing skirt up around her waist. His hands toyed with the edges of her panties. He would find out exactly how interested she was if he delved inside.

"You can't," she said, her voice tinged with regret. She wished she could give in. Rafe and Cam would take over, and she wouldn't have to think. She could simply let them take care of her. But that wouldn't solve her problems. It wouldn't stop de Sade. "I have to see this through. Joe is expecting me back in that room in less than thirty minutes."

They had more questions for her. Questions Rafe nor Cam could save her from.

"I'll get you out of here," Rafe promised. "You watch me."

He lowered his mouth to hover over hers. She could feel his heat and smell the mint on his breath. He looked into her eyes, giving her no place to hide.

"I have to face him."

She didn't have a choice. Maybe she'd never had one. The man who'd ruined her body was here in Bliss. He was pretending to be something he wasn't—upstanding and worthy of trust. Whether any of these men believed her, it didn't matter, because she knew she was right, and now she was pretty sure that de Sade might have been closer than any of them ever imagined.

"I love you, *bella*. I won't pretend. I love you. I'll do anything to protect you." The tip of his tongue came out, and he licked at her lips, igniting every nerve in her body. "I'll even fight you if I have to. I'm just warning you. Now give me your tongue. If we only have thirty minutes, I intend to make the most of it."

She knew she should fight. He really would try his damnedest to get her to do what he wanted, but she needed him. She let her mouth open and sighed as his tongue surged in, sliding over hers. He dominated. His weight held her down, pinning her against the desk. As his tongue played against hers, his fingers found their way under the band of her underwear and into the creamy folds of her pussy.

"You're already ready for me," he whispered against her mouth.

She didn't have a response for that. She was always ready for him. She'd spent years aching for him.

He pulled the panties down her legs, giving up her mouth. His fingers followed the line of her legs as he dragged the silky underwear down. She started to kick off her shoes. She'd worn her canary-yellow, four-inch peep toes today.

"No," Rafe said, gently pushing her hands away. "I love them."

His hand went to the belt on his slacks, and he made quick work of them. He shoved them down and had his cock in hand in no time at all. He grimaced.

She quickly realized what was wrong. "No condom."

"I'll find one."

"Stop," she said. She took his hand and traced the long scar that went across her lower abdomen. "I'm perfectly clean, and you know what he did to me. We don't have to worry about children."

The Marquis de Sade had taken that from her when he'd shoved a knife through her womb. The only way she'd survived was to literally hold herself together. If she hadn't been able to find her way to the street, she would have died.

He stopped, his hand warm on her stomach. He covered the scars there. "I would kill him for you if I could."

She shook her head and started to push Rafe off of her.

"Don't," Rafe said roughly. He kissed her again, softer this time. "Don't let him come into this."

"Rafe, you don't need to use a condom because he took that away from me. You need to think about this. I can't have children because he thought it was a fun way to torture me. He comes between us." And he would until the day he was caught. She'd been hiding for years, but she was ready to face him now. She wasn't sure she was ready to face Rafe.

"I don't give a damn about kids. I want them, but not more than I want you. You think Cam and I haven't talked about this?" His cock still pressed against her, a sure sign that he wasn't lying. He still wanted her. "I wasn't interested in you for your womb. If you want to adopt, we can. If you want it to just be the three of us, then that's my family."

Tears pooled in her eyes. She couldn't imagine him without kids. She couldn't imagine him without a big family surrounding him.

"Please, *bella*. Don't push me away. I won't go." He pressed inside her.

His cock started to fill her. She knew she would probably have to let him go, but not now. Not yet.

She let her hands find the flesh under his dress shirt. She reveled in the feel of him. His skin was warm underneath her hands. She could feel the leashed power in the muscles of his back as he carefully entered her.

"God, you feel so good. Nothing between us. Nothing." Rafe started to thrust a bit more heavily. His cock filled her. He adjusted her hips and slid home with a groan.

So full. So full of him and it still wasn't enough. She still needed Cam. Why? Why did she have to need them both? Why couldn't she be normal?

She looked toward the door, wondering if Cam was out there. Would he be angry that she'd come in here with Rafe? Nate's door had a pane of opaque glass. A brawny set of shoulders could be seen against it, the outline so familiar she nearly cried.

Rafe glanced toward the door, never letting up on the silky

strokes of his cock. He looked back down, a frown on his face. "It was my turn to go first. Cam got to go first last night."

A light joy took over. Cam was standing guard. He wasn't sitting, sullenly angry with her for choosing Rafe over him. They weren't fighting over her this time.

Rafe held himself tight in her pussy. He brought his hand up to touch her face. "We knew when we came after you that we were going to share. We won't make that mistake again, *bella*. It's you and me and Cam, though he is righteously pissed at me right now. He's still a fair man. He knew it was my turn."

They needed to talk about this whole "turns" thing. She wanted to be more than a body they passed between them. She loved it when the three of them were together.

Then she wasn't thinking of anything but Rafe. He pressed her knees apart and began to thrust. Over and over he pushed that big cock inside her. She locked her legs around his waist.

He hissed, his expression turning slightly feral. "That's right. That's what I want. Dig those heels into my back. It won't make me go easy on you. It will only make me fuck you harder."

That hadn't been her intention, but damn if she was going to tell him that. Rafe leaned over and suddenly every move he made hit two spots. His cock hit that magnificent place inside that started her moaning, and his pelvis rubbed her clit.

Laura struggled to contain the wail that wanted to come out of her. He felt so good, so right.

Rafe was relentless. He picked up the pace, making her shake as the orgasm threatened. "Give it to me. Tell me what I want to hear."

She knew what he wanted, and she couldn't hold it back. He was going to make her scream if she didn't give him what he wanted.

"I don't care if everyone out there hears you scream when you come."

"I love you." She did care if everyone heard her, and it was true. She loved him, but it wasn't going to happen. He needed more than

184

she could give him. He needed his career and his family, and he risked both if he became involved in a ménage. Cam had worked hard to get where he'd been, and he'd already given up so much for her. He'd given up his whole career. How could she ask them to give up their chances at a family, too? She would have to make that sacrifice. "I do love you."

He leaned over and kissed her as he pressed down hard. The orgasm bloomed, racing through her system, connecting them in a way they had never been connected before. She felt a heated rush as Rafe released deep inside her. It had nowhere to go, but it still felt right. It still felt like something that should happen between them.

"I love you, *bella*." There was a knock on the door, and Rafe's face fell. "Impatient bastard. I wouldn't bother cleaning up."

He kissed her one last time and then zipped up. She scrambled to get up and off the desk, but the door closed again and Cam was all over her.

"Oh, baby, was he a greedy son of a bitch?" Cam sank his hands in her hair and turned her mouth up, locking his lips over hers. He ate at her lips, biting and licking softly. "He took two thirds of the time, but he only has half the cock."

It had felt like a whole cock at the time—and then some. "Cam, we should talk about this."

She was covered in Rafe's release. Despite what Rafe said, she should clean up, and they really needed to talk. The morning had flown by, her emotions twisting and turning until she'd felt numb. Now her heart was racing and her head spinning. She needed to talk, to explain that she couldn't do this with them. They had to see that it couldn't work.

"I don't think talking is going to help. I haven't talked to Rafe except to tell him he's an asshole and to agree that, given what happened last night, I should go second." He rubbed their noses together, the touch so sweet it made her want to melt.

She had to stay strong. "I don't want to talk about sex. We have to talk, seriously talk."

He pulled up a bit. "I don't know if I can talk seriously until I get inside you."

"That's not going to help." She forced herself to say the words, but she was already twitching, her hips seeking him out.

"It's going to help me a lot." Cam let his hand run down her body toward her pussy. He'd already taken Rafe's place between her legs. His eyes flared as he sank his fingers in. "Holy shit. He didn't use a condom. Motherfucker. That's not fair." A slow smile spread across his face. "Damn. This should gross me out, right? Fuck, I'm turned on. I know I should be thinking about how some other dude's jizz is all over your pussy, but all I can think about is the fact that this makes great lube."

He pulled back and flipped her over in one neat turn. His finger pressed against her ass before she could think to breathe.

"Damn it, Cameron. I'm supposed to be mad at you," she complained.

"You were supposed to be even madder at Rafe, but he got to ride you bareback. He's the one who brought this shit down on our heads, but you let him fuck you. I deserve more. I'm the good one. Doesn't the good one deserve more than the bad boy?"

She groaned as he pressed his well-lubed finger deep in her ass. His cock teased at the lips of her pussy.

"You're both bastards." It was so much easier to fight with Cam.

She practically heard the smile on his face. "Yes, but we're your bastards."

Laura groaned as his cock invaded. She would have sworn she couldn't feel anything else, but her pussy lit up at Cam's thrust.

"What if I don't want you?" Even as she said the words, she lifted her ass up to take him more fully.

"I'd want to die, so I wouldn't believe it," Cam replied.

He gently spread her legs further so he could work his cock in. It was so deep at this angle. She felt absolutely helpless, yet that was all right with Cam. She felt her body softening under him, allowing him to take control. Her breasts were flattened against Nate's desk. God, Nate was going to kill her for desecrating his desk. Nate took his job seriously. There was no way anything sexual had ever happened in his office. Well, it had now. She had to hope Nate had gone to lunch and wouldn't guess what the feds had been doing to their very important witness.

Laura felt the dual penetration of Cam's cock and his fingers.

"Besides, your pussy is sucking me in. Damn it, baby. You have to stop that. I don't want this to end. I want to make it last." Cam sounded slightly drunk. He pushed in and out of her pussy, never letting up on the slow, gliding motion. "I want to fuck you forever. You won't have to deal with anything. You'll only have to deal with this."

It sounded perfect. It felt better than perfect. "We have to talk."

Cam found a rhythm, his hips pumping his cock deep while his fingers rotated inside her. "I'm listening."

She groaned as he added another finger to her asshole. "Damn it, Cam. I can't leave here."

"Is that his plan?" Cam steadied himself before he started up again. "I wouldn't talk to him about anything but this. But I will, baby. I'm pissed right now, but we'll work it out. And I wholeheartedly approve of getting you the hell out of here. We'll hole up someplace quiet. No one has to know where we're going."

"I can't." She clawed at the desk. He was killing her with this never-ending slow fuck. He kept the rhythm perfectly tantalizing, but he withheld her orgasm. It was right there. She shouldn't need another one so soon after the last, but the pleasure was there and she reached for it—only to have him pull back. "Damn it, Cameron. I'm not leaving. I'm going to face this."

"Then I'll face it with you," he swore, and there wasn't a smile in his voice this time. "I won't ever leave you. Not until they haul me out in a body bag. If you run again, I'll find you. I'll track you down, and we'll be right back here. I already talked to the sheriff. He says he could use another deputy. If you stay, I stay. I can't promise what Rafe will do, baby, but I'm here, and I won't let you shut me out. Never again."

She moaned as Cam got serious. He plunged in and pulled out, cock and fingers working in perfect time. She wanted to argue with him. The body bag comment scared the hell out of her. If Cam stood in the killer's way, that rash statement could prove true.

Then nothing mattered but the way he felt. He filled her. She closed her eyes and imagined they were both there, one in her pussy and the other claiming her asshole. Her men, working together. The three of them safe and whole.

She nearly sobbed as she came. Cam stiffened behind her, calling her name over and over as he pumped into her body. His fingers slipped from her ass, but his cock remained.

"I love you, baby," he whispered.

"I love you, too." And she would protect him. She would find a way to protect them both.

* * * *

He watched his pretty rabbit as she tried to sneak out of the sheriff's office. The big asshole who had gone in there with her didn't bother. He had that smile on his face, the one that idiot men had after they were done fucking.

Of course, the other one had that same self-satisfied "the world is mine because I got some" look on his face.

Only his rabbit had the sense to look embarrassed. Too bad she hadn't had the sense to not be a whore.

He felt his fists clench on the file in his hand. He'd spent the morning coming up with some questions to pose to his girl. He'd always wanted to ask her how she'd liked their time together. Back when the wounds were fresh—god, he loved the fact that he'd made her bleed—he would have seemed monstrous to ask her what he really wanted to know, but now with so much at stake, he could have a freer hand. If anyone pushed back, he could merely state he needed to get deeper into the killer's mind. Nothing had worked so far. The profile still wasn't complete.

At least not the one he'd accepted. The one his lovely rabbit had compiled was so close to perfect that he'd been forced to bury it.

She walked by him, glancing up with a small, tight smile. She was beautiful. Perfect golden hair and legs that went for miles. She'd gotten a bit fat for his tastes, but there was still a loveliness to her that called out to him. She seemed so perfect from the outside. Smart. Elegant. Lovely. Of course, underneath it all she was just like the rest of them. Exactly like his mother and his dearly departed wife. Women were whores. They couldn't help themselves. If a man offered them a cock, they took it.

And if Special Agent Kincaid and Briggs thought they were the only ones she was fucking, they were fooling themselves. She had obviously been with that obnoxious SEAL, and perhaps the deputy as well. The deputy had a mouth on him. He would love to shut that mouth, but it would have to wait.

Need clawed at his belly as his rabbit ducked away. Briggs tried getting close to her again, but she shook her head.

"I need some air, Cam." She slipped outside.

"Give her a little time." Kincaid stopped his former partner with a firm hand on his shoulder. "We know she's not going anywhere."

"Yeah, she made that clear."

A very large man with scars covering some of his rough face walked in the door carrying two large bags with handles. "Food, anyone?"

Ah, the luncheon. It was coming from some bar. Yes, that would likely be lovely. He forced himself to smile and join in the general drivel about how good a burger would taste.

He needed something more than a piece of meat. His hunger was growing, and he was going to make a mistake if he didn't do something about that. The last five years he'd been very careful, culling only what he needed to get by. He'd performed his rituals, but in a truncated way that never seemed to feed his beast. He would have to do it here, too. His rituals required time and space, neither of which he had, though a plan was forming in his brain. He'd listened in on the ants and their talk. He knew there was at least one private home that wouldn't be occupied for a while. Something about aliens and taking cover. Once he knew where that space was, he could start planning.

But for tonight, a quick fix would have to do.

"Kincaid, Briggs!" The small-town sheriff barked like he had something important to say. The man stood in his office doorway with a ferocious frown on his face. "Seriously? I thought you were going to use my office to talk to her."

Kincaid had the decency to flush, but Briggs was right back to grinning. "Words were said."

"Yeah, I can imagine what was said. Hope, we're going to need some Lysol," the sheriff yelled. "And you, Briggs—get in here, and we're going to have a serious lecture on respecting your new boss's office. Why don't you step in, too, Kincaid. I have a couple of things we can go over."

He didn't like the way that sounded. The last thing he wanted was that pesky sheriff nosing in where he didn't belong.

He needed a distraction. Perhaps he could serve his needs in multiple ways. He could distract the sheriff, feed his need, and put a little fear into his rabbit.

All he needed was a few moments alone with a lovely lady. He had his pick in this town.

Chapter Twelve

Cam settled onto the seat beside Laura and slid his hand around the back of her chair. She was tense, her shoulders set in a way that made him want to get behind her and rub until she relaxed. He wanted to take her home and coddle her until the tightness around her eyes softened and she let him hold her. He and Rafe could take turns.

"Don't cause more scandal than you already have, Cam," Laura murmured low as she moved his hand away from hers. "I can have you thrown out of here."

He frowned. "No one seemed particularly scandalized."

He wasn't upset. Let them all know. If he could, he would have broadcast the whole thing so there was absolutely no question who she belonged to. He would have made damn sure that fucker Wolf Meyer had a front row seat. Why was he still here? He was hanging around the sheriff's department when he didn't have a formal place here. The ex-SEAL still looked at Laura like something he needed to protect. *Bastard.* And he hadn't missed the way all of the feds looked at her. She was a gorgeous woman, but did they all have to look at her like she was the second coming of Marilyn Monroe?

They needed to get their own superintelligent, funny, blonde bombshell. This one was his. And Rafe's. He and Rafe had things to work out, but Cam wasn't going to fight him. It hurt Laura, and damn it, he liked having Rafe around.

She slid a glance his way. "The boys from Bliss might not care, but I assure you, everyone from DC was shocked at what happened."

Was she worried about that? He didn't give a shit what any of them thought. He'd never fit in with them. He'd always been that weird mix of nerd, country boy, and aggressive asshole that no one had liked in the Bureau. No one except Laura and Rafe. "Well, they don't count. The guys from Bliss were just pissed that I hadn't cleaned up. I received explicit instructions on how to have sex in public places. The sheriff has a pamphlet. I've been assured that if I don't follow the rules, he'll shove me in a cell. There's only two, you know. He told me what happened the last time he put Rachel and Max Harper in jail."

There it was. That smile that made his heart skip a beat. Laura's smile lit up his whole fucking world. "Yeah, that particular incident had the gossips going for a day or two. Rachel has a problem with jaywalking. And being mouthy. Nate was in a bad mood at the time. Max sacrificed himself to go to jail with her. He threw a punch at Nate. Needless to say, they had fun while they waited for Rye to post bail. It was late, and it was their date night. They didn't let the fact that they were in jail stop them."

Now see, that was information he was interested in. There were a couple of trios in this town, and he wanted to know how they worked. "They have date nights?"

Laura nodded. "She goes out with each one at least once a week. I believe Callie, Nate, and Zane do it, too. I can imagine it's a good way to keep the relationships intimate. Conversely, I know the boys have boys' nights out."

The door to the interrogation room opened, and Brad walked in, followed by Rafe. Rafe's face was set in dark lines. He wasn't happy to be on the other side of the table, but for now, it was their best choice. They needed to know what was going on from the inside. Joe and Edward followed. The all looked grim and gray, file folders in hand.

Cam remembered what this felt like. There was a certain adrenaline that pumped through any agent's veins before an interview. Even if the agent knew the person in front of him wasn't who he was looking for, there was a certain amount of power that came from being on the right side of the table. Cam definitely felt vulnerable.

Laura's spine straightened. Cam suddenly wished he already had the badge and gun Nate Wright had promised him. There was paperwork to be done, even in a small town. This wasn't his dream job. Far from it. He wasn't sure he had a dream job. He wanted Laura. That would be enough. If he could marry her and provide for her and find some time on the side to write his code, he would be happy. Still, he'd feel safer when he could legally kill someone again. It would make defending Laura so much easier.

If only she would let him defend her now.

Joe sat down. He was in great shape for his age. Rapidly approaching fifty, the special agent in charge looked years younger. He smiled at Laura as he opened his folder. "I'm sorry to have to go over all of this again, Laura. I know it's an old wound for you."

"I don't know about that. It feels pretty fresh today." She clasped her hands together.

"Let's get right to it." Brad sounded unctuous and self-important. He'd changed his shirt and put on a new tie, but he couldn't hide the way his nose bulged. Rafe hadn't broken it. That was a bit disappointing. Brad was in the middle seat, the driver's seat, and he seemed to utterly relish it.

Brad drummed his fingers along the top of the table. "You became involved in the case roughly a year after it had been established that there was a serial killer working the DC area."

Laura took a deep breath and plunged in. "Yes. It was spring

193

roughly six years ago. I moved from another unit. I had been a special agent for four years before that."

Brad huffed. "That's young to join the BAU."

Laura didn't mention the amazing work she'd done in the Crisis Negotiation Unit. She didn't talk about how she'd graduated at the top of her class from Harvard, where she'd put herself through school. She merely shrugged. Cam wanted to shove her exemplary record in Brad's face. She hadn't gotten into the BAU on her looks.

Brad moved on. "So, you came into the unit as a special agent, and roughly a year later, you turned in a profile of the killer known as the Marquis de Sade. Did you realize at the time that you turned in the profile that Senior Special Agent Edward Lock was the unit's senior analyst?"

What the hell was that supposed to mean? Everyone knew that. Cam sat forward. This wasn't going the way he'd thought it would. He caught Rafe's glance, but Rafe seemed as confused as he was.

"Yes," Laura replied. There was a flustered pause in her voice. "I was aware of that."

Brad smirked as though he'd caught her in something. "Who asked you to turn in a profile?"

She tucked a strand of blonde hair behind her ear. "Um, no one, but I thought it was important. I thought I had a fresh look on the case. I have degrees in psychology and criminal justice. I knew what I was doing."

"But no one actually asked you to turn in a profile?" Brad asked.

Rafe sat forward. "Joe told the whole team that any information we gathered on the case would be welcome. He wanted everyone's thoughts. It wasn't out of line for anyone to work up a profile. We're all trained."

Joe nodded. "Yes. I like to keep the lines of communication open. I think it's important for any team. I worked that way then, and I still work that way today."

Edward adjusted the glasses he always toyed with when

interrogating a subject. He put them back on and stared at Laura like a bug he'd pinned down for study.

Cam started to get a bad feeling about the way this was going to go. "What does this have to do with anything?"

Brad held up a hand. "Mr. Briggs, you're here as a courtesy. If you can't stay out of this interview, I'm going to ask you to leave."

He started to get up from his chair. "I'd like to see you try to get rid of me."

Joe shook his head. "Cam, please. I know this is hard, but Special Agent Conrad has reasons for asking the questions he is asking. We spent time deciding on these questions. We all agreed to them. We're in a bind here. We haven't had a break in this case in years. We need a fresh approach."

Laura put a hand over his, and he reluctantly sat down. His heart rate was creeping up along with the need to kick a little ass. He looked back at the large two-way mirror on the opposite side of the room. There would be a whole bunch of people watching this, and one of them would be his new boss, Sheriff Nate Wright. It probably wouldn't do a bit of good to start his new job by punching his former coworkers in the face. He needed this job. He needed to fit into Laura's world.

He forced himself to relax back in his chair as Brad pelted her with questions about how she became involved with the case. Laura answered each one in short, professional terms. She explained why she'd written her profile. She talked about how she'd collected her data. In short, she told the asshole that she'd done her job.

"How long had you known Jana Evans?" Brad asked, flipping through his large folder.

A long sigh came out of Laura's mouth. "I met Jana Evans our freshman year of college. She was studying journalism. We ended up rooming together for a couple of years. After we graduated, she moved to New York, but I moved out to DC when I joined the BAU. She got a job at a TV station in DC about three years later, and we got back in touch."

Brad smirked as he asked his next question. "Is that the time you started to feed her confidential information?"

"What the hell?" Rafe got to the outburst before Cam could. "Joe, what is this? I was told we were asking former Special Agent Rosen about her ideas on who the Marquis de Sade is."

Joe's left eyebrow rose. Sometimes it was easy to forget he wasn't just one of the guys. "You are also here on my sufferance, Special Agent Kincaid. If we hadn't been friends for many years, I would have kicked you off this case the minute I figured out you were sleeping with a witness."

Rafe opened his mouth to argue, but Laura charged in. "In Rafe's defense, I wasn't a witness when I started sleeping with him."

"And Briggs?" Brad practically sneered.

"Well, it was the same night," Laura said brazenly. "So no, I hadn't met the Marquis de Sade at that moment. We were coworkers. It was probably not the most professional thing I could have done, but it had nothing at all to do with the case."

"You better change your line of questioning," Cam said through clenched teeth. He wasn't about to sit here and let them insult her.

"Or we could stop this entirely," Rafe interjected. "Perhaps we should. A lawyer might be helpful."

He didn't disagree at all. It sounded like a perfect idea. Laura didn't need a lawyer for anything criminal, but a lawyer could fuck with these pricks in a way neither he nor Rafe could.

"I'm not getting a lawyer," Laura said with a resigned huff.

"You will if I call one." He hated fighting with her, but he couldn't let her refuse good counsel.

"Just get on with it," Laura said.

Brad's shoulders moved up and down in a negligent shrug, as though he didn't really care, and Cam believed it. "Fine then. If your cavemen are done, I'll move on. In your original report, you talked about a phrase the man who abducted you used. Do you recall what he said to you?"

Laura's eyes took on a haunted, vacant look. She seemed to go somewhere deep inside herself. "He liked to talk. He talked to me for hours. I don't remember a lot of it, but I remembered that one phrase. He told me that the only way to a woman's heart was the path of torment. He said he knew of no other way so sure."

Cam had looked it up. The real Marquis de Sade had written it. The original de Sade had a lot to say, most of it garbage. The Marquis had believed that all moral principals were fancies, not anything concrete or real.

"That's a bit specific," Brad said. "Are you sure that's what he said?"

Now Laura was the one staring through Brad. "Well, a girl rarely forgets what's been said right before a man in a plague doctor's mask whips her, cuts her, and shoves a knife through her gut multiple times. I was tied down and he'd whipped me viciously. I hate to admit it, but he did have my attention."

Cam felt his gut twist. His brain tended to go to a black place when he thought about what had happened to her. When he read it on paper, it was bad enough. When he heard it coming out of her mouth in that dead monotone she employed whenever the subject came up, it was devastating. She'd been taken and brutalized. She'd been tortured for hours. He loved her. Guilt festered like a sore. He was responsible for her. She'd let him take pleasure in her body and solace in her heart. He owed her protection, and he'd failed.

He wasn't going to fail her again.

"And did you recognize the words?" Brad asked.

Why was he still talking? His voice grated on Cam's every nerve.

"Not at the time," Laura admitted. "Later on, I looked it up. It was right after I'd gotten to Bliss. I was in bad shape. I couldn't get those damn words out of my head. I went into Stella's and asked to borrow her computer. I told her I needed check on something. That's when I found it. It's a quote from the Marquis de Sade."

"Donatien Alphonse François, the real Marquis de Sade, had a philosophy attached to his methods. He was imprisoned several times for abusing prostitutes. One was said to have been held for weeks of torture before she managed to escape out a second story window," Edward murmured. He spoke academically, as if he wasn't discussing the torture of a colleague. "He wrote a lot about sexual freedom. Some of his philosophies are interesting."

"We don't need a lecture, professor," Brad grumbled. It seemed to Cam like the special agent didn't enjoy having his spotlight taken away. And he was being rude. Back when Cam was in the unit, Edward hated to be called professor.

Edward's eyes narrowed on the junior agent. "I have a point. I can see where someone of our killer's persuasions would be interested in the Marquis. That isn't surprising. What is surprising is the fact that he adopted the philosophies the press put upon him. I've been thinking about this for a while. It doesn't sit particularly well with me. I would have thought he would be in control of his press, so to speak. I think this validates my own profile. The Marquis de Sade is immature, socially awkward. He's probably making up for a very bad childhood and intense feelings of inadequacy."

"Or he's controlled the press far better than we could have imagined. I can't believe I didn't think about this. I don't believe the man is immature. He's too smart, too in control. He would never follow someone else's lead." Joe leaned forward, a grave look on his face. "Who was the first reporter to name him?"

Motherfucker. He remembered that first televised report well. It had been the report that made Jana Evans's career. How long had Jana been talking to that son of a bitch? What clues had she hidden in her quest for a freaking local Emmy?

"We should get her in here." Rafe's voice was tight with fury.

"Jana would have told us if she was in contact. She wouldn't let a killer roam free to get a story," Laura said.

For the first time since the interview began, there was a hint of emotion in her voice. It was a slight shake that had Cam reaching for her hand despite the obvious reasons not to. Jana had been Laura's friend, but she'd betrayed her in so many ways. How long had she used Laura to further her own career?

How had it felt to wake up after a nightmare and believe no one loved her? She'd felt betrayed by Cam and Rafe and her oldest friend. For the first time, Cam understood why she had walked away and what she had found here.

"You know reporters and their confidential sources," Brad murmured, making notes in his file. "We'll have to bring in Ms. Evans and have a chat. It's convenient that she showed up here in Bliss."

"Yes, it is." Cam cradled her hand in his, satisfied that she didn't pull away.

Everything he learned pointed more and more to Laura being right. There was a leak in the unit, and that leak might be the killer. He studied Brad, Joe, and Edward carefully. Maybe he needed to rethink everything he knew about them. Maybe it was time to trust Laura's instincts. He wondered how far Nate Wright would let him in. Would Nate allow him to use one of the computers to run checks on his former colleagues?

"I would also like to talk to Mr. Wolf Meyer," Edward said, staring down at his notes. "I ran a check on everyone in this town, and I don't like what I've discovered. This whole town is full of misfits and riffraff. But Wolf Meyer interests me. He lived on a base close to DC right up to a few months ago. He took a trip back to DC at a time that places him in the area when the last victim was killed."

Laura's blue eyes rolled. "It's not Wolf. He's a SEAL."

Edward laughed, condescension dripping from his mouth. "Yes, because a military man would never kill anyone. He fits your profile, dear. I would think you would be thrilled I would consider him."

"You're an ass, Edward," Laura stated. "If you've successfully profiled someone before, it was because it was so obvious a monkey could have done it. Wolf has a core of integrity. He practically glows with it."

"I wouldn't say that," Cam grumbled.

Laura smiled up at him. "He doesn't have your sunny disposition, babe."

Why did everything inside him clench when she looked at him like that? Why did his whole fucking world seem okay because she was accepting him? Sunny disposition? He had to smile back. He was a taciturn son of a bitch most of the time. God, he wanted to kiss her. He wanted to take her out of here.

Laura turned back to the agents. "Please, feel free to talk to Wolf. I think you'll find a conversation with him enlightening. I happen to know he spent an awful lot of time overseas doing things for our country you can't even conceive of. Interview everyone in Bliss. I know you're all damn good at wasting time."

"Insults aren't going to get you anywhere," Brad said, his composure slipping a bit.

"She's right." Rafe's hands slapped on the table. "We're wasting time. She's gone over everything. Why are we treating her like a criminal?"

Joe sighed and rubbed a spot between his eyes. "I know she's not a criminal, but she is a bit of a hostile witness. She left town. I can't be sure she won't leave again." He turned his eyes to Laura. "If I offer you protective custody, will you take it?"

"No," Cam said before she could.

If anyone was going to protect her, it would be him and Rafe. If witness protection got involved, they might or might not accept the two of them coming along, and he didn't trust anyone else.

"What he said," Laura admitted with a weary sigh. "I firmly believe that de Sade is law enforcement. Given what you all now suspect about Jana, he might even be on this team."

"That's ridiculous," Edward spat. "No one in the BAU is a serial killer. It's preposterous. The Bureau has systems in place to ensure someone like that would never get in. What do you have against men, Ms. Rosen? I have long suspected that you don't like men."

Joe pointedly cleared his throat and stared between Rafe and Cam. Cam didn't miss the way Laura's mouth turned up.

Edward shook his head. "I didn't say she was a lesbian. She uses men. Probably a great deal of them."

"Says the misogynist," Laura murmured.

Cam turned to Rafe, who seemed just as lost. He'd known Edward was an unctuous little prick, but not that he particularly had it out for Laura. Though now that he remembered back, he could see all the slight ways the senior special agent had tried to cut out the only female on the team. He was always putting down her intellect even as he praised her wardrobe or the way she wore her hair. Edward had tried to make her seem less than the men.

Edward leaned forward. "You weren't able to prove that claim, were you, Ms. Rosen? You tried to put a black mark on my record, but it didn't work."

"Well, I did leave before my meeting with human resources. I guess that was lucky for you," Laura replied.

Cam leaned in. "What did he do to you?"

"I've heard nothing of this," Rafe said, standing up. "Why is Edward being allowed to question a witness with an outstanding complaint against him? He can't exactly be unbiased."

Joe's bark quieted the room. "Neither can you, Kincaid. There's nothing normal or routine about this fucking case. It involves a woman who used to be one of our own. Will you all sit down and shut up, or I swear this is going to be an empty room in two minutes. I will dismiss you, Special Agent, if you can't keep your shit together."

Rafe's jaw clenched, but he visibly calmed and took his seat again.

"Brad, I would like to get this over with. Please continue." Joe sat back, seemingly satisfied he'd gotten everyone on track again.

Brad pinned Laura with his stare. "I only have a couple more questions for Ms. Rosen."

He was ready to get her the fuck out of here. "Make them

quick."

Brad sneered his way. "You'll be the first to go when we start thinning out the room, Briggs." He pulled a set of photos from the folder.

He felt his stomach roll. He knew those photos. They were the same photos Rafe had been showing when Cam had found him in DC to tell him about Laura. They haunted him. Black and white. Stark. A woman in bondage, her unseeing eyes looking up at the camera. It didn't matter that he couldn't see the red of the blood. He could smell it. Acrid and coppery. He hadn't been at the scene of this woman's death, but he'd seen enough of this killer's work firsthand to know what it had been like. Clinical and pristine, the Marquis de Sade didn't leave evidence in his wake, merely death and heartbreak. Even prostitutes had people who missed them, loved them, mourned them forever. He'd come so close to being one of those left behind.

Brad's voice cut through his introspection. "This is the woman we believe now to be the latest victim of the Marquis de Sade. You can't see it in the black and white version, but she's wearing the same lipstick he put on you. The same lipstick he puts on all his victims. This occurred after you left DC and refused to help further with the investigation. The Marquis de Sade is working again. Do you feel a certain culpability in her death?"

Rafe stood and, before anyone could do a damn thing, had his fist on his partner's face. He pummeled the son of a bitch, and chaos reigned. The room exploded in shouting.

Joe yelled at the two men to stand down. Edward moved out of the line of fire. Brad tried to fight back, but Rafe was meaner and way angrier. The door to the room opened, and Nate Wright entered with his deputy, pulling the men off of one another. The room seemed overheated. It was too loud, too full of testosterone. Cam was about to jump into the fray when he looked down and saw Laura.

She sat as still as a doll, staring at those photos. Her eyes were locked, her mouth slightly open. Guilt was easy to read on her face.

As everyone continued to shout, Cam dropped to one knee. "No, baby, this isn't your fault."

She didn't look at him, but a single tear dropped from her eyes and splashed on the table.

Nate finally managed to pull Rafe off the man who would almost assuredly be his ex-partner as soon as the Bureau could fill out the paperwork. Logan got Brad to his feet.

"I'll call Doc. This one is pretty messed up." Logan didn't seem to be bothered by the blood. The big, might-be-on-steroids deputy looked down at Brad. "You talk to her like that again, and I'll be the one fucking you up, you understand that?"

"Logan." Nate said the word between clenched teeth, and Logan walked out of the room.

Joe scrubbed a hand through his hair as he stared at Rafe. "Damn it, Kincaid. You leave me no choice. You are off this case. You'll catch the first flight back to DC, and I'll deal with you when this is over."

Rafe didn't even blink. He pulled his gun and badge out and laid them on the table. "I quit. You'll have a formal resignation tomorrow."

Joe stared, widemouthed. "You've got ten years in, son. Are you sure you want to do this?"

Rafe swallowed once, but nodded. "One of us will be legally married to Laura as soon as possible. We'll have full legal rights. You won't be able to shut us out. If you try, I swear to god I'll bring the press in, and someone out there will write a hell of a story about how the Bureau is harassing victims because they can't get the job done. You will leave my wife alone."

Joe turned to Laura. "You understand what he's trying to do? He's going to bully you. He's going to shut you off somewhere and hope this all goes away. It hasn't gone away, and it won't."

Laura turned those tear-filled eyes upward. "You want to use me as bait."

"That is not going to happen." Cam stood and did what he'd wanted to do from the moment he'd found out the feds were in town. He picked her up, hooking his arm under her knees and pulling her to his chest. She didn't fight, but she didn't exactly cuddle against him, either. "You can fuck yourself, Joe."

"You going to run away again, Rosen?" Brad's face was still bleeding.

Edward shook his head. "How many more women will die because you're too scared to face him?"

Rafe started toward Edward. Cam was almost to the door when he heard Laura's reply.

"I'll do it."

Chapter Thirteen

Rafe felt his stomach flip as he walked out of the interrogation room.

He'd quit his job. He didn't have a job. He didn't have a badge or a gun or a future.

Cam turned, and Rafe saw the only things he had left in this world. Laura and Cameron. His family. Well, he wasn't about to let the only thing he had left slip through his fingers. "You will not be bait."

"Rafe, not here." Cam turned again. "Let's get her home, and we can hash this out without an audience."

God, where was he going wrong that Cam had to be the sensible one? His fist still ached from the battering he'd given Brad, but he would do it again. They had led her like a lamb to slaughter. He could see it now. They had beaten her down, gotten her emotional, and then pulled the final card out that sent her over the edge. They'd played her like a fiddle, and he was ready to kill them all.

What if one of them knew exactly what he was doing? What if one of them had been watching her with predatory eyes?

"Kincaid."

He turned at the sheriff's sharp bark. Wolf Meyer stood beside Wright. Rafe had a sudden bad feeling that the sheriff had let the SEAL watch things play out. Despite what Edward had said, he didn't believe for an instant that Meyer had anything to do with this. "What is it? If you're planning on telling me to get the hell out of your town, then you can think again."

To his surprise, the sheriff smiled. "No, I was going to congratulate you on growing a pair. You should have done that a long time ago."

"I knew he had a set when he took down that asshole. Conrad was snooping around Laura's cabin, and this guy here gets the jump on him before I could. That's saying something," Wolf admitted.

The sheriff tilted his hat back and regarded him with an assessing stare. "There's a town meeting concerning Laura. You need to be there. Town hall, seven o'clock."

Wolf's eyes rolled back. "Yeah, I have to go set up the computers. Just because mom and Mel are hiding out doesn't mean they aren't civic-minded. They intend to attend the meeting via the Internet, and since the Farley brothers messed up our cell tower, I have to do this all without using wireless. God, I long for a day when they can't get hold of me from that bunker. Maybe I can somehow prove to Mel that aliens can get to him through his dial-up connection."

Rafe promised the men he would be there. If he could get the whole town looking out for Laura, it might make things easier. They could look for someone who shouldn't be there—only he was starting to believe that maybe the killer was already in Bliss.

He wanted to get Cam on the Edward angle right away. Rafe's brain raced as he moved toward the parking lot. Laura and Edward had some sort of beef he hadn't known anything about. Brad was acting like an ass. Brad had been around the Bureau for a long time before he joined the BAU. And Joe. God, was he actually wondering if his mentor was a serial killer?

He wouldn't let it stop him. He would investigate every single one of them until he figured it out. This was what he should have done five years before.

Rafe slammed out of the double doors, practically running to keep up. He stopped in his tracks at what he saw. Standing right there in front of his SUV—crap, it was technically the Bureau's SUV—stood Jana Evans, microphone at the ready. Cam had put Laura on her feet, and they both faced the tiny ball of spite.

"Would you like to tell our viewers about your experience with the Marquis de Sade?" Jana asked in a brisk, professional voice. She wore what had to be a thousand-dollar suit and killer stilettos, but there was a gauntness to her frame that utterly turned Rafe off. "We would all love to know how you managed to escape a killer who never makes a mistake."

Cam stepped in front of Laura, his big body a barrier between her and the world. "You get the hell out of here. Move that van out of the way."

"Not until I get my story, I won't." Jana shoved her microphone toward Laura's face. "This is the one that puts me over the edge. I'll get on at one of the cable giants after this."

"Are you live?" Laura asked.

"No. The time difference wouldn't work, but if you want to do a live shot, I can be back here for the eleven o'clock news at nine o'clock. We would have to broadcast then." Jana practically vibrated with energy. "I would need to meet you a little earlier to get you ready."

Rafe was about to forbid it when Laura nodded at Jana. "Come out to the town hall. We can do it there."

She walked around the news van toward the SUV Rafe had driven out here. Rafe stopped in front of the reporter. "She's not doing this."

Jana gave him a tight-lipped smiled that came nowhere close to her eyes. Her icy blonde hair was in a tight, professional bun. It was so different from Laura's natural honey color. "Laura always does what she wants to, Rafe. You should know that. She won't listen to you now. See you tonight. Don't think you're getting on camera. I already have an FBI source."

He bet she did.

Rafe hopped into the SUV right before Cam took off. Laura had taken the passenger seat, leaving him in the back. He leaned forward, trying to force his way into her space. "What was that about? You can't go on television."

Her stony face stared back at him. "Sure I can. It's what they want. It puts a huge target on me."

"You already have a target on your back," Cam pointed out, his voice tight with tension.

"It will be a beacon when I'm done with that interview," Laura replied.

He could guess what she was going to do. She was going to get on TV and taunt the Marquis de Sade. She would know exactly what to say to get his rage going. By the time she was done, there would be no question about him coming after her. It was everything those fuckers would want. "I forbid it."

"You can't forbid anything," she replied with a sigh.

He chose to ignore her. "How fast can we be in Vegas, Cam?"

Laura turned, her face marred by a nasty frown. "We're not going to Vegas."

"If I break speed limits, I can get us there in ten hours." Cam paused at the street as though trying to make the decision.

Laura stared at Cam. "If you want me to run again, this is the way to do it."

Cam turned toward her cabin. *Pussy.* As if he could hear Rafe's thoughts, his eyes pleaded through the rearview mirror. "What am I supposed to do? We can't make her marry us."

Rafe didn't see why not. "I can think of several ways."

"It's not happening," Laura said, a stubborn set to her chin. "You're going to drop me off at my place, and then you can leave. Both of you."

Cam turned to her. "I'm not going anywhere. I told you that. I told you that you couldn't get rid of me. For god's sake, Laura, we made love not an hour ago."

"We had sex," she shot back.

"You told me you loved me," Cam replied, his voice thick with emotion.

Rafe sat, wishing he'd had the chance to pull her in back with him. He could see plainly what she was doing. He wished he'd done more than ruined Brad Conrad's face. By showing her those photos and playing on her guilt, Brad had undone all the progress he and Cam had made with her. Brad had shoved her back into that place where she was alone and helpless.

He wasn't about to let her stay there. "Can I finish this conversation for you, *bella*? I know precisely how it is going to go. Now you're going to tell Cam that you didn't mean it. You're going to tell him that making love in the sheriff's office meant nothing. You were telling him what he wanted to hear because he was being unreasonable. Cam is going to get hurt and sit there in sullen silence while you turn to me and tell me the same thing. You're going to lay down the law. You're going to push us both out by telling us you never loved us and you like your life here without us. You're going to tell us to go home and forget about you. Am I close?"

She crossed her arms over her chest. "Well, I was going to curse more."

Yes, she probably would have. He shook his head. "You're being a self-sacrificing idiot."

"Is this about the case?" Cam asked, clearly confused.

"No," he replied. "It's far more than the case." He couldn't forget the haunted look on Laura's face as she'd told him they didn't need to use a condom. "She's feeling guilty about a lot of things. She's feeling the weight of those women's deaths. She's also feeling unworthy. She loves us, but she doesn't know how to be with us."

"That is such bullshit," Laura shot back. "I think I know how to be with you, Rafe. I just have to let you pin me to the nearest flat surface. That's all you require."

She wasn't going to get to him that easily. "I don't require a surface at all, *bella*. When I want you, I'll simply lift that skirt, pick you up, and impale you on my cock."

Cam shook his head. "Yeah, baby, I can totally do it standing up."

He couldn't miss the way her fists clenched in her lap as Laura replied. "There's more to a relationship than sex."

He wanted to wrap his arms around her, to touch her, but he held off. "Yes, there's far more. There's also more to a marriage than giving birth to children."

She flushed, her delicate skin turning pink in a heartbeat.

Cam stopped the car in the middle of the road. "She thinks we don't want her because she can't have kids?"

He'd known they would have to deal with this sometime. "I believe Laura is seeing herself as the noose that's going to take us both down."

Cam turned back to the road and started driving again. "You're right—she's being a martyr."

"You've both quit your jobs for me," she said, though a bit of the fire had left her voice.

"I never liked it much anyway," Cam said flippantly. "I was only there for the nookie, and when you walked away, that dried up."

She slapped a hand on the dashboard. "This is serious, damn it."

Cam shrugged as he sped up. "I am serious. I would have quit that job a long time ago if it hadn't been for you and Rafe. I'm not like some of these guys. I don't want to be knee-deep in bodies. It drags on me. I like programming. I liked building the program that found you. I'm going to stay here in Bliss and work my job and come home, and after I fuck you into submission, I'll work on my facial recognition program."

"You are not staying with me."

"So, throw me out," Cam challenged. "When you can pick me up and toss me out, I'll sit in your doorway until you let me back

210

in."

"I won't," Rafe vowed. "I'll slip back in again and again."

"Damn it, Rafe," she hissed under her breath. "Be reasonable. Go back to Joe and get your job back. You know he'll take you back in a heartbeat. Cam might not have loved the Bureau, but you're a lifer, and you know it. You relish that job. It's everything you worked for."

He had loved the job, but he loved Laura more. The job he'd spent his whole life preparing for had threatened to chew up and spit out the only woman he'd ever loved. In the end, there wasn't a choice to be made. He wouldn't love the Bureau with his whole heart. He wouldn't cuddle the fucking Bureau at night. The Bureau wouldn't grow old with him. "I'm not going back. I don't know what I'll do from here, but I can't go back."

"That is insane," Laura said.

"Why? Didn't you walk away from a life that you thought didn't work for you anymore? That's what I'm doing. I'm walking away. The world is a big place. When one thing stops working, you walk out and find something else. As long as I have you, I'll be fine."

She shook her head. "No. You don't have me. I won't do this. I won't be the reason you lose your job and your family. What would your mother say? Or are you asking me to choose between you and Cam again?"

He knew she was making a certain amount of sense, but his sense had been tossed out a long time ago. There were a hundred things wrong about this relationship, but only one thing mattered. He loved her. "My mother can choose to accept me as I am, or she can stop talking to me. I'll still love her. I'll still try to take care of her. I can't force her to respond the way I want. I can only be responsible for my own actions. I can't fix the outside world, *bella*. I can only promise to make our personal world as perfect as I can."

"You won't be happy." She turned and stared out the window.

"Don't tell me how I'll feel," he shot back. "I know how I have felt for the last five years. Broken and useless."

He'd been missing a piece of his soul since the day she'd walked away. His badge, his job, his family meant nothing if he couldn't get her back. He loved his mother, but Laura was his soul. If there was a choice to be made, he'd made it the minute he quit the Bureau. Frustration welled up inside him. A few hours ago, he'd been deep inside her. Now he could feel her pulling away.

She turned from him, her eyes shifting to the road ahead. "You get over it, you know. That broken, useless feeling won't last forever. You find something else to love, and you move on. You make a better life."

Every word from her mouth made his heart ache. "And you found a better life."

"I found this place. I love my friends. Do you know how long it took me to let one of them in? It was years. Nell was such a little flake. She was one of the first people I met here. She made me zucchini bread. I took one look at her and decided that she was safe. She wasn't smart enough to hurt me." Rafe could hear the tears in Laura's voice. "I love her. God, I love her. I wouldn't have given her the time of day when I was in DC. She would have been an amusing airhead, but I have learned more about truly loving the people around me from Nell than I could have imagined. She believes in so much more than I can. And Holly. Holly will do anything for a friend, but I rebuffed her for years because I wasn't going to let another Jana get her hooks in me. I broke my foot one winter. Holly ran out of her cabin, and she got me to the hospital in Del Norte, and she brought me home and fed me. She worked my shift for a week so I didn't lose my job. I hadn't done anything for her. I had been nothing but cold."

"She saw the real you," Cam said quietly.

She took a steadying breath. "I don't know that I knew the real me until I came here. I don't know that I would be this me if I went someplace else. Maybe part of figuring out who we are is finding a place to call home. What I'm trying to say is that it was hard, but I got over it. I'm happy here. You'll be happy one day, Rafe. One day you'll wake up, and your kids will jump all over you, and you'll go to work as the special agent in charge, and your mom will be so proud. You'll look back, and I'll be nothing more than a memory. You'll thank me."

His hands were shaking. He had the sudden realization that this wasn't going to go the way he had planned. She wasn't going to give in because he kissed her senseless. "I won't. If you won't take me, I won't thank you, *bella*. I could handle it if I thought I wasn't the best man for you. Hell, I'm willing to share you because I know you need Cam, too. If you won't accept me, my life won't be filled with kids and this great career. It'll be filled with regret because I know why you're really rejecting me. You can't forgive me. You can't put what happened behind you."

Her blonde hair shook, but she didn't bother to turn around. "This isn't about what happened to me. This is about you and Cam. Neither one of you can be happy here. It isn't in you."

"Really?" Cam asked, his bitterness dripping. "I'm such a city boy. I've never lived in the country."

"You hated it," Laura pointed out.

"No, I hated the small-minded attitudes that put my mother at the bottom of the social feeding order," Cam argued. "I love the country. I love the peace and quiet, and if you think you can force me to leave, you're wrong. You might not want me, but by god, you'll see me. I'm not leaving. If I find this magical, mystical woman who can complete me by spitting out my kids and proving her womb works, then you'll have to watch. You'll have to watch me make a life for myself here and know that it could have been yours. Baby, I can't tell you how much I wish I could change what happened. If I could give my fucking life to have spared you that, I would. I made a horrible mistake and you paid for it, but I'm here now. I've gotten on my knees and begged forgiveness. I can't do any more than tell you that I love you, and I'll try my damnedest to never fail you again. If you can't forgive me, then you'll watch me.

213

You'll watch me live my life here, without you."

Cam pulled in front of Laura's small cabin. It was tiny and far from Rafe's traditional level of comfort, yet he'd been happy here briefly. He'd woken up this morning knowing where he belonged—beside her. Now she was pulling away, and he had the distinct impression that his caveman act wasn't going to work this time. He could force her to Vegas, but he couldn't make her marry him. He couldn't make her accept him. Fuck, he couldn't force her to forgive him.

Maybe he didn't deserve forgiveness.

Laura slammed out of the car the instant it stopped. She walked to her door and disappeared behind it. Rafe felt like someone had shredded his insides. He threw open the car door and got out, utterly unsure of what to do next. He couldn't leave. He thought briefly about walking in after her, throwing her down, and fucking her until she admitted that she loved them, but that wouldn't work in the long run. She would just go back to her self-martyrdom as soon as the flush of orgasm faded.

She hadn't forgiven him. Not even close.

He walked, unsure of where he was going. The early evening air was crisp though it was technically still summer. The grass at his feet was a lush green and sprinkled with wild flowers. Reds and whites and blues and purples dotted the carpet of grass as he walked closer to the river. He stared down at the Rio Grande. It looked deep and cold. It flowed on endlessly.

How the fuck was he supposed to deal with this? Her pain was his fault. He'd served her up on a silver platter because his career had meant more to him than her pride.

God, he wanted to take it all back.

"Don't." Cam was suddenly beside him. "Don't give in to it."

"What are you talking about?" Rafe asked, but he thought he knew.

"The guilt. It doesn't solve anything, brother. I feel the weight of it. I feel it every time I look at that scar on her belly. We fucked up. We can't let it affect the rest of our lives."

"I don't see why not. It affects the rest of hers."

"Only because she's letting it," Cam replied. "I meant what I said. I love her. I won't leave her again. If that means I'm a deputy in a small town, then that's what I'll be. If my penance for failing her is never touching her again, then I'll stand back and protect her from afar, but I don't think she'll resist for long. When I was in the office with her, there wasn't some horrible guilt between us."

Rafe hadn't felt it. All he'd felt was his connection to her. But then she'd rejected him.

Cam put a hand on his shoulder. "I don't think you should leave, either."

He was surprised at that. "Why? If I left, you could have her all to yourself."

"And be alone? I don't think so. She's a hell of a woman. I think it takes two to handle her."

Emotion choked him, and he finally fucking understood. This was why it could work. This pain he felt was halved because Cam took some of it. If Cam was here with him, then he was never alone. Cam would be beside him. A strange sense of love and gratitude flooded Rafe's system. *Love? Damn.* He shouldn't think that way about his best friend, but then again—why the fuck not? He didn't want to jump Cam. He had zero desire to have anything physical with the man. But maybe love was a lot of different things. Maybe love was a word that defied simple explanation.

Family. That was another one of those words that he wasn't sure of anymore. His family, it seemed, was outside the norm.

"Stay with me," Cam said. "We can get her back. I know we can."

Rafe nodded, far too emotional to speak. He wasn't leaving. Not when he'd found his home.

Chapter Fourteen

"I think we should consider hiring a bodyguard for Laura and perhaps some security for the town," Nate was saying into the microphone. "Special Agent Kincaid gave us the name of a company that might be good to work with."

Laura felt like a freak. She'd tried to take a seat in the back, but Holly had shown up and pulled her to the front, explaining that the only reason she wasn't onstage was that Nate had told everyone he didn't want to put her on display.

Nice to know Nate Wright was on the job.

"I have a call in," the sheriff continued, looking down at his notepad. "I'm going to talk to a man named Ian Taggart tomorrow about the potential of sending a couple of his men into town."

She groaned inwardly at herself. She was in a terrible mood. She'd been sitting in this chair for an hour while Nate went over what was happening with the rest of the town. At some point, she'd noticed that Joe, Brad, and Edward had filed in, but they had kept to themselves.

The fact that everyone knew about her past rankled. She wouldn't be proud, strong, competent Laura Niles anymore. She would be that victim, Laura Rosen.

Henry stood up.

Nate shook his head. "I'm sorry. By men, I meant men or women. Although I'm pretty sure the bodyguards are all men. I wasn't trying to be sexist."

Henry shook his head. "No, I wasn't…are you talking about McKay-Taggart? The security firm in Dallas?"

She wasn't about to let the town pay for bodyguards. She had no idea what Nate was thinking. He'd gone over the facts of the case and what to look for. Everyone was supposed to be on the lookout for suspicious behavior. Everyone was supposed to stick together. There was a lot of talk about how Bliss had come through time and time again. She'd felt a bit numb through it all. The only thing that had warmed her was the way Cam and Rafe encircled her. Even though she wasn't talking to them, she appreciated their presence. What the hell was she going to do if she couldn't get them to leave?

She wanted them. God, it welled up inside her until she almost couldn't breathe.

Rafe raised a hand. "It's former Special Agent Kincaid and yes, that's the firm I recommend. I used to work with Alex McKay and Eve St. James. They're former FBI as well, and from what I understand his partner Ian Taggart has actually worked with Stefan Talbot before."

"He's super hot." Jen piped up from the back. "He came and helped get me out of prison. I'm pretty sure he's the one who gave Stef the handcuffs."

"I had my own, love," Stef replied. "But I agree that Taggart could be helpful in this situation."

Henry shook his head. "No. We absolutely can't hire that firm."

Laura sat up a little straighter. She'd met Alex McKay once, but didn't know a lot about the man. Still, Henry was helping her case, so she wasn't about to argue with him.

"And why not?" Rafe didn't have the same problem. "They're excellent. They have a great reputation. If the county won't pay for it, I'll pay myself."

She hated the fact that they were fighting. "I don't need a bunch of bodyguards."

But everyone was looking at Henry. The men were all eyeing him like he was crazy. Henry had flushed a nice shade of red. Nell was staring up at him like she didn't quite understand.

"They don't recycle," Henry said primly. "And I recently read an article linking private security firms to civil wars in the third world."

Nell gasped and the bullhorn came up.

Nate held up a hand. "We'll table this until tomorrow after I have my talk with Taggart." Nell opened her mouth, but Nate was quicker. "I'll ask him about his recycling practices and how he feels about civil wars."

Yeah, that Taggart guy might not want to take the job at all after he got a whiff of their particular brand of crazy.

"Let's move on," Nate said as quickly as he could in an obvious attempt to stop Nell from protesting.

At least they had gotten to the fun part of the evening. Open forum always lifted her spirits. A few minutes later, she was happily watching the show.

"You have got to make a law or something," Max Harper was saying, his voice all growly and taciturn as he faced the small group onstage.

Cam sat on one side of her and Rafe on the other. Despite her locking them out of her cabin, they'd been standing on her porch waiting for her when she emerged to go to the meeting at town hall. They hadn't said a word, simply opened the door to the car. She'd decided not to be stupid. Taking her own battered Jeep would have been an act of defiance. If de Sade was stalking, she shouldn't be alone, and calling Holly or Nell into it seemed like a dumb thing to do.

Cam leaned across her to talk to Rafe. "Is he talking about what I think he's talking about?"

Laura couldn't miss the way Rafe's lips quirked. "I believe he is."

"It's a natural process, Max," Rachel shouted, proving she didn't need a microphone. "How the hell else am I supposed to feed our baby?"

Hiram, Bliss's elderly mayor, leaned forward and spoke into his microphone. "Max, this seems like something private between you and your wife."

"Oh, I wish it was private," Max shot back. "If it was private, I wouldn't be standing here, but my wife's boobs are everywhere now. I would like to see a show of hands of the people who have been treated to the sight of my wife's nipples."

No one took that bait. Laura figured Max would have written down some names for a future ass kicking.

"I'm feeding the baby!" Rachel argued. "I don't know what your problem is, Max. Rye is fine with it."

There was a tap on Laura's shoulder. She turned around to where Jen sat with Stef. Jen's eyes were lit with mirth, while Stef watched the proceedings with the lazy amusement of a king being brilliantly entertained. "I brought chocolate-covered peanuts. Want some?"

Laura couldn't help but smile. "You knew about this particular topic?"

Jen nodded. "Oh, yeah. Rachel is sick of using the privacy blanket when she breastfeeds in public. Paige doesn't like it. So she's started plopping those suckers out whenever Paige cries. Max walked into Stella's the other day and almost had a heart attack when he saw Rachel without her shirt on. I also know something else."

Stef's eyes narrowed. "Are you about to gossip, love?"

Jen flushed slightly. "No. It's not going to be a secret in about thirty seconds."

Rye Harper approached the microphone. He walked up to his brother and placed a hand on his shoulder, as though about to calm

219

his twin down as he so often did. He leaned forward. "I'm with Max on this one."

"Rye Harper!"

"We decided our marriage was a democracy a long time ago, baby," Rye replied. "We're outvoting you."

Nell stood, her pretty face red with indignation. She brought her own microphone up. "I am making an announcement. I intend to back Rachel in this horrible affront to her rights as a mother. As long as Rachel's freedom to do something as gentle and pure as making sure her child is fed is being taken from her, I cannot stand in silence."

"Oh, shit," Laura said as Nell's hand went to the bottom of her T-shirt. Laura had a pretty damn good idea what was about to happen.

She pulled the T-shirt over her head. "My breasts will be free. You can place me in jail. You can silence me, but I will not give in. I vow to remain uncovered until my sisters are free."

She started to get up, but Henry was there before her. *Damn.* Now everyone was going to see Henry's privates, too. This was rapidly devolving.

Henry picked his wife up, shoving her over his shoulder in a neat fireman's hold.

Nell, never one to drop a microphone, held it even as Henry started walking. "Henry? What are you doing?"

Henry walked straight up to Max and Rye and spoke into their microphone. "Handle this one, people. She really will walk around all bare-breasted warrior-like until you figure this out, and then I'll have to break my vow of nonviolence by killing every son of a bitch who looks at her."

"Henry!"

His head shook as though in deep disappointment. "You see. I cursed. I don't curse. This is bringing out all the caveman-like tendencies I normally despise. We're going to join Mel and Cassidy until such time as my wife can keep her nudity to the places it belongs. Our bedroom. Our yard. The Naturist Community. Various clubs. The swimming hole behind the Harper Stables. Stef's guesthouse. That club in Dallas. Yeah, you know the one. Everyone's naked there. See, I know you all believe I have no boundaries. There. Firmly placed boundaries. Oh, and you know, I've rethought. McKay-Taggart is probably great, and we do need some help if there's a serial killer on the loose. We should hire McKay. I'm pretty sure it's the Taggart guy who doesn't recycle. Someone give us a call when it's safe to come out again."

Nell was yelling into her microphone as Henry carted her off to Mel's.

On the computer screen Wolf had set up, Cassidy Meyer grinned and rubbed her hands together. "Company. That will be nice."

Hiram shook his head. "We're shelving this until next week. Max, Rye, Rachel—you work this out. The last thing this town needs is an article on how we're the topless town."

"It might make them forget we're the murder town," Zane called out.

Hiram sighed. "If there's nothing else on the agenda, we should consider ourselves adjourned."

Nate stood up, microphone in hand. "You all remember what we talked about. No female in this town goes unescorted until this guy is caught. If you find yourself without someone to walk with, call the sheriff's department. One of my deputies or I will come and get you. In addition, the men of the town have agreed to be on call, so to speak. I want everyone to take a flyer with phone numbers. Do not hesitate to call." He stared out over the auditorium as if he could intimidate the audience into obeying him. "If I find out that someone's broken this rule, well, you know I don't mind arresting people. It's one of the joys of my life."

Rafe looked across her toward Cam. "Your new boss is interesting."

Cam grinned. "I think my new boss is slightly insane."

Cam's open, easy smile told her he was looking forward to working with the sheriff. She studied him for a moment as he and Rafe talked about what had gone on. Cam didn't seem uneasy. He'd walked around introducing himself to people, telling them all about how he was the new deputy. If he was ashamed of his new job, he didn't show it.

Rafe had been right behind him, though he'd been quieter than usual. She hadn't missed how he'd spoken to Nate and the mayor before the meeting had begun. He'd had a series of notes that Laura hadn't had a chance to peek at. She seriously suspected he was the one behind the "no woman left unescorted" rule.

Holly walked up, a big grin on her face. "I always knew Henry was hiding the dark heart of a predator."

Henry? Laura laughed. "Henry loves Nell. He merely proved he's a guy. Though I was worried for a moment that he would join her in her nude protest."

"Nah," Cam said. "That dude's a total freak. I bet he spanks her regularly."

Rafe concurred. "Absolutely. I was watching him. He would be indulgent, but he's also possessive. She would be able to push him very far, but once his foot is down, it would not come back up."

"Is this that profiling stuff?" Holly asked.

"No," Cam replied, giving Holly that good-old-boy grin that caused Laura's heart to speed up. Holly was a beautiful woman. How long would it be before Cam gave up on her and went after Holly? Could she really bear to watch her best friend with one of her men? Why was she even thinking that? They were just talking to each other. "I'm a guy, too. I know how I am. If a man truly loves a woman, he's bound to be possessive."

"And he certainly wouldn't allow his woman to walk around showing off what belongs to him," Rafe said, staring squarely at her.

Holly's gaze bounced back and forth, as though watching an amusing tennis match. "Well, here in Bliss, we have some awfully liberal clothing-optional laws."

Cam frowned. "No, you don't. I was given all the codes, and I was informed to strictly enforce the dress code. The Naturist Community is the only place where it's relaxed. Well, and apparently the pond behind the Harper Stables and that other place Henry said—the guesthouse—but I don't know what that is yet."

Stef Talbot laughed, a silky sound. "I'm sure you'll find out, Deputy Briggs. Most people do."

Laura threw him her most intimidating stare. Stef's guesthouse was a playroom. It was filled with sex toys and totally equipped for BDSM play. Cam and Rafe were not going there.

"As to that end, gentlemen, would you please join me in my office?" Stef asked. "There's something I would like to talk to you about."

Cam and Rafe stood and agreed to meet with Stef.

Laura pulled Stef back. "What is this about?"

Stef's eyebrows rose, and he went from friendly to intimidating in a second. "You, of course. I understand your men are staying. Did you not think we would welcome them properly? It's nothing more than some guy talk and perhaps a Scotch."

"They aren't my men."

Stef shrugged her off. "Well, then what I say to them isn't your business. Logan is going to watch you."

She glanced back, and the big deputy was standing close by. He tipped his hat to her but didn't smile. Damn, when was that boy going to smile again? "I don't need a babysitter."

"Consider him a bodyguard. And don't even try to tell me you don't need one of those." Stef nodded and walked off toward the hallway that led to the town hall's offices. Stef held the title of Bliss's County Engineer and kept an office there.

Jen put a hand on her arm. "He means well. Don't worry about it. He won't do anything to hurt you." She looked across the hall. "Oh, crap. I think Rachel's about to break her vow not to kill someone around her daughter."

Jen ran off.

Holly stood up and put an arm around her. "Are you sure this is the way you want to go? Those men seem to really care about you."

And that was the trouble. They loved her. They weren't thinking straight. She couldn't stand the thought that one day they would wake up and realize everything they had given up to be with her. "It wouldn't work. I don't want to marry anyone."

"Okay," Holly said, but Laura could tell she didn't believe her.

Wolf walked up, a smile on his handsome face. "Holly, I've been assigned to escort you home. Your chariot awaits, if you consider a big-ass truck to be a chariot, darlin'."

Holly started to smile, but a low voice cut through the crowd. "No."

Laura turned with Wolf and Holly to see Caleb Burke standing close, his hands in his pockets and a ferocious frown on his face. The gorgeous doctor was staring a hole through Wolf.

"No?" Wolf asked.

Caleb shook his head. "No."

"Care to elaborate?"

"No." Caleb walked up and placed a hand on Holly's elbow. "She needs someone to drive her home. It's not going to be you. Come on."

Holly was staring up at the doctor as she allowed herself to be led off.

"Do I smell or something?" Wolf asked. "Because I can't seem to catch a break today."

Laura watched as Holly walked off with the doctor. "He's one of those guys who can't seem to commit but doesn't want to let go."

"Well, I wasn't hitting on her," Wolf protested.

She raised an eyebrow.

"Much," Wolf admitted. "Hey, I'm on the rebound." He turned very serious. "Those men keep watching you."

She turned and saw who he meant. Joe, Edward, and that asshole Brad were talking amongst themselves, ignoring everyone around them. They stared at her in turns and talked behind their hands as though deciding on an assessment.

"They're trying to decide if I'm going to be murdered tonight," she said.

Wolf paled. "No."

"Now you sound like Caleb."

"Damn it, Laura, I know Rafe and Cam offered to take you away. Tell me they didn't."

"They did," she agreed.

"Then why the hell aren't you gone? Why aren't you miles down the road?"

No one understood. "I have to face him. I ran once, and now there's another dead girl. I'm the one who got away. He'll come after me. He has to. It isn't in his nature to leave something undone. He's been stewing for years about the fact that I got away. This is the only way to catch him. If he's allowed to continue, he'll never stop."

"Fine, then let someone else be the decoy," Wolf suggested. "Surely they can bring in someone with your height and coloring."

She'd thought of that herself but discarded the notion. "It won't fool him. He's clever, and for all I know, he would be the one picking the decoy."

Wolf breathed deeply, his chest expanding. "You seriously think he's already here?"

"I know it. He's here, Wolf, and he will come for me." Laura turned and walked off, Logan following behind her. She needed to find a bathroom. She had an interview to do.

* * * *

"Scotch?" Stef Talbot asked, holding up a crystal decanter of amber liquid.

Cam shook his head. He didn't need anything screwing with his faculties. Not even a single drink. He was already a bit nervous about leaving Laura, but Stef had assured him that Logan Green would watch over her. She wouldn't be allowed to leave the safety of town hall. "No, but thank you."

Rafe shook his head as well. It seemed they were in sync. They had been since they stood out by the river and contemplated what the hell they would do if Laura didn't let them back in. Stef shrugged and poured three glasses. He passed them to the men in the room. Nate Wright took his with a nod, and his partner, a big dude named Zane Hollister, took the other.

Cam waited impatiently for someone to tell him why he was here.

The door to Stef's office opened, and the twin cowboys with the wife who liked to feed her child walked in.

"Damn, Stef, give me some of that. Rachel is pissed off," one of them said.

The other grinned. "And not just at me, brother. I told you she wouldn't know what to do if we presented a united front."

"Yeah," the first one said morosely. "Now we're both cut off."

"Max, don't worry. It never lasts long. She can't help herself."

Max frowned his brother's way. "It didn't work. She was sitting in the middle of town hall with Paige hanging off her boob, and this time she actually took the bra off. She's sitting there like an amazon warrior woman and all the other women were standing around in solidarity."

Rye frowned. "Yeah, I was actually a little afraid of them. We might need to back off this one."

"You should have thought about that before, brother."

Stef looked at the two with great affection. It was easy to see they were all friends, which begged the question of why he and Rafe had been called into this meeting of a close-knit group.

"Gentlemen, I appreciate the invitation, but my partner and I need to get back to Laura," Rafe said in a firm but polite tone.

Cam nodded. He would have simply said "what the fuck." Rafe was better at the social conventions.

"Partner? Is he really your partner?" Stef asked, staring at both of them.

What was that supposed to mean? Cam tried to explain. "We used to be partners when we both worked for the Bureau."

They all exchanged looks, heads shaking, eyes narrowing. They seemed to be communicating amongst each other, as though that was the answer they had all expected and it disappointed them.

"That's what we thought," the sheriff said.

"Amateurs." Max Harper had a frown on his face.

"What is this about?" Rafe seemed calmer than Cam felt. Cam felt like he was being judged and found wanting.

Zane Hollister turned. "Look, we all care about Laura. It's easy to see that you do, too."

"Are you attempting to pursue a ménage relationship with Laura?" Rye Harper asked the question academically, without a hint of judgment.

"I don't see where this is your business, but yes," Cam managed. He kind of wished he'd taken that drink.

Stef sat on the edge of his desk looking wholly comfortable as he probed into someone else's private life. "Laura belongs to Bliss. She's everyone's business. We work differently here, gentlemen. You should get used to that."

Zane grinned, his scarred face looking years younger. "Yeah, everyone is up in everyone else's shit here."

Stef shook his head. "Not the way I would have put it. I believe what the big guy is trying to say is that we care for each other here."

"And you two are totally fucking this up," Max interjected.

Dark eyes rolled as Stef replied. "Again, I would have used different words."

Max shrugged. "And taken up way more time with all your pussyfooting around. Let's get to the point. You two are fucking up. You've been fighting amongst yourselves since the day you walked into town."

Rye agreed with his twin. "You two are not acting like partners. When we asked about the whole partner thing, we weren't talking about your work relationship. We were talking about the way you live your lives."

Nate held out a hand. "Don't take this the wrong way. We're trying to help. Normally, we would take a step back and let you two figure this out on your own, but we're worried about Laura. With a killer on the loose, she needs the two of you to get your shit together."

"Trust me, those two are experts at this. They know how to fuck up. They fucked up for years before getting their shit together. You should listen to them," Max said, sarcasm dripping.

Zane stood up, and his face turned into a mask of intimidation. He bared his teeth at Max, and then sat back down and sipped his Scotch while looking up at Nate. "He's right. We were dumbasses for years. We wasted a lot of time that we could have spent with Callie."

Nate put a hand on his partner's shoulder. "That's in the past."

He looked over at Rafe, who seemed to be assessing the situation, as he always did. Though he'd gone through all the training and knew how to read body language and size up a subject, Rafe was the one with the true talent for it. Rafe wasn't on Laura's level, but he knew what he was doing. When Rafe's shoulders relaxed, Cam calmed down.

And Stef Talbot smiled. "There. That's what I'm talking about. Rafe just decided we're not out to get them, and Cam took his cue. Now we can talk."

"Are you sure you're not a profiler?" Cam asked, surprised someone had read him so well.

"I am many things," Stef replied. "But for now call me a concerned friend. Laura isn't happy."

"When she talked to Rachel earlier this afternoon, Rach said she'd been crying," Rye explained.

"She had a rough afternoon." Rafe's eyes were downcast. They had all had a rough afternoon. There had been moments of pure joy, but now all Cam could feel was an aching sadness.

"Yes, I watched the whole thing." Nate took off his Stetson and set it down on the desk. "I also know that you two did what you could to protect her. The trouble is she's not protecting herself. Now, I know a bit about what happened. Stef and I have looked into this. We don't know all the details, but we can read between the lines. Laura handed in a profile of the serial killer that neither one of you agreed with."

He nodded. His guilt was an uneasy knot in his gut. "We backed the senior special agent's report. Laura was upset because we were involved at the time."

"All three of you?" Stef asked.

"We had started a relationship the night before," Rafe explained. "We hadn't worked out the details yet."

"So she was unsure about your intentions," Stef continued. "And then she was taken and tortured."

"But we were there for her," he argued. God, there was a part of him that was still trying to figure out what had gone wrong.

Zane shook his head. "It doesn't matter. Look, I know what I'm talking about. When you've been through something like that, you feel utterly powerless. I know that some people would curl up and sink into the first affectionate person they could find, but people like me and Laura, we leave. I'm not talking about merely walking away. We leave emotionally. We retreat because it's easier than feeling. I was lucky. I had someone who wouldn't let me fade away. Laura has made a comeback, but it took her a while. I don't pretend to know exactly what she's feeling, but everyone here has seen the way she looks at the two of you. She's just scared."

"I don't know about that," Rafe replied. "I think there's a certain amount of anger in there, too. I think she blames us for what happened to her."

"Then you make it up to her," Stef said resolutely. "Are you in love with Laura?"

"Yes." The word came out of both of their mouths at the same time, sounding as though their voices were one.

"Then you have to quit fighting and work together," Nate said. "The whole screwing her in my office was a good play, even if it was a little messy. But you need to take it further. You took turns."

Everyone shook their heads at Nate's announcement.

"Like I said, amateurs," Max whispered.

Max might get that ass kicking everyone thought he wanted.

His twin stepped forward. "You can't view it like that. You have to take that girl down, and the best way to do it is together. You see, women are like horses. They'll kick and buck and resist that saddle until you prove you can handle them. Then they like a real nice, smooth ride, if you know what I mean."

Cam was pretty sure he didn't. "So, like at the same time?"

"He learns," Max snarked.

"We're not idiots," Rafe interjected. "We've taken her together."

"Have we?" Cam asked, suddenly kind of getting what they meant. "We've been in the same room. One of us has held her while the other one fucked her, but have we really taken her together? Have we worked together or just been voyeurs?"

"It's the same way in life as it is in sex," Nate added. "You have to talk things out between the two of you. Cam, you picked her up and walked out today. You didn't look to Rafe. You left him behind to quit his job and deal with all the Bureau shit. Now, that's fine and dandy if that's the way your roles work. Trust me, I handle anything that requires a modicum of delicacy, and Zane's job is to make sarcastic remarks."

He wasn't sure delicacy was the sheriff's strong point. Maybe he and Rafe made a better team. *Damn.* Was he the sarcastic one?

"And to give Callie multiple orgasms," Zane interjected.

"I don't need to hear that, Hollister," Stef said with a sigh. "The point of this exercise is to let you two know that we're here for you if you want advice or need to talk about how to make a ménage relationship work."

"And we need your input, why?" Max asked. "You're in a

ménage with Jen and your collection of sex toys."

Stef nodded and looked awfully superior. "Yes, that's because I'm the smart one. None of my sex toys talk back. Well, that new one from Japan does."

Nate looked at them seriously. "Are you two really interested in trying this? None of that taking-turns shit. You have to be in this together. You have to be a team."

Cam looked at Rafe, almost afraid of his reply. Rafe had far more to lose than he did. Cam's mother would sigh and then get another beer. She wouldn't reject him. Rafe was running a risk.

"Cam has always been my partner," Rafe said. "Even when we weren't working together. Yes, we're serious."

"Then you need a plan, my brother," Rye said with a friendly smile. "We're good with plans."

Max looked at his brother like he'd gone insane. "No, we're not. We're horrible at them. Rachel always sees right through them."

"Well, I'm good at them," Stef said with complete confidence.

There was a loud snort from outside the office.

Every male eye in the room rolled.

"That's ten, love," Stef called out. "Do you want to make it twenty?"

"Fine," a feminine voice called from behind the door. "We'll go. Callie has to use the bathroom anyway. And Rachel needs to feed Paige."

Max flushed. "My life was easier when the only ones hanging off my wife's boobs were me and my brother."

Cam finally laughed. Long and hard. It was ridiculous. It wasn't normal. He was standing here talking about how he was going to share the woman he loved with his best friend.

And he felt happier than he had in a long time.

Rafe doubled over, his hand coming out to balance against Cam's shoulder.

He stayed still so his partner didn't fall.

He was quiet as they started to talk about how to win Laura.

* * * *

His pretty rabbit paced, her arms crossed. She could feel the connection. He was certain of it. There was a tension to her body that let him know she was anxious. She was impatient. He wondered if she'd missed him.

They had an intimate connection—far more intimate than any sex she could have had. He'd held her life in his hand. For the hours they had been together, he had been her god.

He was going to do it again, and no one could stop him. Certainly not the two morons who sat beside him, talking about the case and making plans. They had sat beside him for years, never realizing that the killer they were looking for was right in the room.

This was why he needed her. She was the only one to see through him. Oh, for certain, she hadn't seen past his mask, but he wouldn't make that mistake this time. This time he wouldn't wear the mask. No theatrics between them.

His cock hardened. It almost never did that anymore. Certainly when he was with one of his charges, administering discipline, he would become aroused, but almost never when he was simply thinking about it.

His rabbit did this for him.

He wouldn't be able to hold it in. He answered his colleague on some meaningless point of procedure, but his brain was looking around the room.

So many ladies. And so many of them were naughty.

He would have liked to play with the one who tried to take her clothes off in a public forum, but her husband had saved her.

A pretty redhead walked behind a man.

"You don't have to do this, Caleb. I can get a ride with Laura," the woman said. "I live right next door."

"No." The man simply herded her out the door.

Obviously they weren't married. He wondered if the man with

232

the gold and red hair would drop her at her doorstep. He doubted those two were having sex. These cabins were so easy to get into. No one here protected themselves. He wondered if his rabbit would appreciate a friendly gift.

"I'm heading back to the motel," the Marquis de Sade said, stretching and standing. "Nothing's going to happen tonight. I'll talk to you in the morning."

They nodded and gave him a friendly good-bye.

On his way out the door, he bumped into that obnoxious reporter. She rolled her eyes.

"Excuse you," she said with a huff as she fixed her hair and charged into the room past him.

He watched her ass sway in her tight skirt. She was a loose end. She'd been useful over the years. Jana Evans had been more than willing to report what he told her to report. He'd always been careful with her. He used disposable cells to call her, and never the same one twice. He gave nothing of himself. It had been mere coincidence that his rabbit had been involved with such a piranha.

Of course, piranhas had nothing on sharks.

He turned and followed the redhead and her escort. It was time to announce that the Marquis de Sade had arrived in Bliss.

Chapter Fifteen

"I don't see why I can't go to the bathroom, Logan." Laura had to glare up at the deputy. This close, she could see the tired look in his eyes. Lately he'd taken to wearing a pair of aviators everywhere he went, but tonight he'd left them off, and there was no denying the red rim to his eyes. Logan Green was on the edge of something, and damn if Laura could figure out how to help him.

"Because you could be brutally murdered."

"In the ladies' room?"

He shrugged. "I don't see why not. I was almost brutally murdered in my boss's office. It happens."

And that was the trouble. Months before, Logan had been tortured by members of the Russian mob who had come to Bliss looking for a painting of Jen Waters's. Logan had endured hours of painful questioning. It was a miracle he'd survived, but the sweet boy who loved comic books and napped at work was gone. That Logan Green had died, and Laura wasn't sure how to get to the one who had taken his place. "Logan, you can stand outside, if you like. All the other women are allowed to go to the bathroom."

He looked down at her, an unmoving slab of granite. "I'll let you go, but I stand outside the stall."

She closed her eyes in frustration. She didn't need to go. She simply wanted a minute alone.

"All the other women are not being hunted by a serial killer," he said without inflection.

He had been like this for thirty minutes. He followed her around, not speaking unless he needed to. He'd been a hulking presence as she talked to Stella and her husband, Sebastian, about helping with cleanup, and then Brooke Harper about how they were going to get Nell into a bra before Stef and Jen's wedding. Not once had the deputy cracked a smile.

"Logan, do you want to talk about it?" she asked quietly. It looked like she wasn't going anywhere until Nate Wright decided to un-sic Logan.

There was only the fine tightening around his eyes to let her know he'd even heard her. He looked older than his twenty-three years. The last six months had given Logan a body to die for. It had toned and tightened him until even his face had lost its boyish charm and was replaced with a hard masculinity. But he'd also lost his joy.

"I know what it's like," she said. "You feel utterly helpless. You know what it means to be in someone else's power, and it's horrible. It changes you, but it doesn't have to ruin your whole life."

But wasn't she letting it ruin hers? Hours she'd spent agonizing over letting Rafe and Cam go. Was she doing it for the right reasons? Or was she simply afraid?

No. She couldn't think that way. It was selfish. She wasn't afraid of them anymore. She'd loved them once, but she'd proven that she could live without them, and happily at that. This was her home, and her friends were her family. Rafe and Cam would give up eventually, and they would find a life that made them happy, too. Rafe would go back to the FBI, and Cam would find someone to build a family with.

Logan simply stared at her as though he could read her thoughts. "Sure. Voice of reason, huh? You're totally adjusted,

Laura. I'll take that under consideration."

"There she is!" Jana's flat, Midwestern cadence broke through the chatter surrounding Laura. Laura knew she'd cultivated that accent. Jana was from Jersey. "You look...fine. I think the whole small-town girl thing will sell this story."

She stared at Jana, wondering what to say. Laura had been reconsidering this little plan of hers. Maybe Rafe and Cam were right. De Sade would come after her anyway. All she was doing by taunting him was bringing Bliss back into the spotlight. She was about to open her mouth to tell Jana to go to hell when Rafe and Cam walked back into the hall, looks of grim determination on their faces. Stef, Nate, Zane, Max, and Rye walked after them. Every man walking in looked at her.

What the fuck was going on?

Whatever it was, Laura had the feeling it was going to be interesting.

Cam walked straight up to Jana. "You, go away."

"I will not. I have an interview. Laura promised me. If I don't get my interview, I'm going to run the story anyway. I can make her look good, or I can make her look like the cowardly FBI agent who doesn't care that women are being killed." Jana's perfectly sculpted lips curled into a sneer. "I can make her look like the hero, or I can make her a complete pariah. It's up to you."

Laura was going to defend herself when Cam stared down at the reporter. "And I promise that if you attempt to smear her in any way, I will find a way to make your life hell. I am damn good with a computer. I got a stern talking-to from the government at the age of twelve because I managed to hack into several of their systems. They were kind enough to decide I wasn't a criminal and took an interest in getting me into the FBI. I will turn criminal if that's what it takes to fuck with you."

Rafe turned to her as well. "And I have connections. I will use those connections to ensure that you are not hirable."

Her eyes narrowed. "You can't do that."

Stef Talbot smiled lazily as he stepped forward. "Oh, I assure you I can. I happen to know that several of the heads of the networks are great lovers of art. A well-placed word and your career is in the toilet. If I can't influence them with my status as an artist, I assure you my status as a billionaire and the heir to Talbot Industries will influence them."

Laura saw the minute Jana knew she was defeated. She turned the burgeoning scowl into a placid smile. "Mr. Talbot, I think there's been a misunderstanding. Laura is a dear friend. I'm merely surprised that these men would think to curtail her freedom as a woman."

Oh, not even Nell would have been fooled by that one.

"Well, if you think we're cavemen now," Cam said with a grin before he leaned over and shoved a shoulder in Laura's midsection. Laura found herself in a fireman's hold before she could think to protest.

"Cam, put me down!" Laura shouted, although she was shouting it to his butt. It was a really nice butt encased in some fairly tight blue jeans. She had the sudden, wicked urge to cup that ass because it belonged to her.

That was a dangerous thought.

"No can do, baby," Cam said with an easy confidence. "We've decided we outvote you."

"I didn't realize we were a democracy," she shot back.

Rafe was suddenly on one knee. He gently pulled her head back so she was forced to look into that gorgeous face of his. His olive skin practically glowed in the low light, and those dark eyes of his got her every time. "There are many things we intend to make you understand tonight, *bella*. The first of which is you will not be speaking to that woman."

Cam started to carry her out. She bounced against his body, straining to see as he walked. "Damn it, Cam. Put me down. You can't manhandle me like this."

"Yes, I can," he said, a weird cheeriness to his voice. "I'm

237

doing it right now."

She heard the door open and close, and the world around her got a lot darker as he left the building and walked out into the parking lot. She saw Rafe walking behind them. Maybe he was going to be more reasonable. "Rafe, this is not exactly legal."

"Take it up with the sheriff."

Laura strained, and she could make out Nate Wright standing in the doorway looking out over the parking lot. He did not look like a man about to arrest someone, which was surprising given his predilections.

What had gone on in that meeting? "Let's talk about this. I'm willing to admit that talking to Jana was a mistake, but I'm not going to put up with this. We're adults, and we should discuss this situation rationally."

Cam snorted. "Not going to happen. You're not in charge tonight, baby."

The door to the SUV opened, and she found herself stuffed into the car. Rafe followed hard after her while Cam raced around to the front seat. Before she could scoot to the other side, Rafe pulled her close. His arms circled her.

"We've been going about this all wrong. We've been treating you like fragile glass, but you're not fragile, *bella*. You're strong. You're so fucking strong. You can handle a fight. We're going to give it to you." Rafe's warm breath played along her skin. "Some of the other men seem to think we should tie you up and spank you until you submit."

She was so going to kill Stefan Talbot.

"But I think that would cause more trouble," Rafe concluded.

"I voted for the spanking, baby," Cam said as he pulled out of the parking lot. "I thought it sounded hot."

"We'll see how you like it then," she shot back.

"Yes, I thought that would be your reaction," Rafe murmured as he stroked her hair. He should stop doing that. He was kidnapping her. "So Cam and I compromised."

"We're going to fuck you until you admit you love us," Cam explained.

"I already admitted I love you." Loving them wasn't the problem. She would love them until the day she died, but she couldn't ask them to give up everything for her.

"Fine, we'll fuck you until you forgive us." Rafe's hands delved under the collar of her blouse. She tried to move away, but he held her tight. It occurred to her that she should be fighting this loss of freedom.

When she'd first come to Bliss, she'd had terrible nightmares about being held down. Over the years, those nightmares had shifted and turned into dreams of being wrapped in Rafe and Cam. Fear had changed to longing. She still had the occasional dream that de Sade had come for her, but lately, the end had changed. Lately, when she thought she would die, the bonds that held her down became warm hands stroking her and Rafe's voice telling her she was safe. She would look up and Cam was the one standing over her, a look of love in his eyes.

"I forgive you," she said, emotion choking her. *Damn it.* If it was forgiveness they were looking for, then she would give it to them. She could give them what they needed. She could forgive them, but she was never going to...

Tears streamed down now.

"*Bella*?" Rafe forced her face up.

"I don't forgive me," she choked out. "Oh, god, I don't forgive me."

She let Rafe pull her into his arms, his warmth surrounding her. She was here when all those other women were gone from this earth. Why was she the only one? And how could she have walked away? She'd run so fast and so far, but he'd caught up with her, and what had that cost all of them?

"I should have stayed," she whispered against the fabric of Rafe's shirt.

Strong hands stroked her. "*Bella*, you can't blame yourself."

Couldn't she? The sight of those girls haunted her. She'd known he was lurking, and she'd chosen to hide. She'd picked her pain over what she'd known was right. God, she'd never cried. Five years and she'd never cried.

At first it had been all about surviving. It had been all about putting one foot in front of the other and making it through the day without blowing her brains out. She'd walked out because she couldn't deal with Rafe or Cam. She hadn't been able to face them, much less choose between them. She'd made it through the police interviews by pretending it had happened to someone else. She had pushed it back until she told herself it didn't touch her anymore, but now she could see it had affected her every minute of every day.

"He hurt me."

A stupid assertion. Obviously he'd hurt her, but she'd never said it so simply. She'd told them the clinical details of what had happened to her. She'd explained how he'd bound her and how she'd gotten away. She'd described the knife he'd used on her in technical details, but not how it had felt when he'd shoved it in her torso. He'd used a small knife, and he'd cut her over and over. It had been enough to hurt, but not kill her right away. She'd never told them how she'd felt. She'd never told them how she'd felt when she'd woken up from anesthesia and the doctor had told her that he'd been forced to perform a hysterectomy in order to stop her internal bleeding. There had been numerous other things, but that was all she'd heard that first night.

"I'm sorry, *bella*."

She could feel something wet on her forehead. Tears. Rafe was crying with her. Big, strong Rafe was crying. She clung to him. If he could cry, she could, too. She could be brave enough to do it.

"He made me feel small." She'd been insignificant. She'd been nothing but a body bound to a slab. An insect to dissect. She'd been nothing to him. Hours of torture had led her to the conclusion that she was nothing.

When the Marquis de Sade had left her alone abruptly, it had taken everything she had to fight. She'd gotten one hand free by working it out of the binding. She'd used her own blood to do it. She'd found a towel and shoved it against her belly to hold herself together. She'd found the door that led out to the warehouse he was using and made her way to the street. All the way she'd wondered if it was even worth it. Her feet had moved as though the will to live was something that put her on autopilot. How long had she been on autopilot?

"You weren't small, baby." Emotion choked Cam's throat as he drove toward her cabin. "You were loved. No matter what he did to you, you were loved. So fucking precious to me."

"To both of us." Rafe's hands tightened as though he was scared to let her go. "He can't take that from you. He can't make you small. You're Laura Rosen…Niles…whatever you want to call yourself, and you are loved. Always loved."

It hadn't happened to someone else. It had happened to her. It wasn't technical. It was visceral and emotional, and she'd ignored it for far too long. It was still happening to her because she wouldn't let these two men in. She'd lied to Logan. She'd lied to Rafe and Cam. She'd lied to herself. She wasn't pushing them away for their own good. She was letting that fucker win because he was affecting her life.

She sobbed because she'd held it in for so long. She'd sat up alone at night, a pain in her chest that wouldn't let her go. She released it now because for the first time in years, she was finally safe. The danger might not have passed, but she was safe.

She was loved. No matter what he did to her, she was loved.

"I can't have babies." That hurt most of all. He'd taken that from her. He'd taken her babies. All that mattered was the fact that she would never have a family. The tears became a flood.

"We can. We can do anything we want," Rafe promised, rocking her gently. "You can't carry them, but we can find a surrogate. We can adopt. *Bella*, if you want a family, we'll have one."

241

Was it really that simple? If she let go of the pain, could she have what she wanted? She loved Bliss, but she needed these men. In the end, if she had to choose, she would choose them.

The car stopped, and Cam was in the backseat in seconds, his strong body wrapping around her. "Baby, we can be happy. I promise. We'll do anything to make you happy. This is our second chance, but you should know I'll ask for a third and a fourth and forever. I'll never give up on this."

"Never, *bella*. I quit, and I'm not going back," Rafe promised. "This is my life. You and Cam are my family. Bliss is going to be our home."

Her head came up. She'd been ready to leave with them. "You don't have to quit. I knew if I was going to be with you, I would have to leave."

He shook his head. "No. You said you liked the you this place brought out. I think I'm starting to like this me. Home is where you are. That's enough."

"And I like it here. I have a crappy job with a boss who seems highly difficult and a town that is not likely to recognize my authority. What more could I ask for?" Cam asked with the dippiest grin on his gorgeous face.

Joy, pure and real, burst through her. Love was right there. All she had to do was say one little word. "Yes."

"Oh, now you're in for it." Cam dragged her out of the car. He hauled her up.

Rafe was opening the door to her cabin with a key she hadn't given him. She sent him a questioning look.

"I told you I could sneak back in." He had the most devilish grin on his face. "You said yes."

She nodded. "I said yes. I'll say it again."

She'd said no to so many things in the last five years. She'd said no to herself. But she wasn't going to say no to them. She was done with that.

Rafe leaned over and pressed his lips to hers. "I'll expect you to say 'I do' to us very soon."

She would get married. She'd thought she'd lost that. She could see clearly now how she'd given up on her future. She gripped Cam and pulled his head down for a kiss, too. She loved how different they were. Rafe was overwhelming. He came in like a marauder, trying to conquer everything he touched. Cam was softer, but no less possessive. He was the easy touch.

Cam's tongue touched hers in lazy play. It felt different. There was nothing between them now. Certainly not the pain of the past. There was only the future. She opened herself and let him in. He moved through the doorway even as he kissed her.

"Get her clothes off." Rafe slammed the door.

She was set on her feet, and big hands pulled at her clothes. Her shirt came over her head and a second set of hands tugged at the back of her bra. Her breasts bounced free, the nipples tightening in the cool air. Cam's fingers undid the fly of her jeans and delved inside. He slipped his fingers under the waistband of her panties, seeking her pussy. She shivered as he stroked over her clit.

"She's already getting wet." Cam's voice held a wealth of satisfaction.

She couldn't help it. She was always ready around them. She'd never thought she was a sexual creature, but she became a beast around them. She pushed her pelvis against his hand, seeking more contact. God, she wanted to fuck that hand. "I'm ready. One of you should fuck me."

Cam's hand came out of her jeans.

She didn't like that. "What are you doing?"

An evil, entirely sexy grin crossed his face. "Taking our time. And we won't be taking turns tonight. We're a team, Rafe and I. You should get ready to get packed full of cock tonight, baby."

She gasped, the breath leaving her body. They meant to take her together? They had never done it before.

They both moved back and stared at her.

"Take off the rest of your clothes." Rafe's eyes narrowed on her breasts.

"Leave the shoes on." Cam pulled his shirt over his head, revealing his ridiculously toned chest.

His shoulders were broad and ripped. Laura couldn't help but stare. Rafe unbuttoned his shirt. He was leaner than Cam, but no less hot. His olive skin was perfect and his abs spectacular. She looked down and saw that they were both sporting erections. They would use those on her. One in her pussy and the other would take her ass. They were so big. She would be full of them. She would be surrounded by them.

"Why are you hesitating, *bella*? There is no going back."

"Are you rethinking that spanking now, Rafe?" Cam looked at Rafe and for the first time seemed perfectly comfortable. They had always avoided eye contact with each other during sex.

"Absolutely."

She started to shove her jeans and panties down her legs. She stepped out of her canary-yellow four-inch d'Orsay heels.

"I said keep the shoes on." Rafe's voice was commanding. He seemed to have been taking lessons from Stef.

She kicked the clothes out of the way and put her feet back in the heels. "I heard you, but those are skinny jeans. Aren't the two of you overdressed?"

"Well, I am." Cam's hands undid his jeans and pushed them off his hips. His cock sprang from the confines of his briefs. He stroked it as he looked at her. It was an enormous monster, thick and long, with a plum-shaped head. "Come here and help me, baby."

That she could do. She moved into his space and offered up her lips. Cam's skin was warm, and he wrapped his arms around her as he kissed her, dragging her hand to where he wanted it to go. She caressed the silky skin covering his erection, pumping it in her hand. His tongue plunged lazily into her mouth as he plastered his body against hers.

"Come on, baby. Get me ready to fuck you," he said as he bit softly at her lower lip. "Run that tongue all over my cock."

She sank to her knees in front of him, well aware that Rafe was watching. He hadn't taken off his pants yet, but it wouldn't be long. Once she'd finished with Cam, it would be his turn, and he would be all over her. She looked up at Cam as she licked the bulbous head of his cock.

"Don't play with him," Rafe said, frowning down at her. "Lick his cock all over and then take him deep."

She wasn't sure when Rafe had taken over, but she was willing to play along if it got her what she wanted. She stroked his cock with her tongue, balancing herself on Cam's rock-hard thighs. Cam groaned as she pulled his cockhead into her mouth.

"That's it, *bella*." Rafe was suddenly on his knees beside her. His hands caressed her back, tracing the line of her spine all the way down to the cheeks of her ass. "Suck his cock. Get him hard and ready to fuck you."

Rafe's voice had taken on a rough, rich tone. His fingers played lightly along the crack of her ass. "We're going to fuck you here, *bella*. You know that, right?"

Cam's hands sank into her hair. "Oh, we're going to fuck that ass. I can't wait to sink in balls deep. It's going to be hot and tight. I can't wait to have your asshole milk my cock."

She wasn't sure about that, but she wanted to try. She wanted to be between them. She wanted them to fill her up. She struggled to take Cam's girth in her mouth. Inch by inch she opened her jaw to try to take all of him. She swirled her tongue around his cock despite the tight fit. Cam seemed to lose some of his sweetness as the dominant male came out. His hands tightened on her hair, and he fucked her mouth ruthlessly. In and out his cock worked toward the back of her throat.

"Relax and breathe, *bella*," Rafe encouraged her. "He's almost there."

"Fuck, yeah, I'm almost there." Cam grunted as she took another inch of that dick inside.

He was. She could feel his cock pulsing in her mouth. He would

245

come, flooding her mouth with salty fluid, and then Rafe would take care of her.

"Don't you forget the plan," Rafe said, his harsh tone splitting the air.

"Damn it," Cam cursed, and suddenly her jaw relaxed as Cam pulled out.

"What?" Laura asked, utterly confused.

"My turn." Rafe shoved his slacks down and took Cam's place. Rafe brought her head up and lined his cock to her lips. "You're not in charge tonight, *bella*. You're in charge most of the time, but not now. Take care of my cock while Cam gets you ready."

She was about to ask what she was getting ready for when she felt Cam's hands separate the cheeks of her ass. *Ah, that.* Rafe's cock insisted on entrance. She tasted the salt of his arousal on her lips and sucked him inside.

Cool oil dribbled between the cheeks of her ass. A twitchy, restless feeling came over her. Anxiety mixed with desire, making her edgy.

"Suck me harder." Rafe pressed forward, his cock huge in her mouth.

She laved the underside of his dick as Cam pressed his fingers against the rim of her asshole. She couldn't help the whimper that came out of her throat. She felt helpless, but this time it was a delicious sensation. She could revel in it because these men wouldn't hurt her. There was something freeing in giving over to them, like she was taking back a piece of herself—the piece that trusted and loved and accepted everything.

"Oh, baby, you should see your little asshole. It's fighting me, but it's going to give in. Just like you. It's going to accept everything I give it." Cam rimmed her and finally pushed in, the sensation a jittery pleasure. "You're going to take my cock up this ass. It's going to be beautiful."

Laura whimpered again. She wasn't sure about beautiful, but it was damn sure intimate. They were working together, and it was overwhelming her. She shuddered as Cam pressed another finger in. Her eyes watered a bit. She concentrated on the cock in her mouth.

"That's right, *bella*. Your mouth feels so good. If I don't watch it, this will be over way too soon." Rafe pulled his cock out of her mouth. It was slick and straining upward, unsatisfied for the time being.

She knew all about being unsatisfied. Her pussy was aching. She needed them.

"How many fingers did you get in?" Rafe asked, stroking her hair.

Laura groaned as her ass stretched again.

"Three now. That's enough," Cam replied, his voice shaking a bit. He fucked his fingers in and out of her hole, making her shake. "She can handle a cock."

"I want to see." Rafe walked behind her, his hand gently pressing her forward until her cheek was on the floor and her ass was high in the air. It gave Cam traction to sink in deeper. She felt invaded, overwhelmed. God, how was she ever going to take his cock?

"Isn't it pretty?" Cam used his free hand to pull a cheek aside. She could imagine that he was showing off her asshole to his partner.

"She's lovely. You're right. I want to fuck her ass, too." Rafe's voice had gone to that guttural place that told her a fucking wasn't far behind. God, she needed it. She needed them so badly.

She shivered as Cam pulled his fingers out. She could feel her ass clenching as though it hadn't wanted to give up Cam's flesh.

Rafe knelt behind her, pulling her up on her knees. His hands seemed voracious and greedy as he cupped her breasts. "He's going to clean up, but then we're going to play for a little while longer."

That sounded a bit uncomfortable. She was ready to go. She couldn't imagine being more ready. Her skin was super sensitive, and there was an emptiness inside her that needed to be filled. It was time to take charge. "Come on. Let's go to the bedroom. I want you both."

Rafe's fingers pinched at her nipples. His teeth bit gently at her neck. "That's not the way this evening is going to go. I told you. This night is about me and Cam taking charge. We're going to do it far more often from now on."

She wanted to argue. She wanted to tell him to go to hell, but he was rolling her nipples between his thumbs and forefingers. It sent a lightning strike of longing straight to her pussy. "Rafe, you can't tell me what to do."

He licked along her neck all the way to her sensitive earlobe. He rimmed it with his tongue. "Consider it persuasion, *bella*. You're not alone. You can't make decisions without us. You can't choose the course of your life without talking to us. You will never be allowed to walk away again."

She drew her arms back, her hands cupping the strong muscles that ran over his lean hips. She never wanted to be away from them again. "I won't walk out again. I promise."

"Because there would be punishment," Rafe warned.

Suddenly punishment didn't seem like such a bad thing. Maybe she wouldn't mind a weekend in Stef's guesthouse. But there were things she needed right now. "Please, Rafe."

His tongue played around the nape of her neck. She could feel his cock prodding her ass. "Please what, *bella*?"

He wanted to hear it, she surmised. He wasn't going to let her off easy. "Please fuck me."

His chuckle sent a warm sensation across her skin. "We will get to that. I promise."

Cam knelt in front of her. "Oh, baby, are you already begging for it?"

Now she could feel two hard cocks poking at her, seeking entry. Cam was the weak link. She reached down and cupped him, feeling him swell in her hand. "Please, Cam. I need it."

He kissed her while Rafe let his hands roam all over her body. Cam was breaking. His cock was pulsing in her hand. Any minute he would throw her down and give her what she needed.

"Just a little longer, baby." Cam pulled away and stood back up.

"Damn it, Cam." Laura tried to stand up.

"No." Rafe's arms caged her. "I told you, this is our night. We've waited five years. You said yes."

She had to laugh. She'd given an inch, and now she walking the mile. "I said yes to loving you, to being with you, not to letting you kill me with sexual tension."

Rafe's hand moved lower. Oh, so close to where she wanted it to be. "You'll live. We won't let you die."

Cam's fingers toyed with her nipples now. "We've sworn to protect you."

But not to keep her sane, it seemed. She was dying. They were lighting up every nerve she had in her body. "Please."

Rafe sighed behind her. "We can move forward since she's asked nicely. Cam, take her."

Cam's arms wrapped around her waist, and she was lifted into the air. "You have to stop doing that."

"I don't see why," Cam replied with a chuckle as he sat down on her couch and settled her on his lap. Her back rested against his chest. His cock jutted up, so close to her pussy it had to be getting wet. "It's the easiest way to get you where we want you. We decided that when you're not playing ball, we'll pick you up and move you into position."

She quickly found out which position he meant. His feet moved to the inside of her ankles and forced her legs to spread wide. His arms wrapped around her, a warm cage. She was utterly exposed, her pussy on full display.

Rafe looked down at her. "That's what I wanted. Look at you. Look at that pussy."

"What are you doing?" Laura asked. This was not how she'd seen this evening going. She swallowed. Her heart thumped in her chest, and all of the blood in her body seemed to go to one very wet place.

"Relax, baby," Cam whispered. "We want to play with you."

She moved restlessly as she watched Rafe. He got to his knees and ran his hands along her thighs, making every inch of skin he touched come alive.

"It was pointed out to us tonight that we have neglected you terribly," Rafe said. "We've been selfish. We've taken turns when we should have given you everything."

She wanted everything. "But you're not going to do that anymore?"

"No, we're going to overwhelm you. We're going to make you scream." Cam punctuated his statement by turning his hips up and impaling her on his cock.

She gasped. He was so big in this position. She was caught on his cock, utterly helpless to do anything but take him deep inside her cunt. He fought because the angle was odd, but that long dick wasn't taking no for an answer. He slid deep inside her with a satisfying grunt.

"Better?" Rafe asked. What was he doing? Cam was in her pussy. Rafe couldn't take her ass. Her ass was pressed against Cam's pelvis.

"Better for me. Fuck she's tight from this position." Cam's hands steadied her hips.

Rafe got in between her legs. "It was pointed out to us that we've missed many opportunities because we've been a bit too…what was the word the perverted artist used?"

"Vanilla." Cam rotated his hips, his cock massaging a spot deep inside her that got her moaning.

"Yes, we've been vanilla. We've decided to give that up. We've been a bit afraid of not proving entirely masculine."

Cam laughed behind her. "We've been afraid our cocks might bump and we'll feel weird."

"That's stupid," Laura said, her breath catching as Rafe put his fingers on her pussy.

Rafe winked at her. "Yes, we were told how stupid it is. And we were also given several suggestions on how to avoid the disaster of this morning."

Even through the righteous sexual tension, she had to laugh. She remembered what had happened. "I thought you looked sweet together, all cuddled up."

"Hey, I thought he was you," Cam complained. "And if you do what Zane told you to do, you should know I'll have my revenge."

Rafe was toying with her clit. Oh, god, she was so stinking close. When were they going to stop this slow, delicious torture? "If I know Zane, it involved punching someone."

Rafe lowered his head, proving how dedicated he was to giving up his addiction to vanilla. "He called it aversion therapy. Nate called it assault. I think we can work out our problems without violence."

Cam's cock was rubbing in a rhythmic cycle. Just a little in and out. In and out. "You're not allowed to leave our bed. That way we always cuddle you."

"And if our cocks touch, we move away. No harm. No foul. But you should know our attentions will always be on you, our *bella*." Rafe leaned over and licked her clit.

"Oh my god," Laura cried out.

Cam pulled her back, fucking deeper into her and forcing her clit to stand out for Rafe's use. His tongue caught on the nub and worked her hard. Cam pressed her down on his cock, filling her and hitting her G-spot as her clit exploded. Pleasure rushed through her like a tidal wave. They didn't stop simply because she'd come. Rafe continued to lick her, and Cam maneuvered her on his dick, finding new spots that sent her gasping.

Finally they drew away. Rafe pulled her up and off Cam's cock. She looked back at him and could see his dick glistening with her cream, but still hard as a rock.

"You didn't come?" she asked. Cam's face was set in a harsh, unsatisfied line.

He shook his head. "Not yet. Not until I get in that ass. I'm not coming until I fill your ass, baby."

It wasn't done yet. She felt languid as Rafe carried her toward the bedroom. He rushed as though he couldn't possibly wait a moment longer.

"Ride me," he demanded as he set her on her feet and got on his back.

He was the perfect picture of glorious decadence. His long, lean body was laid out for her, and his cock stood up as though seeking what it was missing. She straddled him and had gotten her balance when he thrust up, his cock invading her pussy. He forced her hips down, impaling her on him.

"That's what I want," he groaned as he pulled her down. "Now give Cam room to work."

She felt Cam's hands worshipping the curves of her ass while Rafe kissed her into submission. Cam's fingers glided from the small of her back, over her cheeks, and down the crack to rim her asshole.

"Do you have any idea how long I've waited for this?" Cam asked.

Years. He'd had a healthy preoccupation with her ass from the first day they'd met. She'd noticed how he looked at her. She'd seen him watch her walk away through the reflective glass of an elevator and thought he just liked the way she looked. Even then he'd probably been thinking about how nice she would look with his dick up her ass. Her Cam was a dirty boy.

"Fuck, Cam, hurry up. I want a turn." Rafe wasn't far behind. Now that they'd left their vanilla-ness in the dust, it looked like she was in for some rough rides. Damn, but she was looking forward to that.

More lube. He spread it all over her asshole, working it deep inside. Before she could process that sensation, she felt the broad head of his cock poking at her, requesting entrance.

"Push out against me, baby. It only hurts for a minute," Cam promised on a low groan.

It wasn't hurting exactly, but it also wasn't comfortable. There was an oddly erotic pressure building. Rafe soothed her by stroking her hair and kissing her, his tongue whirling around hers. Cam gripped her hips. Four hands caressed her. Two bodies enclosed her. All the years without them fell away.

"Does it hurt, *bella*?" Rafe's concern showed on his face. He pushed her hair out of her face. "Cam, stop. She's crying."

"Don't you stop, Cameron Briggs," she ordered. She wasn't about to lose him now. "I'm not hurt. I'm full."

She was. She was full of them, full of love. For the first time in years, she was full of life. Even when she'd thought she'd moved past what happened to her, she'd been living a half life. She could never settle for safety when what they offered her was so much more. Dangerous, yes. Anything could happen. The world was filled with bad shit that could flare up in an instant. A physically stronger person could hurt her again, but what she couldn't lose was this moment. Not ever. She wouldn't ever let anyone close her heart off again. That had been her mistake.

"I'm so full, Cam. I need you."

"I love you, baby," he said, his voice hoarse with emotion. He pressed in, and she felt his cock sink deep.

"*Bella*, I love you so much." Rafe pushed his hips up. "Oh, I can feel him."

"We're together," she said, smiling through those cleansing tears. Finally together.

She'd thought she couldn't come again, but it built quickly. Cam dragged his cock in and out of her ass, hitting nerves she never knew she had. Knowing that their cocks dragged against each other, working in tandem to push her to a peak, did something for her. She came in a giant rush of pleasure and emotion.

Rafe held her tight as he shouted out when he filled her. His cock felt like it grew impossibly large as he spilled inside her. Cam came a second later, grinding into her. She felt hot jets filling her pussy and her ass. She was covered in them.

She fell forward, and Cam came down on top. They shifted to the side, plastered together.

"I love you both." This was her future. These two amazing men.

And then Cam looked over her at Rafe. She waited for the emotion to pass between the men, but no. Cam gave his partner a thumbs-up.

She let her head fall back as she laughed.

Yeah. She'd missed that, too.

Chapter Sixteen

Rafe turned in his sleep and cuddled against the softest, warmest skin he'd ever felt. He let his arm drift around her. He breathed deeply, smelling sex and musk and Laura's own sweet scent. He inhaled it, letting it surround him. Then he opened his eyes because he wanted to make damn sure who he was cuddling.

Laura lay beside him, her beautiful face peaceful in sleep. Her blonde hair was spread across the pillows, tickling the skin of his neck. Soft light filtered in, making her look so lovely. The night before crashed over him. It had been everything he could have hoped for. She'd given them everything. And he was a greedy bastard who always wanted more.

He would never get enough of her.

The scent of coffee brewing wafted in.

"That smells so good," Laura said, the smile on her face telling Rafe she'd been awake for a while.

"Cam is up." And that meant maybe he could get in some alone time with the most beautiful girl in the world. Not that he didn't like sharing her with Cam. He liked it more than he would ever have dreamed imaginable, but he wasn't going to pass up the opportunity to have her to himself. They would be having a lot of date nights. "You know how Cam's appetite is. He's cooking breakfast."

"If I remember correctly, breakfast is the only thing Cam can cook." She stretched, the sheet slipping from her breasts revealing creamy-white skin tipped with the dusty-pink nipples he loved to play with, to suck on.

A deep sense of peace fell over him. He'd agonized over this decision, but it was the right one. This was where he belonged. Close to her. He caressed her cheek, loving the feel of her skin against his hand. Even the fact that Cam was puttering around the kitchen gave him a deep feeling of belonging.

He didn't have a job. Every single day since he'd turned sixteen, he'd gotten up and gone to work in one way or another. He'd been a twenty-four-seven obsessive workaholic, and now he was thinking about fishing.

He was definitely thinking about never leaving this bed again. He let his hand find the curve of her hip.

She moved closer, cuddling against him. "I guess I won't need my electric blanket this winter. You and Cam are like furnaces." She turned her face up to him, her blue eyes sleepy in the early morning light. "You really want to stay in Bliss?"

"Yes." He wanted to figure this place out. It was a weird mystery—part hippie, part pure *True Grit* western. But he did have a few demands of his own. "You can't keep working at the gas station."

Her mouth turned down. "What else am I going to do? Nate is full up on deputies."

"Not for long. Cam is working on his facial recognition software. What if the three of us specialized in missing persons cases? You know people. You know why they might run. I know how to track down a criminal. Between the three of us, we could help some people." He'd thought about it long after Laura and Cam had fallen asleep. It was work that could be meaningful.

She settled back down. "I could get into that."

And he could get into her. He rolled her on her back, making a place for himself between her legs. "But we don't have to go to work yet."

He was about to press his lips to hers when there was a loud knock on the door.

Rafe cursed and rolled off her. It had been easy to forget that there was a whole world of shit out there that he had to deal with.

"I'll handle this, *bella*." He reached for his pants. "You can stay in bed. We'll take up where we left off."

"Not on your life, mister." She wrapped a robe around her body and got to the door before he could. "I'm willing to discuss decisions with you, not allow you to make them for me."

He rushed out behind her, not bothering with a shirt.

Cam had the door open, and Nate Wright filled the doorway. He'd taken his hat off. *Fuck.* That couldn't be good. The sheriff had a deeply somber look on his face.

"Laura," Nate began. "I have some bad news."

Cam took a step back, and it was obvious that he knew what was going on. He took Laura's hand. "They found a body dumped in the woods with a note for you."

Rafe's stomach turned. He'd known that the Marquis de Sade was out there. But this made it all too real. And proved beyond a shadow of a doubt that Laura was right. He knew it deep in his bones. Not only was the killer law enforcement—he was on the same team that was trying to catch him. God, one of his coworkers, one of his friends, was the same man who had nearly killed his woman. Rafe looked at his partner, and he could see they were thinking the same thing.

"Who?" Laura asked, her voice smaller than usual. She'd paled, her complexion turning a chalky white. Rafe reached for her hand. He would do anything to spare her this.

Nate held her eyes. "It was your friend."

Laura stumbled, her body crumpling. Rafe caught her before she reached the floor. A sob tore out of her throat. "No. No."

"Nate? What's going on?" a feminine voice called out. Rafe looked up and saw Holly rushing from her doorway where the big, sullen doctor stood fully dressed with a bag in his hand.

Laura looked up and was on her feet before Rafe could stop her. She ran toward Holly, throwing herself in the other woman's arms. She ran her hands across Holly's face as though she had to prove to herself that Holly was still there.

"Damn it," Nate cursed, stalking toward the women. "Laura, I did not mean Holly. I am so sorry. Nell is fine, too. She and Henry are still holed up with Cassidy and Mel."

"What happened?" Holly asked, wrapping her arms around Laura.

The doctor stepped forward. "A hiker found the body of a woman on a trail near Tooth Rock. Logan's already up there. I was just leaving to head to the scene."

"Who?" Laura asked.

Rafe had a suspicion. If he was right, then the Marquis de Sade had taken care of some old business. "It was Jana, wasn't it?"

"Yes. The victim was Jana Evans," Nate replied.

Laura choked back a sob.

It made sense. Now that the fact that the killer had a connection to Jana had come out, he would have to deal with the reporter. "And you said there was a letter addressed to Laura?"

Nate nodded gravely. "Yes. It's in evidence at the station house, but the gist was that he's coming for her. He called her his sweet little rabbit and promised that their game would be over soon."

"Motherfucker." Cam always had the right words to sum up a situation.

They had to figure this out and soon. It was time to take a close look at all their coworkers. "You won't find anything on the body. He's careful, though this is a change in his MO. He usually leaves the bodies where he kills them."

"I'm looking for his kill site," Nate said.

"It will be someplace remote," Cam advised. "He likes to take his time with his victims. At home he used abandoned warehouses and storefronts. You should look for empty cabins. And we need alibis on everyone. I mean everyone. I want the whole FBI team's time last night accounted for."

"That won't be easy." Nate frowned. "According to your coworkers, they were all in bed by ten-thirty. No one is sharing rooms, and the Movie Motel doesn't have keycards, so we can't tell when someone leaves or accesses their room."

That was a dead end. If Rafe thought for one second he could convince the higher-ups that this BAU team should be pulled, he would call the director himself, but no one was going to listen to him. He'd quit.

Nate shook his head. "The feds are finishing up forensics. They'll transport the body to the morgue, and then I'm sure they'll bring in their own expert. Sorry, Caleb. I know you don't like other doctors in your clinic."

The doctor shook his head briefly. "I'll take care of it. I think you'll find the feds will be more than willing to let me do the autopsy."

Rafe stepped forward. He felt bad for the doctor. It was hard to give up control. "I'm sorry, but Joe is going to insist on his own guy."

The doctor set his bag down. "I already have the go-ahead."

Cam's mouth dropped open. "How did you manage that?"

The doctor shrugged slightly. "I know a few people. I made a call, and now I'm the one doing the autopsy. Don't worry. I won't fuck it up. I've had a lot of practice doing autopsies lately."

The last bit was said with a ferocious scowl sent Nate Wright's direction.

Wright rolled his eyes in obvious frustration. "Damn it, Caleb. I did not invite the Russian mob to town. You can't blame me for that."

The doctor grunted as though he really *could* blame the sheriff. He walked over to Holly and put a hand on her shoulder. "Get dressed and come with me."

Holly looked up. "Caleb, I appreciate you spending the night, I really do, but I have to work."

A stony face looked back at her. "No."

"You have got to stop doing that," Holly complained. "You can't simply say no."

Nate stepped in. "Stella shut down the cafe for the day. We're all closing up shop so we can stay in. It's better that way. Consider Bliss on vacation for a few days. We can all handle it. It should keep the tourists safe. We're sending some business to Creede and some to Del Norte."

Holly's hand curled around Laura's. "All right, then. But I could stay home. I promise I won't answer the door."

Caleb stared at her.

Her mouth turned down in a stubborn pout. "I know—no. Fine. I'll get dressed, or should I go to the morgue in my undies?"

The doctor's lips curled up the slightest bit in a way that told Rafe he would be perfectly fine with that scenario.

"I don't suppose there's any way we could get on that crime scene?" Laura asked, wiping her eyes. She straightened up, and he could pinpoint the minute she put her tears behind her and pulled her professionalism around her.

"I'm supposed to bring you in for questioning," Nate admitted.

"What?" Cam practically screamed the question.

Laura put a hand on Cam's chest. "You know they're going to want to talk to me. The key now is to make sure they don't take me into protective custody for my own good."

"I will not allow that to happen, *bella*," Rafe promised. He turned to Nate. The sheriff was really his only law enforcement ally. "I am convinced that someone on my former team is responsible for this."

"Rafe," Laura breathed as though she couldn't believe what he'd said.

"You knew it all along," he replied. "It's someone close. Cam and I are going to run back to our motel and pick up our things. You have wireless somewhere in this town?"

Nate grimaced. "At the station, but I doubt you're going to be able to quietly investigate people who are standing right behind you. It's a small station. You're out at the Movie Motel? Gene has dial-up."

Now Cam was the one groaning. "I can make it work. We need access to employment files. There has to be something in there. I have three suspects in mind, though you're not going to like them, Rafe."

He was being realistic from this point on. There was no longer any room for friendship beyond Cam's. "We look into Edward, Brad, and Joe. Even before Brad was on the team, he was always hanging around. And he's been divorced three times."

"But his girlfriend from high school was murdered," Cam added.

That fact was not lost on Rafe. "It's why he claims he joined. They all have something in their pasts that could have served as inciting incidents. Edward's never been married, but his mother died in a car accident, and we all remember what happened to Joe's wife."

Joe's wife had committed suicide. He remembered standing beside his friend at her funeral. And Brad had more than once talked about how he couldn't forget his girlfriend, his first love. Edward had lived with his mother. He'd never been married, and as far as Rafe knew, he'd never even had a real girlfriend.

The Marquis de Sade hated women.

Rafe's brain was working overtime. "We need to look at those files and dig up everything we can. If we eliminate these three as suspects, we move deeper."

Cam crossed his arms over his chest and looked supremely confident. "If the information is on a computer, I can find it. I can find files they thought were long buried."

Translation—Cam was a gun. All Rafe needed to do was point

and shoot. But he didn't have to be there while Cam looked. "Cam can take the SUV. I'll go back with Laura."

"Yeah," Cam said. "I would be happier with that scenario."

"No," Laura said, her eyes wide and her voice rising with panic. "No. You are not going to leave Cam alone."

"Baby, I can handle myself," Cam protested.

Tears formed in her eyes. She looked up at Rafe, pleading with him. "Please. I can't lose either one of you. He killed Jana. He could be anywhere. He could take out one of you. You can't be alone. Promise me, you won't leave Cam alone."

His heart ached at the fear in her eyes. "*Bella*, I can't leave you alone."

"I won't leave Nate's side. I won't let them separate us," she promised. "I'll be at the station, surrounded by agents. He won't come after me there, but he could come after someone I love. If he's been watching me, then he knows about us. Please."

He hugged her. He couldn't argue with her logic, and Cam was out of practice. He looked over her shoulder and exchanged a glance with his partner. "All right, *bella*."

"I should go get dressed," Laura said.

"I'll go with you. That way I won't be alone and Caleb doesn't have to tell me no. It's his favorite word." Holly took Laura by the hand and started to lead her away.

"It's not," Caleb said, watching the women as they walked. He didn't seem to notice Laura was alive, and Rafe was perfectly fine with that scenario. The doctor had a serious thing for Laura's best friend. "I don't actually have a favorite word."

Rafe couldn't tell if the man was serious or joking. He got the feeling Caleb didn't joke often.

"Caleb, if you want to go and get started, I'll bring Holly and Laura with me to the station," Nate offered.

"No," Caleb replied. It really did seem like he had a favorite word.

But Rafe was with him on this one. "No."

Cam stood next to Rafe. "We're not letting Laura out of our sight."

Nate scrubbed a hand over his face. "If I don't bring her in with me, it's going to look suspicious. Your SAC has already asked to talk to her. If they think she's going to run, they might take her into protective custody."

"They can't force that on her," Rafe said. He had no intention of letting them get their hands on Laura.

"They can hold her for forty-eight hours," Nate replied. "And I wouldn't be surprised if that's what they do. If you let her come in and talk, I think they might back off."

"All right," he conceded. "I'll take Cam to the motel and meet you at the station. But I expect you to have eyes on her the whole time she's with you."

"Either Logan or I will be with her at all times. And we don't have to worry about Holly distracting anyone because apparently she gets to go see an autopsy," Nate said sarcastically.

"Yes," Caleb replied simply. Rafe admired the doctor. He wasn't about to let anyone intimidate him.

Panic threatened to swamp Rafe. Everything was happening too damn fast. Maybe he should rethink. Maybe he should just take off with her.

Cam looked at him. "I know what you're thinking, man. She won't go."

"We could make her."

"After last night, we can't leave here. We can't make her leave. Our best option is to find this bastard and take him out," Cam said. "Otherwise, we're running for the rest of our lives. Let's get dressed, and I'll get on this. She'll be safe with Nate and Logan. It's broad daylight, and she's going to a police station."

"I'll lock her up if I have to," Nate offered.

"He likes to do that," Caleb said with a growl.

"If you don't like to go to jail, you should pay your parking tickets." Nate pulled out his radio. "Logan, can you read me? I'm bringing Laura in with me. Can you tell me who is at the station from the FBI?"

"The athletic asshole who got his face beat on and the asshole who looks like a professor," Logan replied over the radio. "I guess the corporate-looking asshole is still at the crime scene."

"Thanks, Logan. Very professional." Nate sighed and turned back, giving Cam a stern look. He reached into his pocket and pulled out a second radio. "Be better than Logan. Please." He handed the radio to Cam. "There you go. It's set to contact the station or me or Logan. And unlike our cell tower, it's Farley brothers proofed. I'll keep you updated on who's where at all times. I guess the SAC decided to stay and supervise the forensic team. He said he wanted to view the autopsy when it's ready. I bet the other two will go to that, as well."

"I don't need an audience. I already have to tape the thing." Caleb ran a hand through his hair. "I hate bureaucracy. I hate autopsies. I hate all this crap. I'll wait in the car."

The doctor might hate bureaucracy, but the man had major pull if he'd managed to overrule Joe.

"I'll go wait with the doc. He can be an obnoxious son of a bitch, but he knows what he's doing," Nate said. "When Laura's ready, we'll go. And if you two need anything, let me know. I still have contacts in DC, and I know Stef's dad has some pull."

The sheriff walked off to get in his Bronco, and Rafe was left shaken. Only a few minutes ago, the world had seemed damn near close to perfect, and now it felt like it could fall apart at any minute.

"Come on, man. Let's get dressed," Cam said, urging him inside. He clutched that radio in his hand. "The quicker we start eliminating suspects, the faster we know who she's safe with. Except for Brad. I don't care if he has a rock-solid alibi for every murder. He's still an asshole."

"Agreed." After the way Brad had talked to her, Rafe couldn't really consider him a friend.

But was he a killer?

Hopefully the answer was somewhere out there. Rafe had to pray Cam could find it.

* * * *

"Sweetie, are you okay?" Holly asked the minute they were alone.

Tears threatened and Laura couldn't give in to them. If she broke now, she wouldn't be able to stop. "Please, Holly. I can't talk about it right now. Tell me what happened with Caleb. Take my mind off this for a minute."

"He spent the night on the couch," Holly said with a sigh.

Laura walked into the bedroom and pulled out a clean pair of jeans and a yellow blouse. She tried to still her racing heart. She was pretty sure they could hear it in Del Norte. She forced herself to answer in an even voice. "That's disappointing."

She'd been sure Caleb was ready to make a move.

Holly opened Laura's closet and started looking for something to wear. She was shorter than Laura, but they shared as often as they could. She pulled out a simple black T-shirt and cotton skirt. "I asked if he wanted to share my bed, just to sleep, you know, since he wouldn't leave."

"I bet I know what he said."

"No." Holly did a damn fine impression of the man. She shrugged out of her nightgown and pulled on the clothes. "You didn't have the same trouble."

Holly was staring down at her bed. The sheets were twisted and tangled. Of course, there were also clothes scattered through the house. If Holly hadn't picked up on that clue, her destroyed bed was a dead giveaway.

"I love them." Laura shimmied into fresh underwear, wishing she had time for a shower. Maybe she could use the one in Nate's office. Nate had a decent bathroom. She understood the necessity to move quickly, but she smelled like sex.

"I know. Everyone knows." Holly gave her a soft smile. "I'm happy for you. I'm going to miss you though."

That was bugging her? "No, you won't. I'm not going anywhere. They're moving here."

Holly gave a happy squeal. "Yes! That's awesome." She sobered a little. "Now I can watch another of my friends be happy and settle down."

Laura zipped up her jeans. "Sweetie, that man is crazy about you."

Holly sat on the bed, utterly dejected. "No. That man is plain crazy. I don't know how to deal with him. I swear it's easier to deal with the mobster. At least he talks to me—well, he writes to me because his handlers won't let him call. Caleb is a mystery. He won't talk about his past. All he seems willing to do is boss me around. I've already been married to one man who turned out to be a bully. I don't need another."

Laura turned to her friend. "I don't think Caleb is anything like Scott. And you know it. I've seen the way you look at him."

Holly's hands twisted in her lap. "Someone fixed my roof. You know I had that leak? Someone from Del Norte showed up yesterday morning with a work order and fixed the bad section. He's coming out next week to replace the whole thing. Do you know how much that costs? He had a paid receipt, but he wouldn't tell me who paid it. Wouldn't say more than they paid cash. Do you think that was Stef?"

Stef Talbot was known for his acts of anonymous generosity, but she doubted it in this case. Jen would have blabbed. It was the best thing about Stef getting a wife. She loved to gossip. "No. It was Caleb, and that is the most un-Scott-like thing he could do."

Holly's ex was a powerful politician, but he wouldn't help anyone. He was all smiles on the television when he was campaigning, but off TV he was an asshole of the first order. Sort of like...

She sank to the bed. Jana was dead. Tears filled her eyes. How could Jana be dead? Nate had said she'd been left behind with a note addressed to Laura. Guilt pressed down on her.

"How close were you?" Holly always seemed to know what she was thinking.

"She was a horrible bitch. We haven't been close in years, but I didn't want her to die. God, I wouldn't wish it on anyone." She put her hands on Holly's shoulders. "You stay with Caleb today. You don't walk away or let him out of your sight. You should be okay as long as you're in the clinic, but don't you dare go outside without him."

Holly's green eyes went wide but she nodded. "I won't. I think I should stay with you."

Laura forced herself to move. If she stopped, she would dissolve into tears, and she couldn't do that. Rafe and Cam had a job to do. They needed to get those files. Once they had what they needed and she'd pacified the feds that she wasn't going anywhere, she would really like to get a look at the reports. She'd seen the Marquis de Sade. She'd looked at his work and known who he was deep inside. Now she needed to see the man he presented to the world outside. She needed to find the man the monster hid behind. Maybe if she looked for the mask he wore every day, she could put the two together.

Maybe the motel was a better place to hole up than her cabin. Less windows, less places to hide. Internet.

"You can't stay with me. You're in danger if you're with me, and I think Caleb would say no." There was no way she was letting Holly stay close to her. She'd panicked when Nate had said her friend was dead. Nell was underground with Henry, so her mind had seen Holly's body, cold and still. She hugged Holly. "Stay with Caleb. Promise me."

"All right."

There was a knock at the door.

"Laura, we need to get dressed and go. I put together some toast and eggs. You can eat it fast. I made you coffee, too." Cam sounded hesitant. If she didn't watch it, they would go with her when she needed them working.

"Sounds great." She squeezed Holly's hand and went to force breakfast down her throat.

* * * *

He waited, his breath pulsing in and out of his body. It was a rhythm, and he could hear the thud of his own heart. Had she gotten the news?

He'd left her a gift. Her greatest enemy, torn to shreds. Not shreds, exactly, but he had neatly eviscerated the bitch. She'd cried and begged for her pitiful life. She'd thought that her career would save her. Dumb animal. It had been anticlimactic to push the knife through her belly and watch as she writhed on the blade. He had watched, sitting back and letting her believe she was alone. He would never again underestimate one of his lady loves. She'd cried and begged and found some deity that she'd never believed in before. It had been predictable and utterly pathetic.

She'd been an unsatisfactory substitute for what he really wanted. His rabbit.

Now that he'd seen her again, he knew she was the one for him. His cock hardened. The thought of her was the only thing that got him hard anymore. There had been that one woman, but she was gone and she'd been a whore. His rabbit was a whore, too. She couldn't help it. She was female.

She had to be put down, but that didn't mean he couldn't enjoy her before he did it.

It would be a true gift. An honor to bestow.

It was the least he could do before he killed her.

Chapter Seventeen

Cam stared at the computer screen, willing the damn thing to move faster. It seemed like forever since they'd both kissed Laura and let her leave with the sheriff. It had been one of the hardest things he'd ever had to do, but she wouldn't back down. She'd been adamant about getting this "interview" over with. Laura wasn't one to procrastinate. She was a "rip the Band-Aid off" kind of girl.

The computer beeped quietly, the sound taunting to Cam's ears.

"Hurry it up," Rafe complained.

Rafe had his arms crossed over his chest as he stood behind Cam. Everything about his attitude spoke of his irritation. He'd already talked to Laura twice on the radio Nate Wright had given them.

Cam wanted to punch something. Rafe had been on his ass since the second Laura had driven away. Laura hadn't wanted Rafe to leave him behind, so Rafe was waiting on him to get the files he needed. "I'm going as fast as I can. When was the last time you used dial-up? Seriously, if we're staying in this town, we have to do something about the Internet access."

Rafe stopped and sighed, a long, heavy sound. "I'm sorry. It's not your fault. I don't like this. It feels wrong."

Everything about it felt wrong. It was wrong that someone had been killed in this sleepy little town. It was wrong that Laura was having her life disrupted again.

He waved off the apology. It wasn't needed. He knew why Rafe was edgy. "Did you pull Laura's profile?"

Rafe went to the bed where his briefcase sat and drew out a fat file folder. "Yes. I've gone over it a thousand times. We know he's an organized killer. He almost never does anything without careful planning. He's disciplined and well educated."

"He would have to be to have gotten into the FBI."

Rafe was silent for a moment. "We have all kinds of measures in place to keep something like this from happening. Every agent has to go through testing."

"All of which a highly-intelligent, highly-motivated person with a deep understanding of psychology could fake his way through." Those tests weren't infallible. Nor were the psychiatrists who administered them. "The screening process isn't perfect. Nothing is."

Rafe leafed through the documents. "This is interesting. She talks about how she thinks the killer will use the media. She labels him as intensely controlling and very interested in what she calls his 'legacy.' Sound familiar?"

"Given what we know now, yeah." It was obvious that the Marquis de Sade had used Jana Evans, probably even telling her what to write, and when she had lost her usefulness, he'd killed her. "Do we know where her cameraman was at the time?"

Rafe had talked to Nate, too. "He was in the van. Apparently there weren't any rooms left, and Jana wasn't kind enough to let him stay with her. He was on the computer, video chatting with a couple of buddies. They had a satellite connection. Maybe we should break into the news van. Anyway, they have him down at the station giving a statement, but he didn't hear anything."

Another dead end. But maybe the cameraman knew something

about Jana's source.

The screen changed, and he was in. "Thank god."

Rafe got behind him, blocking out the light from the window. "What can you tell?"

Impatient bastard. "Nothing yet. I just managed to get in the system. Let me copy the files onto a thumb drive, and we can head to the station. I don't care what Nate says. I can go through what I found quietly while we watch Laura. I'm done hacking into the server, so the sheriff doesn't have to worry about me getting him in serious trouble and bringing the feds down on the town. I don't think we need more feds."

It was funny how easily he'd slipped into the role of Bliss citizen.

"And you?" Rafe asked. "How much trouble could you get into?"

Cam shrugged. "All they're going to know is the ID on this computer. I'll dump it after I'm done. I'll take it apart and toss out the parts. You think I haven't done this before?"

He had. Many times. His fingers flew across the keys now that he'd been granted access. He'd been a snot-nosed, small-town hacker before the feds had swooped in to show him the error of his ways. He'd given it up for a long time, but in the last few years he'd taken it up again. Now he was damn happy he was up to speed. A nudge here, a nudge there, and he was in. The files started to download. The FBI kept copious files on their employees.

"I have the police report on Edward's mother's death." He scanned the simple report. "It looks like Toyota versus eighteen-wheeler. The mom's blood alcohol level was over the limit. Other than that, it's kind of boring. He went to Harvard. Top of his class. He's been a dedicated agent for years. Here's the complaint Laura filed. Asshole. He made comments about women in the workplace and how a woman like Laura shouldn't be taken seriously because she was looking for a husband and would leave the job when she had her first kid. I bet that went over like gangbusters with Laura.

271

She left before the complaint could be resolved." He read down the professor's file until he came to the newest tidbit of information. "He recently moved. And listed his emergency contact as a man named Cecil Newberg."

Rafe's lips curled slightly. "Good for Edward. And we can eliminate him. He was out of town the night Laura was attacked. I had forgotten, but he left for a convention that night. At least two hundred law enforcement personnel attended a seminar he gave in Atlanta."

He breathed a sigh of relief. He didn't want to believe that one of his coworkers was capable of this. If he could eliminate the members of his former team, he could move on. He closed the file on Edward and moved on to Brad. "Brad wasn't in the BAU when Laura was attacked."

Rafe stared over his shoulder, crowding him. There was only one desk in the motel room, and it was barely large enough to fit the laptop. "Don't discount him. When he first became my partner, he walked in the door with a file on the Marquis de Sade. He said he was fascinated with the case. He requested the assignment."

He pulled up everything he could on Brad Conrad. Star football player. High school valedictorian. On paper, Brad Conrad was the all-American hero. He'd given up his athletic dreams to pursue justice after his high school girlfriend was killed. He'd single-mindedly pursued a career with the FBI. And he'd fought to get on the BAU.

"He found the body," Cam commented as he read through the information on the girlfriend's death. The police report listed the case as open, but he knew what it really was—cold.

"Yes," Rafe replied grimly. "He went to her place. Her parents weren't home. He found her with her throat slit. He talks about it when he gets drunk. I think it's why none of his marriages worked out. He can't put another woman above her."

"Doesn't fit the MO." The Marquis would never simply slit a throat. He liked to play with his victims. He spent hours and hours playing with them before he finally put them out of their misery.

"Could be the first one," Rafe pointed out. "Serial killers perfect their techniques over long periods of time. MOs evolve. This murder could be the inciting incident. A crime of passion that led him to more calculated murders."

Cam looked up at his partner. "You've worked close to this guy for the last couple of years."

Rafe's eyes tightened, the lines around them becoming more pronounced. "I wouldn't say close. I worked with him. I had beers with him on Fridays. It wasn't a close friendship."

"Still. You've spent at least eight hours a day with the man for the last couple of years. Did he give you any indication that something was off?"

"He's an agent. He works crappy hours for government pay in one of the most stressed-out units in the FBI. Does he have problems? Hell, yes." Rafe ran a hand through his hair. "He drinks too much. He sleeps around. He's got a bad temper."

Well, he couldn't blame the guy for that. He had a bad temper himself. This was going nowhere. He could bring up all kinds of stuff from their past, but it wasn't hard evidence. Hell, he'd have taken a little soft evidence. But it looked like everyone had some dark secrets. "I don't know what I thought I would find in here. I need a white board. We need to skip the profiling crap and figure out who was where on the nights of the murders."

That was something he could use.

Rafe stepped back and started to pace around the small motel room they had checked in to but never used. While Cam had been hacking into systems, Rafe had packed up the few things they had left here on the morning they had checked in. They wouldn't be coming back here. They would move into Laura's cabin.

He thought of all the things he was going to have to do to make the cabin livable. Locks. Lots of locks. An alarm system. Motion detectors. He might have to buy a guard dog.

God, his heart felt like it would stop every time he thought about the fact that this guy was after his woman. Until he was caught, how was he supposed to think about anything else?

"When do you get your gun?" Rafe asked, pulling him out of his dark thoughts.

That was a good question. "As soon as the paperwork is done, but I bet I could convince the sheriff to give me one now. And there can't be a shortage of shotguns around here. You don't need a license to carry a shotgun in Colorado. Hell, up here I bet people expect you to carry."

He would feel better once he had a gun in his hand. For now, Cam felt completely impotent. He couldn't defend his woman. He couldn't even figure out who he should defend her against. What use was he? The least he could do was hurry so she wasn't alone. He trusted Nate. More importantly Laura trusted him, but he wouldn't feel better until she was in his sight.

Cam looked down and made sure he had all the files he planned on taking. He could very cautiously review them at the police station. Maybe he could piece together some dates from the information. He would hole up in Nate's office, and Rafe would make sure he wasn't disturbed while he tried to put together what he needed.

The last file he was waiting on, a police report, finished downloading. On instinct, Cam opened it up to make sure he'd gotten it all. He flipped through the report to the pictures the police had filed. A woman lay on her back, her unseeing eyes face up to the camera. It wasn't anything Cam hadn't seen before, but something about her lips triggered his memory. That color, a shiny mauve. It stuck out like a sore thumb.

Laura's words came back to haunt him.

He put lipstick on me. It was the weirdest thing. It was like he was making me up to be someone else.

It was the one thing the killer had left on all of his victims. A high-end lipstick called Purple Passion. The same lipstick on the woman in the photo. Cam had just found the Marquis de Sade's first victim. The one the killer had never planned on sharing.

Rafe opened the door, letting the sunlight in. "Are you ready to go? It's been an hour."

Cam turned, his stomach in his throat. It was far worse than he'd ever expected. "I know who the Marquis de Sade is."

* * * *

Laura forced herself to get out of Nate's Bronco. All she could think about was the fact that Jana was dead, and there was no denying the truth. The Marquis de Sade was here in Bliss, and he was someone she knew.

Someone she knew had tortured her. He'd drugged her and tied her down and cut her. He'd terrified her and caused her more pain than she'd imagined she could survive.

He'd taken pieces of her.

"Laura?" Nate stood in front of her. He reached out a hand. "Stay close to me. I won't let anything happen. I promise. Your men will be here before you know it."

Her men. She liked the sound of that and the way Nate and the rest of the men had welcomed them. Rafe and Cam wouldn't find it hard to fit in here.

She knew they would hurry. Rafe had sounded miserable when she'd talked to him earlier, but the truth was, she wanted that information. Anything Cam could pull out of the system, legal or illegal, would be welcomed. She wanted to sit down and build a profile. It was there. She knew it. It was all there in the background. Now that she had concrete suspects, all she had to do was fit the pieces of the puzzle together. The truth would be in their history, hidden in the small documents that made up a life.

She could catch him if she tried.

But first, she had to get through this.

"I'd like to see the letter he left for me." She didn't want to see it at all, but she had to. It could give her insight.

Nate nodded. "They have it inside. They brought the physical evidence here, but the body was taken to the morgue. I can probably get you in there if you want to witness the autopsy."

She shook her head. Laura had attended many an autopsy, but never one on a person she'd known. She couldn't imagine being forced to try to view Jana in clinical terms. Despite the trouble they had, they had been friends once. She couldn't see Jana that way. This was precisely why cops didn't investigate crimes against their families or loved ones. Joe should have taken Rafe and Cam off the case the minute he realized she was involved with them. "Just try to see if Caleb will get me a copy of his findings. I know it's not protocol, but…"

"Since when do we stand on protocol? You'll have a copy as soon as he's done." Nate settled his hat on his head and led her through the double doors.

The station was buzzing with activity.

"Sheriff." Hope, Nate's secretary, stood up and greeted him. She was in her twenties, but she dressed much older. Laura and Holly had talked about the admin's odd wardrobe choices, wishing they could give the pretty woman a makeover to accentuate her assets. Today Hope wore a long, shapeless skirt and a button-down brown shirt. The ensemble made her look heavier than Laura thought she was. Her dark hair was pulled into a ponytail, as it was every day. Her scrubbed-clean face was hidden behind large glasses. "Logan went back out. He said the special agent in charge came in and asked him to take extra evidence bags to the scene. They're apparently trying to be very thorough."

Then she and Nate were alone. She would have preferred to have Logan here as well. Two bodyguards were better than one. She took a deep breath. It was broad daylight. Nothing was going to happen to her in a police station.

Nate nodded at Hope. "I appreciate it. Is there anything else I should know?"

"Your wife came by."

Nate's face became thunderously fierce. "Callie left the cabin? She better have a damn good reason for leaving the cabin. I left explicit instructions that she was supposed to stay there with Zane."

Laura half expected the little mouse to run away, but Hope merely frowned at her boss. Her eyes rolled slightly as though she was utterly used to her boss losing his temper. Maybe she wasn't so shy. "Zane brought her in. They brought your lunch and a thermos of coffee. I believe they thought that since Stella's was closed today, you might have a hard time finding something to eat. And not eating makes you crankier than normal. It's sitting on your desk. Speaking of your office, I thought I should let you know that the feds took over yours while you were gone. The special agent in charge had a call with DC. I hope it was okay. He didn't actually ask me. He told me he was going to do it."

"It's fine. Damn, I hope these guys are gone soon. I want my station back. It's too loud. And I haven't been fishing all week." Nate growled a little and opened the door to his office. "Where are they now?"

"Special Agents Conrad and Lock are talking to the cameraman." Hope motioned toward the back of the building where the small interview room was located. "It took them a while to get him to talk. He was trying to make a news story out of this."

Nate grimaced. "Asshole. I hate reporters. You go on into the break room and grab a cup of coffee. Take fifteen or twenty minutes to yourself, Hope. But you make damn sure there are people around, you understand? I'll answer the radio."

Hope nodded gratefully and disappeared down the hallway.

Laura walked into Nate's office and sat down. She thought about calling Rafe up on the radio but decided against it. She'd already talked to him, and she didn't want to disrupt their work. The sooner they got done, the sooner they would come for her.

Nate took off his hat and sat behind his desk. There was a paper sack and a thermos sitting in the middle. It spoke of sweet domesticity. She would have to make sure Cam had lunch when he

277

started coming to work.

The door opened again, and Brad Conrad stuck his head in. He was dressed in a perfectly pressed suit and tie. If he'd been in the field, he didn't show it. Apparently Brad was one of those guys who didn't get his hands dirty. He looked down at her. "You came in."

"I told you I wasn't going to run again." Was he the one she was running from? She rather thought not. Unless he was a spectacular actor. He seemed too emotionally undisciplined. Though he had asked her very leading questions. He'd seemed to delight in her discomfort. "I heard you wanted to talk to me."

"Yes," Brad replied. "We'll get to you soon enough. Don't leave the station. I don't want to have to track you down."

Yeah, she kind of hoped it was that asshole.

"Hey," Nate called out to the special agent. Brad turned, his face bunched in an impatient frown. "Could you show her the letter?"

"Sure. She should know what's coming for her. It's not much of a letter. It's a whole bunch of quotes," Brad explained.

She could guess who the bastard was quoting. "From the Marquis de Sade?"

"Dunno." Brad held his hands up, impatience apparent in his stance. "Someone's looking into it. It's a bunch of crap about how morals are arbitrary and destruction is nature's mandate. It's all pretentious shit. I think this guy is stuck in a college phase."

"Just get her the letter," Nate said, his eyes narrowing on the special agent.

"I'll see if Joe is still around. He's been running all over today. It's been hard to pin that man down. He has the letter." Brad shut the door.

Nate sighed and sat back in his chair. There was a weariness to the sheriff's eyes. How hard had this been on him? Callie was pregnant, less than a month away from giving birth to their first child. Nate should be at home getting ready for his kid and taking care of his wife, but he was dealing with feds and autopsies and playing her bodyguard.

"Nate, I'm so sorry about all of this."

"What?" Nate asked, clearly surprised. "Don't you apologize. This is none of your doing. This is my job. I might complain some. Fine, I might complain a lot, but I love this town, and I'll protect every citizen with my life. Except Max. I'll protect him with my toe or some limb I'm not real attached to."

"Point taken." She wasn't alone.

Nate reached out and grabbed his thermos, opening it. Laura was immediately assaulted with the smell of coffee.

"You want some?" Nate asked. "I can get you a cup. If I know my wife, it's some froufrou flavor. She never makes plain, ordinary coffee even now that she can't drink it. Zane has gotten every bit as bad as Callie. He claims he needs to push the taste envelope because he's a restaurant owner. It's a bar. He makes wings and burgers, not high-end coffee. What the hell does he know? Bullshit, I say. Coffee is best when it tastes a little like overused motor oil."

Laura leaned forward. "Do you drink a lot of overused motor oil, Sheriff?"

He smiled, his handsome face splitting. "Maybe not, but I like a masculine coffee." He took a long drink and grimaced slightly. "Vanilla."

"Then yes," Laura replied. "I would love some. And I'm still hungry, so if you want to split that lunch of yours, I'll take it. You closed down the only diner in town."

Nate frowned. He opened the bag. "It's a sandwich. I don't know if that will feed me. Hope was right. I get cranky if I don't have proper sustenance."

"Fine. Hopefully there's something in the break room." Nate Wright was a greedy bastard. She obviously wasn't going to get anything out of him. "Do you mind if I use your bathroom? I still feel grubby."

He waved her toward the bathroom as he took a long drink of the coffee his wife had brought him. "Feel free. Apparently we have time. I tell you, I don't like being on someone else's timetable. I'm going to call over and see if Caleb's gotten started."

On the autopsy. She stood and tried to approximate a smile. "Okay. You do that. Rafe and Cam should be here soon."

She turned and walked into Nate's private bathroom. She closed the door behind her and took a long, deep breath. The events of the week crashed over her. She choked back tears. She couldn't lose it now. Later, when Rafe and Cam were surrounding her, she could lose it, but now she had to keep her composure.

She walked to the window. *Fresh air*. Nate's office had a window with a broken lock, allowing for the pane to open. Laura opened it and breathed in the cool air. Despite the fact that it was summer, the mornings were still cool. She let her head rest against the sill.

She had to find the strength to get through this. She wasn't alone, and she wasn't walking away this time. She wouldn't leave her home. Never again.

She straightened up. As she went to close the window, she noticed a car in the alleyway. It was a big, black SUV. One of the feds. *Damn it*. Now they couldn't be bothered to park in the lot?

Why wouldn't they park in the lot? There was plenty of parking in the front and side of the building. The alley was narrow, and anyone who parked there would have to walk all the way around the building to get to the front. Not to mention if Nate saw it, he would ticket the person who parked there.

A cold chill went across her skin. It was illogical, unless the person didn't want anyone to know the car was here.

"Nate," Laura called out. She leaned over the sill, trying to see if she could get the plate number off the car. It was almost surely a rental, but at least they could tell who had rented it. "Nate, get in here. You need to see this."

The door to the bathroom opened. Laura turned to give Nate a chance to look out the window.

Brad Conrad stood in the doorway. "You have to come with

me."

She shrank back. She couldn't miss the look in Brad's eyes or the gun he held. Primitive fear threatened to take over. She pushed it back and tried to figure a way out. If she tried to get out the window, he'd be on her before she could get through. She would fit through the window, but she'd land face first and have to scramble to get up. Then there was another problem.

"What did you do to Nate?" Nate Wright wouldn't have allowed this asshole to walk in. Her stomach rolled. *Please don't let Nate be dead.* He was so close to having his family with Callie and Zane. She couldn't even think about it.

Brad frowned. "I didn't do anything, but he's out cold. Look, Laura, you're coming with me. I'm sorry, but I can't take no for an answer."

He reached out to grab her, and she feinted to her left. She punched out with her right hand, catching him in the jaw. Brad groaned, and she pushed her way around him. He fell back, hitting his head hard against the sink. The sound thudded through the room, and she couldn't miss the blood that started to pool around Brad's head. She shoved her way out of the door and froze at the sight in front of her.

Joseph Stone slipped from the small closet behind Nate's desk, a Taser in his hands.

And Laura realized she'd made a deadly mistake.

Chapter Eighteen

"**Y**ou're certain?" Rafe asked, his heart racing as he put the SUV in reverse and jammed his foot on the gas. He was pretty sure he hadn't locked the motel door, but it didn't matter.

Nothing mattered except getting to Laura.

Cam clicked his seat belt into place and turned to Rafe, gesturing toward the computer. "It's right here. I know it's not conclusive, but this is it. This is what we've been looking for. The lipstick connects the cases. Purple Passion. The lipstick is listed in the evidence log for Marla Stone's suicide. Joe's wife is the connection. She's wearing the same lipstick that the Marquis de Sade puts on all his victims. That can't be a coincidence. Tell me you think I'm wrong. Tell me Laura isn't in the same building with the man who almost killed her."

"It was a suicide." Rafe said the words, but he no longer believed them.

"I don't think so. I think she's the first." Cam still had his laptop up and running. He struggled to keep the thing steady. "She slit her wrists. Damn. And she was pregnant according to the autopsy. She said in her suicide note—which was typed and unsigned—that she couldn't handle what she had done and called herself a whore. The police concluded she'd been having an affair with a coworker."

Rafe let his eyes close briefly. "That's why he tortured the victims with shallow wounds to their lower abdomen. That was probably what he wanted to do to her the first time, but Joe has always been a disciplined bastard. He planned it. He knew he couldn't get away with torturing her, so he staged a suicide, but he couldn't let it go. The first victim was killed a year after Marla, and every six to seven months after, he killed again. He was killing her over and over again."

"That would be my take on it," Cam replied. "And after we found the first couple of victims and the news reports started, he couldn't help himself. He had to control his image. He needed more than just the killing. He needed the attention. He asked for our team to be assigned to this case, you know."

"I remember it well." Rafe remembered how Joe had gone over all the evidence the DC metro police had found before deciding it was a serial case and calling in the Bureau. He'd thought Joe was excited about taking on a big case. The bastard had talked about how smart the killer was. He went on and on about how hard it would be to catch this one. At the time, he'd taken it as Joe issuing a challenge to his team.

Joseph Stone had been bragging.

Cam broke through his dark thoughts. Fingers flew across the keyboard in a flurry. "It gets worse. Did you know Joe had a brother? He's in a mental institution and has been for years. He was discovered torturing animals and was accused of raping a neighborhood girl. Do you know who the star witness was in his trial?"

His stomach turned again as he realized how long his boss had been lying. "Joe, I'm sure."

"His brother's IQ is under 80. It would have been easy for Joe to make him the scapegoat. The girl didn't see who it was because the attacker wore a mask, but forensics led to someone from next door. Apparently Joe's mother had some rare plants in her home that tracked to the crime scene. Joe gave up his brother. Joe testified that he'd covered his brother's violent streak for years. The fucker was seventeen years old. And his father divorced his mother for cheating on him. God, what a pattern."

For the normal person, it was a pattern that would lead to bitterness and a host of self-destructive tendencies. But with that rare person, it led to focusing the rage outward. Joe was a super predator. The tendency had always been there. Rafe knew the pattern well. Most serial killers had similar stories. Joe had undoubtedly been the one to torture animals as a kid. Joe had been the one to rape his neighbor. It had been his luck that he'd had a handy scapegoat, or Joe would have been discovered. Rafe could guess how things had gone after that close call. Joe had hidden his monster for years until the inciting incident—discovering his wife was pregnant with another man's child. Then he couldn't hold it in any longer. The fact that he'd planned his wife's death was a testament to Joe's discipline.

If Joe intended to kill Laura, he would have an excellent plan in place.

Cam was staring at the screen as though he couldn't believe what he was seeing. "He's hidden this for years. Do you think he laughed the whole time we were profiling the Marquis de Sade?"

"I bet he did," Rafe replied.

He'd never known the man. He'd worked beside him for years, and he'd never seen the monster behind the mask. Joe had been the one to sit down with him after Laura left. He'd listened. He'd bought him beers, and Rafe had gone over everything that had happened to her.

"The fucker enjoyed listening to me. The whole time I was moaning about Laura, he was enjoying my pain," he said, finally understanding.

Cam nodded, his lips a grim line. "Yes, he would. He would

enjoy the misery he caused. Being in charge of the case had to have given him an enormous amount of satisfaction. He was able to manipulate things his way. And when Laura got too close, he tried to kill her."

"Is the radio working?" They had tried a couple of times already. Bile rose in his throat at the thought of Laura being in the same state as Joe, much less the same room.

Cam switched some dials on the radio he held. "This is Cameron Briggs. Can anyone hear me?" He groaned. "And no one is answering. What the hell? The station is supposed to be manned. I know there are at least five people in that building. Why aren't they answering?"

Rafe hit the gas again, cursing the fact that the motel was on the outskirts of town. "Try the direct frequency for the sheriff."

Frustration dripped from Cam's voice as he closed the laptop and set it at his feet, his whole attention focused on the radio in his hands. "I've done that twice now. I'm not getting anything. I've even tried to switch the frequency to see if I can get anyone in town to answer."

Rafe pounded his fist on the steering wheel. "Something's wrong. I know it."

His every instinct was screaming at him that this situation was ripe with danger. Something had happened.

"I'll see if I can get Logan. Maybe he'll know what's going on," Cam said.

When Nate Wright had radioed in earlier, Joe hadn't been at the station. He'd been on site, possibly making sure he'd cleaned up properly after himself and getting rid of pesky pieces of evidence. Joe had always joked that he, himself, was the smartest man he knew. That arrogance had seemed like a funny quirk. Now Rafe could see that Joe truly believed it. He thought he was above the law.

Cam changed the frequency again and let out a shout of triumph as he got an answer. "Thank god. Logan. Logan, it's Cam and Rafe.

We need to know if the SAC is still at the site."

Logan's voice crackled over the line. "Your SAC is a jerk. He had me bring all this crap out here and now he's gone. I asked some of the forensic guys and no one's seen him. And the forensic guys are looking at me like I'm stupid. I fucking hate that. He wasn't at the station when I left. Is it standard FBI procedure to disappear in the middle of an investigation?"

Rafe's skin went cold. "Who's at the station with Laura?"

There was a slight pause, and then Logan didn't sound quite so pissed off. "Nate. Nate's there. I'll get him on the radio."

The connection got quiet for a minute.

"He wouldn't take her in the middle of the day." Cam's words came out almost like a prayer.

"He'll do anything it takes." God, he needed a gun. Why had he given up his gun?

Logan's voice came back on the line. "Nate isn't answering. No one's answering. I'm getting in my Bronco right now. I can be there in ten minutes."

Ten minutes was too long. He turned onto Main Street. Unlike the other times he'd been on the street, it was almost deserted. The line of businesses and restaurants was eerily quiet. There was one truck parked outside the Trading Post. It was big and black. Rafe recognized it because he'd thought sincerely about firebombing it with its owner inside. Now Rafe couldn't think of a single person he'd rather see more than Wolf Meyer.

He stopped the SUV in the middle of the street when he saw Wolf walking away from the front door of the Trading Post, scratching his head at the *Closed* sign.

Wolf was dressed in a black T-shirt, jeans, and boots. He looked very military and substantial. Rafe hopped out, leaving the engine running.

"Hey, have you got any idea what's going on? Why the hell is everything closed in the middle of the week?" Wolf asked.

He didn't have time to answer the man's questions. "I need a gun."

Wolf Meyer looked like a man who kept a gun handy.

Wolf went from confused to stone-cold professional in a heartbeat. He moved toward his truck. "What's happened with Laura?"

No hesitation from the ex-SEAL.

"We figured out who the killer is, and we think he's after her. Nate took her in to be interviewed while we were getting the files we needed, and now we can't raise anyone from the station," Cam explained.

"Fucker." Wolf pulled back the front seat, and his hand disappeared. "There's no way Nate lets anything happen to her. We have to think that Nate's not answering for a reason."

"Yes, he's either run with her or he's down." Rafe didn't even want to think about that. If Joe had killed the sheriff, he wasn't sure how he was going to live with himself. Of course, if Joe killed Laura, he wasn't sure he wanted to live at all.

"Nate's going to be a tough kill," Wolf said, his voice gruff as he pulled out a black bag. He unzipped the bag and started pulling out what looked like an endless supply of things with which to kill people. He'd definitely come to the right place. "Sig Sauer P226."

"I'm familiar." The minute Wolf put that big black gun in his hand, Rafe felt infinitely better. He checked the chamber and made sure it was loaded and ready to go. "How many more do you have?"

Wolf grimaced. "More than I should have. And a couple of knives. Taser unit. Two shotguns."

"Are you planning on starting a war?" Cam asked, holding his hand out for his weapon. He proved he was familiar with firearms, too, when Wolf handed him another P226.

Wolf reached back in his truck and came up with a scoped rifle. "My mom and potential future step-dad," he stumbled on the word, groaning around it, "they might be crazy, but they're right about this town. It's dangerous. I'm loaded and ready to go. Russian mob. Stalkers. Biker gangs. Hell, aliens. I'm ready to take them all down."

Rafe was grateful for all the help he could get. He'd use anyone if it meant getting Laura back alive and whole. He couldn't fail her again. "Will you come with us?"

"Of course." Wolf slammed the truck door shut. "What are you going to do with this guy? Do you have enough to arrest him?"

"I'm going to get him alone, and I'm going to kill him," Rafe said. Even as the words came out of his mouth, he knew he shouldn't have spoken them out loud, but he couldn't take them back. He meant every word.

Wolf stared at him for a moment. "See that you do. And then tell me what your alibi is. I'll back you up. So will any man in this town. They won't be able to prosecute you. Make sure you get rid of the gun. And wipe it down first."

Wolf sounded like he knew how to play dirty, but then he was sure the SEALs had taught him that. They didn't play fair when the country's safety was at stake, and Rafe didn't intend to play fair, either.

Wolf nodded as he started toward the sheriff's department building. It was only a block away, but it seemed like a mile to Rafe.

Rafe turned to his partner, the only person in the world who understood how much was at stake. "Let's go get her."

He watched Cam swallow down his fear and turn stony cold. "I'm ready."

Rafe walked toward the sheriff's department, his mind set to the task.

* * * *

Cam went in the front door, gun at the ready. Wolf followed behind him while Rafe went up the alley to sneak in the back. Cam's heart was in his throat. He checked his emotions so he wouldn't take one look at Joseph Stone and pull the trigger.

He was shocked at how normal the station seemed.

A young woman dressed in a long skirt and loose shirt walked out into the main room as Cam and Wolf strode in. Her eyes went wide as she saw the guns in their hands. "Deputy Briggs? Is there something I should know?"

Hope. Nate had introduced her as Hope. "Where's Laura?"

"She's in with the sheriff. I was taking a break." Hope strode over to open her boss's door, and then a shriek came out of her mouth. "Sheriff!"

Cam ran. Now some of the others were coming out of the interrogation room. Edward actually called out for him to stop, but Cam ignored the man. Bile welled in his throat when he saw the sheriff slumped over his desk. The desk was in complete disarray. He'd knocked over a thermos, and coffee was everywhere.

"We need to call a bus," Rafe yelled from the small room in the back. "Brad is down."

"I'm fine." Brad sounded cranky, but Cam was focused on the sheriff. Wolf got in behind the big man and tried to pull him up.

"He's got a pulse." Wolf struggled as he forced Nate Wright's big body up. "Come on, Sheriff. It's time to wake up and possibly purge."

Where was Laura?

Chaos ruled all around him. He couldn't place all the voices shouting.

"Call Caleb. Half-alive sheriff is more important than dead reporter."

"We have to get him on his feet."

"What happened to Special Agent Conrad?"

"Where's Laura?"

Where was Laura?

"Stop." Cam's roar filled the room, and everyone stopped. "Hope, get Caleb over here. Edward, you stay. Wolf, get the sheriff into the bathroom. Everyone else, clear the room. When Logan gets here, send him in."

"I need to sleep." The sheriff tried to shove Wolf away.

Wolf wasn't having it. "No, Sheriff, you need to spend a little time in the bathroom."

"Can't. Gotta keep it open for Callie." But the sheriff was on his feet, stumbling toward where Wolf wanted him to go.

Rafe helped Brad sit down. "What the hell happened?"

Brad's forehead was swollen above his right eye, and his face was covered in blood. It seemed to have stopped, but Brad held a towel to his head anyway. "I walked in to ask the sheriff about the recording equipment, and I found him like that. I realized something was wrong, and I tried to get your girl out of here, but she attacked me. I hit my head and then nothing." He turned to Edward. "Where the hell were you?"

Rafe shook his head. "It wasn't Edward. It was Joe. We need to figure out where Joe would have taken Laura."

Edward's face went a stark white. "It can't be Joe. Joe is helping process the body. He told me to handle the cameraman because he needed to focus on evidence."

Cam was sick of everyone hiding their heads in the sand. "He killed his wife, and now he has mine. You're the closest one of all of us to him. Where would he go?"

Edward shook his head as if he was trying to wake up from some nightmare. "He loved Marla. He loved her so much. He was devastated when she died."

"Edward, snap the fuck out of it." Cam needed a different tactic. Just because Edward was blind didn't mean he was stupid. "I need you to focus. You know more about the actual facts of this case than anyone. Stop thinking of him as Joe. He's the Marquis de Sade. Where would he take her? Where would he go?"

Edward swallowed, and for a moment, Cam worried that he wouldn't answer.

"Somewhere isolated," Rafe prompted the profiler.

Edward nodded. "Yes. Isolated. He prefers places that no one looks at. Places that blend into the background. It's why he worked in abandoned warehouses. There was plenty of space and no one to hear his victim's screams. He could work in privacy."

"He's not going to find a warehouse out here." There wasn't anything industrial about Bliss.

A bang resounded through the room as the door slammed opened, and Caleb Burke rushed in. "Where's Nate? Do we have any idea what he ingested?"

"Some type of sedative," Cam guessed.

The doctor slammed his bag on the desk. "Shit. And we have no idea how much? No chance it was anything acidic?"

"I don't know." He felt utterly helpless.

"Joe has a prescription for sleeping pills. I would assume it's that. It's a common prescription. He could easily call it coincidence if anyone thought to ask," Brad said. "I saw the bottle in his hotel room the other day."

Caleb strode toward the bathroom. "Holly, have that charcoal ready."

Cam turned, and Holly stood in the doorway, a mug in her hands and tears in her eyes. Caleb had come prepared. "He has Laura?"

"Yes," Rafe replied. "We're trying to figure out where he would take her."

"Would it be the same place he took that reporter?" Holly asked. It was easy to see that she was forcing herself to hold it together. Her hands shook and there was a pale fragility to her face.

Of course. He already had his kill spot. "It has to be close. He was here this morning. When is the first time anyone remembers seeing him?"

"We all got the call at seven," Brad said.

"I heard him in his room far earlier than that." Edward sounded stronger now. "I have the room next to his. He was in his bathroom running the shower at four this morning. The walls are paper thin, and I'm a horrible sleeper. Anything wakes me up. Unless someone else was using his shower, he was in his room at four."

Now they were getting somewhere. Cam looked into the

bathroom. Wolf had Nate upright, one hand around his waist and the other under Nate's arms.

"You're going to swallow this." Caleb didn't sound like he would take no for an answer.

"Don't wanna," Nate said, struggling against Wolf's hold.

Caleb didn't back down. "And I don't want to get covered in vomit, but that's probably what's going to happen."

Cam did not want to watch that. "Have you figured out the time of death on Jana Evans?"

"According to liver temp, I would say no later than 2:30 this morning." Caleb held up Nate's head and tipped back the small container he held. "I would leave now. It's about to get messy. Ipecac doesn't take long. Wolf, get him over the sink. I need the contents of his stomach for testing."

Cam stepped out as the ipecac began to work. "Did you hear that?"

Cam noticed Logan had arrived. His face betrayed no emotion as Logan stared at the bathroom. "Is Nate going to be okay?"

"I think so," Cam said. "Caleb's taking care of him. Now, we're trying to figure out places to look for Laura."

Logan nodded. "I got that. I heard Joe was in his room at 4:00, and the reporter was killed at roughly 2:30. He's got to be in the area. He couldn't be farther than Del Norte. Creede is forty minutes away. There are only a couple of spreads between here and there, and all of them are occupied right now. We have a lot of land, but our population is small. We all know each other."

"There are no new developments?" Rafe asked, frustration evident in his tone.

"No." Holly's hands were shaking slightly. "You would have to go about a hundred miles east to Alamosa to find any real development projects. We have some summer cabins, but they're mostly privately owned. I could call and see if they're occupied."

"You do that. Have Hope help you." Cam took the mug out of her hand. "I'll pass this to Caleb when he needs it. Also, check on anything that's for sale in the area. He needs to know that the place won't be occupied. He would make sure of it."

The horrible noise coming from the bathroom stopped, and Wolf reappeared, his face a surprising shade of green. For the first time, the man didn't look like the all-American hero. "Caleb needs the activated charcoal. Nate's going to be fine. I'm not sure about me though."

Cam passed the mug. "We're trying to come up with an isolated place within about twenty minutes driving distance. Do you know of any cabins that are unoccupied? Places people would easily identify as empty?"

Wolf passed the mug but kept his eyes on Cam. If anything, he got even sicker looking. "Wasn't this guy at the town hall meeting?"

Edward looked up. "Yes, we all were. Joe insisted on it."

"Then he knows about my mom and Mel," Wolf replied.

Cam went still. "Where is this Mel's place? Everyone is talking about the fact that they won't come out of their bunker until the feds are gone. Joe has to know that."

"He laughed about it," Brad interjected.

"We need to get out there," Rafe said, walking toward the door.

"Mel's place is a no-go. He has all kinds of whacked-out security, including cameras he can monitor from his bunker," Logan said.

"But my mom doesn't. She refused to spend the money. She just planted beets everywhere. She thinks they'll keep the aliens away." Wolf took a deep breath and visibly stilled. He was back to being in control. "Her place is right on the county line. You can easily get there in fifteen minutes, and her closest neighbor is two miles away."

If Wolf was wrong, Laura could be dead by the time he figured out where else to search. He looked to Rafe. He stared at his partner and was suddenly so fucking grateful he wasn't in this alone.

"We're going out there." He turned because there wasn't a moment to waste. "Edward, you wait here, and if Hope and Holly come up with anything, you check it out. Brad, you need to have the doctor check you out. Logan and Wolf are coming with us."

"Stop."

Cam turned, and Nate Wright stood in the doorway looking like death warmed over. "Consider yourself on the clock, son. You do what you need to do and with the full weight of a badge behind it."

Cam nodded and they all hit the ground running.

Chapter Nineteen

Laura came to with a splitting headache and terrible fear in the pit of her stomach. She tried to sit up, but her arms were held fast. Rope bit into her wrists. She was already losing feeling. God, where was she?

Don't let it be real. Wake up. Wake up and be back in the cabin curled up with Rafe on one side and Cam on the other.

She forced herself to focus, to take in her surroundings. She couldn't fool herself. She was in serious trouble. She was naked, her skin chilled. She hated this so much. She looked up at the ceiling. There was a wagon wheel that had been fashioned into an odd chandelier.

God, she was at Cassidy's. She remembered looking at that light fixture the last time she'd had dinner out here. She'd been helping Cassidy and Nell on a project, and that was when she'd met Wolf. She remembered how she'd looked the gorgeous man over and all she'd been able to think about were Cam's shoulders and Rafe's dark eyes.

Where were they? Did they even know she was gone?

"Ah, you're awake. I had to use the Taser a couple of times, dear. I hope it doesn't have any lingering effects. I wouldn't want to desensitize you." Joe came into view. "You know who I am now?"

A monster. "Yes. You're the man who calls himself the Marquis de Sade."

He chuckled lightly. "He was an amateur, a fop who played at dealing pain. I am more than that. Still, he had a lot of interesting things to say. Did you get my present? Or did those cops keep it from you? It was addressed to you."

Jana's body. God, had she ever known this man at all? "I got your message even if I didn't see the actual package."

He pulled latex gloves over his hands. "But I did it for you, little rabbit. I cut out her heart. It was messier than I like to get, but I thought you should see that she actually had one. And I took it apart for you. You're the only one who understands me. That profile of yours was dead on."

Her first instinct was to scream her lungs out. Her second was to fight with all her might, but another thought skittered across her brain. *Time*. She needed time.

"But it wasn't perfect," she forced herself to say in a calm, even voice. "I think I understand parts, but not the whole."

He stopped and looked down at her, brown eyes narrowing. "Well, no one can comprehend all of me, but you came the closest. It was why I had to shut you down. You aren't my usual prey. Not because I find women like you more worthy of life. I don't. You're all the same underneath. It's simply more expedient to prey on the weak, the unwanted. I was making a statement. It was far more important that I remain unfettered to continue to speak."

By speaking, he meant killing. "Why did you stop after me?"

He sighed and turned briefly, coming back with a small tray. "It was a close thing with you. Do you know why I left you that night, darling? You looked lovely all tied up and bleeding. It was rude of me, I know. I've always wanted to explain why I had to leave you there so very unfinished."

His words sickened her, as did the almost affectionate way he spoke. He didn't sound anything like the Joseph Stone she knew. Still, if he was talking, he wasn't stabbing her, and she needed to avoid that. They would come. This time they would come for her. "I did wonder why you left suddenly."

"Well, my two worlds collided," he explained. "I had been careful to keep them apart, but you forced my hand. I thought I was the smartest guy in the world when I was able to fire you for talking to the very reporter I'd set up as my mouthpiece. Do you remember? You introduced me to her at the Christmas party years and years ago. It was when you were working in another department, but you would butter me up because you knew you wanted to be in the BAU."

"Yes," she replied. He was talking. If he wanted to stroll down memory lane recounting all the ways he was smarter than the rest, she would go with him. "I brought Jana with me because she was more outgoing than me."

"She was a whore, dear. She hit on every man in the place. But I digress. I was able to fire you for talking about a case to the press. I thought no one would miss you for a night or two. I didn't realize that you had made...friends with both Kincaid and Briggs. They went looking for you. When they couldn't find you, they made a stink. I was called away to start investigating your disappearance. By the time I was able to get back, you had already made it out of our hideaway."

A sob threatened to escape. She'd always wondered why he'd left so abruptly. Cam and Rafe. They had saved her then, too. They hadn't known it, but their need to find her had saved her life.

She would live through this. She would do it because she loved them. She didn't need survival instincts this time. She had Rafe and Cam.

"I think you'll find the ropes are properly tied this time. The last time, I was a bit too eager," Joe said, testing them again. He pulled at the ropes he'd tied. Laura noticed there was a sheet underneath her covered by a layer of plastic. It was like last time. He'd be able to easily destroy the evidence without leaving pesky blood or fibers behind. She wondered if his baldness was real or if he routinely shaved his head. Hairs left behind at a crime scene had gotten more than one killer caught. "Like I said, you were outside my normal prey, but so much closer to what I truly hunger for."

She shivered. "What do you hunger for, Joe?"

He smiled. "I like hearing my name for once. I like hearing it coming from you. We're close, you and I. To answer your question, I want someone soft and real. Those whores are close to death anyway. Most of them thank me when I finally put them out of their misery. Not you. You fought like you had something to live for. It made the game so much sweeter."

"I'll fight this time, too." She would. And if he believed the experience would be good, maybe he would prolong it. She would survive. She would live through anything if it meant getting back to her men.

He ran a gloved hand along her torso, obviously admiring the scars he'd placed there. "I read you lost your womb, dear."

Temper. She had to watch it. She wanted to spit on him. "The surgery to repair my intestines and uterus didn't go well. I bled out, and they performed a hysterectomy. I was lucky to live."

And she could see that now. She'd been lucky. She'd lost something precious, but she hadn't lost her life. Rafe was right. They could have a family if they wanted one. They could adopt. Their lifestyle would be a challenge, but she knew people who could cut through red tape. Stef Talbot had offered his help in the past, and she'd turned him down because she didn't want to be a charity case. It wasn't charity, she realized suddenly. It was love. It was caring. It was family.

"You're getting emotional, dear."

Laura felt the tears running down her face. She felt his hands on her body. It felt like the ultimate violation. She preferred his violence to this slow, torturous petting. "How are you going to get out of this, Joe? Rafe and Cam know the Marquis de Sade is someone in the FBI."

He chuckled and reached down. At least his hands were off of her. When he came back, there was a small brush in his hand. It was pearl handled and had old-fashioned bristles. Every muscle in her body tensed because she remembered what he could do with that feminine-looking brush. He'd beaten her with something similar. In between "sessions," he had used it to brush her hair.

"You've made it impossible for me to continue, but I think you've freed me in some ways, too." He reached over and started caressing her hair with the brush. His motions were languid, as though he deeply enjoyed this part of his ritual. "My time with the FBI is done. I'll make it to Mexico and on to some friends in South America. I have an appointment with a plastic surgeon. Thanks to my dearly departed wife, I have quite a bit saved up. She had a trust fund, you know."

How long had Joe been killing? She'd written in her profile that there had to have been an inciting incident that started the killer on his path. "Your wife cheated on you."

Joe started. He stepped back, pulling the brush from her hair. "Yes. I gave the bitch everything, and she preferred the gardener. She even got herself pregnant."

That explained it.

"Marla was exactly like my mother. Dear mother left me with an alcoholic, abusive father because she needed to follow her heart. She also left me with my waste of a brother. He came in handy, though." He took a step back, the brush at his side. "Now, little rabbit, it's time for some punishment. Do you know what the Marquis used to say? He said it is always by way of pain that we arrive at pleasure. He was right. Your pain is my pleasure."

He snapped the brush back, and Laura cried out when she felt the sting along her skin.

She tugged at the ropes, but they wouldn't come loose.

Another strike and she cried out again. Fire licked along her flesh.

"We're going to have a fine time, you and I," Joe said with a ghastly smile on his face. "And I have a note written out for those dolts you call lovers. They weren't smart enough to find me, and now they're going to lose you."

"Think again."

Laura's head came off the table at the sound of Rafe's voice.

Rafe stood in the doorway that led from the kitchen to the dining room. He was the most beautiful thing she had ever seen. Her breath caught. There wasn't a single thought that he could be hurt. He was here to save her. Everything would be fine now.

Joe shrank back. He dropped the brush, an almost bored look on his face. "I didn't expect that."

"I'm sure you didn't. You never expected anyone to put it together," Rafe replied.

A smirk lit Joe's face. "It took you long enough. Do you have any idea how much fun it's been to watch you chase your tail?"

Rafe ignored him. "Does he have a gun, *bella*?"

Laura shook her head. "Not where he could get to it before you could shoot."

Joe shrugged as though he'd been caught in a minor lie rather than exposed as a serial murderer. "Well, I suppose you'll take me in now."

Cam moved in from the opposite direction, from the living room. Both of her men carried guns leveled at Joe. "That would be the procedure."

Cam looked down at her, his eyes seeming to take in every mark on her body.

Joe chuckled, a wicked sound. "And you're a good boy, aren't you? Both of you. I'm counting on that, you know. Let me tell you how this is going to go. You're going to take me in, but you'll find most of the evidence is utterly tainted. Good luck pushing through a case where the lead investigator is also the suspect. You won't have a shred of evidence that will hold up. I made sure of it. I'll get out on a technicality, and you should know, I'll come for her again." He smiled. "Perhaps this will be a fun game, too. I know I'm smarter than any judge."

Laura wanted to be sick. He really would. And he was right. All of the evidence was contaminated.

Joe reached a hand out for her. "You're mine, little rabbit. Bars aren't going to keep us apart. This game isn't over until I hold your heart in my hands."

"We're not playing games, Joe," Rafe said, his eyes cold.

He nodded at Cam and fired. Her men fired one shot a piece. Joe's body staggered under the impact. Two holes opened up in his chest, bright red blood blooming through his clothes. His eyes flared, and he looked down at her. He reached a hand out toward her.

Rafe moved quickly, shoving the dying man away. "You don't touch her. Not ever again."

Cam's face came into view. "Baby." He put a hand on her hair, and she could hear the emotion choking his throat. "Baby, are you okay? God, he hurt you."

She shook her head, wanting so much to get her arms around him.

"I need a knife!" Rafe called out.

Cam pulled off his own shirt and covered her with it. "Wolf and Logan are here, baby."

Wolf entered the room, looking down at the body on the floor. Logan followed after him. Wolf passed Rafe a knife, and he went to work on her bindings.

"I'll have you out in a moment, *bella*," he promised.

Logan was already on his radio. "Yeah, Sheriff, we're going to need to call in some help. We found her. Laura's fine, but Deputy Briggs and Special Agent Kincaid were forced to put the suspect down. He was going to kill her."

Rafe turned back and sent the deputy a grateful smile. He passed the knife across to Cam, who cut through the last of her bindings, and she was free. Rafe pulled her up and into his arms.

301

She was deliciously crushed. Even the pain from the strikes she'd received now reminded her that she was alive and they were here.

"*Bella*, I was so scared." Rafe didn't seem to care that her ass was hanging out, but Cam came around the other side and covered her with his body. His arms wound around her.

"I was terrified," Cam admitted.

"I'm fine." She sighed and let herself sink into their warmth. "I knew you would come for me."

She felt a tremble go through Rafe's body. "Always, *bella*. Never, ever doubt it."

When they carried her out, she didn't look back. That part of her life was done, and it couldn't hurt her again.

Chapter Twenty

Laura watched as Stef and Jen Talbot had their first dance as husband and wife. They were wrapped up in each other like vines twining together, swaying to the music. The Bliss Reception Hall had been completely decked out to look like a romantic forest complete with greenery and trees along all the walls. Stef Talbot was a billionaire who could have bought his own private island to have a wedding, but he and his bride had insisted on the Feed Store Church and the Rec Center.

"They look good together," Holly said, locking arms with Laura. For days, Holly had tried to keep a hand on Laura. Laura hadn't been able to miss the way her best friend refused to let her out of her sight.

She leaned over, brushing Holly's head with her own. "Those two definitely belong together. Jen is the perfect woman to deal with King Stef. She makes him laugh." And she put him in his place from time to time. Everyone needed that.

"Caleb never laughs," Holly said with a sad sigh. "Why do I

like him so much? I'm starting to wish I didn't."

Her poor friend. Caleb Burke was a puzzle and a half. He'd been all over Holly when there was a threat, but he'd backed off the instant the threat was gone. He was right back to sitting in Holly's section at Stella's for breakfast, lunch, and dinner and staring without ever asking her out. She didn't envy Holly dealing with Caleb, but it was obvious her friend was totally into the doctor. "Give him a little time. When is Micky coming into town?"

That was the way to get Holly's mind off her heartache. She lit up at the mere mention of her son spending a week with her. It had been a long time since Holly had been able to spend time with her seventeen-year-old son. "He'll be here in a couple of days. He's got a tiny bit of time between his summer pre-college camp and football camp. I'm so excited. And now that the serial killer is gone, I don't even have to worry about him being murdered."

"Always a good thing."

Bliss had settled back into a peaceful, sleepy existence. They'd only added two murders to their total this time around. The mayor of Bliss had called it a win.

Laura had gone back to work, but only until Bart found a replacement for her at the Stop 'n' Shop. She'd promised Rafe she'd get her PI license and join him in building a real business. She meant to keep that promise. He was passionate about finding missing persons and reuniting loved ones.

Cam was finding his place. He was a hard-working deputy and spent every night perfecting his software. Callie was rapidly approaching her due date, and Cam had already been told he would be in charge of Bliss while Nate was on paternity leave. Given Cam's longtime law enforcement experience, he'd been given the second in command job. Logan had taken the news well. Or rather he'd seemed to. He'd shaken Cam's hand, and then Cam had had to pick him up at a bar two towns over later that night. Cam was busy with his new job. Well, when he wasn't busy making love to her. He and Rafe seemed happy to spend as much time in bed as possible.

Nell joined them, her face shining in the twinkle lights of the reception hall. "Hey, you two. Stef had a vegan cake brought in. It's delicious."

Trust Stef to make sure everyone had what they wanted. There were three different cakes. A bridal cake, a groom's cake, and a vegan cake. Not a one of them was vanilla. "That's great, Nell. I'm glad you decided to give up your nude protest in order to attend the wedding."

Nell shrugged. "Well, friendship is more important, isn't it? Rachel gave me her blessing. She said she found a nice cover on the Internet that allows her to see Paige when she feeds her. I think she should be allowed to run around topless if she wants to, but I got outvoted. Besides, the bunker was too quiet once Mel and Cassidy left. Henry was completely irrational about the whole topless thing. I was surprised." She turned, and her face went from bright and shiny to serious. "But he's being reasonable about one thing."

"Really?" In Laura's opinion, Henry's response to Nell's topless protest was one of the more rational things he'd ever done. She knew what would happen if she tried that. Rafe and Cam would do way worse than take her to a bunker. "What is that?"

"I know what happened to you. I know that you can't carry a baby anymore," Nell said quietly, her eyes softening.

Laura felt Holly's hand on her shoulder. Being reminded of what she'd lost didn't hurt the way it used to, but the thought still brought tears to her eyes. "When the time comes, we'll see about adoption."

"And that would be great," Nell said, taking both of Laura's hands in hers. Nell's brown eyes shone as she looked up at Laura. "If that's what you decide to do, I am all behind you. But if you want to, you could choose a different path. You kept one of your ovaries. I could be your surrogate. My womb works, at least I think it does. And Henry and I decided a long time ago that we would forgo having children, so you wouldn't be intruding."

Laura was utterly shocked. Nell had many principles, but this was one of her most sacred. "Because of population control. Nell, you believe in that."

Nell gave her a watery smile and squeezed her hands. "I believe in you more. Like I said, friends are more important. And you and Rafe and Cam would raise an amazing kid. It's something to think about. If you want to, we would like to give you that gift."

Now Laura cried for a different reason. She hugged Nell, pulling the delicate woman into her arms. "Thank you."

Laura might never take her up on the offer, but it was a balm to her soul that Nell had offered.

"It's something to think about." Nell pulled back, and a little smile curled her lips. "And if we need to do it the old-fashioned way, you know I think Rafe is cute as a button."

"Bad girl!" Laura said playfully as Nell winked and scurried away to dance with her husband.

Holly had tears in her eyes as she leaned forward and kissed Laura's cheek. "I'm going to get a drink. I love you, you know. You and Nell, you're my lifelines. Now you get out there and dance with those hot hunks of yours."

Holly turned and started a conversation with Marie and Teeny.

"So, this is what a wedding's like in Bliss, huh?" Cam asked, nodding to Holly as she walked off. He handed Laura a glass of champagne.

She stared at her loves. Rafe was right beside Cam. They looked amazingly gorgeous in tuxedoes. Rafe was tall, dark, and broodingly handsome. Cam was an all-American hottie. What had she done to deserve them?

"Were you surprised when the bride danced down the aisle? I think Stef was," Laura said.

The ceremony had been joyous, utterly reflecting the quirky beauty of the couple involved. There hadn't been a dry eye in the house. Laura had even caught Max wiping his eyes when Stef had pledged to love his bride forever.

"I liked the bales of hay," Rafe admitted with a broad smile. "I haven't been to a wedding where all the guests sat on hay."

"That's because you've never gotten married in a Feed Store Church before," Laura replied. "You get a beautiful wedding ceremony, and all the attendees get ten percent off their next feed order. I think that's the only reason James Glen came. He says he's allergic to commitment of any kind."

She looked across the room where the said commitment-phobe was talking up Brooke Harper. He might not want to get married, but he was definitely looking for some company. Wolf stood beside his closest friend. He didn't look like he would mind spending some time with Brooke Harper, either. Two cowboys strode up, trying to get into Brooke's space. Laura searched her memory. They were brothers. Shane and Bay Kent. They were friends of Stef's, but Max and Rye Harper couldn't stand the two cowboys. Brooke was about to get herself into a very interesting situation. Wolf stepped back like he didn't want to get too involved. When he saw her, he smiled and raised a glass.

She smiled back and did the same.

And found both of her men frowning down ferociously at her.

"Hey, I was just saying hi," she said.

"See that you keep it that way," Cam replied.

She threw back her head and laughed. "Because I need a third guy. Trust me, baby, my dance card is totally full."

"It's full of us," Cam said, getting close to her. He invaded her space, his hips moving. He bumped against her in time to the music. "We can keep you dancing, baby."

She felt Rafe at her back. "We can dance all night, *bella*."

They could dance forever. They *would* dance forever.

The music flowed around them as they swayed together. Laura was surrounded by her men and her friends and her future.

She almost didn't notice when the double doors to the reception hall opened, and a big, broad figure filled the doorway.

"Oh my god," she breathed as she realized who it was. "Alexei?"

"Who's Alexei?" Rafe asked as he looked around at all the people staring at the new guy. Everyone had stopped.

The big, gorgeous Russian walked in, a broad smile on his handsome face. He glanced around the room, and his focus lasered in on Holly. The room seemed to stop, every eye following the former mobster as he made his way toward the woman he'd saved.

Laura watched as Holly turned, and her eyes widened. Alexei had dressed for the occasion, wearing a perfectly tailored suit that clung to his muscular form. He was hotness personified, and Laura wasn't surprised that Holly practically drooled.

Alexei walked up and stopped mere inches from his target. He towered over Holly.

"Hello. My name is Howard, and I am be coming from Orlando."

Holly seemed breathless as she looked up. "Is that your witness protection name?"

"Yes." Alexei started to reach a hand out. "But we can pick new one if you do not like this one. The trials are over. I am free to go where I like to go. I go with you."

"No!" Caleb Burke's favorite word didn't fall out of his mouth this time. It was pushed and with great force. Caleb's face was a mask of indignation. Unlike normal, his emotion could be read plainly on his face.

Another song started. This one a happy, bouncy tune.

Holly was in a mess.

"Dance with us," Cam whispered.

"Be with us," Rafe said just as provocatively. "We found a closet that's unlocked. There's plenty of room. We need you, *bella*."

Their hands were on her hips and getting dangerously close to her breasts. Laura's heart sped up. It always did when they were around. "Take me there."

Holly would figure it out. She was caught in between two men, and that was an amazing place to be. Laura gave her best friend a wave as Cam and Rafe led her off.

It was time to dance.

* * * *

Caleb, Holly, and Alexi and all of Bliss will return in Found in Bliss.

Author's Note

I'm often asked by generous readers how they can help get the word out about a book they enjoyed. There are so many ways to help an author you like. Leave a review. If your e-reader allows you to lend a book to a friend, please share it. Go to Goodreads and connect with others. Recommend the books you love because stories are meant to be shared. Thank you so much for reading this book and for supporting all the authors you love!

Sign up for Lexi Blake's newsletter
and be entered to win a $25 gift certificate
to the bookseller of your choice.

Join us for news, fun, and exclusive content
including free short stories.

There's a new contest every month!

Go to http://www.lexiblake.net/newsletter/ to subscribe.

Found in Bliss

Nights in Bliss, Colorado Book 5
By Lexi Blake writing as Sophie Oak
Coming October 9, 2018

Re-released in a second edition with new content.

Holly Lang has a hard time trusting men. Eight years ago, her husband tossed her aside and took her son away from her. Finding the little town of Bliss has given her a second chance at life, new friends, and sense of belonging. Unfortunately, Bliss also seems to have filled her days and nights with dreams of two beautiful men. She can't stop thinking about the gentle but haunted Dr. Caleb Burke, and the exotic and dangerous Alexei Markov.

Caleb Burke isn't your ordinary town doctor, but he's always dedicated himself to trying to be a good man. His journey to this quirky little town was not an easy one. Some of the stops along the way left him scarred in more ways than one. But when he first sees Holly, it's like someone threw open the blinds and let the sunlight into his life for the first time in years.

Alexei Markov is nothing like Caleb Burke. Working as a hit man for the Russian mafia, he was forced to do unspeakable things. He suffered through all the moral compromises to fulfill one simple goal, killing the man who murdered his brother. When a mission led him to Bliss, he found something more precious than vengeance. A woman named Holly Lang. Throughout months of living in witness protection, testifying against his former employers, all he could think about was finding his way back to her.

After returning to Bliss, Alexei and his strange new ally Caleb discover that they aren't the only ones interested in Holly. Someone else is stalking her and appears to want her dead. The only way to discover the identity of the killer is for all three to face up to the secrets of their past and work together to fight for everything they have found in Bliss.

* * * *

"No." He said the word. He said it a lot, but this time he really, really meant it. Caleb Burke watched as that big Russian stood over sweet Holly, his dark eyes promising all manner of comfort, and he knew he wasn't ready to let her go.

Of course, he also wasn't ready to take her.

Fuck.

"No?" Alexei turned to him, seeming to notice for the first time that he wasn't alone with Holly. Moments before, the Russian had walked into the reception hall where Stefan Talbot and his new wife, Jennifer, were hosting their wedding party. He'd marched in like he owned the place and zeroed in on Holly.

Alexei looked the same as he had months before, but it was easy to tell he'd changed. There was a relaxed set to his shoulders he hadn't had the last time he was in Bliss. But then the last time Alexei Markov had been in Bliss, it had been as a member of the Russian mob.

"Get your hands off her."

"My hands are entirely to myself." And Alexei still had trouble with English.

"Caleb, what's wrong?" Holly asked, her face turning to him. Wide green eyes stared up at him in confusion. She was so gorgeous. Every time she looked at him, he felt it straight in his gut. And his cock. *Damn it.* He had to turn away from her.

"You shouldn't be here." Caleb couldn't take his eyes off the Russian. It was nothing less than the truth, though he had selfish reasons for pointing it out. "You're supposed to be in witness protection."

Alexei shrugged, his eyes going back to Holly as though her

313

presence was a magnet he couldn't avoid. "I told you. The trials are over. All the men who worked with Pushkin have been put in proper jails. I finish my testimony last week. I am here today. I am free man."

Free? After everything he'd done? Alexei Markov had blown into town eight months before as a mobster. Just because he'd turned state's witness and saved Jennifer Waters and Callie Hollister-Wright didn't give him a free pass. He tried not to think about the fact that the Russian had saved Holly, too. Alexei had thrown his own body over hers, taking the bullet that would have ended her life. It didn't erase the crimes he'd committed before. "You killed a bunch of people, and they let you go free?"

"He only killed them to save me, Caleb. And Stef got a couple, too. No one's talking about putting him in jail." Holly was already reaching for the Russian's hands, her face turning upward in greeting. "I'm so happy for you, Alexei. I'm happy they let you come back to Bliss."

A cloud crossed Alexei's face telling Caleb everything he needed to know.

"They didn't let you come back, did they?" Caleb asked. "You're on the run."

"No running. I take taxi and then train and then bus. Bus drop off at the Trading Post. It was closed, but Ms. Teeny was kind enough to leave note on door telling me about the wedding." After his quick explanation, Alexei turned back to Holly. "You look like beautiful doll."

Caleb grabbed at his tie, loosening it. The damn thing was a noose around his neck. Why had he come to this thing? He should have done what he always did. He should have stayed at home until someone needed him. He should have barricaded himself in his office and stared at medical books until his eyes wouldn't stay open one second more and he was forced to fall into that hell he called sleep. Yeah, that would have made for a great night. But no, he'd gotten on this monkey suit and headed to the Feed Store Church to attend a wedding, all because he'd wanted to watch Holly walk down the aisle. He'd wanted to see her in a beautiful dress and imagine for one second that she was walking toward him and he was normal. That he was twenty-two again, marrying the right woman this time with his whole life ahead of him.

Not once in that daydream had he included a second man in the scenario, though given where he lived, he should have known that would happen whether he liked it or not.

"Thanks," Holly said to Alexei, her face lighting up.

Caleb flushed. He hadn't told her she was beautiful. He'd nodded at her. Why couldn't he talk to her? He'd been good at this once. He'd gone to parties and balls. Why couldn't he talk to one small-town waitress?

Because she was the *one*, but he was too fucked up to deal with it.

"You do look really pretty." He forced the words out of his mouth. He didn't say the ones that were locked inside. She didn't look pretty. She was beautiful. Inside and out. Holly Lang practically glowed in his mind. With auburn hair that curled and caressed her porcelain shoulders, Holly was a vision of everything feminine. She stirred his cock and his mind. He thought about her all the time.

Yeah. He wasn't going to say any of that.

Holly turned toward him, a vibrant smile on her lips. When she smiled that sunshine-goddess, center-of-his-whole-fucking-world smile, he always thought he would turn into a puddle of goo at her feet. *Yeah. That would be really sexy, Burke.*

"Tell her more, Caleb. You do well." Alexei was smiling at him like he was a toddler who'd finally managed to walk.

What the hell was that about?

Siren in Bloom
Texas Sirens Book 6
By Lexi Blake writing as Sophie Oak
Coming November 6, 2018

Re-released in a second edition with new content.

For psychologist Leo Meyer, peace and comfort come through strict discipline and order. It's one of the reasons he was chosen by Julian Lodge to be the Dom in residence at his club. His time there has been a near-perfect existence filled with a daily routine free from the chaos of emotional attachment. With the exception of his brief relationship with Shelley McNamara, that is. She may have been the only woman he ever truly loved, but he was confident he had put her out of his mind until she walked into his club on the arm of another man.

Shelley McNamara is tired of waiting for her new life to begin. After finally finding freedom from an abusive marriage, she is eager to discover who she really is. After her encounter with Leo Meyer, she knows that the first thing she wants to explore is the lifestyle he exposed her to during their brief time together. She's been promised her new Dom will be an excellent fit, but she can't imagine anyone could fill the hole left by Leo. Until she sees Master Wolf.

After a devastating injury forced his retirement from the Navy SEALs, Wolf has been restless and lost. Hoping to reconnect with his estranged family in Dallas, Wolf accepted a new job working for Julian Lodge. His first assignment is training a beautiful woman named Shelley. Her fiery nature unlocks feelings he didn't know he was capable of after a life spent in combat. The closer they become, the more certain he is that she is his ideal mate. The only catch is that her relationship with Leo may not be as resolved as they both believed.

Just when Shelley believes the looming shadow of her deceased husband has finally cleared away, a dangerous killer arrives at her door seeking retribution. Leo and Wolf will have to put their grievances aside, leverage all their training, and work together to keep her safe and claim her heart.

About Lexi Blake

Lexi Blake is the author of contemporary and urban fantasy romance. She started publishing in 2011 and has gone on to sell over two million copies of her books. Her books have appeared twenty-six times on the *USA Today*, *New York Times*, and *Wall Street Journal* bestseller lists. She lives in North Texas with her husband, kids, and two rescue dogs.

Connect with Lexi online:

Facebook: Lexi Blake
Twitter: authorlexiblake
Website: www.LexiBlake.net

Other Books by Lexi Blake

ROMANTIC SUSPENSE

Masters And Mercenaries
The Dom Who Loved Me
The Men With The Golden Cuffs
A Dom is Forever
On Her Master's Secret Service
Sanctum: A Masters and Mercenaries Novella
Love and Let Die
Unconditional: A Masters and Mercenaries Novella
Dungeon Royale
Dungeon Games: A Masters and Mercenaries Novella
A View to a Thrill
Cherished: A Masters and Mercenaries Novella
You Only Love Twice
Luscious: Masters and Mercenaries~Topped
Adored: A Masters and Mercenaries Novella
Master No
Just One Taste: Masters and Mercenaries~Topped 2
From Sanctum with Love
Devoted: A Masters and Mercenaries Novella
Dominance Never Dies
Submission is Not Enough
Master Bits and Mercenary Bites~The Secret Recipes of Topped
Perfectly Paired: Masters and Mercenaries~Topped 3
For His Eyes Only
Arranged: A Masters and Mercenaries Novella
Love Another Day
At Your Service: Masters and Mercenaries~Topped 4
Master Bits and Mercenary Bites~Girls Night
Nobody Does It Better
Close Cover
Protected

Masters and Mercenaries: The Forgotten
Memento Mori
Tabula Rasa, Coming February 26, 2019

Lawless
Ruthless
Satisfaction
Revenge

Courting Justice
Order of Protection
Evidence of Desire, Coming January 8, 2019

Masters Of Ménage (by Shayla Black and Lexi Blake)
Their Virgin Captive
Their Virgin's Secret
Their Virgin Concubine
Their Virgin Princess
Their Virgin Hostage
Their Virgin Secretary
Their Virgin Mistress

The Perfect Gentlemen (by Shayla Black and Lexi Blake)
Scandal Never Sleeps
Seduction in Session
Big Easy Temptation
Smoke and Sin
At the Pleasure of the President, Coming Fall 2018

URBAN FANTASY

Thieves
Steal the Light
Steal the Day
Steal the Moon
Steal the Sun

Steal the Night
Ripper
Addict
Sleeper
Outcast, Coming 2018

LEXI BLAKE WRITING AS SOPHIE OAK

Small Town Siren
Siren in the City
Away From Me
Three to Ride
Siren Enslaved
Two to Love
Siren Beloved
One to Keep
Siren in Waiting
Lost in Bliss
Found in Bliss, Coming October 9, 2018
Siren in Bloom, November 6, 2018
Pure Bliss, Coming February 2, 2019

89244727R00197

Made in the USA
San Bernardino, CA
21 September 2018